OUTLAW

ALSO BY K. EASON

On the Bones of Gods Series

Enemy

OUTLAW

K. EASON

Published by 47North, Seattle

www.apub.com

Amazon, the Amazon logo, and 47North are trademarks of Amazon.com, Inc., or its affiliates.

ISBN-13: 9781503935907
ISBN-10: 1503935906

Cover design by M. S. Corley

Printed in the United States of America

To my parents

CHAPTER ONE

The stolen sword hissed past Snowdenaelikk's head, smashing through branches instead of her skull, scattering pine needles and shards of bark. Fair enough. That big-boned toadfucker was swinging like he had an axe, not a legion blade. Broad strokes, graceless, with all his weight behind them. All a woman had to do was get out of his way.

Which she had, except the once; and then he'd damn near sliced off her arm. Blood all over, tingling fingers, lucky she still *had* all five. At least it wasn't her sword arm. Thank luck for that. Thank whatever spirits

not the God, never again the God

watched over half-blood conjuring heretics. She struck back at him, left-handed. Put a deep cut above his right knee, crossways and up, into the meat of his thigh. He staggered back. Snow showed her teeth, more grimace than grin, and came in again. Moving rough, but still fast. Still hard.

She folded sideways, made him pivot after her on his wounded leg. Felt the hiss and whistle as his blade cleaved past her. Angled herself and gave ground, step by slow step, and tried to remember the motherless terrain. Spring-melt mud underfoot, mixed with slush. The rotted half log one, two, *there* to step over it. The trio of saplings. She found the big evergreen with its head-high scatter of branches, turned so that it wasn't quite at her back.

The Talir came at her again, an ugly backstroke that would open her up like a fish. She ducked and twisted at the last moment. He tried to correct, couldn't. Snagged his blade on the big evergreen, a shallow slice through the bark that scrubbed all the force off his strike and slowed him down.

She jagged in close, aiming for the spaces in his stolen armor. The Dvergiri weren't a large people, even the women; the Talir was four kinds of idiot not to have patched the gaps. She drove the seax—not a stabbing weapon, not meant for this—into his ribs. Worked the blade into the space between bones, hoping to catch a lung. And then she pulled the blade out, dragging on skin and muscle, a hitch at the end when the seax caught suction before wrenching free. She spun away. Focused on keeping hold of her blade and her last meal and staying upright.

The Talir's shout ended in a gurgle. She'd got the lung, then. Meant this toadfucker'd die without a chirurgeon's help. And the nearest chirurgeon wasn't interested in helping him. The nearest chirurgeon had her own wounds to occupy her attention.

Snow took herself a safe distance before she looked down at her right arm. The fingers were cold, numb, locked into claws. The forearm bone wasn't bent. Wasn't grinding. Might be nerve damage, yeah, or cut tendons. The chill on her skin had nothing to do with shock. Please, she could *make* the fingers move, even if she couldn't feel them, please—

And there, yes, she could. Snow clenched her teeth hard on a back-surge of nausea. Not enough air for her lungs. High-pitched whine in both ears. Her vision hazed soft on the edges. She blinked. Still hazy, and a headache lancing in behind. And that meant—

Briel.

She had time to brace her whole left arm against a friendly tree before Briel's sending caught her, taking over eyes and ears and everything. Spinning trees, spinning forest, a svartjagr's aerial impression that did not help Snow's balance at all. Briel was worried because Snow was somewhere under those trees, where Briel could not find her. And there was guilt on the tail of that worry, because Briel had been somewhere else when Snow had got hurt, with Veiko, up near the ridgeline, where a svartjagr's wings could stretch without worrying about inconvenient branches.

Briel sent a jumbled report, sound and image overlaid and not necessarily connected: a Talir woman gone down screaming, a man staggering backward with Veiko's axe in his skull. Another thrashing body down with Logi on top. So Veiko was fine, having help from the dog and the svartjagr.

She still felt a splash of relief when Briel sent another impression, pure Veiko this time. Grim satisfaction. Fine and unhurt. Of course he was.

Out, Snow told Briel, before Briel relayed her condition to Veiko. She came back to a new headache to keep her arm company. Came back to the dying Talir. Down to breathless little moans now, wheezing pink froth. White-ringed eyes as he drowned in his own blood. Pity said help him or kill him, don't let him die slow. There were scavengers in the Wild who might not wait their dinner for his death.

Fuck pity, Snow. Pity's for the weak.

Tsabrak's sentiment. Tsabrak's whisper, blowing cold along her neck. Tsabrak's pointed smile, crooked and sharp as a broken blade.

Let that toadfucker drown in his own blood.

Not a lot of mercy in Tsabrak. But good advice, sometimes, like: never trust a downed enemy as helpless. Tsabrak had made that mistake exactly once, and caught metal in his back as a lesson. Had gone crawling through Illharek's Suburban alleys until he collapsed at a certain half-blood, half-trained chirurgeon's feet.

And found *her* pity, fuck and damn. She could've let him die in that alley. If she'd just stepped over him, her life would've gone some other direction and she wouldn't be here, fighting with a Talir raider in the fucking forest and risking her arm and her conjuring.

You sorry for saving me, then?

No. Sometimes.

Fuck and damn. Tsabrak's voice in her head, that was bad enough. She could dismiss it as memory. But Tsabrak's shadow beside her—look sideways and there he was, no matter how hard she blinked: Tsabrak as she'd last seen him, rain-soaked, his sleeves plastered against his arms, hair clinging in strands to his cheeks. That wasn't memory. That was . . . something else. Ghost-trouble.

She didn't look straight at him. Didn't want to see *through* him, fuck and damn. Shouldn't talk to him, either, but—

"That why you broke my finger, then, before you gave me to Ehkla? Remind me of your toadshit lessons?"

You did manage.

"I'll manage now, too. Shut up and go away."

Left to her own, she would let the ravens eat the Talir in strips, skin to bone. But the last thing they needed, any of them, was some angry ghost rising at sunset. She rearranged her grip on the seax. Skirted wide and yeah, there—gasping or not, frothing or not—he had enough strength left to swipe at her. Determined toadfucker. He should be past moving. Should be past speaking, too, but there he was, muttering the same drowned syllables over and over, which made her head spin a little faster and her ears buzz like wasps.

She could blame blood loss for that buzzing, or shock. She had half a dozen good physiological reasons to go dizzy and close her eyes and look for balance in the dark. But memory played on the back side of her eyelids: violet fire on the cracked plaster walls, blood running in channels as the godmagic took hold. Gut-tangled, itchy-skinned nausea, then and now.

She could imagine sense in the Talir's syllables. Could imagine a name rising up through the foam and blood. Tal'Shik.

Godmagic.

She stomped hard on the Talir's wrist. Bones broke. The maybe-prayer dissolved into sobbing fragments. The sword hilt slid into the mud as his hand spasmed open, baring his palm and the tattoo on it. Tal'Shik's godmark. Fuck and damn. Taliri raiders in winter were nothing unusual, even this far south, even this late in the season. But Taliri godsworn were *real* trouble. And here this toadshit was, trying to kill her. Not an accident.

Snow chopped hard at the Talir's neck. Ugly cut, awkward, that glanced off his jaw and stuck in his spine and did not, by any measure, remove his head. But the praying stopped. So did the gurgling, and the foaming. His fingers flexed once, then relaxed.

Death had a particular smell. A particular shape. A chirurgeon knew all of death's faces, if she'd earned an Academy master's ring. And a chirurgeon might imagine that death was the end of things. *She* had, until she'd been dead herself. There was *dead*, and then there was staying that way. And the angry dead, they were a problem.

Snow braced a foot on the dead man's shoulder. Her arm was hurting now, all the battleshock numb running out with her blood. She'd be on her ass soon enough, she didn't get her own bleeding stopped.

But the Talir might get back up after dark if she left the job unfinished. So she wrestled with the blade until her vision fogged and her chest hurt. Only way she knew to keep dead *dead* was take the head off. That was Veiko's advice. And Veiko's damn axe would be useful about now, yeah, all of Veiko would be.

"Snow! Snow, you all right?"

More of her luck, that the first person to find her would be Dekklis. Szanys Dekklis, First Scout, Second Legion, Sixth Cohort, currently absent without leave and leagues from her garrison, and blaming Snow for every step of that journey. Dek wouldn't have a mark on her, bet on that, she'd have more than one corpse to her count, and she'd've done it without any help.

Hell if Snow meant to lose a fight with her own motherless blade with Dekklis watching. She straightened as much as she could without letting go of the hilt. Shrugged. "Fine."

"Fine," Dekklis repeated in the tone that meant *toadshit*. "You're bleeding."

"Noticed that."

"Badly."

"Noticed that, too." Snow eyed her. Dekklis had long, bright stains on trousers and tunic, was red to her wrists. "And you?"

"None of this is mine." Dekklis picked her way through the trees. Not even breathing hard, rot her anyway. "Looks like he surprised you."

"Came out of nowhere. Damn near took my head off before I even got my blade out."

"Big man." Dekklis squinted upslope. "Broken branches up there. Lot of loose gravel. Seems he should've made noise. Where's Briel?"

Which was Dekklis's way of asking *what the hell happened?* Dek knew very well that no amount of good fortune would have let the Talir get that close to Snow. Implied: Snow must've fucked up.

Which she hadn't, yeah, but she wouldn't own what *had* happened, either. She would not say, out loud, *yeah, Dek, listen, I've been seeing Tsabrak since we left Cardik, and sometimes he talks to me.*

Dek might believe her. Dekklis, too, had learned that the dead didn't always stay that way.

"Briel's with Veiko, playing scout. Besides." Snow rolled her eyes upward. "Lot of low branches in here. She'd do me no good. Get herself tangled, yeah?"

Dek's eyebrows said *toadshit*. Dek's mouth said only, "All kinds of bad luck for you, then. No Briel. No Veiko. Sneaky Talir."

"Looks like." Snow tried again to get her blade loose, hard pull and twist. Damn near fell, yeah, but she got it. She thanked a flash of good luck for the tree at her back. Rested against it and waited for the world to resettle. Maybe one more strike, if she hit it clean.

She didn't. Glanced off the collarbone this time and started a new cut in the Talir's neck. The seax stuck again. Snow swore.

Dekklis grunted. "He's dead, Snow. You noticed?"

Szanys Dekklis was Illhari highborn, had a mother in the Senate. It wasn't proper to believe in ghosts or gods or heretical superstition. Dek might know better, but she wasn't friends with that knowing.

"You think that means anything? Look at his hand, Dek."

"Hell and damn. Tal'Shik."

"Did your corpses have the mark?"

"Not that I saw. Either of them."

"Then I got lucky with this one. Figures I'd get the godsworn. A man, though. That's different."

"Maybe he came for you deliberately. Maybe that's how he got close with you not hearing. Tal'Shik's not in love with you, Snow."

"Not in love with Veiko, either, and *he's* all right."

"Briel says?"

"Yeah."

"Figures." Dekklis made a face. Came around the corpse and wrapped her hand over Snow's on the hilt. Squeezed hard and pulled and got the blade out. Kept her hand on Snow's wrist after, hard and steady. Kept Snow upright. And scowled hard at her right arm. "We need to get that bleeding stopped."

"After we're done here."

"Now."

"What, you're a chirurgeon now? Don't tell me my business."

"Saying you can't slow us down, that's all."

"Or what, you'll leave me here?"

"Or we'll have to do all this again, with another ambush. They'll track your blood."

"They've *been* tracking us, maybe since we ran from Cardik. Look at him. No supplies. No bow. He's getting fed somewhere at nights, and *they* have to be close. Best chance we have is to hurry."

It was Dek's habit to argue with her. Snow watched her jaw set just so, watched her suck a mouthful of air and hold it. And then Dekklis let it out, in a gust. "Where's your partner?"

"Why?"

"Because we need his axe. Neither of us has a weapon that takes heads."

"He's coming." Fast enough she could hear him, crashing downslope like an angry bear. Briel had reported her injury, bet on that. Veiko was worried.

Veiko had reason. That cut was deep, bleeding harder than she could stop with a little pressure and a fistful of cobwebs.

You need to get that stopped. Tsabrak squatted beside her, arms on his knees. *You don't want to lose that arm. You're my right hand, yeah? That means you need yours.*

"Fuck off," she whispered. "Not your anything, yeah?"

But Tsabrak was right, and Dek, too, rot her anyway. Snow needed to deal with the wound now. She might not be much of a conjuror, but she'd be none at all if she lost a hand.

Then Logi was there, kicking up pine needles in his haste to reach her. Behind him, Veiko, whose eyes bounced from dead Talir to Snow and then to Dekklis, who moved into his path.

"Where's Istel?"

"Scouting. He thinks there may be others nearby. Briel is with him." Veiko was only a little out of breath. He came and squatted beside Snow. Frowned at her arm. Didn't ask *are you all right?* because he had both eyes and wits enough to know the answer.

Snow shrugged away his concern. "Godsworn over there needs your axe. Don't want him getting up later."

"Give it to me. Let me do it," said Dekklis. "You help *her.*"

Snow picked the wound clear of shredded sleeve and debris. "I need a needle. Thread. Silk, Veiko, in my pack. You know where. Dek, when you're done—I need you to hold the wound shut for him."

"You're the chirurgeon," Dekklis snapped.

"Not asking you to sew, am I? Asking Veiko. I've seen his needlework."

Veiko blinked. He was on the edge of arguing with her, yeah, see the protests gathering up in his eyes.

"I know," she said. "You've never stitched skin. So pretend I'm a shirt."

There was more than needle and thread in her pack. She debated, while Veiko rummaged through her kit, asking him to get the moss-flower for her. It would scrub the edge off the pain. Dull her wits.

You don't need it. Tsabrak's ghost was careful to keep her between himself and Veiko. Cold, cold breath on her cheek. *Need all your wits, yeah? There's more Taliri. They're close.*

Veiko threaded the needle with steady hands as Dekklis beheaded the dead man with two efficient whacks.

"Roll his face into the dirt," Veiko murmured. He came back to Snow. Looked at the wound and shook his head.

"Start at the top, where it's shallowest." She pinched the flaps of skin together. "Don't get too close to the edges, yeah? You'll rip through. Little stitches, that's right."

"Move, Snow, let me do that." Dekklis was steady, pitiless, lips clamped tight as her hands.

Which *hurt*, fuck and damn. But it slowed the bleeding. No one told Veiko to hurry. No one had to.

By the time Istel came pelting back, they were ready.

"Got trouble," Istel said in his quiet voice. "Found the rest of the party. Less than ten, more than two. Too many for us. We need to run."

* * *

The mist rose off a river three times as wide as Cardik's, shrouding every-thing in a prickling damp. Veiko could wonder if he'd slipped somehow.

9

Stepped into the ghost roads by accident. Except that was an Illhari stone road underfoot, and a downwind stink that said too many people. A sudden sense of openness that meant fields, maybe, and farmsteads. There had been both around Cardik. That they were back on the roads now meant they had to be close to Illharek.

Snowdenaelikk walked beside him, narrow and dark and silent. Thinking. Angry, according to Briel's uneasy impressions. Although what might have angered her, in this barely-morning, the svartjagr did not know. Briel's concern did not stretch much past her own close interests. She might not like Snow's mood, but she would not fret over the cause.

That was Snow's partner's job.

"Does your arm hurt?" he asked finally. Expecting temper from her, sharp denial.

Got back quiet and the slow turning of her head in her hood's shadow. He could see the pale smear of her hair. The Dvergiri-dark wedge of her face. Blue eyes, too, with enough light. They were dark holes now, bottomless.

"This place." Snow stumbled over something. Swerved into him, gentle bump that must have hurt her, from the hissed and indrawn breath. "Fucking Illharek."

It is your home, he almost said. Didn't, being wiser now than he had been. Dvergiri was not an easy language. The Illhari were not an easy people. And because Veiko traveled with three of them, and two had a habit of arguing about things long since past changing: "Do not let Dekklis hear you say that. She did not want to come."

Snow glanced ahead. Frowned. "Dead if we stayed in Cardik. She knows that."

"Yes." Leave off the obvious: that Dekklis might have preferred dying to running, and that the only reason she had come south was that Illharek itself—republic and city—was also in danger. Tal'Shik's vengeance wouldn't stop with Cardik. The goddess would come south, and she would take back everything that had been hers before the Purge, unless Szanys Dekklis, senator's daughter, could convince the Senate to act. Then the legion could deal with the Taliri while Veiko figured some way to put his axe between the dragon-goddess's eyes. He owed her that. "This is the wiser choice."

"This is the *necessary* choice," Snow shot back in the same tone she had said *be sure to draw the stitches tight.*

A wise man would let that silence hold and keep walking.

CHAPTER TWO

No one noticed them.

Dekklis had worried about that from the instant they set foot on the road. She wasn't concerned for herself, or Istel. They wore no armor, no legion insignia, and a pair of Dvergiri might go unremarked just about anywhere. Even Briel might go unremarked, feral svartjagr being common enough around Illharek. But Veiko was half a head taller than anyone else on the Riverwalk. Head full of straw-colored braids, an axe in one hand, a bow on his back, that big red wolf-shaped dog beside him—he'd catch some attention. And Snowdenaelikk. Half-bloods weren't especially uncommon, but she was damn near Veiko's height, and the Academy topknot would draw stares.

But no one looked twice. Not the merchant women, with their bondies and their wagons. Not the farmers, pushing their produce in handcarts. Everyone in her own world, occupied with her own tasks, and to a Purged hell with everyone else. It was only just past dawn, and already the Riverwalk was crowded. Handcarts, oxcarts, overburdened bondies staggering in their mistresses' wake. Pole boats and rafts choked the Jokki River, keeping mostly good order, never mind all the shouts and cursing.

So perfectly, painfully Illharek, and so typically *Illhari*. Dekklis caught herself smiling. You got used to Cardik's rhythms. You got used to

courtesy, Dek, that's the word

life in a city where half the population weren't citizens, where a good chunk of the traffic on the streets was traders or hunters, not merchants or highborn. Where people locked eyes and nodded and checked for weapons—only citizens having the right to wear metal.

Illharek had no such rules. The city trusted its resident aliens and visitors to behave themselves, or face Illhari justice.

Dekklis imagined Snowdenaelikk's lip curling, her razored *Illhari injustice, yeah? That's what you mean.* Dek felt heat crawling under her skin, as if Snow were looking at her now, with those words hanging between them.

Years since she'd been back here. She hadn't expected to return until the Sixth did, and maybe not even then. She had three older sisters. Had planned to retire

hell you did

in Cardik. Take her pension plot of land and what, turn farmer? Sell it, more likely, and turn sellsword.

All of those plans had gone to smoke and blood and ashes, like Davni and a dozen other villages. Like Cardik itself by now, unless the gates and the Sixth had held it against the Taliri and Tal'Shik.

Dekklis's smile dried up and fell off. She had nothing behind her but ashes, and nothing in front but Illharek. From here, the city looked like a great black hole in the earth, like the rock had grown a mouth and teeth and frozen in the act of biting. The Jokki coming out, the broad paved road beside it, like twin tongues in a dragon's throat. You could call the city of Illharek the heart of that dragon. It had been, in Tal'Shik's time.

Dek's memory supplied the vault of Below, the witchfires that wreathed and ran along the silhouettes of buildings and glowed blue and cold in lanterns. Memory supplied the tall twists of stone, buildings stacked close on the narrow streets. The lattice of bridges over river and pool and chasm, adding layers and height to the city, so that the highborn might not touch foot to cave floor for a week, might not need to descend to the Suburba at all. The damp cave-cool that did not vary with seasons. The absolute black where the light would not reach.

Had been a time she'd missed all that, when she'd first marched north with the Sixth. So proud of her new posting, and so terrified of open sky and the wide Wild. Now she slowed down and looked up at the shredded blue overhead, where the mist gave way to sun. Felt another stab under her breastbone.

Call that a heart, Dek.

"You look like a tourist, Szanys." Snow's voice, gravel and razor, from just off Dek's shoulder. "You miss this place that much?"

Dek turned to look at her. Took in the half-blood's mocking smile, the eyes grim as northern winters. Shrugged. "I did once. You?"

Flash of teeth. "It's home, yeah?"

"Right. Home." A fourth daughter's rebellion had made her seek the legion, which she had compounded by seeking a scout's posting in the Sixth. Dekklis imagined the accumulated years of her mother's disappointment. "Snow. I can't take you with me."

"To House Szanys? No? You saying your mother wouldn't welcome me?" The half-blood chuckled. "No intention, Dek. Trust me there. Is that where you're staying?"

"I don't know yet. Barracks, maybe. We're still legion. Send Briel if you need me."

Snow raised both brows. "All right."

Dek made a grab for Snow's arm as Snow began turning away. "Where will *you* be? In case I need to find you?" Expecting prevarication. Argument. Evasion.

Got a midwinter smile instead. "My mother's house. The Street of Apothecaries, seventeenth shop from Tano docks. There's a hammered-copper sign out front that looks like a bundle of sweetleaf."

Whatever that was. "I'll find it."

"Better you don't. It's not safe down there for the highborn, Szanys."

Because the Suburba relied on the cartels to keep order. Collections of criminals who held down neighborhoods and ran drugs and, "Aren't they your friends?"

The half-blood's smirk this time was bitter, and the edge cut both ways. "Not sure where I have friends anymore. Like you said. The God doesn't love me any better than Tal'Shik does."

"Then be careful. We need to know what *they* know about Tal'Shik. That doesn't happen if you're dead."

"I'll handle the cartels, Szanys. You handle the Senate. I'll check the Archives, too. See what I can find about godmagic. I'll send Briel when I know something. You need me, send a bondie with a message. I'm sure even House Szanys has people who know the Suburba."

Dekklis thought that might be an insult. Dredged up the wit to say something back. Too late.

Snow was already turning. She threaded her arm through Veiko's. The skraeling had his free hand locked on his axe, as if he meant to pull it out and cut himself a path out of here.

Skraeling manners, skraeling superstitions, that damn direct stare that he had—you forgot how young the man was. A few years past twenty, maybe. Cardik had, Dek recalled, been the largest place he'd ever been, and all of Cardik would fit into the Suburba's dockside.

"Dek."

Istel didn't look any happier than Veiko. Cardik-born, surface-bred Istel. He was Illhari, pure Dvergir. He could pass as a city native until he opened his mouth. Border accent. Border manners. And what the native-born Illhari would forgive an outlander, they would not forgive in another Dvergir.

Right now, Istel didn't like the new attention being paid them—because what skraeling and conjuror had not earned, stopping to talk in the middle of the Riverwalk had. Eyes on them now, mostly hostile. Strangers breaking around them, muttering unkind assessments of their ancestry.

Wouldn't dare, Dek thought, if she were in uniform. None of them would *dare*. But she was slinking into Illharek in travel-stained wool and leather, in the company of skraelings and half-bloods. Didn't look like a trooper. Sure as hell didn't look highborn.

"Dek?" Istel asked, a little more urgently. "What's wrong?"

"Nothing," she lied. "Come on."

Illharek was an old city. The newer parts had been conjured out of living rock, shaped and slick and graceful, but the garrison came from the time before the conjurors had learned how to shape the stone, before the Academy grew out of the walls above First Tier and the highborn moved their houses higher still. The garrison was Old High City solid, great granite blocks stacked together so that a child's fingers wouldn't fit into the cracks. It occupied most of the First Tier, barracks and buildings and training plazas, all walled off. A city within a city. The solid line of defense between Suburba and the rest of Illharek. You wanted to get into the Tiers, you had to come past the garrison's gates.

What about the Suburba, Szanys? Who protects those people?

Foremothers defend, if Snow's subversion didn't persist when the half-blood was nowhere near. Dekklis had called Snow contagious once. Might've been truer than not.

Foremothers knew she'd infected Istel. Turned a good partner

don't you mean silent?

into someone who argued, into someone who'd threatened—

I'll go if you won't, Dek.

—desertion. Dek had no doubt at all that he'd've come south with Snow and Veiko without her if she'd insisted on staying in Cardik.

Had no doubt it would've come to blows between them if she'd tried to make him stay.

So ask why she was in Illharek, then. Ask if it was loyalty to the Republic or a simple reluctance to cross swords with Istel that put her on the road to

home

the garrison gates. Statues of Illharek's heroes lined the road at intervals. There, Tuovi the Tyrant. There, Ana the Just, and Ragna Half-Blood. All of them in legion kit, the modern stuff, with the short sword that had not been widespread until the Purge, which came after Tuovi and Ana both. They had been founding foremothers. They had been godsworn. And *they* had remained from that darker time, having stories more important than their heresies. But the others, names and statues who had also been godsworn—they had been dragged down and melted for steel to forge the first swords of the Republic's legion.

That's rot, Szanys. You know that. Propaganda. They used the same weapons before, during, and after the Purge.

Snowdenaelikk's wisdom, no doubt from the Archives, which the Academy kept in violation of Senate order.

Toadshit, Dek. Senate knows about them. Senate wants them around. It's more propaganda—see the Purge, see the scrolls burning, see Illharek casting off its old ways. That's theatre. Any Suburban street-singer can tell you that.

Dekklis hoped Snowdenaelikk was right about that. Hoped that the Academy had the records that might tell them how to turn aside a godsworn army. How to fight godmagic.

And Dek hoped, with a dark little kernel of spite, that Snow was wrong. No archives. No answers. One moment of *oh toadshit* to erase the habitual, arrogant smirk on her face, that half-blood heretic who had a knack for landing on her feet, who couldn't even stay dead. Be nice, just once, to see her fail.

Except if Snow failed here, if she was wrong about what the Academy knew, then it was the legion who'd bleed first.

The legion said death in defense of Illharek was honorable. But the legion hadn't seen what Dekklis had. There was nothing honorable about dying spiked and bled out in a godsworn rite like K'Hess Kenjak. The legion oath said life and honor for the Republic. That of the two, honor was the more precious. And maybe Dek was a heretic, too, now, because she wasn't sure she believed that anymore.

Damn certain she didn't want trooper bodies stacked up like cordwood. *Damn* sure she didn't want more dead like Kenjak.

It was always the green ones died first in a war. K'Hess Kenjak had been green as they came.

There'd be a lot of Kenjaks if Snow was wrong.

She and Istel hadn't been green when they'd become partners, because scouts came out of experienced ranks; but they'd been young. They'd gotten older because they were

lucky

good at what they did. Because they could trust each other. Because, until Snowdenaelikk, Dekklis had never doubted her partner's motives. Until Snowdenaelikk, she wouldn't have thought to look and see if he was still following her.

Which he wasn't. Hell and *damn*. Hanging back now, Istel, arms folded and shoulders hunched. Only his voice came after her, bitten to the quick.

"Dek."

"What?"

"What are you doing?"

She could hear the shouts behind the garrison wall. Training noises. Thwack of wooden swords, a centurion bawling abuse at new milae.

She pitched her voice to carry. Hell if she'd walk back to him. Let them shout like debating senators. "Obvious, isn't it?" and pointed.

He threw a narrow-eyed stare at the garrison walls. Cut the gap between them with quick strides. Came a hairsbreadth from taking her arm, hell and damn, *that* was how much Snow had corrupted him. He caught himself at the last. Splayed stiff fingers, palm out, *sorry* and *wait* together.

"We don't have any orders, Dek."

"So?"

A flash of the old Istel, eyes sliding off hers. He stared at the garrison walls. Worked his mouth around stillborn sentences. Then: "The praefecta will ask to see them."

"What, now you're fretting protocol? Orders? The consequences of breaking the rules? Didn't bother you back in Cardik."

"I didn't think we were coming *here*! I thought we were going to warn the Senate!"

"You didn't think!" hissed between teeth, because the guards had noticed them arguing by now, because passersby had. "How do we warn the Senate? I talk to my mother. I *don't* go up there wearing fourteen days of road dirt and a scout's uniform. You listen to me. This isn't Cardik, savvy? You lay hands on a woman here, you shout at her, people notice. You're in Illharek, and you need to remember that. You have no family here. No property. And the legion won't risk the Senate's temper defending one border-born *man*. Listen, Istel. Most of the command here *is* highborn. To them, you're nothing."

And there was the rebel Istel, the one Snowdenaelikk had created up north. Sudden direct stare and raised chin that would get Istel on report if he pulled it with any other officer, that would get him flogged if he tried it on any other highborn.

And what are you, Dek?

Just as infected as Istel, clearly, because she didn't mind the stare or the defiance half as much as she worried she might've said too much. Hurt him, foremothers defend her, insulted him, and when did a daughter of Szanys care about either? But if he walked away from her now, she might not see him again. If she lost him in the Suburba, even Briel wouldn't find him.

She could grab his arm and raise no attention. Did, and gripped hard enough to bruise. "Listen. Before you do something stupid. The praefecta's an old friend of mine. We came up together. She will *never* think I've gone absent without leave."

It took him a few heartbeats. "You're going to lie to her."

"I'm saying I won't *have* to lie. I'll say we were the best chance to get word out of Cardik, which is true. That we ran damn near fourteen days overland to get here. *That's* true. That we found more Taliri in the woods than just normal bandits, and they came after us. Also true. I'm not going to say Cardik's smoke and ash by now, because we don't know that it is. I'm not saying anything about godsworn, or Snow, or Veiko. That means *you* don't."

That should have fixed it. Should've patched the gap between them, gotten her Istel's best *no shit, Dek* face when he knew she was teasing him.

But this was an angry Istel, sullen, who dropped his eyes to the street. Bitter, quiet: "I don't say anything. Let you do the talking. That's how it works here, yeah? Do I savvy?"

What did you expect, Szanys?

"Yeah," she muttered, and swung toward the gate and the guards. "You savvy."

CHAPTER THREE

Snow had warned him about Illharek. She had told him *no sky* and *no light* and *no green things*. She had described Illharek in broad gestures. Made models of it, out of fruit peels and pips and crockery, on the table in the flat they'd shared at Aneki's.

There's the main cavern, that's here, but there's all these side passages. Tunnels, too.

That go where? he had asked, fascinated by the spoons radiating out of the central bowl. He could not imagine a place that matched her description. It was fantastic, impossible, like the noidghe's hearthside stories had been in his childhood.

Deep pits. Streams that feed into the lake. Paths to other cities. Sometimes nowhere at all.

He knew there was a deep lake called Jaarvi, at the bottom of the cave where the underground rivers collected. He knew the Jaarvi fed the Jokki, which was the main river coming out the cave-mouth, the one with the massive road beside it, and the barges and boats clotting its surface. Snow had told him that the buildings in Illharek clung to the stone and stretched up, stacked in layers. That there were bridges connecting levels and walkways that stretched between layers over the basin and the lake.

Like spiderwebs, yeah?

Like spiderwebs, *no*, unless the resident spider was far larger than any Veiko wanted to meet. He looked up in snatches, trying to scope the shape of the place. Some of the bridges overhead were honest rope and planking, swaying as people crossed them. Some of them were what seemed to be stone, arched impossibly across gaps and chasms. He could see buildings clinging to the walls higher up, like some strange fungus, visible as little clots of tiny blue lights. Witchfires, he knew that, but they reminded him of eyes.

"We won't go up there," Snow said casually. "That's highborn territory." And when he only stared at her, "It's a joke, Veiko. Highborn, high places. Yeah?"

"It is not a very good joke."

"No pleasing you." She guided them past a small collection of goats, driven by a ragged woman and a more ragged dog, who barked from the herd's far side and would not come any closer.

"Logi," Veiko said, and glanced down. Logi's head was up, his nose and ears working madly—but he had not drifted a fingerwidth from Veiko's thigh.

Snow leaned close. Put her chin on his shoulder and let her voice drop low. "Keep Logi close, yeah? We got dogs in the Suburba, but they're smaller. Common as rats. People eat them sometimes."

And then she was moving again, following some instinct he did not have. She seemed to know where the gaps would be in the crowds, and had a disturbing habit of darting and dodging.

Give him wind and a sky, he could find his way. Even in Cardik's streets, that had been true. Illharek would require a new set of skills. Well. He was a hunter, or had been. He would manage this new, wretched forest.

Follow Snow closely, step where she stepped. *That* was the challenge. Felt like a newborn takin trailing its mother, all clumsy lurching and graceless steps. At least she was not looking at him. She had eyes on the crowds and the jagged rooflines. They signaled something to her besides *noise* and *chaos*. Signs he needed to learn if he meant to navigate this place.

She turned suddenly onto a narrower, steeper street. There were shops on both sides here, shutters thrown wide to show slabs of raw meat hanging from low ceilings. Chopping noises, the wet sound metal made in flesh, the smell of old blood. The buildings went up several levels, what Veiko assumed were rooms and flats, their windows shuttered against the noise from the slaughter pens and the cave-chill, which deepened the farther they descended.

He supposed the shutters would not help against the stench. There were too many bodies in too small a space, cooking smells and peats-moke and slaughter. At least there was no sewage in the gutters, which parts of Cardik had had. Snow had told him that Illharek enjoyed proper Illhari engineering. Called it *plumbing*.

Veiko didn't know the word. Wondered if *plumbing* was as suspect as those aerial walkways. He cut a glance upward again. They were directly under a bridge now, one of the plank-and-rope variety. It sagged in the middle, where a Dvergir marched ahead of an overburdened Alvir. Easy to imagine a bundle tumbling through the air and landing on some unwary head.

And impossible, while engaged in that imagining, to keep his attention on the street. So Veiko heard the disturbance before he saw it: a ripple of shouts and swearing and *stop her* and *thief*. He dragged his eyes off the bridge and down and *there*, yes, a wrinkle in the forward progress, people crimping aside for a Dvergir child, perhaps eight or nine, running as if wolves were after her. Veiko marked the glint of metal in her hand, and the bulging sash looped around her chest and waist that clearly served a purpose besides holding the too-large tunic on her body. She rabbited through the crowd at apparent random, ricocheting off pedestrians.

Snowdenaelikk had mentioned cutpurses. Veiko put a hand on his beltpouch, shifted his pack higher on his shoulder. Reached down for Logi's ruff and snatched at empty air.

No dog beside him. No Snow, either. He stomped down on panic. Looked and found Snow's ice-colored topknot bobbing through the crowd. He squinted down into the forest of legs, and yes, there, a snatch of red fur. A man could feel a little put out that they had not noticed him missing. He resettled the pack again, squared his shoulders, started after her.

A gap in the crowd opened up, suddenly, right in front of him. The child changed direction, came straight for that gap. Veiko took a fast step back and a hard jag sideways, so that the girl cannoned instead into a man of sturdy middle age, carrying a basket of apples. The man toppled. The apples thumped and rolled.

The child pinwheeled for balance. Caught it not an arm's length from Veiko. Looked up at him and smiled. It was, Veiko thought, the same look a weasel might give to a chicken. And then she spun and dove into the crowd.

Flicker of motion off to his left. He started to turn to meet it. Heard, "Grab her!" and then a body much larger than a half-starved child slammed into him. His bad leg tweaked from dull ache to deep burn and did not, thank the ancestors, give way. He gritted teeth and caught the woman who had hit him by the elbow. Kept them both from going down, somehow.

The woman shoved at him. "Let *go*, yeah?"

He did. Held his hands up, empty. Aware, peripherally, of the crowd making room around them. Of someone shouting and someone else swearing and the smell of bruised apples.

The woman glared at him. Average height for a Dvergir woman, average build, in trousers and a scarred leather apron. Working clothes, worn and patched. Youngish face, narrow-eyed and thin-lipped. Veiko marked the long seax on her hip, which looked just like Snow's. Marked the second knife in her left boot.

"Hey," she said loudly. "Why'd you grab me? I almost had her. You a thief? You working with that girl?"

Veiko blinked. A pinch of heat bloomed under his ribs; that was anger, followed by a spreading cold that was not quite fear. He had played this game before, in Alviri towns and villages, when he came in to trade. Then he'd had both dogs and a ready story—

My brothers are camped in the hills nearby.

—and there had been sensible villagers who did not see a profit in fighting when a man had things to trade. Now, here—no visible goods, no sign of dog or partner. A whole forest of Dvergiri around him.

"No harm," he said in his thickest accent. Stared at her with what he hoped was a convincingly blank expression.

The Dvergir's eyes lit like lanterns. Her face bent into an expression that reminded Veiko of Briel before she snatched a flatcake off someone's plate. "You all alone, skraeling?"

"No harm," Veiko repeated. He wished he dared turn a shoulder and walk away. Wished he dared take eyes off this woman and look for Snow. Do that, and he might catch a knife in the back. The woman had that look. Smile going stiff on the edges.

"Come with me. I'll help you." She made a grab for his wrist.

Veiko dropped his hand to the axe without thinking. Knew his mistake in the next heartbeat. Hard glint in the woman's eye now, rising mutter through the crowd. She loosed the seax at her belt.

"Give you ten on the skraeling," someone said, and another, "Motherless outlanders." A third voice called out, "Take him down, Gert!"

And then, suddenly, it got darker. The shadows seemed to rise up out of the seams in the paving stones, out of the creases and folds in clothing, from the edges of everything. Like a black wind, dimming torches and lamps to mere flickerings.

Sudden witchfire bloomed, running along the street. The air shivered, and then Snow appeared out of apparent nothing, trailing a snarling Logi, as Briel swooped overhead and keened like the angry dead.

A man could laugh at the look on Gert's face. A man could make fists of both hands, too, and hold very still. No little fear in the crowd. No little anger, if he understood the hiss and whispers well enough.

"—toadfucking conjuror—"

"—half-blood—"

"That's *Snowdenaelikk*."

Snow ignored them. Ignored him, too. Looked only at Gert and said softly, "Skraeling's got friends, yeah? He doesn't need you, *Gert*. Abattoir's out of your district, yeah?"

Gert's eyes were huge. "Snowdenaelikk. I'm sorry. I thought—"

"I know what you thought."

Veiko believed he'd seen every shape Snow's face and mood could take. Had seen arrogance, yes, had seen pride—but not this cold-eyed stare that sliced past her curved blade of a nose. He didn't know her in this moment. Did not *want* to know her.

"Apologize to *him*, not to me."

Spreading quiet around them, growing empty as the crowd began to peel away. Gert looked around her. Licked her lip. She made a little bow at Veiko. "Apologies."

Veiko dipped his chin. Would not say *it is no matter,* because clearly it was. Not that Gert was looking for any response out of him. Her eyes were on Snow, who said nothing. But she flipped her wrist, and the witchfire faded. The shadows soaked back to their corners and edges.

Snow turned her back on Gert. Walked away, long loose strides that looked nothing at all like retreat. He guessed he should follow her, without fearing Gert still behind him with her seax and her boot knife. He guessed that he should not mind having to follow Snow, like a dog or a bondie, as if he had no choice.

Do you?

At least Logi was waiting for him this time, ears back and guilty. Fell in at Veiko's heels just as Veiko fell in behind Snow. They made a little train, Snow and he and Logi, for the remainder of the street. Then Snow took another left and down and dropped back. Let him draw even with her.

"What were you doing?" she snapped before he could say anything. "Logi went after a rat, I grabbed for him, I thought you were behind me, I swear to—" She clipped teeth together. Hissed through them. "Going to put a leash on you both, yeah?"

"You knew that woman."

"She's motherless cartel, yeah? Street gang. What passes for the local law in the Suburba."

"Like the Warren."

"Not by half. Tsabrak *owned* Cardik. Nothing happened in the Warren he didn't know and wasn't running. Here it's not like that. The Suburba's a lot bigger. More factions, more politics. More enemies. You have a territory, you keep to it, or you start a war." Snow was angry now, which meant that he'd scared her. "Damn lucky there was only Gert and not Rata's whole toadshit *gang*. You're not local, yeah? You got to stay close. Gert probably figured she could get you alone, shake you out—"

"Sell me?"

"Maybe. Don't look at me like that. Warned you that could happen."

"There is no—" He shook his head.

"Law? Order? Honor?"

Safety, but it was not danger that bothered him. It was feeling like a fool. It had been the same in the ghost roads before that. New terrain, new enemies, new rules. At least in the ghost roads, Helgi had been the only witness to his mistakes.

And Tal'Shik. And the God.

He had been lucky then. Lucky now. Best he learn the rules before that luck ran out.

"Gert was afraid of you."

"She was afraid"—Snow ran her fingers across the dusting of hair on the bottom half of her skull, tugged the end of the topknot—"of this. And down here, afraid means polite. You're lucky that witchfire worked. My little finger still doesn't bend all the way."

"That is because it is still broken." His heartbeat was steadying out again. Deep breath that strained the tightness in his chest.

She rolled her eyes at him. "Listen. Gert shouldn't be here. That's why I came through the Abattoir in the first place. These are *Ari's* streets. If Gert's here, then either Rata's moved up or spread her territory. And either way, means something's happened to Ari."

"Ari."

"Tsabrak's man. Godsworn. This was our—his—territory." He watched the anger run out of her, watched quiet fill in behind it. Thinking again, ancestors defend them.

Veiko left her to it. Concentrated his efforts on staying beside her as she led them down twists of street and alley. The streets coiled in on themselves like the narrow guts of a strange stone beast. The buildings took on alien shapes, odd bulges and angles that looked as if hands had squeezed them out of raw rock. He caught himself looking up more and more often at the city brooding above them. The distant bridges, slim as wires, on which he could no longer see moving shapes.

A bundle might fall a very long way indeed.

On his lips to ask *how much farther?* when he smelled the lake. Cool, wet, with the peculiar smell of still water, and a great deal of it. He sifted through memories of maps made of fruit and flatware. Of Snow's voice, naming rivers.

The Jokki is the biggest, comes out the main mouth. There's a handful of smaller ones running out of the lake into side tunnels. Not much citizen traffic through those, traders, mostly, who don't want to deal with the Riverwalk's traffic. You ever need out fast, you take one of those passages. Then there's the Karas, the Tebir. You want the Tano, though. It's closest to the docks, and it goes Above.

So that must be the Tano there. Actual torches studded the tunnel opening, braziers throwing orange light off rocks as pale as a twilight snowfall. A wooden platform extended over the edge of the lake. There were fair heads on the dockside, moving too straight to be bondies, shouting and laughing and visibly male. One Alvir, two Taliri. A trio of

Dvergiri women stood on the docks, one marking a tablet, the others watching the unloading with folded arms.

"Oh no." Snow hooked his elbow. "No gawking. No stopping." She drew him against the wall, out of the trickle and flow of passersby. Rocked up on her toes, so that their shoulders touched, and looked where he had. "What, never seen a boat unloaded before?"

"In Cardik," he said, "the Taliri burned villages."

"Cardik's near the border, and the Taliri burn villages this far south, too. But some of them settled after the war. Took the ink. That's the difference down here. You look on any of those folk, you'll see the Illhari mark. They're citizens."

"Ink solves old grudges?"

"Business solves old grudges. You've got people with enough to eat, reasonably safe—they don't want to ruin that. Besides. Cardik caught a bad case of godsworn. That's always a problem."

"Tsabrak was godsworn."

"And he's dead, too, isn't he?"

"And Ari?"

"Also godsworn, and cartel. But he wouldn't have gone after an outlander in the streets. The God never liked slaving."

Veiko thought about the girl and Gert, the naked stares from the onlookers, and felt the tweak under his ribs again. "It seems that this might have been a wiser path to take into the city. There are far fewer people to see either of us."

"True. But down here, you and I aren't the problem. Istel can slouch. I don't think Dekklis knows the word. Walks like a highborn, yeah? Not who I want in my company."

"And I am?" Wished the words back as he said them. Too much like complaint and self-pity, and she *had* warned him.

But Snow cocked one of her real grins at him. "Look at me, Veiko. It's a family custom for our women to keep company with foreign men."

CHAPTER FOUR

The copper sign still hung over the shop door. Corrosion had crept across most of it. Only a few bright metal patches remained to catch the lamplight off the docks. Snow's mother had insisted on polishing that toadfucking thing, but Sinnike and Daagné had never liked the bright metal. Had hated polishing it even more. But they would do it anyway if her mother still lived to command it. So her mother was dead, then. Not a surprise. She had not been a young woman when Snow left Illharek. Had been full of disapproval for her eldest daughter, any pride she'd had for Snow's Academy topknot scrubbed away by Tsabrak and the cartel. They'd barely been speaking at the end. Relief on both sides when Snow went north.

So there was no reason at all for the twinge Snow felt under her breastbone. She dropped a step. Stumbled and waved Veiko's concern away with a gesture that sent fire stitching up her arm.

"Motherless fish guts," she said. "In the gutter. Didn't see 'em."

Veiko looked at her sideways. "It does not smell like fish."

"So just say, 'Toadshit, Snow,' and have done."

"I do not see any toads, either."

Took a lot of practice to see what passed for his sense of humor. There, in the little creases at the corners of his eyes. Most times she'd grin back, try to encourage those moments. Foremothers knew Veiko didn't make many jokes. He knew something was wrong with her. He was clever enough to see it, even without Briel's help. But she felt his concern, through the svartjagr's link, prickling through her chest.

Damned if she wanted to explain.

My mother's dead, yeah? Didn't think I'd mind so much.

She shook her head. Looked elsewhere, fuck and damn, found herself staring at the sign, at the shopfront. Fresh paint on the street-level shutters, a god-blinding yellow and orange that wouldn't be cheap. A more modest blue on the second floor, where the men and the bondies lived. The third-floor garret had no streetside windows. Only a double-wide, shuttered door that opened on an iron balcony clinging like a vine to the stone beneath it. Her flat once. Might still be if Sinnike and Daagné had kept any part of their old agreements.

All of the store's shutters were still closed, her mother and sisters having never believed that an apothecary need open early.

First candlemark is for bakers and farmers.

For bondies, too, and husbands. The house had never kept many of either. The ones it had would all be awake now, moving behind those walls. Snow took a deep breath. Imagined the chaos in the kitchen. The smell of baking bread.

Veiko was still watching her. And not just Veiko, no, eyes all up and down the street. Shutters cracked like half-closed eyes, some of the bolder faces peeking out open doors. She hadn't been gone so long that the neighbors wouldn't remember her. Bet they were whispering now, bet the story would be all over the Suburba by fifth mark. That had been her plan, yeah, get *Snowdenaelikk's back* out on the streets and see who came out of hiding.

She grimaced. Locked eyes with Veiko. "This is my mother's shop. She's dead, or the sign would be copper, not green, because she'd insist on polishing it. That puts my sisters in charge. And they won't be happy to see me."

He blinked. Quick frown, sharp nod, and a hand dropped over his axe.

"Not like that," she said. "At least, I don't think it is."

"Mm." His hand didn't move. His eyes did, flickering past her. Marking the placement of windows and doors.

She didn't say *take your hand off that axe.* Let the neighbors see him. Let *that* news travel the streets, too. Might save them some trouble later on, when certain people heard about an armed skraeling in Snowdenaelikk's company.

Right now, all she wanted was *off* those streets. Her arm hurt. Every bit of her ached. And as much as she didn't want her sisters right now, this was the safest place she knew. Fuck and damn, Rata running things in the Abattoir? That made her sisters seem like a basket of kittens.

Snow walked up to the door. Banged the heel of her left hand against the wood. One-two-three, and wait, and again. Listen to the echoes, imagine the startled stare from whoever had door duty this time of day. A child, yeah, bet on that. Some fair-haired bondie brat.

Snow put her face close to the door, so that her breath warmed the wood. Smelled like oil and varnish, smelled like

home

age. She smoothed her hand across the grain. Remembered the bolt and bar on the far side, the black iron lock. Remembered the ring of keys on her mother's belt that Sinnike would carry now. Not that Snow needed keys. She could pick the lock. Force the door. Scare the hell out of her sisters, too, and the poor brat on the other side.

Who chose that moment to say, all thin-voiced bravado: "The shop is closed. You will have to come back at fifth mark—"

"Tell Sinnike that Snowdenaelikk is here."

Half a beat, then, "Domina is busy."

Oh, so that's how it was. "Then tell Daagné."

"She is also busy."

"Listen." Snow caressed the wood. Breathed the oil and paint smell of it. "If *my little sisters* are busy, you get Kaj or Paavo and you get this door open. I'll wait. But not long."

One beat. Two. And then a scampering sound as the child abandoned his post. She imagined a run for the kitchens to roust whoever might have the authority to open the door, or—if the boy mentioned her name, yeah, and bet he would—who would go and summon the dominae.

A whisper of leather and wool, a whiff of two weeks' hard travel as Veiko leaned in beside her. He tapped the door with long fingers and cocked his head at the echoes. Nodded as if the wood had whispered something very clever to him.

"It is not very thick."

"We're not hacking it down." But it tempted. Have the whole street turned out to watch, and tales spread halfway to the Abattoir by third mark. And Sinnike's face. "Kid doesn't know who I am, is all."

"Aneki's newest thralls knew your name."

"I was more likely to come to Aneki's door." Which was probably ash and grease by now if the Taliri had taken Cardik. If Tal'Shik had got her revenge. A hundred motherless *ifs*.

Logi's ears swiveled forward. Deep *oof*, which meant *someone's coming*, same time as Veiko's, "Logi," that meant *stay*.

The interior lock rattled. Briel sent an image of the giant cave-toad that made its meals climbing into svartjagr nests. Warty, unlovely, pasty-pale, devouring the pups whole.

Well. Briel had never quite understood the idea of *sister*. But she had it close enough.

The svartjagr dropped onto Snow's shoulder as the doors swung inward, her tail slapping across Snow's ribs and belly, pulling tight. Hard flap as she stopped herself, which sounded like snapping canvas, sending a gust ahead into the opening doorway that made the woman on the other side flinch and gasp.

Except it was Daagné in the doorway, not Sinnike. A very pregnant Daagné, who managed to rearrange the shock on her face into something approximating a smile.

"Snowdenaelikk."

"Daagné. You're looking well. What are you, sixth month? Seventh?"

Daagné smoothed her hands over her belly. Pregnancy suited her. Smoothed out their mother's jagged features, rounded her cheeks and plumped her lips. Always the prettiest of them, Snow thought, and the worst at hiding her feelings. Daagné's eyes jumped from Snow to Veiko. Lingered there, checking for collars, as fear chased across her face like clouds in a summer wind.

"Seventh." Off balance, the smile slipping. "We didn't get word you were coming."

"I didn't send any." Her finger ached. Her arm throbbed. Briel's excess of sending had shoved a hot poker through the back of both eyes.

Feel like toadshit, sister, we've been running most of the night, you mind letting me in?

She strangled that. Knew damn well why Daagné wouldn't invite her inside. That was the domina's privilege, and that title was Sinnike's, wherever her place in the birth rank. And *that* begged the question:

"So where's our baby sister? Surely not still in bed."

"She. Um."

"Asked you to come out here, yeah? See if I was real? See what I wanted?"

"I." Daagné threw a glance sideways, past the lip of the door. So there must be someone else standing back there, listening. Logi was proof of that, with his shuffling paws and both ears pricked forward. So was Briel, who snaked her neck out and hissed.

"Fuck and damn, Snowdenaelikk, leave her alone. I'm here."

If Daagné had softened, then Sinnike had hardened into their mother's double. That same skin-stretched-over-bone tightness to her. Same way of looking past her hatchet nose as if she had a highborn's sigil under her collarbone instead of a citizen's glyph. But she, like Daagné, was full-blood Dvergiri, so she had to look up at half-blood Snow. She did, glaring, sharp as javelins.

"Can't say this is a happy surprise. Why are you here?"

"Never promised I'd stay away, did I?"

"No. You didn't." Sharp cut to Veiko. Appraised him, up and down. "And look what you've brought with you. I don't see a collar."

Veiko shifted. Temper came off him like heat from a forge. Briel caught it, sifted it through her own understanding.

Nest-stealer, egg-eater, more vividly, so that Snow's vision hazed at the edges. Snow took a handful of Briel's tail where it wrapped hard round her ribs. Squeezed warning. *Peace,* she wished at her. Thought of the night sky in winter, spangled black that went on forever. *Peace.*

Briel's claws relaxed a notch. Veiko did. Which left Snow wishing *peace* at herself to far less effect. Heard her own anger, cold and quiet: "This is Veiko Nyrikki. My partner. And that's Logi. I'm sure you remember Briel. She remembers you."

Sinnike's nostrils flared. "What do you want?"

"Last time I checked, I had rooms on the third floor."

"What, *here?*"

"You put someone else in my flat?"

Headshake, which might mean *no* or *fuck you.* "Where's Tsabrak?"

"Not with me. We want to have this conversation on the street?"

"You don't need my permission to come into this house. *Eldest* sister."

"Call it courtesy, then, that I *am* asking."

"Courtesy." Sinnike snorted. Folded aside, drawing Daagné with her, and dipped a neat little bow. "*Welcome,* then, sister, to your mother's house. You and your . . . partner."

Snow went through the doorway first. At least the interior hadn't changed much. The stone bench with its ceramic tile surface. Bundles of herbs hanging above it from a wrought-iron grid. The set of shelves on the back wall ran floor to low ceiling, studded with jars and bottles. The firedog squatted in the corner, its door sagging open. Fresh coals glowed inside, tiny newborn flames battling the damp.

The curtain between household and shopfront fluttered. Snow guessed everyone else was clustered back there, bondies and husbands alike. Guessed that whispers of *Snowdenaelikk* had run through kitchen and chambers by now. And yeah, there, the other face she'd

dreaded

expected, standing in the shadows by the curtain. Fair-skinned man, gone pallid in sunless Illharek. No collar on his neck now, only the Illhari citizen's glyph, inked black where the metal had left a scar. Dvergiri wore their citizenship much lower, in the hollow nearest the shoulder, where a shirt would hide it. Non-Dvergiri didn't dare, freeborn or freed. There was no difference under the law between the marks, no, every citizen was equal. But Dvergiri were *assumed* to be Illhari, and everyone else was assumed bondie or outlander unless they wore the ink visibly. This man had been all three, but he'd worn the citizen's mark longest of all, almost the whole stretch of Snow's life.

Still. He had changed. There were lines she didn't remember collected at the corner of his eyes and mouth. His braid seemed thinner, silver shot through the ice blond.

"Snow," he said, and the smile might've blinded her. Same one he'd turned on her mother a thousand times. It made her stomach hurt.

"Kaj." She shrugged her bag off her shoulder. Handed the strap to him. Ignored the *are you all right?* in his eyes. Blue like the summer sky at midnight, yeah, damn near black. She had a pair of her own, to stare out of mirrors.

She turned a shoulder and cut his stare off.

"Veiko. Kaj can show you where we'll be staying." Snow looked at Kaj again. "The third floor, yeah? Both of us."

Sinnike twitched. "There's room for him in the men's quarters."

"No. My flat." Draw the syllables out, shape each letter. "And don't be such a motherless prude. Who cares where he stays? What are we, highborn?"

Sinnike scowled. *Not proper* hung between them, unspoken. So did *like our mother.* She sliced her hand down and sideways. "Kaj. Show Snow's *partner* to her flat."

Kaj bowed to Sinnike, then to Veiko. "Please," he said, and took two loud slapping steps on the tile. A small herd of feet pattered behind the curtain. Kaj took a strategic pause before he tugged it aside on an empty hallway. "This way."

Snow felt Veiko's stare on the side of her face. Felt his unease prickling through Briel, tangling with the svartjagr's own.

"Take Briel," she said. "Will you?"

You forgot how strong a svartjagr's tail was, how sharp her talons, until you had one stuck to your shoulder and determined to stay there. Tough battle on a healthy day. Beyond a broken finger and a mangled arm, yeah, going to lose the fight right here.

Veiko saved her. Bigger hands, stronger, he could have peeled Briel off. Didn't have to. Briel worried for Veiko's good opinion. Uncurled her tail with no more resistance than a kitten's. Quick hop and she settled onto Veiko, draped herself across his shoulder like a careless arm.

Fickle little wretch.

Another time Veiko might've made one of his arid jokes, might've let a smile leak from eyes to lips. Now he only gazed at Snow, with the set to his mouth that said he did not approve of her sisters, her household, the whole toadfucked city.

Both of them, then, in agreement.

"It's all right," she told him. "I won't be long."

He nodded. Called Logi and followed Kaj and didn't look back. Kept his hand on the axe, yeah, and didn't limp, although she knew damn well his leg ached at least as much as her arm.

Sinnike watched him, too. Snow knew what she saw. Long ice-colored braids, frayed and slipping across his back. A man who had to duck to go through the doorways, wearing

skraeling

hunter's kit. A man with a svartjagr balanced on his shoulders, *her* svartjagr, when Briel had no good reputation for liking people. A man who looked too much like Kaj.

Sinnike's scowl got deeper, more corrosive. "Daagné," she said, "you go, too."

Daagné almost argued. Spark of protest in her eyes. She squared up and opened her mouth. Wilted the instant Sinnike looked at her, and fled as fast as her melon belly would allow.

"She might've stayed," Snow said mildly. "This is *properly* her household, yeah? Unless the law's changed."

"The law hasn't." Sinnike crossed to the curtain. Twitched it aside and peered behind it and grunted. "But our sister's an idiot. You know it. Our mother did. *She* does."

"I'm sure you've told her so often enough."

"You think she should run the shop? Deal with the cartels and the Academy and everyone else who comes through that door? All Daagné wants is babies and the fucking that comes first."

"That's nothing new." Snow dragged her eyes around the room. Took a lungful of herbs and household. "Place looks good, Sinnike."

"We're pleased that the domina—"

"Oh, cut the toadshit, yeah? I'm not here to claim it."

"Then why? You come back with some uncollared skraeling, insist he sleeps where you do, what am I supposed to think except you're pregnant and back for your rights?"

"Careful." Snow didn't raise her voice, didn't look at her sister. But she stretched her left hand toward the firedog. Crooked her fingers, all but the littlest. It was easy, so easy, to shift the fire's patterns *just so*.

The flames in the firedog guttered a sudden blue, warm orange gone to cold witchfire. Grim satisfaction at the sudden silence, yeah, and what she knew was a Tsabrak-shaped smile on her lips. "I'm not pregnant. And Veiko's not some gelding who'll dip his chin and *yes, Domina* anything with tits. Putting him among your men would be like putting a wolf in with dogs. You'd have a rebellion by the end of the week."

"So you're protecting this family now, is that it? By causing scandal?"

"What scandal? You think anyone but you cares who sleeps where?" Snow crossed the room. Selected one of the bottles off the shelf behind the counter. Tipped it toward the firedog and examined the contents. "What is this?"

"Tincture of mossflower."

"It's the wrong color."

"I added rasi."

"Rasi?" Snow pulled the stopper out. Sniffed. "Why?"

"Mossflower stops pain, but it makes you stupid. Rasi lets you carry on conversation, yeah? Keeps you alert. I'd've reckoned you knew that."

"Where are you getting it?"

"My business, yeah?"

"Rot that. You buying from Stig?"

Sinnike frowned. "Stig washed out of the Tano right before Festival. Kjotvi disappeared right after. Ari went missing last month. Now Rata runs everything from the Abattoir to the docks. I thought that's why you came back, yeah? Settle Tsabrak's toadshit out for him."

"No." Fuck and damn, that was a pile of answers. Told Snow why Gert was running up in the Abattoir. Told her that Rata was probably pulled pretty thin, too. But she still didn't know who had Rata's back, because no way that toadfucker had the brains or the bodies to throw

Ari, Kjotvi, and Stig off. They had the Laughing God on their side. They were godsworn, same as Tsabrak.

And Tsabrak was dead, wasn't he? Tsabrak and the God had made deals with Tal'Shik and her godsworn. Snow'd seen how that had turned out. That same thing might be happening here, too, if Tal'Shik had fingers in the Suburba, too, and not just among the Taliri.

And if *that* were true, then those agents could be anyone. Anywhere.

Fuck and damn, we're too late, Szanys.

Snow tilted the bottle again. Studied the blood-thick swirl at the bottom. "You know who's helping Rata drop the God's people?"

"I don't know. I don't ask. I buy rasi from her, that's all. You leave your heresy in the streets where it belongs."

"Who's talking about heresy? This is smuggling. Senate banned rasi after the Purge, yeah?"

"No one will know."

"No one except any competent herbalist."

"It's *medicine*."

"It's addictive. Guaranteed repeat customers. It's a good idea. Brilliant. You could sell the recipe to the Academy and walk away. Let them make it legal."

"Since when are you worried for legal? I got this shit from *your* friends first."

"I'm worried about *you*. Rata's dangerous because she's stupid. Stig wasn't."

"Stig's dead, yeah? So Rata does *something* better."

"All that toadshit you spouted about how I brought shame on this house, how I put everyone in danger, and now you're in bed with a cartel."

"You did all right. Say I learned from you, eldest sister. Besides. You always said you didn't give a motherless shit for running the place. So. Now you care how I do it?"

"No. You're right. Your shop." Snow put the bottle back with insincere gentleness. Turned and looked at her sister again. "Daagné's on her, what, second? How many do you have?"

"One. A girl."

"Congratulations."

"Huh. Daagné tell you her first was a boy? She insisted on keeping it. He's oldest."

"He's no threat to your daughter's inheritance."

"Way the Senate's been voting lately, he might be. A lot of Reforms coming down. Eldest child inherits, not eldest daughter—that's the rumor."

Old argument, worn smooth between them. Snow rolled her eyes. "The day the Houses let men run them, we all turn Alviri. What's her name, your brat?"

"Aina." Sinnike stabbed at the firedog's guts with a poker. "Fuck and *damn*, will you put the fire back?"

Snow uncurled her fingers. The witchfire warmed, changing back to orange. She came around the counter and propped her hip against the edge of it. "Listen. I'm not here for you, or for this place." She took a breath. Told exactly as much of the truth as Sinnike needed, leaving out heresy and godsworn and toadshit her sister didn't need, might not believe, might tell the wrong pair of ears. "The Taliri are moving south. Raiding."

"The Taliri are always raiding."

"I'm not talking caravans. I'm talking whole villages burned, up near the border. Alviri villages. Those refugees came to Cardik. Half of them ended up selling themselves into collars, and the rest looked for revenge. So. There was a riot inside the city, same time the Taliri rushed the gates. And not a raiding party, either. A small army."

Sinnike was staring at her. "So what are you saying?"

"That Cardik's probably ashes. I reckon we'll start seeing refugees *here*, sooner or later. And let me tell you, baby sister, they are not like the toadbellies we have in Illharek. Our Alviri are tame. The ones from the borderlands are feral. They hate us. Dvergiri. Illhari. They don't see a difference. Anyone with ink, light or dark skin, doesn't matter. And those are the Alviri who will come here. They'll rot this city from the inside, and when the Taliri get here, it will crack."

"And what, now you're all concerned about the Republic? I doubt that." Oh yes, Sinnike was their mother's daughter, arms folded tight across her ribs. "You haven't taken a step without Tsabrak's say-so for a decade. So where is he in all this?"

"Dead. Took a trooper's sword during the riots in Cardik. I'm not here on his business. Not anymore. He wanted that riot, and I didn't. We disagreed. End of our association."

Another few beats of quiet as the Suburba's morning routine leaked through the shutters. Inside the shop, only the firedog's crackling mutter for company, and the kitchen's distant rattle.

"Then let me ask you again," Sinnike said, softly now. "Why did you come back? It's a big Republic. More cities than this one. Why come back *here*?"

"Two reasons. First one." Snow pushed her sleeve back. "This needs a little help. Took a sword cut."

"Fuck and damn." Sinnike came around the counter. Looked with a professional's eye at puckered stitches, at the wound's livid lips. "What'd you use on it?"

Not *what happened?*, not *who did that?* Snow felt the crooked grin crawl onto her face. "Cold water."

"Cold?"

"Couldn't build a fire. Not a lot of time. Taliri were on us."

"Who stitched it?"

"Veiko."

"Huh. Not bad." Sinnike turned Snow's right arm carefully. She pretended not to see the godmark on her palm. "You'll scar. Don't imagine that bothers you."

"Not especially. More concerned about wound rot."

Narrow look. Sinnike laid her knuckles on Snow's cheek. Frowned. "Halfway to it, yeah? I'll make a poultice."

"Send up the water, and I'll do it. —Not *like* that. I trust your skills. I just want it quiet, yeah? You. Me. Veiko. No one else needs to know. You brew down here, everyone will." She started to tug her sleeve back down. Sinnike grabbed her left wrist. Twisted her hand none too gently into the firedog's glow.

"How'd you break that finger?"

"I didn't. Tsabrak did. Part of our disagreement."

Sinnike traced the line of the bone. Still swollen at both ends, still tender. Snow clamped her teeth together.

"Just the one finger. Doesn't sound like Tsabrak. I figured he'd take a whole hand."

"He didn't want to ruin me. Just, you know. Make it harder to conjure. Or fight."

"Sounds like Tsabrak." Sinnike let her go. "And the second reason you're back?"

Snow looked up at the ceiling, crossbeams and plaster. Veiko would be in the apartment by now, probably pacing, certainly worrying. Feel that much, prickling through Briel. "We're here to stop the Taliri."

CHAPTER FIVE

The flat was larger than the one they'd shared at Aneki's. This one had a separate bedchamber off the main room and a firedog in both. Stone walls, stone floors, even here on the third level, against Aneki's squeaking wood and drafty walls. There was also a pump in the corridor outside, and a latrine closet. Kaj had shown him both, his eyes hanging slyly on Veiko. Had explained their purpose in careful Dvergiri.

Kaj had apologized for the dust, too, once he'd got the door open. A broom, he promised, a mop, a boy to clean. A bucket for the pump, some pots for cooking. Fresh linens. *Here*, the window, the balcony, the view wasn't much, but you could smell the Tano. And then he was gone again, leaving the door open behind him.

Veiko stayed on the balcony. Set Briel on the railing. Waited there, arms crossed, as Logi looked for mice in all the flat's corners. He breathed the tang of too many people, too many ovens and fires. And under all of that, a dampness that clung to the back of his throat and crept in under his clothing. Not a smell so much as a taste, a presence.

Illharek.

He looked up, followed the cave walls as high as the light would allow. The walls sloped inward here, funneled down toward the lake and the Tano. That meant there were no bridges overhead. No witchfires, either. An absolute black, and echoes, and the immeasurable, invisible mass of stone.

Only a fool's hands would sweat, thinking about all that rock. Only a fool would gasp like a landed fish, imagining that the darkness had weight. Only a child feared the dark. Snowdenaelikk could drive the shadows aside, could call witchfire out of the black.

Any Dvergir can.

Which he was not. Would never be. He might comb out his braids, trade leather trousers for loose cloth, and he still would not pass for anything except

skraeling

outlander. Too tall for an Alvir, too fair for a Talir.

Too much like Kaj.

There were scars on Kaj's neck. Old and faded, but still visible. He had an accent far fainter than Veiko's, an Illhari's single braid. The Illhari sigil inked into his skin. And he had Snow's axe-jagged features, or she had his. The same midnight eyes, the same ice-colored hair. Obvious to anyone, what their relation. But Snow had said nothing. Take that as an indication of where Kaj ranked in her estimation.

Snowdenaelikk had told him once that all manner of people

even yours, Veiko

came to Illharek. She had asked once last winter, during those long nights in Cardik, what his people called themselves. She knew that there were different tribes: the Jaihnu, and the Pohja to the north, and the K'Rel in the frozen marshlands of the east. She knew that he was Jaihnu. Just as she must have known Kaj was. She must have seen the sameness in them, and she had said nothing to him. So he might wonder where *he* fit in her estimation, too.

"Chrrip." Briel bent her head around to look at him. Nipped gently at his fingers. She did not understand his thoughts. But she understood the roil and upset in his head and his gut, and she did not approve.

He rubbed a knuckle across her skull. Hard bone under skin like fine suede, softer than the membrane on her wings, and tougher. Batsnake. Svartjagr. Illhari natives who lived wild in the caves. Snow had promised to show him their nests.

"Chrrip." Briel leaned into his touch. She, of them all, was happy to be here. Sent her impression of

diving and turning

flying in darkness that made Veiko's eyes ache.

"Go," he told her.

She launched off the balcony, dip and flap before she caught air. Veiko watched the pattern she took, climbing breezes and drafts that he couldn't feel on his skin, couldn't smell. He trusted that she would not bump against the stone walls that he could not see. Trusted that she could navigate that absolute dark.

Cardik had been strange, but at least it had a sky. This place—oh ancestors. Veiko had never missed the ghost roads before. It was a dangerous place, but he knew it, and its rules. Don't step in the river. Don't feed the ghosts. Don't lose your spirit guide.

But in Illharek he knew nothing at all, except trust Snowdenaelikk.

He closed his eyes. It took drugs

poison, Veiko, be honest

to put him close to the glacier in the ghost roads. But he imagined the steady thump of his heartbeat, like a drum. Imagined the wind coming off the ice, and the flat pewter sky. Imagined Helgi beside him, tail curled over his back. Close enough to touch, there, reach down and feel Helgi's cold nose in his palm, and Helgi's hot breath. Hear Helgi's growl, warning and query together.

Except that was not Helgi. Helgi's voice was deeper. That was Logi's growl and—as Veiko opened his eyes and turned and grabbed, on sheer reflex—Logi's fur sliding under his hand. He grabbed a fistful, earned a yip and a glare over Logi's shoulder, but the dog stopped. Crouched, and the growl got louder.

And there, the reason why. Kaj had come back with the boy. But it wasn't broom and bucket that had Logi's attention, no, it was Kaj spreading the contents of Snow's pack across the dust-coated table. It was Kaj with a scroll in his hands, plucking at knots.

"Stop," Veiko said, sharper than was courteous for the guest that he was. But he had a handful of irritated dog, and a mindful of Briel, and the weird doubling of sensation that was Snowdenaelikk filtered through svartjagr. She

I/we

was no happier than

I/we

he was, blurry sense of

coming

agitation and the farthest end of her patience.

It would be dangerous for Kaj if she came and found him rooting around in her things. So Veiko said again, "Stop, please," and then, "Stay!" He released Logi. Wished

peace

at Briel. Crossed back into the dim and rescued Snow's pack himself. He felt over its surface. Found a second scroll under his hand. A small book. The spare shirts were already out on the table. The pouches and the small bottles, too, but not lined up neatly. Scattered, as if Kaj had pushed through them fast. As if he'd had some idea what he was looking for.

Or he'd wanted everything out and visible before Veiko noticed what he was doing.

"Put it down," Veiko said. "The scroll."

Kaj did, though his surprise curdled into defiance almost before the scroll touched wood. He pinned Veiko with a direct stare.

"There is nothing to worry about," Kaj said. Slowly. Careful of the syllables. "I will not steal from her."

Veiko hooked the scroll with a fingertip. That was imagination, that his flesh tingled where it met the stiff vellum. "Do you know what she is? What she can do?"

"Better than you, I think."

"If that is true, then you are a fool to touch any of this." Definitely, he felt tingling. Veiko pushed the scroll back into her pack. Ran a quick eye across the pouches and bottles. He thought that was all of them. "What were you doing?"

"It is custom," Kaj said, as if speaking to a child, "for a servant to unpack a guest's belongings."

"Is it also custom, to"—Veiko fumbled for the word—"to unwrap and look at scrolls?"

"You mean *read*." Kaj smiled. And then, very softly, in a language Veiko had not heard for a long year of exile: "Let me say it again. This is an Illhari courtesy, Veiko Nyrikki. Servants unpack a guest's belongings. It is part of hospitality. And Snowdenaelikk is Illhari. I tell you—she expects this. Do you understand me?"

"I do," Veiko said, in the same language. Tasted like rust on his tongue, rough edged and bitter and strange. "And I say—she never mentioned this custom to me, and I have never seen it."

"You are not long off the mountain. What, a summer? Two? Do you know so much about Illhari customs, having spent so much time among us? Perhaps she forgot how young you are and thought you understood." Arrogance pulled the corners of Kaj's mouth, shaped like a smile.

"Snowdenaelikk is my partner. I know better than you what she wants."

"Partner, is it? Who are you? Some youngest son without prospects, come south to win your fortune? Some ragged hunter who can barely feed yourself? *Partner*. A winter's amusement, I think."

Veiko's skin grew hot. "I am a noidghe."

"Hunter's braids. No drum. I don't know what kind of noidghe you must be."

Veiko wondered that himself, in the deep quiet of night. He thought—each time he opened his eyes to the glacier, under the silver sky—that he should not be there. That he was just what Kaj said, a hunter, a youngest son without prospects. A murderer and an outlaw. But he was noidghe, too, whatever else, and Kaj had stopped just short of calling him *liar*.

Veiko gripped the axe handle until his bones ached. A man did not draw a weapon as a guest in another's home unless he courted blood feud.

"Among *my* people," Veiko said slowly, "a man does not insult a guest in his house. Perhaps it is different for the Illhari. Perhaps you can tell me, since that is so clearly what you are."

Pink crawled from Kaj's neck to the roots of his hair. The citizen's mark floated black on his skin. He opened his mouth around something poisonous, possibly fatal.

And then Snow said, from the doorway, "Right. What's all this?"

The bondie boy dropped his broom. Veiko took his hand off the axe. Kaj almost smiled, and the gleam in his eye made Veiko grind his teeth.

"Veiko is confused about our customs," Kaj said in rapid, fluent Dvergiri. "I have tried to explain, but his grasp of our language is poor. I think he's afraid I'm stealing from you."

Snow had a copper basin cradled in her left arm, heavy enough that the cords stood out on the back of her hand. She cleared a careful place among the pouches and bottles. Nudged her shirts aside. Set the basin on the table and traced the rim of it with one finger. Then she looked at Veiko.

He drew a deep breath and let it out slowly. Looked back at her and said nothing.

"Kaj. That will be all. Thank you." Quiet, oh ancestors. The anger smoked off her.

For a moment, Veiko thought Kaj might argue. A flicker of something in those indigo eyes, a tension in the mouth. And then gone, so fast that Veiko wondered if he had imagined it.

"Domina. As you wish." Kaj bowed, stiff and Illhari proper. Took himself out the door with a servant's quick obedience. Snow stared after him, drawn up in a brittle quiet. Glacial fury coming off her, seeping through Briel, who was not at all interested in coming back down, no, who wanted very much to stay high and away from Snow in this mood.

No blaming Briel. Veiko entertained a brief wish for his own wings.

The bondie chose that moment to pick his broom up off the floor. Snow snapped around at the scrape and glared at him. One breath. Two while the boy looked as if he might drop it again and flee.

"Go ahead," Veiko said in the same tone he might use with spooked takin. Gentle, careful, avoid a stampede. "It is all right. Finish your work."

The boy looked at Snow.

"Go ahead," she repeated. "Finish. Then fill the basin with water, yeah?"

"Domina," he squeaked, and Snow grimaced. Took herself out onto the balcony, collecting Logi on the way. Left Veiko to follow or not, as he chose.

He followed, after a heartbeat. Came up beside her and put his hands on the railing. Gripped hard and counted his own breaths, one for each gripping finger, one for each toe, and started over.

"That didn't take very long, you making friends," Snow said when he'd gotten through each of his hands twice and begun again on his right foot. "At least no one's bleeding."

"I did not start it."

"I know that. You caught him snooping."

"He claimed it was Illhari hospitality."

"Oh, it is. It's a very polite way of spying on your guest and assuring yourself that she isn't carrying extra weapons, or poison, or anything else of interest. Which I was. The scrolls. The books. And poison."

"A father should not spy on his daughter."

He had wielded axes less sharp than the look Snow cut at him. "Did he fucking say that? He's my father?"

"No. But it is obvious."

"You don't talk about those things, Veiko, not with Illhari. It's draw-weapons rude, yeah?"

"To talk about fathers." Months among her people, so that her language was more familiar than his own, and still, she could surprise him. "That seems foolish."

"Foolish. Huh. So whose name do *you* carry? Nyrikki. Your father's clan, yeah?"

"Yes." He sensed a trap. Couldn't quite see the edges.

"Right. But your mother's the only parent you know for certain. Your father's a *guess*, yeah? Only she knows for sure. So tell me who's being foolish."

It was like realizing that solid ground on which you had stepped was, in fact, fragile ice under snow. Sudden crack and then ice water up to your knee, and the twin rush of *stupid* and *dangerous*. The most important thing to do was stay calm. Too much reaction, you might fall in deeper. Might not get yourself out again.

And so, no inflection: "You do not know my mother."

"No. I don't. But how many men do? *You* can't say. Your *father* can't. *She* can."

"My mother," he began. Stopped, took a breath, started again. "My mother is honorable."

Snow grinned unkindly. "So it's draw-weapons rude for me to suggest that she is the only parent you know for certain, yeah?"

He bit off one word, spit it out. "Yes."

"So then."

"A child will look like its father. *I* look like mine."

"And there's a shortage of blue-eyed, fair-skinned giants where you're from?"

"I do not think that my father looks that much different than yours."

Oh ancestors, the look on her face. Logi whined. Thrust his head and shoulders between them, tried to squeeze his whole self into the gap. Deliberate nothing from Briel, who did not want to be noticed. Svartjagr were wiser than dogs. Wiser than men, too, who continued an argument for its own sake.

He braced for retaliation, but Snow said nothing. Silence so loud he could hear individual voices at streetside, loud enough it was thumping in his ears along with his heartbeat. The bondie's broom rasped loudly behind them, scraped across raw nerves.

"Enough," Snow snapped. She twisted neck and head around, threw words like stones. "Fill the basin. Then go. Leave the broom." Watched, narrow-eyed, as the boy scrambled to do as she asked.

Then she said, low-voiced, so that Veiko had to lean closer to hear her, "Highborn alliances are built on no one knowing exactly who sired whom. Dek's got probably five men who might be her father. That's five other Houses won't move against hers. Good planning, yeah? It's the same law that says I'm legal owner of this place because I'm eldest daughter. It doesn't matter my mother fucked her skraeling bondie and kept the issue out of sentiment. I am my *mother's* daughter, yeah?"

It was one thing to hear *skraeling* from villagers and strangers. Quite another to hear Snow spit it out like bad beer. She put a great value on understanding the whys of things. She put great value on having him understand, too, when he would be content knowing only what to do. So he tried, this time, to put himself in her place and figure out the why of her lapse.

She simply hadn't noticed. She wasn't even looking at him now, instead staring blind and quiet at ancestors knew what. Not the people below in the street, who carried on about their noisy business. It was a different cadence of Dvergiri down here than what he'd heard in Cardik. Faster, slurred and liquid. Like Snow had sounded when he first met her. Like she had sounded just now, words spilling out faster than her wits.

Had been a time Veiko would not have minded her silence. A man's secrets—or a woman's—were not his concern. But that had been before he had

saved my life, yeah?

interfered in Snow's business. Before she had returned that favor, time and again, until only a lawspeaker might untangle their debts.

Veiko took one more step on the ice. "What has you so unhappy?"

"You mean, besides my sisters and Kaj? Being back in this godsrotted city again? Besides that?"

"Yes."

He watched the temper drain out of her. Watched weariness fill in behind, running deeper than flesh and bone. "I reckoned we might have a little trouble, yeah? That's why we came down through the Abattoir. The God's not happy with either of us right now. I wanted to see if he'd passed along the word about you and me. See if Ari came at us."

"And if he had?"

"We'd've talked it out. Or fought it out. Settled it, yeah? So we can worry about what's important."

"You might have mentioned this plan sooner."

"Didn't want Dek to hear. She'd appoint herself escort. Spend a day arguing her out of it, yeah? And I'd still be afraid she'd follow us."

"I think Istel would be the more likely for that."

She looked away. Hunched up like a wet bird. "Best reason of all to keep quiet. Point is: I figured on trouble. Figured we could handle it. But no Ari. Instead we got Gert. She's Rata's dog, and that means we need to see Rata. Today. Now. As soon as I deal with this arm. Don't argue, Veiko. Listen. Sinnike tells me that Stig's been dead since winter. And Kjotvi." She showed him the God's sigil on her palm. "That's three senior godsworn."

"It is a bad season for the God's people." Veiko shrugged. "Perhaps Ari had enemies."

"Damn sure he did. But he had the God with him, too, yeah? Unless he didn't. Unless there was some reason the God didn't get involved to save them."

"Perhaps he was displeased with them." Veiko remembered the last time he'd seen the God, kneeling on the bank of the black river. Remembered the God's blood on his axe. "Or perhaps he could not help them. Perhaps he lacked the strength."

"Yeah. That's what I'm—sss."

The bondie came back with the basin. Snow watched the boy stagger over to the table. Watched him set the basin down, with only a little sloshed over the side. Watched him retreat all the way through the door. Then she moved: crossed and leaned against the door, head cocked. A smile, finally, tight and thin.

"There. Now he's down the steps."

"You thought he meant to spy."

"Kaj doesn't like not knowing things. The whole household will be watching us, every move." She crossed back to basin and table. Dipped her finger in the water.

The air felt suddenly heavy. Blanket warm, summer thick, wrapped and squeezing and—

Gone. Steam curled off the water.

Veiko blinked. "That is useful."

"That's showing off. A little patience and a fire would accomplish the same end." She rummaged among the mess on the table. Plucked a pouch out of the mess, and one bottle. "It's just I'm not patient, yeah?"

"I had noticed."

"Huh." A drop from the bottle. A pinch from the pouch. She made eyelock with him. Held it as she eased her sleeve back, bared arm and stitches that pulled tight in her flesh. Lowered her arm into the basin, slow exhale that made its way into her voice.

"We need a bath and a rest, but that can wait until we're back from Rata's. Ah, *shit*, that hurts."

"The water is too hot."

"It's not the water that stings. —Hold it, will you?"

He steadied the basin as she rolled her arm back and forth. He did not like the color of the water. Did not like the seep from the lips of the wound, or the way her hand shook. Did not like the look she cast at it, most of all. Narrow eyes, thoughtful, not at all pleased. She'd looked at him that way last winter when his leg would not heal.

Veiko knew better than to tell Snow her business, or ask for a diagnosis, either. She would say *fine*, and he already had the expression on her face for proof. Were it *his* arm, she'd have him flat on his back, going nowhere while she brewed potions and changed the dressings herself.

"I will go with you to see this Rata," he said, already anticipating the argument. Already marshalling his own. "You cannot—"

"Of course you will."

"What?"

"I said when *we* get back, Veiko. You're coming with me."

His wits scattered. He'd prepared for battle, and she'd come from a direction he had not expected. "I thought you would go alone."

"Fuck no. Need you at my back. Why? You prefer to stay here?"

"No. But I do not know the streets."

"Best you learn them. Best you memorize every alley."

"Snow. It is not wise to go at all. Not with me, not alone. Your friends—"

"Ha."

"—are dead. That is not accident."

"Of course it's not. But I don't know details yet. And until I do, I need Rata wondering what I'm doing back here, and who you are. I need her worried about me, not the other way. So we'll go down there, you and I, and *I'll* worry her while *you* make sure no one sticks anything sharp in my back. Then we come back. Be *seen*, you and me, for a couple days. Public baths. Taverns. Walking up and down the street. And then you disappear." Her words came fast now, tumbling like water over a cliff. "The hills around Illharek aren't all farmland, yeah? There's canyons. Forests. A lot of empty space. I think it might be a good idea if you explore it. Stay up there. Then I go out to find you, stay gone a day or three, maybe bring you back with me. We don't set a pattern. We don't settle any one place. We keep them guessing where we are, or if one of us is alone."

"And when I am"—he jerked his chin upward—"disappearing. Then where will you be?" Knowing what she'd say.

"Places I can't take you. Places Rata won't follow me. Into the Tiers." She matched his gesture, chin pointed up. "Don't worry, yeah? No one will see me unless I want it."

She meant conjuring. There would be no backlash in Illharek. No reason she could not conjure as easy as breathing. Except she had a raw wound in her arm, and the beginning of fever turning her eyes flat and bright. Had a broken finger on her other hand, and that might hurt her conjuring in ways Veiko did not understand. A noidghe did not depend on hands or cities for what he did. A noidghe walked the ghost roads and spoke to ghosts and once led a dead Snowdenaelikk's spirit back to her body. He did not want to do that a second time. Wasn't sure that he could.

He would as soon argue the sun purple as change Snow's mind once she'd set it. She had some kind of plan. Well. It was her city. Her people. Only a fool told someone else her business. A fool, or a partner.

He put his own fingers into the water, paying no attention at all to the heat and the color and the stick-to-the-back-of-his-throat fumes coming off it. Took Snow's wrist and turned it, so that the stitches grinned up out of the water. And drew his fingers across the fine bones of her wrist, onto her palm. Stopped, with his thumb in the solid middle of the God's sigil.

"They were godsworn, your Stig, Kjotvi, and Ari, and they are dead."

"I'm not either of those things. Godsworn or dead." She closed her hand over his. Hid the God's mark under a striping of dark and light fingers. "I thought we'd have trouble from *him* after Cardik. I think we might have bigger worries." Her eyebrow arched, mouth drawn tight in one corner, eyes drilling into him. Expecting him to figure it.

"You think Tal'Shik is responsible."

"Some way. Somehow. This *smells* like her work. Ari. Stig. Kjotvi. That's pre-Purge stuff. Either that, or the God's really dead."

"I did not hit him *that* hard."

"Tal'Shik might've jumped him afterward. What if he *is* dead?"

"Then we have one fewer enemy."

"Then so does Tal'Shik. The God's the one thing between her and Illharek, yeah? We need him."

As if the God were an honored ancestor. As if Veiko wanted anything more than to finish what he'd started with axe and anger. He recalled that ghost-roads cave, black and gaping. Remembered the God standing sentry, bargaining for Snowdenaelikk's soul.

Veiko's guts knotted around old fury. "The Laughing God will not be your ally."

"Maybe. Maybe not. Maybe he's decided making nice with Tal'Shik is stupid, too." Snow untangled her fingers. Pulled her hand, her arm, out of the water. She pretended great interest in the stitches. "I've seen Tsabrak, Veiko. Out of the corner of my eye. In shadows. Started in the forest, yeah? Haven't seen him since we got *into* the city. Yet."

Veiko had been kicked by a takin once, square in the chest. He felt like that now, again. Tsabrak was a dead man's name. It was not a surprise, no; Snow had the power, same as he did. She had crossed the black river and returned. That made her a noidghe, same as he was. So of *course* she would see the dead.

But *that* particular ghost. The hollow ache in his chest turned bitter. Backed up in his throat. "Has he said anything?"

She flinched. "His usual toadshit. *You were my right hand. Look out, there's a Talir about to gut you.*" She side-eyed him. "Why can't you see him?"

Asking him, dear ancestors, as if he held the wisdom. Which he did, by her standards. There *were* no Illhari noidghe. At least he'd grown up knowing what noidghe did. At least he had ancestors who might've walked the spirit roads.

She might have ancestors, too. Her father was Jaihnu. And only a fool would bring that up now.

He wished he could reassure her, but, "I don't know. I have seen ghosts who wish to be seen. Tsabrak would have no reason to speak to me. You were important to him. Perhaps that is why you can see him."

"Fantastic. Do I answer him? Ignore him?"

"Listen if he speaks. But ask no questions and make no deals. The dead always want something."

"He might know where the God is. If *anyone* does, it'd be Tsabrak." He had seen the range of her moods. Knew what the half-cocked smile meant, which looked reckless and wasn't. That was fear, which Snow did not manage by running away. No. She ran straight at it. And she was no good at bargains.

This was stupid. Foolish. But it would give him something to do when she exiled him to the Above and the forests and went about her own errands: "Let me look for the God in the ghost roads. Trust nothing Tsabrak says on the matter. *I* will find him."

Snow blinked. Her mouth flapped like Briel's wings for a few beats. Then she said, simply, "Thank you."

"Do not thank me yet. The Laughing God might be truly dead."

"Then we'll find another way to stop Tal'Shik."

Ancestors, that was almost enough to make Veiko wish for the God.

CHAPTER SIX

Veiko took some convincing to leave Logi behind and follow her onto the street; it was not the destination that he balked at so much as the journey. She coaxed him onto the balcony, then up the ladder and onto the roof. He did not mind that climb, or soft-footing across the roof tiles. But the second ladder—an erratic tracery of iron rings and spikes jutting out of the bricks, hand- and toeholds most of the way to the street—stopped him cold.

Might stop her, too. The fucking arm was a problem. Not pain, she had that damped out. But weakness. Muscles and sinews abused past endurance. At the least, she'd pop stitches. Fuck and damn, and no help for it. She lowered herself over. Ground her teeth together and *made* the fingers lock. She'd never fallen off a wall. Not about to start now.

"Follow me," she said. Paused halfway down when he hadn't. Looked up into Veiko's whole face gone to ice and stone.

But then he swung a leg over and let her guide his foot to a place where the brick jutted out. She kept her hand on his leg, held him steady as he found his hold on the wall.

"There are stairs," he muttered. "People will notice."

"No," she told him. "No one will even look this way."

Which got her a tight little nod that made his braids swing and bob. And then he came down the wall, quick as he could manage.

He learned fast. Barely a scuff as he dropped down beside her.

"Your first wall, yeah?"

"Yes."

"You're wasted as a hunter. We can use a man with your talents in the Suburba."

Another witchfire stare. Silence, which meant profound disapproval. Which might mean a little pride, too, mixed in.

She took a right turn, up the Street of Apothecaries. A decade earlier, Rata had run her gang out of the rotting corpse of a two-story tavern, with moldy, vacant flats on the upper floor and a cellar that wasn't honest enough to keep beer. So killing Ari should've meant a move up. Ari'd run his cartel out of the Abattoir, from a back-alley office that smelled like sweat and old blood. A definite improvement over the tavern. Except Snow had seen Gert up there, Rata's second—third, maybe—which argued that Rata was exactly where she'd always been, a stone's throw from the Tano, down on the docks.

Please, she still was. Snow didn't think she had a wasted trip's worth of energy left.

She let the conjuring drop. Stalked down the middle of the street, with Veiko beside her, like she owned the scuffed stonework.

But we did own it, Snow. Remember?

She'd walked on Tsabrak's right side back then. His tall, pale-haired shadow, his right hand. Now she had her own taller, paler shadow. People needed to see him. To see her. She wanted the word to run like rats before a fire. *Hear* the muttering. *Feel* the stares.

Feel Veiko, too, winding so tight you could hear him creak.

"This," he murmured, "is unwise."

"Not entirely."

Gust of air, which was Veiko's exasperation. "Do you want a fight?"

"There won't be a fight." She said it with confidence. Had to make Veiko believe it and convince herself, too. There'd been a time Rata wouldn't *dare* take on the God's people.

Which you aren't anymore.

Rata didn't know that. Rata thought Snowdenaelikk was still Tsabrak's right hand. Pet conjuror. Pet killer. The God alone knew what rumors were attached to her name. And after that Abattoir encounter, Gert would've scuttled back down here with her own report, probably puffed up so that Gert didn't look like an idiot for running from witchfire and shadows. Lightning and fireballs, the stone streets melting like ice.

Tsabrak had encouraged the fantasies. *His* doing, that half the Suburba thought the half-blood Snowdenaelikk could turn a person's blood into oil and set her on fire, while the other half thought she could poison the whole Senate before breakfast.

Dekklis had thought so once. The difference between Dek and the Suburban cartels, though, was Dek wouldn't let fear slow her down. And Rata—

Rata might've killed Ari. Might've killed Stig. So maybe Rata wouldn't scare so easily, either, these days.

Well and good. She could manage more than shadows and witchfire, too. Maybe she did want a fight, to cause someone else pain to match the throb in her arm.

The stone ceiling hung lower, this close to the Tano, bulging and dripping and glistening like a snail in sunlight. Pallid white, brilliant pink, rusty orange all smudged together. The stonecutters said it was different minerals that made the colors.

Pretty enough, if you liked rocks. If you didn't mind the dark smears of charcoal and grease from the smoke holes. Or the noise. Everything echoed down here, water-slap and voices and the hundred other sounds of people going on with their lives.

Veiko looked up exactly once. Hunched his shoulders and looked away fast.

"It won't fall."

"I know."

"Ceiling goes up again soon. Don't worry."

"I am not worried." Staring straight ahead, eyes on the lakeside, on the boats and the rafts.

So he did not see what Snow did, looking up: Briel crawling upside down on the rock, wing tips and talons dug deep in cracks only a svartjagr could find. Amazing how fast she could move like that. If you didn't know where she was, you wouldn't see her at all. Liquid shadow.

Well done, Snow sent at her. Got a warm rush of good feelings in return and a glimpse of the world from Briel's vantage. Upside down, dizzy-quick, a flash of streets and buildings. Then came the second layer, the svartjagr's deeper impressions, the world sketched in shapes and spaces. Solid stone and buildings, the flexible, treacherous Tano, the freedom of the open air. Briel, like Veiko, would be happier once the cavern opened up again.

Soon, she told Briel. And *stop.*

Sending didn't hurt like it had before Briel had added Veiko to her pack. There was no blindness, but the headaches were still formidable. Snow wished she could pinch the bridge of her nose, rub her forehead. But it would not do to walk onto Rata's turf massaging away a headache. The old Snowdenaelikk, the one Rata remembered, admitted no weakness.

I remember that version of you, Snow. I think she's still there.

Tsabrak's silhouette, solid dark against the shadows. There for a blink. Snow turned her chin away. *So you're back. Don't know why. Don't need your help.*

No telling if the ghost heard. But at least he stopped whispering.

Briel got her wish soon enough. The bloated stone overhead retreated as they crossed into the warehouse district. The buildings were lower here, which contributed to the effect of increased ceiling space. Two stories, not the standard three, blank walls unmarked by windows.

Snow cut a sharp left between two of the warehouses. Another left, and then a right, into the alley that cut up behind them. And there, exactly where she remembered it, Rata's tavern. Cracked paint on the walls, another ten years faded. Another ten years of mold creeping through the seams.

There were two women lounging on the bench outside. One large, one wiry, neither one dressed like a dockhand, neither one sagging drunk. Both armed, although neither reached for her weapons. They wore Illhari steel, same as Snow, the seax meant for quick cuts and murder that wouldn't last a sustained battle against legion armor.

Snow's gut clenched slowly. She reckoned for each woman on the bench, there was another two pair of eyes watching. Another blade. Fuck and damn.

"Hm," drifted down from somewhere above her left shoulder. Veiko's way of saying *look there* and *I think that's trouble.* He didn't break stride. But he did drop a hand to his axe. Snow read that in the sudden shift of the two on the bench, straight and suddenly alert.

"Hey," called the larger of them. Her voice boomed up the alley, ricocheted off the walls. "Tavern's closed, yeah?"

Snow didn't answer. Kept walking forward. Kept her own hands clear of her hilt and her knives. Open palms. Fingers wide. Friendly gesture that meant unarmed, unless you were a conjuror. In which case open hands meant *going to scorch you to ash, toadshit, if you try me.*

Please, let them think that. Please, let them recognize her.

Tsabrak's ghost laughed a chill breeze across her cheek. *Who you asking for help, Snow? You think the God's listening?*

"Hey," said the wiry one. "That's far enough."

Far enough to have a conversation, anyway, that the whole street wouldn't hear. Snow stopped. "Here to see Rata."

"What for?"

"Just to talk. That's what neighbors do, isn't it? Talk?"

Eyes flicked between her and Veiko. "We don't want trouble with you, Snowdenaelikk."

So they *did* know her name. Maybe the God was listening after all. Snow heard the ghost chuckle. Shrugged him aside. "I don't want trouble, either. Just talk, like I said."

The women looked at each other. Stood up and took a step each toward the ends of the bench. "Right. Talk. Come in, then."

There were a couple ways it could go inside. The first was an attack the heartbeat they stepped over the threshold. That would mean clubs and knives, the odd sword. Maybe even a crossbow. But Snow had her seax, and Veiko had his axe, and there was always conjuring. Even if Rata had allies among Tal'Shik's godsworn, even if they were already there, that way would be expensive. And loud. And messy.

It won't go down like that, Tsabrak whispered.

The other way, the usual pattern for business, was that Snow would walk in, and Rata would be there with enough muscle to impress her visitors. Rata would offer them a place on the bench, which would necessitate asking her own people to move. That would put a couple more armed bodies *behind* her and Veiko, which Snow would pretend not to notice. She and Rata would have a civil conversation, sitting at the table like old friends. Snow would convince Rata that she and Veiko weren't a danger to whatever Rata had running, and Rata would decide that picking a fight with Tsabrak's right hand was too expensive.

She will. She's afraid of you, Snow. Everyone is. That's my gift. My legacy.

And oh, she wanted to blame woundfever for the voice; but then she turned her head and found Tsabrak, all hipshot arrogance, arms folded to keep his hands close to his knives.

Shut up, yeah? Or your legacy dies here.

If it played out right, she would walk out of here with Veiko in less than a candlemark. Rata would need time to sort out what to do about her, and by then, please and thank you, Snow would have some idea what she needed to do about Rata.

You kill her, Snow. Didn't I teach you that?

You taught me a lot. Now shut up.

But Snow could weight her own dice before casting, couldn't she? And so she snagged a fistful of shadows—out of the flaws in the pavement, out of the place where the door met its hinges—and swept them ahead of her. It only took a little flex of the finger, a little push, just so, and the darkness flowed through the tavern like fog. Not enough to black the place out, not enough to choke out the candles or the firedog. Only enough for sudden deep twilight, and only as long as it took her to cross two steps inside. Then:

"Blink," she told Veiko, and released the shadows.

The lanterns flared up, flame boiling against the glass. The firedog belched like a dragon. A heartbeat, two, to assess the room, while everyone squinted and flinched. Snow counted faces like Briel would. One, two, three, *many*.

Rata sat there, at the main table, an empty bench across from her. She had people behind her, and people ranged on either side of the door, lining the walls. Gert numbered among them. And every fucking one of them was armed, yeah, and bristling metal.

Veiko's shoulder touched hers, quick as a kiss. Then he shifted out of her periphery, moving to cover their flank and her back, clearing his right arm in case he needed to pull the axe. Damn sure everyone in the room could see that.

Snow smiled wide. "Rata. My good friend. You look well."

"Snowdenaelikk." Rata squinted. "I heard you were back."

"You're well informed."

"Huh." Big woman, Rata. She'd started as cartel muscle up in the Abattoir. Prosperity had padded her silhouette. More than one idiot had mistaken fat for soft.

Rata's eyes skated sideways. "Is Tsabrak with you?"

Yes.

"No."

Rata nodded. "I hope he's well."

Not exactly.

Snow wished she had some idea what this woman knew already, what she didn't. Took a chance. "Well enough."

Rata poked her finger in a lazy circle and picked at a splinter. She was trying very hard to seem nonchalant and failing at it. That was sweat on her forehead, and not from the heat in the room.

"Want you to know. I had nothing to do with what happened to Ari."

That was pure toadshit. The Abattoir hadn't just fallen into Rata's thick-fingered hands. Snow shrugged. "I'm here on my own business, yeah? Me and my partner. Nothing to do with anyone else."

"Huh."

Rata cut a look past Snow. Lifted her chin. Bodies moved along the wall, rustling like wind through dead grass. Attack or stand down. Snow made a left-handed fist. If she called fire in here, the whole place would go up, but she'd take Rata first. *Damn* sure.

Then Veiko let his breath out, not quite a hiss. Shifted back, so that his shoulder brushed hers again. She felt the tension in his muscles. Caught an echo through Briel, of a thumping heart and faint disappointment. Snow let her hands relax.

Rata gestured at the empty bench. "Come sit down. Have a drink. Maybe breakfast? You and your . . . partner."

Tsabrak

dead, yeah, go away

would've taken the invitation, draped himself over her bench and dared Rata to try something. Tsabrak *had* done that, more than once, and walked out alive—knowing his limits, and Rata's, and having Snow standing behind him. Tsabrak had had the God, then, too. Snow had only Veiko, only Briel.

Snow gestured at the mud on her boots, the stains on her shirt. "We're not fit for company. Wouldn't've come like this, except I didn't want any more misunderstandings, yeah? *I'm* back. This man here's with me."

Calculations swam behind Rata's mud-colored eyes like catfish. "I appreciate that."

That wasn't an apology. Either Rata had taken Snow's word that she wasn't here on Tsabrak's business, or she had decided Snow wasn't much threat at all. More likely, Rata hadn't made any decisions yet, except that violence now would cost too much.

Good enough.

"I'll see you," Snow said, and pulled the shadows close again. Turned around, never mind the itch between her shoulders that said *knives* and *murder*, and walked out, dragging the dark behind her. Walked past Veiko, who pivoted to watch Rata this time. But he didn't back up, no, didn't retreat with her. Planted his feet and stood there, in the middle of the tavern, until she got to the doorway. Then, as Briel's report of

empty streets

flowed between them, as the shadows rolled toward him like fog, he turned and came after her. Back straight, head up, as if there were no one at all in the room. Past her and out while Snow leaned in the doorway. She flashed Tsabrak's smile to Rata, the one that meant *you're dead, yeah? And you won't see it coming.* Flipped a wave and took all the light with her, left total darkness and

"—hell was—"

"—toadfucking conjuror—"

"—see the size of—"

raised voices behind her.

"We're making friends," she muttered sidelong.

Veiko grunted. "I did not think that your intent."

"No." She couldn't hold it much longer. There was a range on conjuring, unless you were very skilled or very talented. She had just enough of both to know her limits. She let the darkness go before they'd even got to the corner.

Many, Briel sent, and an impression of people spilling out the doorway. Bet they were cursing at her, yeah, but no one followed.

Come on, she wished Briel, and *careful!* when Briel imagined skimming over the *many,* keening like a whole pack of svartjagr.

"Briel's trying to get killed," Snow muttered. "Picking a fight."

"I understand where she learned the habit. Did you get what you wanted?"

"Rata will think twice about coming after us, so yeah. And." Gravel in her gut, her chest, her throat. "She killed Ari, or she knows who did."

"Mm. And what does that mean?"

"I don't know yet. We've kicked over the rock. Now let's see what crawls out."

* * *

It felt strange, wearing no armor. Felt stranger to go without the sword on her hip, only a knife, to go without the bow. To go around without Istel, hell and damn. That left a hole at her back that felt more like *naked* than missing leather and steel.

Dek looked down, checked the folds and drape of her robe. Damn stupid costume, what the highborn wore. Silk and lovely. Long and heavy. Belted and arranged and impractical. Couldn't dodge a stray dog in that thing.

Not that there were stray dogs in the upper Tiers, or many animals at all. Livestock got only as far as the Abattoir. Dogs roamed throughout the Suburba. Cats might make it this far up, to hunt rats and mice in the street. But they wouldn't live in the household. Live animals were for farmers and outlanders and the poor who needed to keep down the vermin. It was different in Cardik, where dogs and cats ran all over the city and people didn't notice. Didn't mind. Kept them as pets, as companions, as help.

She tried to imagine Logi clicking along on her mother's stone floor. Tried to imagine Veiko behind him. Bring *them* along and she could wear a general's plume on her helmet and her mother would never notice. Bring them along, hell, she'd scorch any chance to make her mother hear her.

Dekklis *could* have gone with full legion armor and sword and her partner in attendance. There was no protocol against it. The fourth daughter of House Szanys could come to her mother's house, under the Senate's law, with her scout-partner or an honor guard out of the garrison or, foremothers forbid, a half-blood Academy-trained conjuror-chirurgeon heretic if she so chose. Her mother's staff would not deny her entrance. But her mother had not been happy when her youngest daughter had gone to the legion. And while her mother would never say *get out, Dekklis*, she would look somewhat askance at armor and sword.

So why not wear your scout's kit, yeah? Come on, Dek. It's not like you're infantry.

Damn Snowdenaelikk, anyway. Even imagined, she looked for trouble. Dekklis tried not to imagine herself wearing a legion scout's greys and browns, with the short bow on her back and the hood pulled up over her hair. Tried not to imagine herself creeping through the long hall from doors to parlor, past the blind jet stares of the busts of her foremothers. She would dodge behind their pedestals, blend herself with the shadows, dash across the bright tile spaces.

She caught herself grinning at nothing, like an idiot. Caught the servant's sliding stare. He was a young Dvergir, some unwanted son whose prospects were better as servant in a senator's household than as some fourth husband down in the Suburba.

That, or his mother indentured him. Think of that, Szanys?

Snow wouldn't approve of either option. Snow would curl her lip and sneer about how far the Reforms had got, wasn't that admirable, to let the boys stay uncut so they're stronger servants, *fine* planning on the Senate's part.

Hell and damn. The boy was new, anyway. He hadn't recognized her on the doorstep. Had looked at her and bowed and invited her inside, please come in, Honorable.

That simple. She could've been anyone. A fishmonger out of the Suburba.

Don't smell bad enough for that, Szanys.

Until she said her name, and then it was all bowing and bobbing and *Domina*, the titled inflection instead of simple courtesy, a boy embarrassed that he hadn't known who she was.

Afraid, Szanys. That's what he is. He doesn't want the whip.

That thought wiped her idiot grin away. Szanys Elia didn't, as a rule, beat her servants or her bondies. But Dekklis had three older sisters, and how *they* dealt with house staff, well. The boy was certainly anxious.

Dekklis hauled a deep breath through nose and mouth and followed the servant into the atrium. Memory hit her like a fist. She remembered that bloodthorn when it had been two stalks in a clay pot. Now it had creepers as thick as a woman's wrist, studded with its namesake. She paused beside it. Looked at the remains of its latest meal at the bottom of the pot. Only bones. Her favorite tapestry was still hanging on the long wall: Szanys Tukku and her spear besting an Alvir chieftain. The chieftain looked a little bit like a toad on a spit.

No need to ask where she'd gotten her notions of joining the legion.

"If domina will wait here." The servant bowed.

He didn't wait for her answer, turned and light-footed down the servant's passage. Quick gust as the door opened, swirling incense and morning bread and sweet lamp oil. Dekklis heard laughter, high-pitched and child-hysterical. Her sisters' children, no doubt. There had been only Jikka's daughter alive when Dek left, whose name she could not recall. Maja had been pregnant; probably she had several by now. Disar, too. They might've kept the boys, even, for making alliances later on.

Dekklis prowled the room's perimeter. Wished she could damn the rules and just go through the main doors, there at the atrium's end. Her mother's offices were just on the other side. But the servant had to announce her, had to return and fetch her—through those doors, when it was her turn. That was propriety when one was a visitor. And she was. Damn sure. This wasn't home. The motherless servants didn't even know who she was.

She looked up finally. The ceiling had changed. A new sculpture hung where the old twisted wire lanterns had been. Some silvered steel and glass confection that threw torchglow back in rays of yellow and orange. It looked like someone's conception of sunlight, if that someone had never actually *been* Above.

The servant's door cracked and snicked. Dekklis turned toward it, expecting the boy again, and found her second oldest sister staring back at her, having just come out of a doorway where only staff should go.

"Dekklis! It *is* you." Maja crossed the room in two long strides, pushing chairs aside, and gripped Dek's arms. "I thought Veli was lying. He said there was a woman claiming to be you but that she wasn't dressed like a trooper. I suspected trouble."

"And you came to meet it unarmed."

"*Trouble* in this house means a client Mother doesn't want to see. Sometimes they're stupid enough to lie about who they are. I thought I'd come check." Maja winked. Let go Dek's arms and stepped back. Looked her over. "*You* weren't expecting any trouble, little sister. Not dressed like *that*. Where's your uniform?"

"In the barracks." Maja's hair was loose, which was not proper for receiving guests. Nor was her belted silk robe, or the slippers. Downright indecent for strangers.

"You must have known it was me. You wouldn't've come out like that otherwise."

"What? Ah." Careless shrug. "Worst I'd do is offend some stuffy old woman. Mother might thank me for it."

"Has she changed that much?"

Maja laughed out loud. She was the tallest of them, long boned and strong featured. The one who'd always drawn their mother's disapproval, until Dekklis had gone down to the garrison. It was her laugh, Dekklis thought. Too loud. Too long. Too wild.

"Mother doesn't know how to change." A second shrug. "I hadn't heard the Sixth was back in Illharek."

"It isn't."

"So you're on leave, then?"

"No."

"And I know better than to ask if you've resigned your commission. So what, then? You're here on legion business, forgot how to write a letter home to tell us, and decided to visit without the uniform because you think our mother will forget what you are if you dress like that?"

Dekklis's turn to shrug. She frowned past Maja, at the mosaic on the east wall. Interlocking geometrics, orange and green and rare purple. She'd loved it as a child. Now it made her head ache. "I need her to listen to me. That's easier if she's not already annoyed."

"Oh, she will be. Mother's got Senator K'Haina in her office."

"Which means . . . ?"

"Which means." Maja threaded her hand through Dek's arm. Guided her past the scattered chairs, toward the ornate doors at the room's farthest end. "We have time to talk, and there are nicer places to sit than out here. Where are you sleeping?"

"The garrison."

"Of course. My sister, proper soldier. And you probably choked down some grey slime and called it breakfast."

"Bread, and it was fresh."

"Huh. Well. I'll have the kitchen find something better than legion baking." Maja fished a key on a cord out of her robe. Slipped it into the lock and turned.

"Since when do we lock interior house doors?"

Maja blew air through her nose. Not quite a snort, no, not her sister. "Mad times, Dekklis. That's all."

"Hell."

"Legion language, in this house?" Credible imitation of their mother.

"Maja."

Maja jabbed the key back into the lock. Twisted hard, as if the mechanism offended. "It's been unsettled, lately. People have gone missing."

"People."

"Men. Highborn men. It's been adults so far, and everyone's gone missing *outside* their house, but Mother's worried about the boys." Maja leaned against the door, arms crossed. "You know how she gets. She won't let them go out, even with escorts, for fear someone will snatch them."

"So why lock the main doors and leave the servant passage unsecured?"

"It isn't. See?" Maja pointed down the hallway, toward the little alcove that hid the servant's door. There had been a curtain there once, hiding an ornate metal gate, more form than function. Now the curtain was gone, and the delicate gate had become a wrought-iron monster.

Something Maja wasn't telling her. Mad times, sure. But their mother wasn't paranoid. Dekklis walked down to the iron gate. Squatted beside it and traced the bolts and hinges. Recent work. The plaster and stone were still raw from the drilling.

"You have the key to these locks?"

"All of us do."

Where *all* meant Maja, Jikka, and Disar. And Mother.

"None of the consorts?"

"Of course not." Gust of perfume as Maja crouched beside her. Her hair slithered over her shoulders, ink and shadow, fell into the gap of her robe. "You want a key, Dekklis, I'm sure Mother will get you one."

"I don't want a key." Dekklis stood up. Wished again for the comforting weight of armor. For Istel. "So the consorts are locked in. That's what you're telling me?"

"For their *safety*. That's why K'Haina's here. Worried about her precious son. Wants Mother to reassure her he's in good hands. Bah."

Dekklis recalled a young man with broad shoulders and loose curls. Big eyes. Gentle manner. Someone Istel would eat for breakfast, right along with his grey legion gruel.

Someone Maja might, too, judging from the look on her face. "I say, whoever's doing it, welcome to that one. I'll take him down to the Suburba myself and lose him in the alleys."

"Maja."

"Don't *Maja* me. You haven't had to breed with him. Be grateful for it."

The hallway was not so long between here and their mother's office. The doors were not that thick. And Maja's voice could drill granite when she was angry. Which she was: Maja never had much cared for a second daughter's duty.

Mildly, Dek said, "Boy's got no more choice about being here than you do." Exactly what Snow would say, hell and damn.

"What, you've turned Reformist now?"

Reformist sounded like *toad-eater* on Maja's lips. Dekklis bristled. "I'm Sixth Cohort. That's K'Hess Rurik's command. Lot of men in it."

Don't mention your partner, Szanys. That's right.

Some of Maja's anger leaked out. What filled in behind it was no more appealing. "Really? K'Hess has *command* of a cohort? What did his mother do to land him that post?"

Suddenly Dekklis saw Maja as Snow might. All silk and soft skin, all privilege, never spent a night outside the House walls.

She heard the muted outrage in her voice. The defensiveness. "He's a good commander."

Maja heard it, too. "You bedding him?"

"Of course not. He's my superior officer."

Maja rolled her eyes. "You haven't changed a bit, have you?"

"More than you think," Dekklis said tightly.

Then came an eruption from her mother's office, voices climbing and competing for volume. Dekklis took a step that direction. The same servant—what had Maja called him? Veli?—emerged from a passage. Flicked a nervous glance at Dekklis, at Maja. Dipped a bow.

Bang as the doorway opened. A woman swept out, taller than Maja, draped in Senate crimson, her hair coiled around her skull in the traditional style. Senator K'Haina, no introductions needed. You could see where her son got his big eyes, oh yes. See where he got his soft hands.

Nothing soft in the look K'Haina arrowed at Maja.

"Second daughter," she spat.

Maja bowed, a fraction too late and too shallow. "Senator." And added, as K'Haina tried to go past, "My sister, Senator. Szanys Dekklis."

A flicker in K'Haina's eyes. The senator paused. Turned a shoulder to Maja and faced Dekklis squarely. "The soldier, isn't it? The youngest?"

Dekklis would *not* bow to this woman. Hell no, and damn what was proper. She snapped out a legion salute. "Yes, Senator. First Scout, Second Legion, Sixth Cohort."

"Dekklis," dry-voiced from the doorway. No smile on their mother's face. Raised brows. A glitter in her eyes that might be some gentler emotion. Might be irritation, too, that the first words she'd heard from her daughter in almost a decade had been rank and assignment.

So much for trying not to antagonize her. Should've worn her armor. Should've brought Istel.

Told you, Szanys.

Maja grinned. Said, too loudly, "Mother, *look* who came all the way from Cardik."

"Cardik?" K'Haina's eyes narrowed. "What brings you—"

"We shouldn't bore Senator K'Haina with family chatter. Please, Maja. Show our guest out." Never a request, with their mother.

75

Whip-crack orders. *Should've been in the legion, Mother. You'd've been a praefecta by thirty.*

Instead, at thirty, Szanys Elia had been a mother of three daughters, pregnant with Dekklis, and junior consul and head of House Szanys both, having survived the fever that her mother and sisters had not. The whole weight of House Szanys's survival had landed on Elia's shoulders. The memory of that weight was still stamped into her face. Lines around her mouth, her eyes. The adamant line of her jaw. Delicate woman, Elia. Small. Lovely, in the same way that flights of svartjagr were beautiful, swirling out of the caves at sunset.

Right before they swooped down and tore you to pieces.

Senator K'Haina looked like she wanted to protest. Opened her mouth and shut it again.

Elia bowed. "Thank you for your visit. I will consider your advice. —Second daughter, please."

Even Maja wouldn't argue with Elia. Tight-lipped, "Yes, Mother," and a serviceable, proper bow. Veli melted out of sight, probably grateful, while the second daughter of House Szanys played servant and showed K'Haina out those double doors.

"This isn't a family visit," Elia murmured, "is it?"

"No, Mother."

"Mm. Well." Elia looked at her. Interest flickered in those garnet-dark eyes. "Best you come inside and tell me why you're here."

The last time Dekklis had been in her mother's office, she had been wearing her armor, squeaky-stiff from the quartermaster. Asking forgiveness, not permission, for joining the legion. And not even that, not really. Dekklis hadn't regretted that decision.

Her armor had changed over the years. The office hadn't. Still crisp and neat, stylus and tablet at the edge of the desk, a stack of today's business in the basket. There were remnants of polite tea on the side table. K'Haina hadn't touched hers, by the look of it. Elia took her cup up again. Sipped, delicately, and sat on the edge of her desk. She didn't invite Dekklis to sit in one of the client chairs. Those were padded, cushioned. Comfortable. The chair *behind* the desk, Elia's, had been in the House since its founding. Unadorned wood, naked, edges worn smooth. No cushions for Szanys Elia. No softness, ever.

That her mother was sitting on the corner of the desk implied, if not the intimacy of family, at least informality. Dekklis shifted into parade rest, her knees just a little unlocked, shoulders settled over her hips. The ribs she'd cracked last winter twinged a warning. She was going to ache later.

Elia set her teacup aside. "Do you want some?"

"Thank you, no."

"Then I suppose you should tell me what you do want. And why you're here, and." Elia cocked an eyebrow. "In civilian garments. You identified yourself by rank to Senator K'Haina. I take it, then, you haven't resigned."

"No, mother. And I'm not on leave. I need a favor."

"A *favor*."

"I need to address the Senate. Cardik's under siege. The Senate needs to send troops *now*."

"Wait." Elia raised a hand. "A *siege*?"

"Taliri. An army of Taliri. They didn't have any siege engines, just numbers."

And a dragon, Szanys. You should probably mention that bit.

Elia's lips tightened. "Do you have proof?"

"You mean, did Praefecta Stratka send a formal request? No." Dekklis didn't hesitate. Plunged past the lie in one breath. "I'm here on First Spear K'Hess Rurik's orders. He sent me out—me and my partner—before the siege closed completely."

"With no written message."

"There wasn't time, Mother. They were closing the gates. They *might* still be holding. But they need help. They need the First."

"It's not a trivial thing, Dekklis, to convene the Senate, much less to have you address them."

"You think a Taliri army is trivial?"

"You exaggerate. The Taliri raid in parties. Perhaps an alliance of a couple of tribes."

"*Hell* I exaggerate. I saw—"

A dragon-avatar rising out of the riot and ruin. An army surrounding Cardik's walls. K'Hess Kenjak impaled, whole villages burned.

Maybe some of that showed on her face. Maybe Szanys Elia remembered her youngest daughter wasn't prone to dramatics. "Start at the beginning," she said. "Tell me all of it."

Dekklis filled her lungs. Held it a heartbeat. Then she told her mother everything: the raids on Alviri villages, the riot in Cardik, the armies at the gates. And—

"Their leader was a godsworn named Ehkla. A half-blood Talir godsworn to Tal'Shik. It's a sacrifice, Mother. All of it. Tal'Shik wants revenge on Illharek for the Purge."

Elia sat up straighter. "Don't use that name. That's heresy."

"I *know* what I saw. For the love of all Illharek. Don't pick now to be orthodox."

"I'm a senator. Orthodoxy is required. How do you *know* there are godsworn involved?"

"I saw what they did to K'Hess Kenjak. They killed him the *old* way. I know it was prayers carved on that pole." Which she couldn't know without help. Elia knew that. Dekklis forestalled the inevitable *how.* "I had someone with me, a conjuror I met in Cardik. She confirmed they were godmarks."

"And who is this conjuror?"

Rurik had taken *my friend in the Warren* for sufficient identity, but that had been Istel talking then, one man appealing to another in solidarity. Mothers and daughters, *highborn,* didn't rely on anything so fragile as trust.

Dekklis tried anyway. "She's Suburban. Couldn't get a posting down here, so she went north." Snow would kill her for saying that much. That kind of information could be verified, might come with a name if Elia decided to look.

Which Elia didn't seem too inclined to do. "Suburban" had made her sit back on the desk again, her face set in classic highborn prejudice.

"And this second-rate conjuror *told* you it was Tal'Shik's marks. How would she know that?"

Because she's a heretic. Hell and damn. Snow had said, *Don't you mention me, Szanys.* She'd been right in that warning. Dekklis sifted truths, picked what she hoped was the less damning. "She says the Academy keeps archives, from before the Purge."

Elia surged upright. Honest anger in her eyes, honest alarm that reports of dragons and burning cities hadn't inspired. "She said that? To you?"

Not *what Archives?* That was telling. Dekklis shrugged. "I didn't believe her at first. But you seem to know what she means."

"I need a name, Dekklis."

"No, Mother, you don't. Because if you have a name, you'll go after *her*, and she isn't the problem. The Taliri army is. Tal'Shik is. For the love of our foremothers, are you listening to me? They're coming south. We dodged raiders the whole way, groups of them. Godsworn, Mother, I saw one myself." She held up her hand, palm out. "The godmark, right there. Tal'Shik's mark."

Elia raised her own hands. Warding. Surrender. Maybe just plain *shut up.* "All right." Her tone said it wasn't, not by any stretch. "I will try to summon the Senate, and I will ask that they hear your report. But I won't mention Tal'Shik. And neither will you. You can tell them about the Taliri. You can tell them about the riots in Cardik, you tell them about the villages. But you leave off the bit about Tal'Shik, you savvy? They won't believe it. They certainly won't believe how you know it. Heresy aside, daughter, you'll sound mad."

The senators wouldn't credit a half-blood heretic conjuror's information, she meant. Might not credit a First Scout from the Sixth without orders, either. But Elia believed her. *That*, plain on her face, in the arrangement of lines around mouth and brow. That was her mother thinking, adding facts together. That was her mother coming to a conclusion she didn't much like.

"Something's going on, isn't it? Mother. Tell me."

Elia shook her head. Dek's mother slipped away, leaving the senator, stiff spined, square jawed. Only a flicker of something in her eyes that might have been—could not have been, not in Elia—fear. "Promise me, Dekklis. You *don't* mention Tal'Shik in the Senate. You don't mention her outside this *room*."

As if she were a child again. As if she hadn't spent the last fifteen years in armor, and the last ten of those under an open sky. Some things didn't change, hell and damn, and Snow had been right about that, too.

So, as if she were a child again: "I promise."

Like hell.

CHAPTER SEVEN

There was a singer out on the Arch. That wasn't unusual, in and of itself. Minstrels gathered on the Arch at sixth mark like crows on cold carrion. Sounded about like crows, too, most times, croaking and flogging their lyres, trying to wring coins out of passersby. Sometimes a clot of toad-throated singers would plant themselves in the middle of the street, so that you had to pay to make them move.

But this singer had a pretty voice, high and delicate. Sounded like a boy, too, not a girl. Ten years ago, you wouldn't've heard a gelding singer on the Arch at sixth mark. This one's presence suggested that they were back in fashion, just like deep-red dyes and blunt-toed slippers. Except blunt-toed slippers hadn't gone out of fashion with the Purge, and deep-red dyes weren't one of Tal'Shik's godsworn legacies.

The Reforms had stopped just short of banning castration—allowing, as the law said, a mother to preserve her son's vocal talent. In practice, it meant that poor women had options besides exposing the infant to the Wild. If the boy had a voice, she could cut him, let him earn coin as a singer. But it was more likely, if the boy survived infancy, that his mother would indenture him to a brothel, or a highborn household. Tsabrak's mother had chosen that path—had gotten lucky, too, that she'd contracted him to a proconsul. Better money than brothels, if you caught a highborn's eye.

Lucky, Snow. Is that what I was?

The shadow-Tsabrak skulked at the corner of her eye. His voice was clear, close and cold against her ear. She resisted the urge to reach up and brush him aside. Made a fist of that hand instead and studied the crooked small finger. Tsabrak's last gift to her. It made a focus for her anger, made it easier to shove the rest of her feelings about Tsabrak—a tangled mess, fuck and damn, everything about him was—aside.

You were lucky. She kept the law, yeah? Released you after your years were up. A brothel might've kept you. And then what? I'd've walked past a whore in the street, even one as pretty as you.

The ghost said nothing, so that Snow thought he might've given up, please and thank you. And then:

You're right.

Fuck and damn. Even winning an argument with him brought no satisfaction. Just an ache that went deeper than bone and muscle and lodged somewhere in her chest, where it hurt to breathe.

Snow twisted on her stool. Strained and stretched far enough to threaten her balance. She couldn't see the singer from here, not without abandoning her table. He sounded like he'd stationed himself farther down the Arch, where it crossed one of the Second Tier crossbridges. Pity. There was a shortage of entertainment here, on the Academy's end of the Arch. Oh, it might technically count as part of Second Tier. But the Academy was far older than the structures around it, older than the Arch itself. Conjurors had shaped it out of a massive stalactite, threaded its floors and windows with black Illhari steel. The Academy had since spread to the neighboring drips and jabs of rock, so that the whole business looked like a lacework of stone and steel. A monument to Illhari pride, and to conjuror arrogance.

Small wonder musicians wouldn't come up and play at its feet. They'd have to sit here, in the courtyard just outside the gates. Have to chirp and warble for the amusement of students and masters and Adepts, who came in and out of those gates with little patience for street entertainers.

Snow turned back to the remains of her lunch. Stringy meat in a stale roll, watered beer. Toadshit food never went out of fashion where there were students too poor and too busy to cross the Arch in search of better fare. She had been both. The memory dragged a smirk out of her that hardened and sloughed away. She'd eaten her share of shit up here. Paid for it, too, with more than copper bits.

She fingered the rim of her right ear. Four rings there. One, the silver with the garnet, marked her as a master chirurgeon. There were three others, narrow threads of gold. One of those could've been silver with a little more study. She would never have been an Adept, but she could've mastered fire, at least. She'd always had a talent for it.

But then Briel had happened. Little hatchling Briel, a cast-off project of one highborn second son, Perkal Vik. Snow had mended the svart-tjagr's wings and earned the chirurgeon's master ring, but she'd learned something else, besides.

Where your true talents are, yeah?

It was a tricky thing to kill a man and get the body off the Second Tier. Trickier still to conceal the evidence of murder from an Academy of conjurors and chirurgeons.

Try impossible, yeah? The ghost made a cold patch at Snow's back. Ghost-Tsabrak came and went as he pleased, yeah, just like he had in life. *You had help.*

The Laughing God, the ghost meant. And himself, too. Tsabrak had been the first of her wounded things, beneficiary of a third-year chirurgeon's skills. She'd benefited in turn, because Tsabrak knew how to dispose of bodies. But the God and Tsabrak hadn't been there when Perkal Vik's mother had searched the Academy in person, cell and corridor. They hadn't been there when she'd threatened Senate inquiry, and Senate sanctions, unless her son was found unharmed.

That, Snow reckoned, was the reason she'd gotten away with it. The threat to Academy autonomy had closed its ranks against the ordinary divisions of sex and class. Suddenly there was evidence—a letter, some things missing from his chamber—that suggested Perkal Vik had taken a boat up the Tano and gone east. There were whispers of an affair with a common-born boy, one of the servants. A scandal that, if Senator Perkal pursued it, would taint her whole House. Suddenly there were witnesses who'd say, under oath, they'd seen Vik and the servant together.

Dekklis would have an opinion about the quality of those oaths. Dekklis would have an opinion about Academy insularity, too, but she'd understand it. She was legion. They, too, protected their own. And Dek had enough of a sense of honor that she might see the justice in what Snow had done.

And why do you care what she thinks?

A good question. Snow didn't have any answers. Confronted the remains of her lunch instead and considered calling Briel down for the leavings. Reconsidered in the next moment. Briel wouldn't want this toadshit. She'd turned picky over the years. Gotten used to better fare than this. Briel didn't attach sentiment to substandard food eaten just outside the Academy's front gates, sitting among students with unringed ears and plain queues. And Briel would attract a lot of attention.

Not that Snow hadn't drawn attention already. She wore the rings and the topknot of an Academy scholar, but she dressed like a northerner, and the hair in her topknot was half-blood fair. It didn't take paranoia to guess she was the subject of whispered conversations, held behind hands and turned backs. She could have dressed southern if she'd wanted to waste time in the markets, outfitting herself. But all the silks and linens in Illharek wouldn't hide her hair, or her height. Half-bloods were unusual here but not unheard of. Let people notice, let them talk.

Not what you told your skraeling, was it?

Fuck's own sake, Tsabrak, shut up.

No, what she'd told Veiko was simple truth. He would draw attention up in the Tiers, yeah, same kind he drew everywhere. But in the Suburba, people wouldn't stare at an outlander, because that outlander might become your customer, might belong to one of the cartels, might be one of ten kinds of trouble you didn't want. Here on the Arch, on the Second Tier, anyone that pale should be wearing a collar or showing ink where a collar had been. And no one up here, collared or not, would wear skraeling braids and carry an axe and look everyone in the eye.

Veiko had argued—

This is unwise.

—when she'd sent him Above yesterday. Had scowled and thought *fool* at her. Had imagined failed conjuring and broken bones and her body lost in the lake, which Briel had passed along to *her*, thank you, along with a headache that meant Briel was upset, Briel was worried.

Any luck at all, Veiko would've got that headache's twin. Any luck, he'd still have it, same as she did. She'd told the man not to worry. He understood about Rata. He understood that he would be no help at all in the Archives. His own people didn't even write, fuck and damn, *how* could he help her? But he worried about her just the same.

Same as she worried when he walked the ghost roads and left his body behind, which was what *he* intended to do, in his free time. Practice being noidghe.

Veiko had some reason to worry for her, to be fair. Her finger was mostly healed now, down to throbbing, with occasions of on-your-knees-and-gag pain when she bumped it into something. The arm just *hurt*, deep and constant. The chirurgeon part of her understood that wounds took time to heal. But the rest of her had no time for it, with Tal'Shik and Taliri and fucking Rata and her cartel. That part of her fretted and drove half-healed flesh as if it were whole.

Besides. She didn't need to fight in the Archives. Didn't need anything but her wits and her intellect, and *they* were in fine shape. What she needed was help getting inside. And that help hadn't arrived yet. Fuck and damn.

At least there was one good thing about Illharek: you could get decent jenja here, and without spending fistfuls of coin. And you could light it without flint and patience or risking half a city block to backlash.

No, the drawback to conjuring in front of the Academy's gates was that everyone around you knew exactly what you were doing, and everyone checked your earrings and reckoned the limit of talent and skill. A handcount of heads turned as Snow drew fire out of air and stone and lit the stick of jenja. Students, mostly, and one woman in a junior Adept's robes. That one's lip curled a little, too, when she caught Snow's eye. Might be the three gold rings. Might be the fair hair.

Same toadshit as always.

Snow slid off the stool, abandoned the remains of her lunch on the bench. Walked past Domina Curled-Lip and toward the shops that ringed the plaza. Same goods you could get down in the Suburba, at twice the price. Rent went up with the distance from the Suburba. But no one up *here* would go shop down *there*. Highborn families had bondies to run errands for them, but the Academy forbade bondies in its walls. That's what students were for, scut work and errands. And fucking few of them would dare the Suburba; they'd pay what the shops asked up *here*, even if custom said any coin left from their master's shopping became *their* profit. They were, most of them, highborn. They had no idea how to bargain. No idea how to navigate the Suburban streets.

That had been her advantage. She knew the neighborhoods. Knew how to cut coin, how to weigh bits of copper, or silver, or gold. She knew what things were worth, and she had the accent to bargain with Suburban shopkeeps. She'd got to be damn popular, too, once people figured that out. Mark that one advantage for the half-blood.

Snow paused in front of an apothecary. Smaller than her mother's shop, brighter, whitewashed. Glass jars and bottles lined the back wall, each one labeled—trusting a clientele that could read and who might not recognize the contents without written help.

That was the second advantage Snow had had that her classmates had not, when they'd got to basic herbalism. She knew where the moss-flower grew, because she'd gone and picked it. She knew how to dry snailsilver so that it didn't go brittle, because she'd done it. She knew how to tell toadwort from nettle without reading the motherless label on the toadfucking jar, because her mother had dragged her through every field within a day's walk of Illharek and made her learn.

Snow hadn't admitted how she'd come by her knowledge. She'd let her fellow students imagine genius and raw talent, imagine reasons how the half-blood from the Suburba was better in this one thing than all the daughters of the First Tier. It had been Belaery who'd found her out, the only other half-blood. Belaery's mother was from the Second Tier, a merchant with highborn clientele. Belaery didn't have a Suburban accent. Belaery'd had a bondie tutor, just like a highborn daughter. And because of that, Belaery's we-don't-talk-about-it father, whoever he'd been, hadn't mattered. That, and Bel had been lucky, favoring the Dvergir half of her parentage, in features and frame.

Snow remembered envying the crowblack twist of Bel's queue. Remembered Bel catching her staring, and sidling up after class.

I can get you some, Snowdenaelikk.

What?

The dye I use. I can get you some.

Remembered staring at her, yeah. *What motherless dye?*

I'm a half-blood, too, confessed in Bel's midtown accent that sounded like money. *I'll trade you. The dye for your help on exams.*

It wasn't quite the beginning of a friendship. But alliance, oh yes, they'd forged that. Belaery didn't like not knowing things. She'd gone with Snow to the Suburba on a dare—

The fuck you afraid of?

—and made her own contact with Snow's mother, who'd seen a wealthy future client in Belaery's pretty face.

That had been the beginning of an alliance of half-bloods, and of new business for her mother's shop. Bel had started buying her supplies down in the Suburba—making the walk herself and telling everyone else about it. No few customers had come from that. Sinnike still had them on the books. Makaer and Jhaen, Breszy and Ylisan Kel. And Uosuk Belaery, the merchant's daughter who'd gone on to earn four master rings and an Adept's ring and robes. Who, Sinnike said, still asked after Snow's health and well-being when she came shopping.

So it had been easy enough to send Bel a message. She'd written it out on paper, in the ornate Academy script that Bel had helped her learn.

The letter curls this way, Snow, see?

Rolled it and sealed it, ribbon and runes traced on the paper. Handed it to Kaj—

Read it and your eyes will burst, yeah? So don't.

—to deliver. And Kaj had come back and said Adept Uosuk Belaery had asked Snow to meet her at sixth mark, third day, at the Academy's front gates.

Well. It was somewhat past sixth mark, but Bel hadn't ever been punctual, and—

"The snailsilver here is no good," said a midtown accent, drawn out slowly. "You can tell. The edges are curled up and brown."

Snow's mouth twitched. She lifted her chin. Didn't look at the woman who had come up beside her. "So where do you suggest I go, then?"

"I know a place." The accent shifted, suddenly. "Down in the Suburba, yeah? I can show you."

"I think I know where it is." Snow looked at her finally. "Thought you weren't coming."

"No. Just late." Belaery unfolded a smile. She had the four silver master rings in her right ear; the one in her left was the braided silver and steel that meant *Adept*. "I wasn't sure I believed the message, except that no one mangles script quite like you. Then I wasn't sure I would recognize you." She inspected Snow like a potential purchase. "Life in the north must agree with you. You look just like you did when you left."

"So do you." Same classic Dvergiri beauty, same slender, not-too-tall frame. Same unbroken midnight hair, pulled up in a tidy conjuror's topknot. "You're still dyeing your hair."

"It's still easier."

"I reckon." The jenja was down to smoke and charred butt. Snow flipped it into her palm. Willed it all the way to ash. There was a flash and hiss as the fire did as she asked. She brushed her hand off. Didn't look up. "Congratulations on the fifth ring. *Adept*."

"Thank you." There had been a time Bel would've threaded her arm through Snow's and they would have walked together like sisters. Bel started to reach. Caught herself and stopped and let her hand drop. "I never expected to see you again."

"I didn't expect to come back."

"And yet, here you are." The midtown manners fell away, taking the wide eyes and wider smile. This was the Bel Snow remembered, narrow-eyed and flat-lipped. "I was just down in the shop, what, four days ago. Sinnike didn't say you were coming."

"Sinnike didn't know."

A nod, as if that matched Belaery's expectations. "And you didn't come up here out of sentiment, just to visit."

Was a time Snow would've borrowed Belaery's midtown manners, and

lied

protested no, she'd come to see Bel first, business after. But now: "I need to get into the Archives."

Bel hitched an eyebrow. "You don't need me for that. You're on the graduate rolls."

"I wasn't sure about that. Since, you know."

"Oh, toadshit. No one cares where you went, or what you do now. You earned your rings here. That matters more than your dubious associations during and after." Bel's eyes glinted with a sudden wicked humor. "How's Briel?"

"She's fine. Somewhere up there, gliding around."

"They never found Perkal Vik."

"I didn't reckon. If they had, you'd've told Sinnike, and she'd've thrown that at me along with the rest of her toadshit."

Belaery pulled out her tight and brittle smile, the one that meant her humor was growing fangs. "Even if they locked and barred the door, Snow, you're telling me you couldn't get into the Archives?"

"It's easier with keys and a faculty escort. Besides. Your pre-Purge Dvergiri is better than mine."

"Pre-Purge Dvergiri." Bel squinted at the Academy gates, as if she could see through wood and iron and stone. "I'd ask if you're in trouble, but I don't think you'll tell me the truth."

Snow hauled in a mouthful of air, wished for more jenja, and blew her lungs clear. "Well, then you're wrong. I *am* in trouble."

"Mm."

"So's Illharek."

"That sounds dramatic." Bel's smile flickered. Went out like a candle in rain as Snow looked at her. "What the hell are you into?"

"Met a woman up north. She was a half-blood like us, only her other half was Talir. That's where I met her. With Taliri. She had ink on her hand, like I do. But not to the God."

Belaery blinked. "You're serious."

"The Taliri have been burning the north all winter. Leaving men on poles, yeah? The old ways. *Her* ways."

Silence now. Wide eyes.

"That half-blood I met—she knew godmagic. I saw her work it. I saw." Against her eyelids, in between blinks: blood running up the walls, violet fire, a woman's flesh stretching into something else. "I saw an avatar. She knew the rituals, yeah? She *knew*. She was never a student here, Bel. She's never been in the Archives. And I'm damn sure she can't read pre-Purge Dvergiri. So tell me how she learned them. Tell me how she became godsworn. There's only one fucking way. From the source, yeah? From the fucking goddess."

"What happened to her?"

"I think she's dead. I don't know. I—" Snow bit the word off as a clot of students came too close, all chatter and waving hands. Waited until they passed, and dropped her voice, "I tried to kill her, yeah? Pulled a building down on her. But I didn't stay to see if it worked. The Taliri were all over Cardik by then. Fucking army, Bel. We just ran."

"We? You and Tsabrak?"

"Tsabrak's dead. Me and my partner. And a couple of legion soldiers."

Belaery blinked. Shook her head slowly. "The Senate needs to know about this."

"One of the soldiers who came south with us is a senator's daughter. She's handling that report. Listen, Bel. My partner—he's from a northern tribe, not Taliri. He's got some tricks for dealing with spirits. And *he* says that's all *she* is. Just a really big, old ancestor spirit. I want to know if he's right."

Belaery's fingers clenched around a gesture that was part warding, part reflex. "And you think that information's in the Archives?"

"I think so. If we go far enough back, we might find out what she was before everyone started calling her a god."

"She's heresy. She's superstition."

That was the midtown conservatism, that was Illhari law, that was—

"Toadshit. You know better."

"What you're asking, Snow. It's treason."

"Yeah."

"You're serious. You really believe this."

"Yeah. Same way I believe in sunlight and water."

Bel chuckled. Dry little sound, like lizard claws on tile. "Fuck and *damn*, Snowdenaelikk. I was expecting you to lie to me. Now I wish you had."

* * *

The air was too thick. The sky was too far away, and too blue, and the wind was too gentle. There were trees Veiko did not recognize, and flowers, and grasses. There were birds, too, whose songs he did not know, whose colors seemed bright and garish.

At least there were crows. Raucous congregations of them, studding the alien trees, more than he'd ever seen at once. And there were roads—paved Illhari things, wide and official, as well as honest dirt paths—cross lacing the forests. Smoke spread long fingers into the sky, from woodcutter's huts and small farms. And in the open places there were either villages or the great sprawling houses of Illhari highborn, with their fields spreading around them, and still more huts and habitations. A man could not go high enough, or far enough, that he did not see someone's smoke, or cross a dirt path in the forest made by two feet instead of four.

A man could not get above tree line, either. The hills here were still rocky, still steep, still treeless in places. But they were not high enough. They were not Wild, in the way that the northern forests were.

But there *was* a sky above him. And a sun, and a moon, and the spangled black of night skies. He could hunt in these forests. He could survive here.

There were small red deer. There were rabbits, and squirrels that were nearly as big as rabbits, and foxes. There were large ground birds that he thought would make good eating, but they were clever creatures.

Wary. He had not managed to get close enough to one yet to confirm their edibility. Had not gotten close enough to even draw his bow.

With two dogs, he might've had some chance. The birds did not fly well. But he had only Logi now, and Logi was not at all certain what he should do about a bird whose eyes were level with his own. Helgi would not have minded; Helgi would have worked out how to sneak up on the birds. Helgi would have taught Logi, too, because Helgi was older. Wiser.

Dead.

It was foolish to miss Helgi. Foolish to mourn him. Veiko still had both dogs. One of them lived in the ghost roads now, that was all. His guide in that place. And the other—

"Sst!"

The other had his nose too close to the cookpot. The dog was getting Briel's manners, and none of Briel's wits.

Veiko pulled the pot off the fire. Balanced it on a rock and stirred the contents with a stick. Soup, made with an unfortunate squirrel and what he thought were local onions. The soup smelled like onions, anyway. He sampled the stick. *Tasted* like onions.

With luck, he would not poison himself.

Logi flopped beside him. Sighed.

"You had your dinner."

A second sigh. Logi flattened his ears. Put his chin on his paws.

"No." Veiko left the pot on the rock to cool. Poked the fire down while he waited. A hunter, even one turned noidghe, did not make a habit of sitting downwind of a fire, and the breeze here was fickle. Gusted upslope and down, throwing smoke at him no matter where he tried to settle. It had filled the whole campsite, like the winter fogs that crept across the tundra. Twined among the trees and greyed his world down to fire and dog.

Every animal for a league would smell it. And two-legged trouble might, too. The soup had cooked long enough, then.

Veiko stood. Grimaced at the tweak and tightness in his thigh. Better than it was, but not right, and it made him slow getting up, and that might be trouble—

There was a figure at the edge of the forest, on the very fringe of his vision. Veiko turned toward it, and it disappeared. Nothing but trees and smoke over there. Nothing but his pack, suspended from branches, and his bow.

A chill crawled under his skin. He was acutely aware of Snow's absence. Of the naked space at his back, where she should be. Veiko looked at Logi—smoke or no smoke, the dog should have noticed someone that close. But Logi had eyes and ears for the soup, and nothing else.

And in front of him, there: a woman, standing just beyond Logi, etched against the forest. She wore the same grey as twilight and smoke and held a bow in one hand. There was an axe on her hip, smaller than his and double-headed. One edge was a cutting smile. The other was smaller, longer, thinner, no smile at all.

He had his own axe in his hand by then.

She vanished. Just took a single step back, and the smoke swallowed her whole. Veiko made himself kick dirt over the fire like he had a hundred-hundred times before. He would put the fire out and wait for the smoke to clear. If Logi sensed nothing, then there *was* nothing—

You know better, noidghe.

The voice came from his left. He spun toward it. The woman was there, pretending to lean against a tree. This time the chill settled all the way in his bones. She was a ghost. One of the dead. And not one he recognized. His ghosts were all Dvergiri—K'Hess Kenjak, Teslin and Barkett. She was no Dvergir. He could see that much detail in the gloom. Too small for a Dvergir woman, too pale. An Alvir, maybe—

I am no more Alviri than you are, Veiko Nyrikki. Her features were blurred by smoke, but Veiko thought she was smiling. It was not a kind expression.

"Who?" he said.

That is the wrong question.

Veiko made himself let go of the axe. Made himself smooth his hand over Logi's head. That was fur under his skin. That was *living*. And she—that woman who spoke his language, *she* was—

Dead. Yes. A ghost, yes. But those are not answers.

"I have not called you."

A man could imagine that her smile had slipped. Imagine exasperation on blurred features. Hear it clear as a mountain lake, echoing off the inside of his skull.

No. You did not. You did not call the Dvergir boy, either, the first time he came to you.

"K'Hess Kenjak."

I have no care for his name. She tipped her head sideways. Her braids swung and swayed, caught in a breeze that Veiko could not feel. *I have come a long way to find you, and I begin to think you are not worth that effort.*

"What do you want?"

I just told you. But at least you are learning the questions. Perhaps my journey has not been a total waste. Come. She beckoned. Her edges blurred, until she was only a column of brighter grey against the smoke.

Veiko glanced at his pack. He had a supply of Snow's poison in it, for walking the ghost roads. But he had wanted a safe camp first, and some knowledge of the landscape and of possible dangers. It was one thing to travel the lands of the dead while he was safe in Snow's flat. Quite another to try it alone, in a strange forest.

The word you want is foolish, said the woman. *A noidghe does not need lowlander herbs to walk our path.* Come, *Veiko.*

A noidghe did not let spirits command him, either. The God and Tal'Shik had both tried and failed.

No mistaking her expression this time. Disgust. Amusement. Irritation. *I am no Dvergir. And I am not a mere ghost. Meet me on the glacier. I will wait.*

She and the smoke vanished together. Clear forest around him, fallen to twilight. Logi watched him, ears canted back and sideways, and all the fur on his back ridged up stiff.

He could gather his gear and hike back to Illharek before moonrise. The Tano tunnel had a gate, but it was never locked, rarely watched. Snow had told him that. Snow had told him, too: *Come and go by darkness, Veiko, it's safer.*

He had not made a habit of seeking safety, not since he'd put himself between Snowdenaelikk and two Illhari soldiers in the northern forest. That had been an impulse that earned him enemies, both living and dead, and a limp he would have for the rest of his days.

Veiko touched his pot of soup. It was cold, with a rime of frost that was already melting in the spring warmth. So much for his dinner. He put it on the ground. Called Logi over and sat down beside it. For a moment he watched Logi eat. Red-furred Logi, who had not quite grown into his bones yet, who did not have any hesitation about eating Veiko's cold dinner straight out of the pot.

Then Veiko closed his eyes and remembered another dog, larger and grey as old steel. Whispered, "Helgi," and held out his hand.

A nose brushed his fingertips. A head followed, and a warm body too broad and too tall to be Logi. Veiko took a handful of fur. Pulled himself up, using Helgi as balance, and left his body slumped beside the dead fire.

He took one step, then two.

Veiko dragged a lungful of air that was drier and colder than what he'd find in the Illhari forest. A third step, and he felt the sudden emptiness around him. Smelled the wind coming off the glacier. Felt it slicing past leather and wool.

He opened his eyes. A herd of takin milled along the edge of the glacier. Helgi stood beside him, ears up, tail curled, staring out onto the ice. Veiko knew what he'd see before he looked.

The woman was waiting for him, arms folded, wearing a grim lack of expression. She made Veiko feel ten summers old again, and very foolish.

"Hah," she said. Her voice came out to meet him, sharp as broken stone. "Good. You *are* a fool. And you are proof that luck favors fools. Or children. Which are you?"

"I am not a child."

"No?" She walked up to him, stopping just inside the polite distance for strangers. Not an old woman, but not a young one, either. Hair the color of dead leaves, laced with silver. Lines around her eyes and mouth. "Perhaps not. But you are very young, Nyrikki's son, and very far from your ancestors. It has been a long journey to find you."

Veiko guessed then what she was. "You are an ancestor. My ancestor."

"Indeed. And do you know who I am?"

He did not. She was no one he'd ever met. No one from his village, or the closest neighboring settlements. She was not Jaihnu at all, from the shape of her coat, and the embroidery worked into the leather, and the number of braids on her head.

"I can see that you are Pohja." They were tundra dwellers, and lived the whole year above tree line, following their takin herds even in winter. They could not be bothered to farm the land or build permanent dwellings. A wild people. Strange.

She snorted. "Your grandmother was Pohja. Did she tell you that?"

"I never knew her."

"Pity. *She* was no fool. She would have known me. —What else am I?"

He would have said noidghe, because she was here. But the noidghe in his village, the only one he had ever met, had not worn braids. That man had been shaved bald as an egg, with tattoos on his skull, and earrings. This woman wore hunter's braids, more than a dozen, in the Pohja fashion. He could just see the feathered tips of arrows poking over her shoulder. The bow in her hand was short and made of horn instead of wood. A Pohja hunter's weapon.

She nodded, as if he had spoken aloud. "You have wandered a long way from your ancestors. It required a hunter to find you. Did you think we could not be both noidghe and hunter? *You* are."

"I did not know."

"That is true. There is a great deal you do not know. Best you realize that now."

"I do not know your name."

Her eyes narrowed. "Names have power in this place."

"You know mine."

"And so I have power over you."

"None that I do not grant you."

A blink. A near smile. What might have been a flicker of approval in those pale eyes. "So. Good. Call me Taru. That is a fine dog you have."

"His name is Helgi," Veiko said, and felt like a fool again, at the look she gave him.

"Names have power," she repeated. "A dog—even one as wise as this one—will answer to his name when a man might not. How do you think your enemies called him away, that first time? Do not give power away lightly. And you should thank your fine grey dog that you have survived long enough for me to find you. You have made some poor decisions, Veiko, and you have made some bad enemies. I am here to teach you better."

CHAPTER EIGHT

Dekklis had never been inside the Senate's curia chamber. She'd marched past it a hundred times on maneuvers and stood guard outside it during some of the more heated debates. Killed people on its steps, too, during the bread riot of '06. There had been blood glazing the plaza then, filling the cracks between tiles. She'd gotten her first and only glimpse inside the curia chamber that day, when she'd looked back from the

slaughter

riot and seen a handful of faces peering out the great doors. A flash of benches, an impression of a vaulted, open space. And then her foot had slipped, and she'd got back to the business of stopping the riot.

Riot. Hell. Starving people. Some had been citizens. Some hadn't. The Senate had, in its magnanimity, granted pardon to the citizens who'd participated in the riots, and allowed Illhari burial for those killed. But the rest of the corpses, bondies and resident noncitizens, had been dropped into Jukkainen's Gap, one after the other, for the rats.

And for the svartjagr, who wouldn't refuse a fresh corpse. Predators when they had to be. Scavengers if the meat was fresh.

Opportunists, Snow said. *Not unlike most people.*

Svartjagr were a constant presence in the High City, circling and swooping between the bridges. Clinging to the buildings around the plaza. Maybe a dozen here already, studding the otherwise smooth flutes and spires. Waiting, Dek reckoned, for the street vendors to set up for the seventh-mark break, when the public hearings began. Then the plaza would fill up like a bucket in rain.

It was mostly empty right now. There was the usual legion guard, one trio on either side of the big double doors. They might've been stone themselves, conjured out of rock and shadow. There were bondies, too, who'd come with the senators, who weren't allowed in the chamber. Male and female in the mix, all fair-skinned Alviri, clustered together like birds around grain, flitting from one group to another. Every now and then one would come up to the guards and tease them. Try to break that legion discipline that said *stare straight ahead and don't blink.* And foremothers defend, *what* teasing. Dekklis wasn't sure whether to admire the guards for their control, or wish that they'd take the flat of their swords to the bondies. Teach a little respect.

But these bondies belonged to senators: you could figure that from the quality of their tunics, the precious metal gleam off their collars. They'd absorbed a little bit of their owners' arrogance. No fear. And, to be fair, little evident *need* to fear. Up north, guards on the civic buildings weren't just for ceremony. These clearly were. Uniforms all polished steel and oiled leather over unfaded red and black. Hell. Dekklis figured that armor hadn't seen much more wear than a walk from the garrison and back again.

"Soft," Istel had muttered when he saw them, and exiled himself to the edge of the plaza. He was there now, elbows on the wall, looking over the edge and down at the Suburba.

Istel had developed a deep disapproval of the First's troopers in the past four days he'd had to share quarters with them. Didn't like their attitudes, or their accents, or the way they handled weapons.

Be lucky if they can fight off a kitten, Dek. Look at them.

It did no good to remind him that *she* had come out of that garrison, that *she* was a product of that training. Istel was Sixth Cohort, and the Sixth encouraged that kind of elitism in its troopers.

No. Be honest. K'Hess Rurik, First Spear, encouraged that elitism. K'Hess Rurik had come out of Illharek's garrison, like she had. Was highborn, like she was. Was a man, like she wasn't—which meant he'd never been permitted to stand guard on the Senate plaza. Had he stayed in Illharek, he'd never have risen past centurion. But up north—where the majority population wasn't even Illhari—there a highborn man might climb all the way to First Spear of his own cohort.

But he wouldn't get higher than that. Not in the Illhari Republic, not even after Reforms.

And Istel—who had scrounged a set of armor from the garrison stores, who'd spent an afternoon creasing and scuffing its newness—Istel was a tanner's son from Cardik's Warren. He wouldn't get higher than he was now, a Second Scout in an irregular unit in a northern cohort. Istel was second to her first, the same way Barkett had been second to Teslin. Neither she nor Istel would've minded those facts last spring. Neither one of them would've thought about it any more than they thought about the sky's exact shade of blue.

Blame Snowdenaelikk for changing that, Snow and her heresy and her motherless—

"Chrrip!"

A svartjagr was gliding over the plaza. When Dek looked up, it arrowed and damn near dove at her. Snapped its wings out at the last, leveled out, so that she could see the spidery tracing of scars.

That was Briel.

"The hell do you want?" Dekklis muttered. Briel *chrripped* again and cut a tight circle over Dek's head. That was Briel's notion of courtesy. A warning.

Dekklis braced just as the sending slammed behind her eyes: the Academy's distinctive silhouette, from what had to be fifty paces above the Arch, high enough that the people down on the walkways looked like children. A gut-wrenching dive and dip, and Dek-Briel glided past the vendors that lined one of the bridges. Dizzy echoes of cooked meat and baking things, a svartjagr's sifting and ranking of smells, charred meat and hot bread high on the list, a carnivore's disinterest in fruit or wine. And there, past the vendors, calmly peeling shells off roast rednuts, was Snowdenaelikk. Who looked up as Briel streaked past, and grinned, and mouthed *Dekklis*.

The sending faded. The headache filled in behind it, like mud through an iron grate. Dekklis cracked her eyes open. Foremothers knew if that animal could hear her, but, "Tell her it's not a good time, yeah? Tell her *not now*."

Dekklis gritted her teeth. She'd talked herself raw, convincing her mother to convene the Senate. But she'd won, and now—when Dek was going to do what Snow had dragged her back here for in the first place—*now* the motherless half-blood wanted a meeting.

Hell and damn.

"Chrrip." Briel cut a tight circle over her head. "Chrrip?" The sending threatened a second visit, images pushing across Dek's vision.

Insistent toadshits. Both of them.

Dekklis pinched the bridge of her nose. "Fine," she muttered. "Tell her *wait*, all right? Savvy that? Wait. I'll be there."

Warm flood of satisfaction, and Briel broke off her circling. Flapped to the far end of the plaza, nearest the bridge, and landed on the short wall beside Istel.

Dek watched Istel jump, hand to sword. Watched him settle. Hell and damn, watched him reach out a hand to Briel while she kept her wings wide for balance and stretched her nose to his fingers.

Foremothers defend them. What the bondies hadn't managed, Istel had: all six guards on the Senate doors were looking at him, visibly and obviously. And that got the bondies to look, too, and then all twelve people in the plaza had eyes on Istel.

Who was looking over at *her*. Who beckoned to her, as if she were a servant, to come at his summons.

Temper, Szanys.

She turned a shoulder and pretended not to notice. Would not—dared not—walk over there now, with bondies and troopers watching. That tale would be all over the Tiers by nightfall. Bad enough Szanys Dekklis kept company with a man who treated the local wildlife like a stray cat. She didn't need to add herself to the gossip.

At least Istel had the sense not to call out to her. But she saw him coming, from the corner of her eye, a brisk legion march straight across the plaza. There was no way to walk away from him now or to gesture him back. So Dekklis folded her arms and pretended great interest in the mosaic under her feet. Wished Istel *wait*, and hoped that he understood why she wouldn't look at him. Please, foremothers, he didn't pick now to get stubborn and difficult.

Maybe Istel heard her. Maybe Briel passed the message along. Whatever the reason, he stopped. She heard his single hard exhale, as if someone had hit him. And then his footsteps retreated, with that same legion briskness.

She would pay for that later. She'd get to spend the rest of her day with a sullen partner, when Istel hadn't known how to *be* sullen before Snow. Hell and damn, she missed *that* Istel. This new one—

She didn't finish the thought. Hollow tang from behind the curia doors, before they swung a body's width open. Her mother stepped into the gap. Looked fast around the plaza until she spotted Dekklis. Then she extricated one hand from the official robes and beckoned.

This summons, Dekklis would answer. She walked over, conscious of the bondies' eyes on her. Of the guards', too. She looked to them like a scout in mismatched armor, that was all, and not the sort of person with whom a senator would have personal conversation. Knew how she looked to her mother, too—that same shabby scout, who was also the fourth daughter of House Szanys, who need never wear battered armor. Who need never wear armor at all, and chose it anyway.

Dekklis was conscious of the sword's weight on her hip, and the fresh oil smell on the leather. Of her mother's scowl as she came within earshot.

"You couldn't've worn a proper uniform?"

"We're scouts, mother. Not regulars. Reckoned we should look the part."

"Mm." Elia's gaze floated past Dek's shoulder. Settled and hardened. "That's your second?"

"Istel. Yes." Dekklis peered past her mother. The curia looked smaller than her remembered glimpse. Darker, despite the firedogs and braziers and the heat rolling out. It stank like wax and perfume and incense and a hundred bodies in heavy robes in a space too small and tight.

"The consul has declined to summon you for testimony."

"What?"

"She says." Elia frowned at the guards. Came down onto the steps as if she only wanted a breath of cool air. Low-voiced: "She says there is no need to hear your report."

"That's absurd. Mother, did you tell her about the Taliri? About Cardik?"

"Of course I did," Elia said coolly, as if she were giving dinner commands to the kitchen. It took a daughter to see the set to Elia's fine jaw, and the way her lips pulled tight at the corners. "But it is the end of the winter season. The Taliri do not raid in summer. *Everyone* knows it. No doubt they will withdraw."

"They won't withdraw. If they haven't already stormed the gates—" Dekklis made herself shut it down, calm it down. No shouting on the Senate steps. "So what, she—the Senate—thinks I'm lying?"

"You're not here officially, are you? You have no letter from Praefecta Stratka."

Who was the consul's daughter. Their House had no love for Szanys. Never mind Cardik's praefecta was dead now, or worse.

"She think I've deserted?"

Elia folded her arms across the robes. Her bracelets chimed and winked. "The consul did not make that allegation. But she did suggest that you may have—oh, what was it? That you may have exaggerated the threat in order to excuse your own error in judgment."

A woman who was also a soldier did not say, out loud, *the consul is full of toadshit*, especially when there were other troopers to overhear. Dekklis imitated her mother's stance: arms folded, chin level, gaze drifting. "What did Senator K'Hess say about it?"

"She did not attend."

"What? Didn't you send for her?"

An eyebrow. "One does not send for a senator who is also a proconsul, Dekklis. One issues an invitation. Which I did. Nor is she the only absence. Haata and Saarvo also missed this morning's session."

Senate sessions weren't mandatory. Absences weren't that unusual. But K'Hess, of all people, had to know there was something wrong in Cardik. She'd already lost one son to Taliri. Had probably lost a second when the city fell. And Haata and Saarvo had made their fortunes opening the northern routes. They, too, had a stake in Cardik's future.

"That doesn't make sense."

Elia rearranged her mouth into her best politician's smile. "The families have been in some disarray, of late. K'Hess is no doubt relieved to have two of her sons safe in Cardik, with her *first* son gone missing. I'm sure she saw no need to attend this session."

Dek was amassing quite a collection of blank-faced *whats?* this morning. She skipped the utterance this time and simply stared. K'Hess Kenjak was the *fourth* son, and he had been very dead since before midwinter. His mother had to know it by now. Even if Cardik's praefecta hadn't sent the obligatory message, Rurik would have. Son to mother, reporting a brother's death.

Unless the messages hadn't arrived. Unless the consul was lying about what she'd heard and hadn't. Because *damn* sure Senator K'Hess knew neither of her northern sons was safe, that safety up there was pure toadshit, and—

And Elia knew it, too. Which meant Elia wanted Dekklis to reckon what Elia wasn't saying.

All right. Dekklis scraped her wits together and *thought*. K'Hess's first son—who was that? She shook out her memory. Came up with a dim recollection of a solid-framed young man with the proud K'Hess features. She couldn't remember which House he'd gone to, but he'd stayed in Illharek, and he was missing now. Maybe Haata and Saarvo had missing sons, too. Maybe that was the reason three senators with clear personal interests in Cardik weren't there to vote on hearing First Scout Szanys Dekklis's report.

"K'Hess has another son. The second one."

"Consort in Stratka," said Elia. "Yes."

Stratka was the consul's House.

A soldier served the Republic, might even die for it; but for the foremothers' sake, don't look into its guts. That was politics, a senator's job. Nor could a soldier ask a senator *what the hell does this have to do with Cardik? Are you telling me it's politics, why they won't hear me? Are Saarvo and Haata missing sons, too? Are you saying blackmail and conspiracy, Mother?*

Here, now, on the Senate steps, with everything far too quiet, a soldier could only say, "You didn't mention *her*."

"No." A heartbeat. Hesitation, unheard of from Szanys Elia. "I'm sorry, daughter," soft as snowfall.

Dekklis drew up stiff. "May I return to my duties?"

Elia returned the salute. "Dismissed, First Scout." She turned on her heel and climbed back up the steps, through the curia doors. They thumped together. Sent a puff of incense and heat rolling out like an impatient breath.

And then it was only clear plaza between her and the bridge. Dekklis marched past bondies and guards. Collected Istel with a look. He fell in beside her as she stepped onto the bridge. Said nothing for the first ten paces. Then: "What happened?"

"Nothing. You saw. They didn't want to hear my report."

She felt Istel's stare on the side of her face. "Your mother say why not?"

"My mother." A breath. Two. "There's something wrong with the Senate."

It was the start of an old legion quip that Dek had never liked, that she'd never repeated herself. Istel knew it. The silence stretched and creaked before he delivered the next line. "Yeah. What's wrong, is it's only made out of highborn."

***

The half-blood was standing exactly where Briel's sending had shown her, leaning against the wall on the middle level of the Arch. She had jenja in one hand, a deliberate blankness to her face that meant *trouble*. She threw a look at Dekklis and Istel, sharp as any knife, and went back to staring out over the edge.

"Took your time, yeah?"

Dekklis settled beside her, on the side without the jenja. Made a face at the smell. "Briel didn't tell you we were coming?"

"She's a svartjagr. She doesn't actually talk."

Oh yes. Very unhappy. *Angry*, with a touch of *scared*. And, Dekklis realized, alone. She looked both ways up the bridge.

"Where's Veiko?"

"Out." Snow jabbed the jenja stick toward the dark overhead. "Up there. Above."

"He left?"

"No. Fuck and damn, Szanys, don't be an idiot. He's doing what he does. Talking to the dead. That's easier for him to do in quiet places. And safer if he's not *here*." Snow took a hard drag on the jenja, so that the tip turned hot and red. "I'm hardly going to haul him all over Illharek, yeah? Can't take him to the Academy, either, not yet."

There was a *why not?* begging to be asked. Dekklis rolled it over her tongue. Swallowed it for later. "Is that where you were today, then? The Academy?"

"Yes, that's where I've been for the past, oh, two days, after I stomped all over the Suburba with Veiko and pissed everyone off before that. But let's talk about *you* first, and what you've done with your week so far. Briel found you on the Senate plaza. That seems promising."

"Guess she told you that?"

"*Showed* me, Szanys, and I have a fucking headache to prove it. So what happened?"

Dekklis leaned her elbows on the wall. Stared down at the Jaarvi's black mirror, and the Suburba's twisting streets. They looked like guts, laced with witchfire and lanterns.

"The consul wouldn't hear my report."

Dek had expected a wide-eyed *that's some toadshit* look like the one Istel had given her. Got flat nothing instead, Snow's whole face locked down to stone and steel. "Why not?"

"You don't ask the consul for explanations."

"Guess, then."

"Something's wrong in the Senate. K'Hess was missing. So were other senators with interests up north. And the consul stopped just short of calling me a liar to my mother's face."

"Are they sending a cohort up to Cardik?"

"The consul insists that raiding season is over."

Snow cut a look sidelong. "Your mother do something to fall out of favor? Or is Illharek's consul particularly stupid this year?"

"The consul's Stratka, mother to our praefecta in Cardik. They're old enemies of K'Hess and us, too. It's political."

"Toadshit stupid politics if they cost us Cardik," said Istel. "Don't look at me like that, Dek. You know it."

"You're in uniform."

"You want my opinion, *First Scout*, what the consul's doing is more treason than what I'm saying."

"He has a point, yeah?" Snow blew a gust of smoke over the Arch. Frowned and looked past Dek at Istel, who had tucked in on Dek's other side. "Sorry. You want a stick?"

Hell and damn if he didn't smile. Lit his whole face up, stripped away years. And *when* had he stopped doing that? "Love one. Thanks."

So Dekklis had to wait while Snow handed Istel a stick of jenja and she conjured up fire out of nothing and Dek pretended it was a common sight, flames coming out of someone's fingertips. But she did note the broken finger on Snow's left hand, thicker than its siblings and crooked. She glanced at the right hand, which had all its fingers, pinching Snow's own jenja between them. Marked the angle of the arm, and the stiffness, and the way Snow held it away from her body.

She almost said something. Snow *was* a chirurgeon. Snow had dragged Veiko

back from the dead

through an injury that should've cost him a leg and fever that should have killed him. She did not need Dek's advice on her own health. Had said as much, in the forest.

But Dekklis had seen Veiko's recovery stretched across long winter months. He still limped, too. Probably always would. A soldier could fight with a limp. A hunter could hunt. A whatever-else-Veiko-was, *noidghe*—which involved things Dekklis did not like to think about— did not need two healthy legs to traffic with ghosts. But everything Dek knew about conjuring

not much, yeah, Szanys?

emphasized manual dexterity. A conjuror needed both arms, and both hands, and every single finger.

Snow caught her looking. Asked "What?" in a tone that said *I don't want to hear it.*

Dek shrugged. "My sister says there's a rash of missing highborn. Males. All of them between sixteen and twenty-six. About ten in all, what I hear."

One fair eyebrow hitched its way up Snow's forehead. "Missing."

"As in, they go out of the house, they don't come home. Their own mothers' houses, or their consorts' houses. Doesn't matter."

"And they're not feeding the catfish in the Jokki?"

"They haven't washed up anywhere."

"Weighted at the bottom of the Jaarvi, then. Or one of the deep chasms."

Hell and damn. Dek forgot who Snowdenaelikk was sometimes. Forgot what she'd done, and for whom. "This is your experience talking? Where you hid bodies for the God?"

"This is *sense* talking," Snow said, which wasn't denial. "So. Highborn men. All right. Your sister the paranoid type?"

"Not remotely. My mother, who *is* paranoid, is worried about my nephews, too. My other sisters say *their* friends have lost consorts. So I asked around the barracks. And here's the thing. No one who isn't highborn knows toadshit about it. And the highborn don't want to discuss it."

"I'm sure they don't." Snow frowned. She leaned forward, close enough Dekklis could smell the jenja smoke on her clothes. Flipped her hand and studied the palm as if she'd never seen the God's sigil before. "I think the problem's bigger than I thought."

"Meaning . . . ?"

"Meaning, Tsabrak's people are also dead or missing. But here's the thing. They're godsworn, and godsworn are *hard* to kill. And the woman who's taken over down there isn't smart enough, or good enough, to've done them herself. I reckon she's had help."

Dek stared at her. Shook her head, wordless, strangling on *hell and damn* and *you can't mean it's—*

"Tal'Shik," Istel guessed. "She's got new godsworn, and they're in the Suburba."

"Smart man." Knife-smile, flash and draw blood and gone again. "And maybe up here, too, with what you've told me."

"Ehkla's dead," Dekklis said flatly. "You killed her back in Cardik. What godsworn can these be?"

"I flatter myself to think so. But she said she had sisters."

"Taliri sisters!"

"We assumed Taliri, yeah, and only Taliri. And I think we were wrong." Snow smiled tightly. "That's why I sent Briel for you, Dek. Not for the joy of your company, yeah? Because I've been in the Archives. Found out some things that you need to see."

CHAPTER NINE

Of course, Dekklis wanted to see proof. Snow had expected as much—knew, from the moment she offered heresy for evidence, that she'd slam into that highborn stubborn that Dek did better than anyone Snow had ever known. Most of the men in the Academy came from highborn families, but the girls there were mostly midtown, like Bel, with a scatter of Suburban talent. Highborn daughters went on to politics and officer ranks in the legion—taking over, because it was just what they did. They had a habit of thinking that what they wanted should be what *was*, and hell with any contrary evidence.

Well. That was predictable, too. Fire was hot. Water was wet. And highborn were—

"Impossible," Dek said, there on the Arch. "I don't believe it. You're wrong. You have to be."

Snow had tied down a smile. Twisted her mouth into a different shape. "I know what I read, yeah?"

"You might have gotten it wrong."

"I might have. Except I didn't." Snow paused two beats so they could glare at each other. These were steps in a dance Snow knew well. Dekklis argued. Dekklis wanted proof. Dekklis was afraid. "Fine, then.

You come to the Archives. Meet me at the Academy gates, two days from now, tenth mark."

"Why wait?"

Because Belaery would be there at tenth mark and ten. "Because there's rules against people like you in the Archives. Two days, it's the Adept Council open session. Required attendance for students. Easier to get you inside, yeah? So come then, and I'll show you the motherless scrolls. *You* read them. Tell me I've got it wrong."

Belaery would cough up a snail when she saw Dekklis. Adepts with aspirations had to be careful of rules. But Bel was smart. She'd reckon Tal'Shik a bigger threat than Szanys Dekklis sniffing around in the stacks. Dek couldn't even read half the documents. She was no danger.

Tell yourself that.

And if not, if Belaery couldn't get past her objections and see sense, well, Snow had a lot of practice handling the unwilling. She'd spent more than ten years with the Laughing God's people, with *Tsabrak*, running business and keeping order on the wrong side of legal. If Belaery wouldn't listen, then—

What, Snow, you kill her?

If it came to that. Snow's stomach shied away from the idea. Clenched and chilled. Tsabrak would have, with no hesitation. *She* might hesitate, at least in making the decision; but if she had to do it, well, she would. Tsabrak had taught her that there was no room for sentiment when it crossed business.

Is that what this is?

Business. Revenge. Something more tangled than either. Call it *stop the Taliri*, and leave it at that.

***

The archivist—who looked more like Suburban street muscle, lacking only a seax—had waved Snow into the library without more than a cursory glance. She knew Snow by now, had seen her in Adept Belaery's company, prowling the old stacks. The archivist's indifference was Snow's good fortune; she had Dek right behind her, wrapped in *look away*, and that kind of conjuring was fragile. A good hard stare could crack it, or a noisy misstep, or even basic suspicion.

A second good fortune: the Academy did not bother with wards inside its own walls, on its own archives. The Academy trusted the archivist and her biceps to guard the place, reckoning that no one who had any right to the place would need to conjure at the doors. And they certainly never reckoned that someone would be brazen enough to try smuggling a highborn inside.

Snow had done better than *try*. She'd succeeded. Because there was Dekklis seated at the great table, with a half-dozen scrolls scattered around her in various stages of read and unrolled. Snow's witchfire hovered over her head like a nosy svartjagr, adding its light to the witchfire braziers lining the room. There were no candles in the Archives. You didn't bring fire into the library. That was a rule even Snow wouldn't break.

Dekklis was staring somewhere past the scroll in front of her, into the dust and shadow on the witchfire's far side. Didn't glance up until Snow put a new scroll down beside her. Then she startled. Shivered.

"I was just thinking."

Snow dropped onto the bench beside her. "You're supposed to be reading."

"Remembering lessons," Dek said, as if Snow hadn't spoken. "Want to hear what I learned as a child? That the Alviri tribes united under Eirik the Bloody and drove us Below. Superstitious, primitive people, the Alviri. They were afraid of us, because we were smaller than they were, and darker, and all that kind of toadshit. So the Dvergiri built Illharek in our exile, and we stayed Below a long time, learning metalcraft and conjuring. The Alviri did nothing in all that time except sacrifice to their gods and steal each other's livestock. Oh. And kill any Dvergir they could catch Above, which wasn't many of us. And then one day, we got our revenge. We came out of the caves, and we broke their chieftains, and we imposed order. Then, once we conquered them, we Purged their gods. *And*, Snow, I learned—as an afterthought—that we Dvergiri had been superstitious, too, once. That we'd followed a god when we first went Above. But we learned better. Like children who grow up."

Snow shrugged. "That's all any of us learned, Szanys."

"But it's not what happened." Dekklis flicked at the scroll in front of her. "So tell me, Snowdenaelikk. Is it also superstitious to refuse to talk about the past? To say what actually happened?"

"Superstitious? No. Political. If you want to change history, you change the story. The trick is making sure everyone's story changes and there's no one else telling a different version."

"And we told the wrong story."

"We told the story that served Illharek at the time. Truth is, the Purge left Tal'Shik alive. And the Laughing God. But they were the tough ones. Maybe the lucky ones. You know we had a whole collection of gods once?"

Snow took her hard-won scroll and laid it in front of Dekklis. Unrolled it gently and weighted the edges with stones worn smooth with years of handling. "There. Look. This treatise was written by Mairut the Blind. Before she was blind, of course."

"I can't read that."

"Sure you can. It's in Middle Dvergiri. Sound it out. Letter by letter."

"I can't *read* the letters!"

"It's just *script*. You saying a half-blood can do something better than one of you highborn?"

Dekklis slipped Snow a look of pure poison. "Just read it to me."

"All right." Snow smoothed her hand across the parchment. She hated that spidery archaic hand, with its ink-wasting curls and gouges. Reading it wasn't her best skill. But Dekklis didn't need to know that.

"In early times, the Mothers—for there was no other word for sovereigns, then, the Senate having not yet been imagined—ruled Illharek as a council. Of the council, there were two parts, consisting of the higher order, which were the Houses that had been present and contributed to the founding of Illharek, and the lower order, which were the Houses that had come to power since the Sunless War, and which concerned itself on the greater part with trade and commerce and agriculture. But the higher order, whose business it was to govern, and whose word was law, was most engaged with that practice known as theurgy, which is to say, congress with the spirits of Illharek. And of these spirits, several were known. Now, of this theurgy, we can say—"

"Summarize, can't you? Hell and damn."

"I see why you went into the legion. Not much of a scholar, are you?" Snow's laugh was an airless clicking. "All right, Dek. A summary. *Theurgy*'s a fancy old word for making nice to the gods. Bargaining, yeah? What you give them, and what you get in return. It started out as a science. Very precise. I say my morning prayers, and you, god, grant me success in my business dealings. Or whatever. But then the high council, the one with all *your* relatives in it, got the idea that if you just *gave* to the gods, you were proving something. It was like—" She snatched for the word out of empty air, fingers clipping together.

"Ass-licking." Dek hitched the corner of her mouth up. "Works in the legion."

"Well. Worked for Tal'Shik, too. Next thing anyone knew, that's just what you did. No more science, this for that. Theurgy turned into worship. You just offered up your prayers, you made your sacrifices, and you hoped that Tal'Shik liked you best that day."

Dekklis looked as if she had eaten a bite of rotten meat. "Superstition."

"Oh no. Superstition's all toadshit, yeah? This actually worked. The favored Houses rose. Of course, *favored* changed faster than weather, but maybe since Illhari didn't get out Above much, they didn't notice the similarity. Veiko would call it poor bargaining."

"And what does Mairut the Blind call it?"

"Much the same thing, with a lot more words. She gets really eloquent, near the end, when she's all pissed off. Calls for a return to proper theurgy, calls for the councils to show some sense. Says that, where is it, there: 'This slavish devotion to one fickle ancestor is an affront to all that makes Illharek great. It is indistinguishable from the babbling of the Alviri.' That didn't make the council very happy, since most of them were godsworn and licking Tal'Shik's hindmost parts. A coalition of highborn—that's in the official records—had Mairut arrested. They confiscated all of her property and burned it. They broke all her fingers. And then they gouged out her eyes."

Snow imagined the woman who'd made those marks on the parchment, and felt that familiar rage she'd damn near forgotten. "She was an Adept. The Academy had some influence. Senate couldn't kill her. But she was also midtowner. She didn't have enough family to save her hands or her sight."

A muscle ticked in Dek's jaw. "You think it'd've been any different, she was highborn?"

"You know it would. You think your mother'd let some senator blind you?"

"She might if she knew the company I keep." Dek started to say something else. Turned her head, mouth opening, while the witchfire crawled across her face like a sunrise. Then her eyes narrowed, suddenly, at something past Snow's shoulder.

Snow guessed the reason before Bel even spoke. "You're not talking about *me*, I hope."

Dek uncoiled slowly, like a snake in cool weather. Propped her hip on the table, put a boot on the bench. Casual enough, unless you knew Dek. "I'm guessing you're Snow's friend."

"Belaery." Snow turned around, fast and smooth. "There you are."

"Snow." Bel's most polite tone, which meant nothing good. "I'm sorry I'm late. And I'm sorry I didn't remember that you were bringing a guest."

"Well. I didn't tell you. Bel, this is Dekklis. Friend of mine from up north, yeah? Dek, this is Adept Uosuk Belaery."

Belaery hadn't come any closer. She looked like she might stay right where she was, in the canyon between shelves. "Dekklis," she said, as if tasting the syllables. Her eyes traveled over Dek's face, marking bones and build and features. Settled at the neckline of Dek's very plain, very northern sweater, which came just high enough to cover the Szanys sigil. "I don't remember seeing you before."

"That's because you haven't."

Snow sighed. Dek had this effect on everyone. Take that legion stare that drilled into people, mix it with her highborn sense of *do what I say*, yeah, and you had trouble.

Belaery was an Adept's ring past having to take that attitude from anyone in her immediate acquaintance. Her eyes glittered like glass. "That doesn't sound like a northern accent."

Dek hooked a finger in the sweater's neck. Pulled it down and sideways and flashed her sigil. "I'm not northern."

Fuck and damn, like putting two cats into a closet together. Circle and snarl, everyone's figurative fur sticking straight up.

"Dek found the first sacrifice," Snow said. "She saw the avatar, too."

That got two sets of eyes on her, two flavors of the same *you told her that?* outrage. At least they weren't scowling at each other anymore. Some improvement.

"You told me," Bel murmured, "that the woman who found the sacrifice was legion."

"First Scout, Second Legion, Sixth Cohort," Dek said, matching Belaery for tone and volume. "That a problem for you, *Adept*?"

"Yes. It is. You shouldn't be here. Snow. A word?" Bel turned her shoulder on them both. Retreated partway up the aisle and pulled the shadows solid behind her.

"Be lucky if she doesn't turn me inside out. You hear a squish, you better run," Snow said, and left Dekklis wearing a crumpled-brow *are you serious?* stare.

Bel wouldn't do anything like, Snow was reasonably certain. Uosuk Belaery had never even scuffed her knuckles in a bar fight. Brilliant anatomist, yeah, but a toadshit chirurgeon. Bel liked her subjects on parchment and in theory.

Then again, Adept Uosuk was several rings past needing her fists to do damage, and it looked like she might've remembered that. She really could turn Snow inside out. Or she could haul Snow in front of Academy administration for breaking the rules. Cut off a finger, yeah. Maybe two, for bringing a senator's daughter into the Archives, into the heart of Academy knowledge and power. Belaery could *end* her conjuring, with a few well-placed words.

Same way Szanys Dekklis could end her freedom, with a warrant for her arrest.

Real fury on Belaery's face, real betrayal. Snow felt guilty for that and dismissed that guilt in the next breath. There were bigger issues here than Bel's feelings. It was a pity Dek and Bel didn't like each other, but Snow hadn't expected they would. They were two sides of the same arrogance, conjuror and highborn, with a history built on mutual distrust and dislike and dependence. If the Senate sent its legion out against the Taliri, then the Academy would send its Adepts. One wouldn't go without the other. One wouldn't let the other go alone.

But now they had a mutual, urgent problem. Belaery would understand that. Or. Snow measured the space between herself and Bel. Marked the width between shelves, and the arc her blade would take when she drew it. One step, one cut, no mistake. —Or she wouldn't. That was that.

Then, only then, did Snow meet Belaery's furious stare.

"She shouldn't be here. Toadfucking *highborn*, Snow, what are you—?"

Snow cut her off, cool and quiet: "We need Dekklis to understand who Tal'Shik is. Where she came from."

"We, is it? And why can't she understand what you *tell* her?"

"Dek's not like that. Has to see it herself. She's—"

"I see what she is. *Highborn.*"

Snow took a bite of air. Held it. Let go. "Got a better word. *Ally.* How do you think we're going to get the Senate involved without her? She can explain it to them. Her mother's a senator, for the La—love of precious things."

"We don't *need* the Senate."

"Of course we do. Tal'Shik fucked up before, yeah? She only cared about highborn, and what happened? A few highborn dissidents got the idea of the Purge together, but it was plain Illhari who did most of the killing and dying. You think the senior Adepts are going to deal with Tal'Shik's godsworn all by themselves? Or with Tal'Shik herself? You need the legion for that, and for the legion, you need the Senate."

"You said you had a partner." Belaery licked her lip, as though the word tasted bad. "A skraeling. You said he knows how to deal with the gods."

"I said he deals with spirits."

He hits them with axes.

"Which is all Tal'Shik is. So bring him here. Show me what he can do. Prove it. If you have to show some highborn soldier the scrolls, to make her believe, then you can damn well show *me* what your partner can do. Make *me* believe."

And imagine Veiko's response to that kind of demand. Imagine what he'd say if Bel used that tone and looked at him as if he were some sort of trained animal.

Snow shook her head. Offered a smile that tried and failed at apologetic. "You wouldn't like the proof. Besides. It's not just Tal'Shik that's the problem. It's Taliri. They're coming. And one skraeling noidghe can't stop that. We need the Senate's help."

"So you say. Your word, Snowdenaelikk. That's all I have."

That was a good imitation of highborn contempt, yeah, not bad for a merchant's daughter. But Bel hadn't seen Tal'Shik's avatar ripping through Ehkla's body. She hadn't seen the ruined village of Davni, or K'Hess Kenjak's angry ghost. She hadn't bargained with the God, hadn't died and been dragged back from the dead. Bel was a sheltered Illhari spouting the same *I don't see it, so it's not real* toadshit. In that, she and Dek were almost the fucking same.

Snow grabbed Bel's wrist. Squeezed with a hand that had learned to swing a blade and climb walls. Not a conjuror's delicate grip, oh no. Bel knew it. Her eyes pooled wide, flickered between alarm and outrage.

Snow cut her off before she managed a syllable. "You want proof? All right. Here's how it works. You die. You wake up in a black river, just like it says in Virka's *Customs of the Northern People*. And then, if you're lucky, someone comes down there and leads you back out. You want to experience that? Because I can arrange it. Let you meet my partner that way. Then maybe you'll listen, yeah? Once you've coughed the black river out of your lungs. Once you start seeing ghosts."

"That's toadshit!"

"It's not." Dekklis came around Snow's left side. Grim-eyed, unsmiling. "I've seen it. Ghosts walking around killing people. Dead women breathing again. Wish I hadn't."

Bel pulled her hand loose. Took a step back and cradled it against her chest. "That's not possible."

"I said the same thing. I was wrong. So are you." Dek shrugged. "Why's that so hard for you? You people call blue fire out of nothing. You." She flipped her hand at the walls, the floor, all of creation. "You shape stone. You do *things*. Why are ghosts so impossible? Why is anything? You've got all these scrolls. All this history. You can read. Figure out what the godsworn did and undo it."

"There's no one left who can do what's written in here. Listen. Conjuring's one thing. Godsworn's something *else*." Bel cast wide-eyed alarm at Snow. "Tell her."

"Dek. Godsworn's something else." Snow uncurled her fingers. Looked at her palm and the godmark. "Different sources of power. Different rules. Conjuring doesn't care who you are, long as you have the skill. Gods, now. Gods play favorites. And you have to bargain. Give them something, get something back. We know what Tal'Shik likes. You willing to stick a pole through some third son to get her attention?"

"Maybe someone else is doing that already." Dek leaned against the shelves. Crossed her arms. She might've been another student, debating the merits of Jussi's *Treatise on the Treatment of Festering Wounds*. She looked at Snow. "Did you tell her about the missing highborn sons?"

Snow mocked up a frown and tacked it onto her face. "No."

And on cue, from Belaery: "*What* missing highborn sons?"

So Dekklis told Belaery while Snow pretended to listen and watched instead: Bel's slow uncoiling, and the way she leaned toward Dekklis. The way her suspicion melted into curiosity, Belaery having found a puzzle she hadn't solved yet, new information.

"You think, what, Tal'Shik's got godsworn in the city?"

Dekklis shrugged. "Worse than just inside. I think they're in the Houses."

Snow tried to say *in the Suburba, too* and damn near choked. Ari and Kjotvi and Stig's names turned to mud in her throat. It was one thing to consign imaginary highborn to Tal'Shik's poles. Another to put

Ari and Stig on them, too, and present them to Belaery as evidence. Snow had known those men.

Is that loyalty? Could it be? I thought you were done with us.

Tsabrak's voice, plain as steel, raised a chill on her skin. Tsabrak's scent, knife oil and jenja, sudden and stronger than the mildew and dust. She felt his breath on the exposed curve where her neck met her shoulder. She would not look down and left, into that shadow there where the shelves met. Would not.

Dekklis saved her. "You think of another reason highborn men would go missing? Because they're not running to the legion. And I don't know where else they'd go."

Belaery pursed her lips. Glanced conspiracy at Snow. "We've had highborn men disappear from the Academy before, haven't we?"

All the dust in the Archives had collected on her tongue. "Only one I remember. Real toadfucker. Liked to vivisect svartjagr."

Dek snorted. "These missing highborn haven't cut anything more dangerous than bread. Pampered sons, all of them."

"These could be political assassinations. Revenge." You could feel sorry for Belaery. She looked so hopeful.

"Word you want is *sacrifice*," Dekklis said. "Those men are rotting on poles in one of the deep caves. Bet they've got godmarks carved all over them."

"You're both right," said Snow, and got them both staring at her. "These are highborn sons. They're valuable. You take them, make it look easy, and you sow paranoia. And you send a message. The ones who've gone missing, Dek—they belong to Reform-minded Houses?"

Fuck and damn, the look on Dek's face. Made you pity anyone she faced in battle. "Shit."

"And if the unofficial penalty for pushing Reformist politics is missing sons, then how long do you think those Reforms will last?"

Belaery recoiled into an arms-folded bundle of denial. "The *hell*. What about the Taliri, then? Why are they even involved, if this is all toadshit Illhari politics?"

A headache built behind Snow's eyes, thumping and flashing like a spring storm. "I think Tal'Shik's broken her pattern. I think it doesn't matter to her anymore *who* fights for her favor. I think the more she has involved, the better. That's how it was in Cardik, yeah? Alvir against Dvergir. Toadfucked chaos. All that power, straight to Tal'Shik."

Dekklis gazed into the empty air between aisles. She looked like she was seeing Cardik again, riot inside and siege outside and the legion caught between. Snow heard that grief in her voice, and the anger. "So Tal'Shik wins. Either the Taliri overrun us, or—what, we take her back? Undo the Purge?"

"If it came to a choice between Tal'Shik and losing Illharek, Dek, which would you pick? Which is the greater treason?"

Bleak stare. "I don't know."

"Exactly. And you've seen what she'll do. The rest of them haven't. Listen." Snow made a fist of her right hand. Ignored the barbs and hooks that shot up her arm. Conjured up solid quiet and wrapped it around the three of them, so that someone could stand beside them and not overhear. "Tal'Shik's just a spirit, yeah? That's all a god is. A spirit. Veiko told me that. And how to deal with her is *here*, Bel. Dekklis is right about that. The Archives can tell us how the godsworn do what they do. That means we can figure out how to undo it. *We* can fix it. Give the Senate another option. Dek can make them listen."

Please.

Dek hadn't had much luck so far, but none of them had. And Dekklis didn't say *I can't* or *not possible*. Nodded, as if Snow had asked something simple.

"Godsworn conjuring." Belaery wrung out a smile. "You're asking me to reconstruct a dead discipline. That's its own treason, Snow."

And a sixth ring if she succeeded, which could mean High Adept. Snow saw that ambition catch and burn in Bel's eyes.

Blow on those flames. Fan them. "Damn near impossible."

"Mm." Bel was already thinking. Drifting away, like Bel did when she fixed on a problem, muttering under her breath and squinting at scrolls. Faintest pop as she passed through Snow's conjuring, and then her footsteps vanished.

Dekklis leaned so her arm touched Snowdenaelikk's. "You trust her?"

"Not as much as I trust you."

Dek choked on a laugh. "I suppose I deserve that."

"You do. Listen, Dek. If I'm right—if the men disappearing aren't random—then you're in the best place to do something about it."

"How do you reckon that? They're all spiked somewhere in a deep cave. Veiko's the one who talks to ghosts."

"Because you kill all the hostages, you lose all the leverage. Not all the highborn men in Illharek are missing yet, yeah? You said K'Hess wasn't coming to Senate meetings. That suggests she's got a live son someplace."

Dekklis said nothing for a long moment. Then, "I'll see what I can find out."

"Do more than see."

Which earned Snow a grim little smile. "You're talking more treason."

"Probably."

"So, since we trust each other so much, you and I, what will you be doing while you've got Belaery and I engaged in illegalities?"

Snow looked at Tsabrak standing there in the corner. At the lines and angles of the shelves she could see through him. She tasted bile and iron. Please, Veiko had found the God.

"Same thing, Szanys. Same thing."

CHAPTER TEN

". . . and then Eign and Yrse made it all the way to Cardik—but of course it wasn't Cardik, then—before Yrse's mother caught them."

There was no need to ask what happened next. Even if Dekklis hadn't heard the story before—and she had, *everyone* had—she could guess. Yrse was second daughter of Stratka, from the days before the Purge. Eign was a fourth son from a much less important House. It didn't matter how smart he was, or how gifted with music, or whatever—that part of the story shifted with Sindri's mood, each retelling. The plain fact was he could never be a Stratka consort. Even now, after the Reforms, that wouldn't happen. But *now*, Eign would be whipped and cast out of the House. *Then*, well.

"And then they died," Dek said flatly. "Yrse slit Eign's throat, then her own, before her mother's guards could take them."

"Yes, but." Sindri rolled onto his back. Folded his fingers together on his belly and stared dreamily at the ceiling. "They died together, Dekklis. She protected him."

If a knife in the throat counted as protection. Hell and damn. K'Haina Sindri's only acquaintance with the business end of a blade was cutting meat. Damn sure he had no idea how much blood came out of a body. Yrse would've been smarter to jab the knife behind Eign's jaw, up into the brain. Much neater.

And much less dramatic. Dekklis swallowed the comment. No point in hurting Sindri's feelings. He'd get enough of that, with Maja.

You're welcome to him, sister.

Dekklis pushed herself onto an elbow. Twitched a smile at Sindri when he glanced at her. "It's a good story."

"It's the *best*." Sindri sat up as she did. "You're not leaving yet, are you?"

"Not quite yet."

Sindri flopped back. Reached up and traced the scar on her hip, gift from a dying bandit two winters back. Dekklis controlled the urge to slap his fingers away. There'd been a *reason* she never wanted a consort. It would've been more bearable if that cow-eyed admiration was fake, but Sindri was sincere. She was one of his toadshit heroes, some warrior from the exotic far north, battling bandits and being brave, or whatever it was he imagined legion life looked like.

Not predawn marches, damn sure. Not K'Hess Rurik's bellowing in his face. Not the actual blood and stink that came with battles. Not ghosts, or godsworn, or young men his own age dying on poles.

She closed her eyes. Let Sindri imagine that his touch was the reason, that she liked him tracing spider-fingers down her leg. Held her breath, and her patience, and waited until his hand trailed off her knee. Then she opened her eyes. Looked at him, unsmiling.

"You think it's true? Eign and Yrse. That he actually climbed the Tiers to sneak in to see Yrse?"

"It's true." Sindri had told her this before, too, but he didn't mind the retelling. He sat up, put his face level with her. His eyes were huge, dark, wide and earnest. "There's handholds in the rock between First Tier and Second."

She knew that was true, having checked that part of Sindri's story first. Easily verified, with a little help from Briel. But she nodded now, like she'd never heard him say it. "But *inside* Stratka. Secret doors? Really?"

Sindri nodded again. Leaned closer. Dekklis smelled her own sweat and scent on his breath. Controlled her flinch and grimace as he whispered, "Dasskli Birkir—he's consort to Stratka—showed me once, before all this stupid curfew. There's a door in one of the wardrobes that leads to a secret passage. You get in near the back entrance, through a mosaic. You have to press the matron's *eye*."

A smarter man might've asked *why are you so interested in secret doors?* She had a story prepared: that she had a message for K'Hess Soren, consort to Stratka, from his brother. That wasn't quite as romantic as forbidden lovers, but it was close enough to true. But Sindri hadn't asked. Sindri just seemed happy that he knew something that interested her.

Please, foremothers, K'Hess Soren was less like *this* boy and more like his brothers, or she might end up making the same choice Yrse had.

She glanced at the candle. It had burned all the way to fifteenth mark. Still two marks before she was due to meet Snowdenaelikk, to learn things no highborn daughter should know about getting past locked doors. But first she had to escape her own house.

Getting away from Sindri was easy enough. He protested, very prettily, and pouted, and extracted promises that she'd come back in two days, thirteenth mark. Dekklis felt a sliver of guilt. In two days, during a special late session of the Senate, she'd be somewhere else entirely, with a completely different highborn man, replaying the more successful parts of Eign and Yrse.

K'Hess had four sons. Two had gone to Cardik, part of the Sixth. Kenjak and Rurik. Her first, Ivar, who'd been consort to M'Hjat, had gone missing. The last K'Hess son left in Illharek was the second born, Soren. And *he* was a consort to Stratka. Small wonder K'Hess wouldn't take messages, why she'd refused all meetings. Soren was leverage against her silence.

Don't you see, Mother, what the consul's doing?

Elia did. Damn sure. But Elia could not march into Stratka and demand the release of K'Hess's son from a perfectly legal arrangement. No, Elia had to trade on her House reputation, which was formidable, and argue on the Senate floor. She could raise support by presenting her arguments in front of as many senators as she could muster in a special late session. Elia was a good politician. She had talked Haata back into chambers. Had hosted a dinner with Saarvo and won *her* back, too. So this session would be full, despite the late hour, the entire plaza jammed with bondies and servants.

Which would leave the First Tier houses skeleton-staffed, and—please, foremothers—mostly unguarded. Because Dekklis had determined that if K'Hess Soren's presence in House Stratka was a problem, then the simplest solution was get him *out*.

If Snow could—would—teach her how to pick locks. If she could convince Istel to run a distraction for her. If a thousand other things didn't go wrong in the interim. Sindri could always run that pretty mouth to someone else. He was lonely and bored. Unhappy with the new curfews and confinement, when he'd been accustomed to afternoon visits in other Houses. A little kindness went a long way. Maja might neglect him, at best. Torment him, at worst. Maja had noticed Dek's new interest. *You're welcome to him* didn't mean Maja would leave him alone. Hell and damn, Sindri would probably expect a rescue from her, his legion hero, to save him from her sister.

She had to rescue herself first.

Dekklis smelled Maja's perfume two heartbeats before her sister stepped out of an alcove that shouldn't've held a full-grown woman. Maybe House Szanys had its own secret passages. Or maybe she'd just been too busy thinking about Sindri and not her surroundings.

Getting soft, Dek.

Maja set herself in Dek's path. Grinned a combination of conspiracy and condescension. "You're getting predictable. Every other day, seems like you're in the men's wing."

It was a daughter's privilege. Even a fourth daughter's. Dekklis shrugged. "Well, you don't want him. And I don't have anything else to do."

"Oh, I don't mind. But I can't say I understand it."

"He's pretty," Dek said, which was true.

"Pretty." Maja's smile hardened. "That's all?"

Oh foremothers. She didn't have time for this toadshit. "And he doesn't cost money."

Maja recoiled. "Dekklis! You've been to a *brothel?*"

"Of course I have. Oh, don't look at me like that. It's what soldiers *do*." Dekklis leaned close. Turned her face down and away, so that Maja would imagine shame. "Just don't tell Mother, yeah?"

"Of course I won't. Only," and Maja leaned close, smiling, and this time she reminded Dekklis of a rock leopard about to leap, "you have to tell me what it's like."

"Lots of half-bloods and toadbellies, mostly. It's Cardik," she added when Maja pulled a face. "Some of the brothels double as bathhouses. There's a whole street of them, down by the hot springs. They're all very professional. And very expensive. You don't want to hear all the details, do you?"

Maja did, of course she did. Probably gathering blackmail material, or gossip to spread among her friends: the legion little sister, the rebel, going *northern* in her manners.

So Dekklis told her about Aneki and Still Waters, about the bondies she knew by name. She dredged up Teslin's stories, too, and Barkett's, and Istel's, and filled her sister's ears with them. And by the time she escaped, she'd lost most of a candlemark to

lies and toadshit

telling Maja exactly what she expected to hear. She didn't quite jog to the garrison. But she moved at a fast northern march, the sort Rurik enforced whenever they didn't have real road underfoot. And so she discovered her tail, by luck and accident, as she descended the narrow spiral bridge between First Tier and Second. She was going just a little bit faster than a normal pedestrian's pace, reached one landing and caught the railing, used her momentum to swing herself around to the next ramp. Motion above caught her eye: someone turning around fast, walking back up the ramp. There was no place for that someone to've come *onto* the bridge, except behind her. And maybe that person had forgotten something, had turned around fast and gone back to get it, except who needed a cloak in Illharek? Who needed a hood?

People like Snowdenaelikk. Trouble.

Dekklis got herself off the bridge at the first opportunity, dodging into a neighborhood of lesser Houses on the Second Tier. She crouched behind a conjured sculpture of svartjagr in flight—ugly thing, amateur, that rendered its subject neither graceful nor menacing—and waited. And yes, there, came that same shrouded someone, moving much faster now. And then that someone turned its head just so, and one of the witchfire streetlights cut through the hood's shadows and splashed her features into bright relief.

Dek recognized the woman, by face if not the name, from the barracks. She considered, for a brief white-hot moment, coming out of concealment and confronting her. Considered even more briefly just knifing the woman in the back and dumping her over the edge of the bridge. It was a long way down to the Suburba. No one would recognize the corpse once it landed.

Messy, Szanys. Amateur.

Snow would have laughed at her, and then Snow would've woven the shadows that much more tightly around herself and gotten off the bridge, off the Tiers, and disappeared into the Suburba. Dekklis, lacking those skills, waited until the woman got tired of looking around and left, which took far too long. Plenty of time to regret she'd never asked Snow to teach her that trick with the shadows. Plenty of time to get angry, really and truly, while she worked out who'd put a tail on her in the first place. She didn't want to think it was Dani. They'd gone through first training together, she and Praefecta K'Hari Dannike. She expected better of an old friend.

Idiot, Dek, you know that?

Then again, Praefecta K'Hari might follow orders first, friendship second, like a good soldier. Which Dekklis herself had been once. And now she was plotting treason, consorting with heretics. It might not even be Dannike who'd put the tail on her. She'd asked a lot of questions about missing highborn men, hadn't she? Hell and damn. Could be anyone.

This toadshit was what happened when an honest scout started playing politics.

She wished for Istel at her back, again and always. But Istel had his own work. Her orders, to keep him from outright rebellion. Politics wasn't a man's game. Intrigue wasn't. So she sent him into the Suburba.

Protect Snow, she'd told Istel. *She's got enemies down there.*

She watched Istel go, every day, from the walls, conspicuously—so that if anyone wanted to shadow him, she would see it. Let one of Dani's city-bred, city-trained First Cohort greens follow a scout from the Sixth. Let them try.

But no one ever did follow him. No one bothered. Dek thought that it was because no one thought he could *do* anything. The First, based in and around Illharek, was made up of women. Highborn, midtown, even some from the Suburba. But women, almost to a body, especially in command. Istel didn't rate their attention—lowborn, northern, male.

Tell me I'm wrong, Szanys. Tell me that this is the best way. Tell me how wise our foremothers were.

She found Istel in the barracks. Alone, because the First was all women and did not practice the Sixth's habit of mixing sexes or commissions. Istel had the whole room to himself, five other empty bunks. Dekklis's own quarters lay in the officer's wing, where Istel could not go without orders or express invitation. Hell if she'd summon him like a damn bondie. Easier to go to him.

He had his gear spread out over two bunks. Weapons stacked neatly on one, bow unstrung, quiver, arrows fanned out beside it. He sat on the second, armor spread out around him in pieces. Scout armor was simple stuff, compared to infantry. Primarily leather, some patches of wool, bits of dark Illhari steel studded strategically across breast and shoulders. Irregular patterns of stitching and textures, the better to blend in with forests. Down here, among polished infantry, Istel had no camouflage. Could not, like she had, borrow a cuirass and march through the Tiers.

He heard her. Of course he did. Stiffened just the littlest bit, across the neck and shoulders, when he heard her come to the doorway and stop. He dipped the corner of a rag into a small tub of mink oil. Started working it into the chest piece he had in his lap.

"Snow went back up to the Tiers."

"I know. Meeting her in a mark."

His back got a little stiffer. A little straighter. Wanting to ask her why, wanting to go with her, wanting—hell if she knew what. Things to go back to normal, maybe, which they wouldn't, *couldn't*, in this motherless city.

"I need a favor, Istel."

He paused midswipe on the leather. Looked at her, frowning. "A *favor?*"

"I can still ask for one, can't I?"

"Reckoned it'd be orders." Softly, flatly, only a trace of bitter. "First Scout."

"Cut that toadshit." It came out sharper than she'd intended.

"Sir," he said, and ducked his chin. But his eyes stayed on hers. Maybe looking for his partner under the legion cuirass. His frown deepened.

"What happened, Dek?"

Easier just to say *nothing* and just get on with her

order

request. Easier, and very Illhari, and *hell*.

"Someone followed me today. I lost them in the Tiers. She's from First Cohort," she added as Istel opened his mouth. "I don't know her name."

"Huh." Istel sat very straight, very still, the cloth and oil forgotten. "You know who sent her?"

"No. But it's not good."

"You want me to go with you? Or follow, keep her off you?"

"No. I can shake her. I did once already. I won't bring her to Snow."

Istel grunted. He wanted to ask what she and Snow were meeting about, clear as water. And equally clear, he didn't think she'd tell him.

The less you know, Istel, the safer you'll be.

"So," he said after a too-long pause. "This favor of yours. If it's not helping you deal with this tail, then what is it?"

Dekklis came and sat on the bunk across from him. Leaned her elbows on her knees. "Optio Nezari."

Istel grimaced. "What about her?"

"She doesn't like northerners."

"She's made that clear enough. Always saying some toadshit whenever she sees me—which you already know." Istel's voice sharpened. "It's just hazing, Dek. I can handle that."

"I know that. But next time she says something, I want you to take offense. Start a fight. She'll be in the courtyard at breakfast tomorrow. Make sure you're there, too. Make sure something happens."

Istel raised both brows. "The hell?"

"I need enough time to drive a stake into the garrison roof."

"For what?"

"Istel."

"Right. Best if I don't know. Safest. Whatever." He stared at the barrack wall. His jaw worked, tick and tense and loose again. "This something you and Snow came up with?"

"No. She doesn't know, either."

He turned to her, startled. And relaxed, some of the wariness draining out of his features. "Okay. I'll do it."

"They might court-martial you. That's possible. Or put you in the subbasement cells."

"I said I'd do it, Dek. Nezari's a toadfucker."

"If they leave your punishment to *me*, and they should, I'll have to strip you of your commission. But only for a few days." Please, foremothers, she still had enough traction with Dannike. "I'll recall and reinstate you."

"I'm still saying yes, Dek. This all helps your credibility, doesn't it? Highborn Illhari going tough on her northern subordinate. The praefecta might throw you a party once I'm out the gates." He didn't quite smile. "You won't tell me why, though, will you? You trust me to throw my commission away, but not with whatever plans you've got."

If she failed, if they caught her, she might find herself prisoner, locked in a cell in the garrison subbasement, looking down through the window slit at the Jaarvi's distant black surface. She might face a trial, conviction, maybe even execution: a long fall from the Senate Spire into the Jaarvi, which was how highborn traitors died.

But Istel. He could end up in an indentured's collar. Branded. Gelded. Plain and simply dead, too, but not quickly. Better living and angry than dead with her.

Hell and damn, Snow would laugh at her.

So little faith in your plans, Szanys? In your partner?

As if Snow herself never had doubts, never hesitated, never sliced Veiko out of her reckoning. *He* wasn't sniffing around the Suburba, was he? *He* was Above, safe from whatever toadshit Snow was into.

"It's not a matter of trust. Listen. I get caught, they might throw me in prison. But I'll get a trial. You they'll execute outright. Savvy that?"

She watched the fight run out of him. Watched him retreat behind a face wiped carefully blank. "Savvy, Dek. I'll do it. But you go fast, driving your stake into the roof. I don't promise I'll let Nezari live once I get started."

CHAPTER ELEVEN

"This place is a ruin." Taru crouched at the river's edge, peering into the black trickle. "There are almost no spirits in this river. Almost none"— and she waved a hand at the barren earth, bleached rock and sand— "anywhere. What manner of place is this Illharek?"

"The true Illharek does not look like this." Veiko could see the resemblance, but this cave was smaller, more essential, somehow: a slash of absolute black bleeding out from between two slabs of stone, as if a mountain had collapsed and begun to devour itself. Far quieter than Illharek, far more menacing. Or perhaps it seemed so only because he could remember the Laughing God oozing out of those shadows like living ink.

"This is the true Illharek." Taru stood up. Brushed imaginary dust off her leggings. "Have you paid no attention to my lessons? Flesh reflects spirit."

"Flesh also shapes spirit. I have listened, wise ancestor."

"Huh. Does your partner-who-refuses-to-be-noidghe say what happened here, with this Illharek? Why it is so barren?"

"I do not think she knows." Veiko cocked an eye sideways. "I do not think I do."

"Nor do I." A long span of quiet, with no sound except boots and paws in the sand, and the whispers of the river-dead. "What does the living Illharek look like?"

"There are forests. Fields. A city inside of a much larger cave."

"So there should be spirits here, and there are not. Fled or destroyed, I cannot say."

"That is a rare thing indeed."

If Taru's look could draw blood, Veiko thought, he would badly need Snow's expertise with needle and thread. But her voice was mild:

"Why have we come to this dead place?"

Snowdenaelikk's need. Snowdenaelikk's desire.

"I am seeking a spirit."

Taru snorted. "A spirit. *Here.*"

"One with whom I am familiar." Veiko took a step closer to the cave-mouth. Helgi moved with him, with alert ears, nose and attention directed into that darkness.

There was *something* in there.

"Laughing God!" Veiko called. He drew his belt knife. Heard Taru's disapproving hiss. He half glanced over his shoulder at her. Then he turned the knife's point out and stabbed at air and emptiness. He drew the sigil carefully, the way Snow had showed him. A tepid, ill-tempered yellowish flame followed the tip of his blade, lingering in the still air. When he had finished, the God's mark floated at eye level.

"Laughing God!" he called again.

Helgi growled, very softly, and Veiko moved his free hand toward his axe. But then the sigil guttered and faded, turning to smoke and a fine sifting of ash.

"The spirit you call chooses not to answer you."

Veiko had grown used to southern customs, where a person's face announced his feelings. But he was not so out of practice with his people that he did not recognize smug when he saw it, in the barest hint of Taru's raised brows.

He was certain his own irritation was obvious to her. "I have summoned him by name and sigil. Were he here, he would have to answer."

"Ha. No. *Laughing God* is not a name. It is a description. Your spirit was wise enough to keep his name to himself."

This god was not wise, Veiko was certain. Equally certain he did not want to argue with her about the God's nature or tell her how he'd come by that knowledge.

"Laughing God is the name by which he is summoned," Veiko said patiently. "If he had another, he has forgotten it."

Taru threw him a sharp look. "A spirit who forgets his name—however much power he may have otherwise—can give you no great wisdom. Why are you seeking this one?"

"My partner believes he can help us against Tal'Shik."

"The spirit who marked you already. The dragon-woman. The one who *has* a name."

"All of those things, yes."

"Your Laughing God will be no help against her."

"My partner thinks otherwise, and so I must find him."

Taru sighed. "Must. I don't understand this *must*. You can spend the rest of the day shouting into that cave if you like. Your Laughing God is under no obligation to answer you if there has been no exchange of power between you."

"I gave him the edge of my axe."

"In exchange for a soul's freedom, which you achieved. That bargain is over."

Veiko shrugged. He turned the blade around, made as if to grab the metal itself, bare-handed. "I can make a new bargain."

Taru grabbed his wrist. Her fingers were cold, and surprisingly strong. "You will not use blood. That may call your spirit out if he's hiding, but it will give too much of yourself away."

Pity he had not known that earlier, then. Kenjak, Teslin, Barkett . . .

But it would not have mattered. Then, his need had been urgent.

And what is it now?

Snowdenaelikk's need. And a partner's promise.

"Perhaps I should go after him."

"A noidghe might do that," said Taru. "Hunt a spirit to its lair, challenge it to battle to learn its secrets, and in victory acquire its power. But that is a journey for a noidghe far stronger than *you*. If you lose the battle, the spirit will instead acquire *your* power. Further." She stepped close to him, drilled a finger into his chest. "This is not your quest or your battle. These are not your secrets that you seek. Let your partner look. She is a noidghe herself if she has come back from this place. And she has prior relations with this God."

Which was precisely the problem. Veiko did not want to explain all of the intricacies of Snow's relationship with the God to Taru. He *really* did not want to see the look on Snow's face when he reported his failure. She would be disappointed, yes, but that was the least of his worries. What she would do next—that was.

"My partner," he said. "If she were to seek your help, Taru, would you give it to her?"

Taru did not answer at once. Stood beside him, arms crossed, gazing around at the dust and stones and the ribbon of black river. Then, softly: "We did not have much business with Dvergiri when I wore flesh. And what business we *did* have was purely that. They came in search of wurms, and wurm-parts. But mostly they were busy with the Alviri and the Horse Tribes."

"They call themselves Taliri now. There are no more horses."

"So you say. Another Dvergir achievement. Truly, Veiko, you have fallen among barbarians. To destroy every single horse—that is a horror."

"It was a conjuring," Veiko said. "And it won them their war."

"Did it? Is that not your Dvergir woman's difficulty, that this same war is beginning again? What creatures will they destroy this time? What lands?"

"She is not my woman. She is my partner. And this war will not be the same."

Taru said nothing. Let her silence speak for her, as bleak and blasted as the land around them. And Veiko was left to the un-peace of his own thoughts, in which he wondered if she might not be right.

***

Dekklis rested on the garrison roof, flat as she could make herself. Thank all the foremothers that whoever had built the garrison favored level roofs instead of the snow-proof sloped peaks in Cardik. Bad enough she had to creep along to the edge. Far worse if she had to worry about going over before she was ready. There wasn't anything on the other side of the edge except *down*. A few bridges along the way to the distant Suburba, smaller arteries mostly left to servants. One of those was a rope-drop from the garrison roof, more or less. If her spike held. If no one saw her.

She eeled to the edge and peered over. Tugged the sweater up over her belly. It had been Teslin's and so was far too large. Pure undyed Cardik goat's wool, standard wear in Cardik winters. It had earned her more than one odd look round the barracks, where the cave ambient didn't rate that kind of warmth and weight.

But a smallish woman could hide a coil of rope underneath that much wool. Same rope that a highborn soldier could liberate from the quartermaster's stores without a second glance from the mila on duty.

Dekklis shook the rope out. Checked it for kinks. Knotted it round the spike she'd driven into the stone a day earlier while Istel had done her favor. His fight with Optio Nezari had drawn all the sentries out to watch while the garrison officers were locked in their morning meeting.

Dek hadn't expected him to win. Had worried, as the shouts from the courtyard half drowned out her hammering steel into stone, that Istel might've forgotten that he'd do her no good with broken bones. And when she'd gotten down there—roundabout across rooftops so it looked like she'd come from the officer's wing—hell and damn, there was Istel covered in dust and blood, and Nezari not much better off, and both of them emotional, irrational, and trying to kill each other.

It had taken three troopers to haul Nezari back, on Dekklis's command. Istel had picked himself up on his own. Spat blood and stood there while Dekklis questioned his parentage and intelligence and wondered aloud whether to stake him out for the svartjagr. Then she had turned on the rest of them, enumerating their faults at such volume that the praefecta herself had come out to see what in all hells was the problem and brought the rest of command as a witness.

Dek had worried then that she might've gone too far, that Dani would take charge of both offenders. But Dani had looked over the bloody mess of two soldiers, at the ring of slack-jawed trainees and sentries, and proved—

Illharek's legion's gone soft, Dek, bunch of rabbits.

—what Istel had alleged all along.

A word, Optio, she said, that was all, and Nezari had gone off to foremothers knew what discipline. Dani'd left Istel for Dekklis's discretion. And Dek's discretion meant another tirade, a tantrum ending in *Get out of my sight,* public exile from the garrison, and disappointed troopers who'd rather the blood and the beating.

Which meant Istel was limping loose in the Suburba right now, absent *with* leave, and that Dek had no partner for this liberation of K'Hess Soren. Safer for Istel, anyway. The Senate had enacted severe penalties for kidnap, for assassination, and the half-dozen other events that had been settled, before the Purge, by blood feud. Two, maybe three, of which she intended to try tonight.

Dekklis scrubbed her palms against her sweater. Took a wrap and fist of rope and let herself over the edge of the roof.

***

There was a lot of shadow gathered along the Tano path. Too much for this time of day. It was burning down to the fifteenth mark Below, which meant late afternoon. There was no pedestrian traffic, just her; but there were barges, still, floating into Illharek. Their crew lit lanterns as they passed out of the daylight, little yellow stars bobbing above the decks. Snow's own witchfire bobbed at her shoulder, small and discreet, casting blue along the stone path, grey where its light failed.

And its light failed very much, very hard, just ahead. Snow knew there was a side passage there that would let a traveler angle north, bypass Illharek outright, and connect with the road that ran along the Tebir tributary. There was a whole maze of tunnels in between, cut and conjured by the builders for the road crews. Rude hollows, meant for bondies and blankets, meant to be temporary. Some of those had turned into way stations for those travelers who walked along the Tano and the Tebir. Empty most of the time. Foot traffic Below was a matter of economics. If you could afford better, you didn't walk.

But this maze, closest to Illharek, was occupied. Suburbans called it the Tomb and sneered at it with the lip-curled contempt of the more fortunate to the less, the same look the highborn wore when they looked down into the Suburba's tangled guts. The only people who lived in the Tomb were the truly destitute, and criminals too desperate or violent for the cartels.

Once, the God's people had ranked among those kinds of criminals, counted as scavengers, like svartjagr, skulking in the shadows. Tsabrak had changed that. Recruited and organized and trained his people, built a cartel that ran half the Suburba and had fingers from Cardik to the Redstones.

We are invisible, he said, *because they don't want to see us. That's our advantage.*

Invisible in part because of tricks *she'd* taught them. Shadow-weaving, which would make exactly that sort of darkness.

Briel didn't seem bothered. Probably hadn't even noticed those shadows, being preoccupied with the narrowness of the passage, the shallowness of the ceiling. Not much room for a svartjagr to fly. She had resorted to crawling the walls, claws gouging into cracks even a rat wouldn't dare. That had her attention, not a patch of particular black on the path.

If there was reason to worry, Briel would have known it. Would have alerted Snow to it.

The darkness chuckled, cold against her ear.

Maybe Briel's not as clever as you think, yeah?

Veiko had said *Talk to the ghost,* yeah, but Veiko didn't know what a motherless toadfuck Tsabrak could be. Tsabrak hadn't liked Briel. Had, let's be honest, been more than a little afraid of her. Maybe a little bit jealous. Ari and Stig and the rest of them hadn't liked the svartjagr much, either. Or maybe it was a half-blood conjuror they hadn't liked, Tsabrak's *woman*
ally, whose skills they needed, whose loyalties they'd never been able to reckon. She made a fist of her right hand, where the God's sigil was. Same ink on her palm they had, but she hadn't sworn the same oaths.

Snow. Listen to me. The ghost fluttered against her neck. Cold fingers plucking at her collar.

Air and shadow, that's all he was.

Go away, Tsabrak.

Cold spots on her wrist, like gripping fingers. *Listen. Look. I trained you better.*

Chill-prickles all over her skin, and nothing to do with the temperature or ghosts. She put her hand out. Clenched her fist, and the witchfire died. Strained her eyes through the sudden darkness. Ghost-Tsabrak might be lying. Live-Tsabrak had often enough.

Briel noticed her hesitation. Paused where she hung on the rock. A moment's dizzy flash, Briel's tip-tilted perspective, the air a solid mass of patterns, currents, above the water. That world shifted again as Briel started to turn back.

Go, she wished Briel. *Go ahead. Find Veiko.*

Sentiment, whispered Tsabrak. *She could help you.*

"I won't need help," Snow whispered. And if she did, Briel wouldn't be able to do much. Not against who Snow thought might be up there, in that patch of too-dark.

She picked out the weak smears of lantern light from the passing barges. Drew it toward herself, thread by thread, stretching the glow and forced the shadows aside, so that black became darkwater grey. There were figures standing there, lumped and indistinct. She knew at least one of those shapes herself, and he was no ghost.

Ari.

Tsabrak had been a classic Dvergiri beauty, small framed and slender, long bones and big eyes. Ari, however, showed evidence of a Talir or two somewhere in his ancestry. Not close enough to be half-blood, but still. He was taller than average, broader, heavier. Mud-yellow eyes, which a Dvergir might inherit honestly, and walnut-dark hair, which no pure Dvergir would. The Ari Snow remembered had worn his hair long and loose and plain, deliberately undyed, deliberately not in the fashionable queue. The Ari Snow recalled had been a good bit thicker, too, muscle slabbed over bone. This man was lean as a winter wolf, all his vanity cropped to a stubbled dust on his skull. But those were Ari's eyes, burning with godlit fury. She counted at least a handful of people with him, hinted and half-solid. The shadows inked and ebbed, living darkness, pushing back against her light. Fuck and damn. She'd taught shadow-weaving to anyone who had asked, hadn't she, and thought herself some kind of rebel.

Damned stupid, yeah? Arming the enemy. Adepts knew that.

One conjured witchfire could blast them all into brightness. One conjured witchfire could prompt Ari's friends to jump her, too. The Ari she remembered was talk-before-violence. Please, that this version was, too, however feral he looked.

Snow kept her hands loose. Looked Ari over, crown to toes. Raised both eyebrows. Slow drawl, no shake in her voice: "Huh. Thought you were dead, yeah?"

The shadows rippled as bodies shifted position, came into focus. As knives came out. But Ari raised a hand. Peeled her an unfriendly not-smile. "Disappointed?"

"Don't be an idiot." She matched his not-smile. Showed teeth. "Didn't reckon Rata was smart enough to do you. Didn't reckon she was stupid enough to tell me the truth, though."

Another shift and eddy in the shadows. Faces drifted into focus, stormy, ugly, violent. Strangers, most of them. Only one she recognized, Hraf, who'd been a boy when she left. Cold fingers moved in her gut. These were Ari's men, not Tsabrak's.

Fuck and damn.

This time Ari half turned his head before the movement stopped. Only his eyes flicked back toward her. "You been back a while, yeah? Word's out on the street. Reckoned you'd look for us."

"Where should I look? I checked the places *I* knew."

"Not all of them."

He meant the shrine. The place she'd been exactly once, and then in Tsabrak's company. Ari knew very well why a lone woman, conjuror or not, Tsabrak's right hand or not, wouldn't walk into that place. She shrugged. Paused, got enough spit in her mouth to keep talking. "I reckoned if you were alive, you'd find me. I've been prancing all over the motherless Suburba."

Ari let his weight shift back on his heels, just a little. "That you have. Meeting with Rata, too."

"Once, to reckon where you were." She caught movement on her periphery, some motherless toadshit trying to flank her. "Call off that dog, Ari, or I'll feed him to you."

Ari gestured, and the movement stopped.

"The fuck is *she*," came Hraf's voice from the shadow, "to talk to *us* like that?"

Tsabrak would've answered *she is your better* and splashed a little shame onto preexisting resentment, make the dislike really stick. What he'd always done, to keep her from becoming one of them.

Ari only sucked on his teeth. "This is Snowdenaelikk. There's a reason she was Tsabrak's right hand, yeah?"

"I know the reason." Hraf had almost grown into his nose since last she'd seen him. It still sounded like his voice had been squeezed through it. "Tsabrak was fucking her."

Snow laughed. "We have that in common, yeah? Except Tsabrak wouldn't take you north with him, no matter how sweet you were in bed."

Hraf growled, really growled, like Logi. "You told him not to take me."

"I told him you were an idiot, yeah? That you don't know when to shut up. And I was right, *clearly*." She raised her right hand, palm out. Conjured a witchfire to run down between her fingers, drip and coil around her wrist. Used its light to push back hard at the shadows so that she could see every one of them.

She marked their stances, their placement, their weapons. There were six of them, counting Ari and Hraf. Five pairs of eyes flashed to her hand, five pairs rounded out at the dripping witchfire. Only Ari didn't blink or flinch, like it happened every day that a half-blood called blue fire out of nothing.

"Hraf, leave off. She's godmarked," Ari said. "Just like all of you. And if the God doesn't mind her, *you* don't. Savvy that?"

That was the Ari she knew. Temper sunk out of sight, eyes gone cool and flat. As likely to put a knife in your back as buy you a drink, yeah, that was Ari. But he hadn't killed her yet. Hadn't even tried.

An idiot might think that meant she was safe. Ari would have his own ideas why she was here, why he thought Tsabrak's right hand had come south. She could play on that. Gamble on what Ari knew and didn't, and trust that the God hadn't passed along any messages, by whatever means gods talked to godsworn.

"I'm back because Cardik's gone." Pause, to let the ripple and murmur rise and fall. "Taliri hit it. Whole army of them." And to Ari, as if the rest of them weren't fidgeting like a cage of hungry rats: "They had godsworn with them. Tal'Shik's."

Hraf and two others made warding gestures against the speaking of her name. Dek would call it superstition. Veiko would call it good sense.

Ari only grimaced. "Fuck and damn. And Tsabrak?"

Snow glanced around. The ghost had disappeared again. And he'd so loved attention, too.

"Dead. We were betrayed." Truth. And a lie: "I wasn't with him when it happened."

"How'd you survive?" Hraf said, sharp and too loud.

"I ran," Snow said flatly. "Got out before the siege landed. The Alviri were rioting, yeah? The legion was distracted."

Ari frowned. "The Alviri were rioting? Why?"

Ari could be testing, seeing what she'd tell him. But he seemed genuine. Maybe the God hadn't included all his godsworn in his plans. Maybe that had been Tsabrak's special honor, to know that the God had planned treachery and alliance with his worst enemy.

Didn't need to see the ghost, or hear him, to know what Tsabrak would think of that. Curled lip, cold eyes.

Oh, such an honor. See what it cost.

"Taliri were burning out villages all winter," she said. "Lot of toadbellies in town without Illhari ink. They weren't happy with their prospects."

Ari said nothing. His brows leveled. His mouth did. "You've got your own toadbelly. Some skraeling. He has the street talking."

"So?"

"So Rata's got coin out for information about him. Lots of eyes looking." He rolled his, up and back. "She's paying for help from the Tiers. People like *you*."

"You're saying Rata's got coin to pay *conjurors* to find him?"

"I'm saying that's the rumor. What makes him so special?"

Snow pretended to look past Ari's head at the dockside, at the light-bleed from lanterns and candles. Honest flame. Candles and oil came in on the river, cheap goods, brought and traded by people who still used the word *witchery*. The Suburba was a superstitious place. If Rata'd brought her own conjuror down looking for Veiko, that was serious.

And dangerous. A conjuror wouldn't be fooled by irregular schedules. A conjuror would watch, only watch, and never be noticed. *She* could do that, and she wasn't the best watcher coin could buy. She had to warn Veiko. And Ari wouldn't be inclined to just let her walk away, not now, not easily.

"This skraeling knows things," she told Ari. "About godmagic."

He rolled eyes at her. Red lines all through the white. "What kind of things?"

"He's hurt Tal'Shik once, yeah? Might be able to do it again. That's why they want him."

"Toadshit," said Hraf.

Ari ignored him. "Maybe *we* should talk to him, he's that important."

Oh fuck and damn. Snow moved closer to him. Put her hand on his sleeve. Smelled a man who'd gone too long without washing. Stale sweat. Old dirt. Fear, which she'd never connected with Ari.

"Listen. He's skraeling, yeah? Let me handle him. He'll bolt, he sees more than me coming. The skraeling was part of Tsabrak's plan, yeah? Let me settle it. Then I'll come back. Tonight. Meet me just inside the gate, yeah? Fuck and damn, Ari, I've been *looking* for you. We have work to do."

She felt Ari looking at her. Watched the lines mapping his forehead, his eyes, his mouth. Felt his hesitation, and the shift as he reached resolution.

"We do," he said after a moment. His gaze wandered over her, face to feet and back. "Never thought I'd say it, Snow. But I'm glad to see you."

CHAPTER TWELVE

Veiko was picking his way over the ridge when Briel found him, just as the sun dropped behind a bank of western clouds. She sent him an image of Snowdenaelikk, waiting at his fire. Not wishful-Briel, no, the hard clarity of things-which-were.

Veiko watched as Briel crossed the sunset, her wings like smoked glass. Then she passed into shadow. Passed out of his awareness then, as if he'd slammed a door between them. He could push her aside when she was distracted and have the inside of his skull to himself. But she could do the same. There were insects to snap at. Bats to chase, who were nearly as much fun as cats. A whole sky overhead, and trees below, and she had made her report.

His partner, whom he had not seen in days, was waiting for him. He was glad he had gotten two rabbits, at least. They were not large this early in spring. Not fat. And he had not planned on a guest.

Veiko was most of the way down the ridge now, circling toward his campsite. Grey skies. Grey air, where the river mist rose up and twined through the trees. He smelled pine and growing things. Smelled the death and blood he carried. Logi *oofed*, nose up and ears pointed—smelling Snow, no doubt.

"Go," Veiko said, and Logi bolted in a scrabbling of leaves and claws. Veiko had some sympathy with the impulse. But he made himself walk at a sane pace, minded where he put his feet and where the branches were. A hunter could not let himself get careless, and Snow would hardly leave before he arrived.

He took careful steps. Deliberate. While his belly tightened and his heart thumped.

"Idiot," drifted through the trees. "Will you *sit?*"

A whine, which meant Logi had. He was still sitting when Veiko arrived. Flattened his ears in greeting and shuffled his paws and stayed where he was.

Veiko suspected witchery, for that sudden and absolute obedience. He could be a little bit jealous. Or he could just be

happy

pleased that he would have company for dinner besides Logi's big-eyed greed.

That company squatted beside his fire, feeding it sticks.

"There you are," she said without looking.

"I was hunting."

"Reckoned." She turned then and tipped her little half smile into the corner of her mouth. "Ah. Rabbits."

"Rabbits are simplest. It is much harder to hunt with only one dog." He noted the pack beside her, lumped around its meager contents. She had come for a day, maybe two, but she was not packed for long journeys. "Why are you here?"

"Can't I be lonely?"

"Perhaps. But I do not think that you are."

"Huh. Fine. Because my sister's going to drive me mad. Belaery's busy with some toadshit Adept business. And Dekklis asked me to teach her to pick locks."

Veiko snorted. "That seems unlikely."

"That seems like trouble. I didn't ask why. Reckon she wanted me to know, she'd tell me." Snow snapped a stick in half. Studied the jagged edges. Tossed both pieces into the fire. "Rata's got people looking for you. Conjuror, maybe. Or godsworn. I was worried they might've found you. Obviously they haven't. Unless you've got bodies stashed in the forest somewhere."

"No."

"Didn't reckon. I'm leaving Briel with you. She's another set of eyes, yeah? Besides. She misses you."

"No." An old argument. Comfortable, like worn boots. "You need her more than I do."

Snow hesitated, like she wanted to say something. Then she reconsidered, visibly. Cast her gaze around the campsite and jerked her head sideways, at the drum where it sat drying beside the fire.

"Taken up music, have you?"

It was a crude thing, a simple cross frame with a skin stretched across it. The frame had taken the most effort, needing several strips of wood and bark and the same glue Veiko used for fletching arrows. Arrows, he had decided, were far simpler.

"It is a noidghe's drum." Veiko squatted beside Snow. Laid the rabbits out on the ground and drew his knife.

She snagged the nearest. Turned it over in her hands. "I'll get this one. Goes faster with two of us."

He had tried to teach her how to skin and gut, last winter. Had taken her hand in his and wrapped her fingers round the hilt.

It is not like cutting a person, he had told her. *Hold it like this.*

She had plucked the knife out of his hands. Slipped it between hide and meat with a skill that made him wonder what exactly chirurgeons learned in their apprenticeship.

You're right. Dead things don't squirm.

She cut a little slower now than she had then. Her broken finger refused to clamp tight around the knife's hilt, which made him wonder how the cut on her arm was healing. He eyed her sleeves, which seemed long and thick for the warmth of a late-spring evening.

Snow caught him looking. Cut him a glance that made him understand why Logi would not move from his place.

"The arm's fine, yeah?"

"You are the chirurgeon." The Dvergiri word came more easily now. Sounded less like he'd gotten a mouthful of stones.

"Glad someone noticed. So. Why does a noidghe need a drum?"

"For beating."

"Oh, you're funny. —Do you want the hides?"

Before the winter solstice he would have said yes. He had traded furs in the Alviri villages to the north, before Tal'Shik's Taliri began burning whole settlements, and the legion came out of Cardik. Before Snowdenaelikk.

He stroked the fur. Sighed. "No. Logi can have them."

Motion out the corner of his eye: a dog creeping forward, swinging around the fire on Veiko's side. Logi stopped when Snow looked at him. Whined and sat.

"Tell me how you do that."

She chuckled. "Same way you get Briel to do whatever *you* ask when she argues with me." She tossed a rabbit head across the fire. Logi leapt and caught it, hunched and bit down, hard.

Snow made a face halfway between grin and grimace. Pitched her voice over the crunching. "Tell me about the drum."

Quick cuts, because it did not matter if he nicked the hide. He pulled the skin free. Laid it on the skull. "It is for walking the ghost roads, instead of using the poison."

Half a beat of silence. "What, you just woke up one morning and thought, ah, that's how I make the drum, I don't need to try and kill myself anymore?"

"I have gotten a teacher. One of my ancestors found me."

Her eyebrows fluttered up. "You mean a ghost."

Veiko imagined Taru's expression, should she hear herself called *ghost*. He decided it best that Snow and Taru never meet. "A noidghe must be taught by another noidghe. There are songs to learn, and traditions, and skills. Most often, the teacher is still living. But since I am near no others, my teacher came to me. She is also a hunter, but even so, it took her some time to find me."

"She."

The look on her face was exactly like Logi's the first time he'd discovered that kittens have claws. Veiko let the smile creep onto his face this time. "Women can be noidghe. It is a matter of talent, not sex."

"Old woman?"

"Not particularly."

"Huh." Snow had reduced her rabbit to its component parts. She wiped the blade on the fur and delivered the edible bits to the cookpot in bloody handfuls. "So how does it work? You beat the drum, you're in the ghost roads?"

"An apprentice beats the drum. The noidghe's spirit leaves his body."

"You don't have an apprentice."

"No. But there are skills one learns in the making of a drum that I should have, whether or not I need it to walk the ghost roads." He sent his own rabbit into the pot after hers. Stared down at his hands. "I have learned many things out of order."

"You've done all right. Bargained your way past Tal'Shik, yeah? And the God. Hurt them both."

"I have been fortunate."

"That what your ancestor tells you?"

You are not untalented, Veiko Nyrikki, but only a fool relies on his luck instead of his skill.

"Yes. And she is right to say so."

Snow's eyes flashed. A retort moved across her face like thunder before it lodged behind her teeth. Veiko watched her swallow it.

Her eyes dropped. She was suddenly very busy with her own hands, getting every last smudge of blood off.

"And have you been fortunate in finding the God?"

"No," Veiko said. "I have tried, but there is no answer. Perhaps you should look for him."

She pressed her lips in a line. "I can't call him. Only godsworn can do that, which I am not."

"You should try again. You were not a noidghe before."

"I'm not noidghe now, yeah? Noidghe have"—she waved her hands—"drums. Noidghe have ghost-ancestors who find them and teach them things."

"You also have ancestors."

"I don't have *noidghe* ancestors, Veiko. Listen. I've been through just about every scroll in the toadfucking Archives. Nothing about *noidghe* in there, yeah? We've got godsworn. We've got theurgists and thaumaturgists. But Dvergiri don't have anything *like* noidghe. Not before Illharek's founding, damn sure not after."

The Dvergiri did not recognize the ancestry of the father. He knew that, oh ancestors, he knew it. But that did not eliminate the connection. "*You* might."

"What did I just say? There's no—" Then she understood. Stopped midsyllable. Her jaw shot sideways, tightened until he heard her teeth grind. "You mean Kaj."

A wise man would stop now. But he was not, for all Taru's efforts, a wise man. Deep breath, then: "All of us have noidghe, Jaihnu or Pohja, it will not matter. Somewhere, in your father's line, there will be a noidghe. Snow." Veiko leaned toward her. Tried to catch and hold her eyes. "I made the drum for you, as much as me. Let me help you walk the ghost roads."

The storm built in her eyes, turning the dark blue to black. Lips stretched flat, her face pulled tight across jagged bones. Then the storm broke. Her gaze skated away. She found somewhere else to look, into the trees and shadow.

"I can't."

He had never heard *can't* out of her before, not in that tone. It was as if the sky had turned green. "Why not?"

"I died, Veiko. I know what's over there."

He remembered a barren glacier. Remembered the black river and the mindless dead bobbing below its surface. Remembered the one that had nearly claimed him, and the river's kiss on his skin. "As did I."

"No." Her mouth twisted. "You didn't. Don't tell me my business, yeah? I sat there, I held your hand, and you came godsrotted close, but you never died. *I did.* Dek says so, and fuck and damn, Dek should know a corpse when she sees one. And Kenjak pulled me out of the fucking river. You said Helgi didn't let you fall in."

"Some noidghe die more completely than others, but we all touch that water."

"More of your ancestor's wisdom?"

Delivered more gently than Taru could, but, "Yes."

"Well. I'm in no hurry to come close to it again, yeah? Not for the God. Not for Tsabrak. I want nothing to do with that place."

"Yet you ask me to walk there, on your errands."

He had not meant it as challenge. A statement of fact only, so that she understood that *he* could do this thing and thus, so could she.

And so he did not expect the look he got from her, and a voice like the winter wind. Coldly, so coldly: "You're not willing, say so. You think I owe you for asking, say that, too."

Midwinter dark was warmer and more welcoming than her anger. He felt its echoes, through Briel, like an icicle pushed through his chest. Felt Briel's distress, too, tightening from throat to belly. His guts dropped as the svartjagr banked. A flicker of trees-dark-sky, and a sense of returning. A spear tip behind his eyes. Briel coming fast, frantic. And beneath that, his own anger, welling up.

Effort to keep his voice steady. "You do not owe me."

Years of svartjagr sendings had worn grooves in Snow's face like water through stone. Those grooves deepened now. Cracked her anger like glass. She clipped out a *sorry* that barely cleared her teeth. Turned a shoulder and rummaged through her pack. Came back with a stick of jenja pinched between her fingers. She lit it in the fire. Took a deep lungful. Blew out a spicy-smoke cloud that hung like fog over the fire. He studied her. Leather jerkin laced tight over an Illhari linen shirt, and probably a shift under that, and he could still see the curve of ribs and spine through the layers. A spare woman, always, but she seemed even thinner. Gaunt. He might blame her woundfever for that. But she did not look like a sick woman. Looked like a moose hunted ragged, chased by dogs and men, and oh ancestors, he would not tell her that.

Said instead, "I thought you had stopped smoking jenja."

"I ran out. That's different. Sinnike keeps it in stock. Just say what you mean. I look like toadshit."

"I have never seen toadshit."

Tattered ghost of a smile, which never got off her lips. She pinched her nose between two fingers. Winced and squeezed. "Fuck and damn, Briel, leave off."

A man might hear *Veiko, leave off* just as clearly. And a man might keep his mouth closed this time and let the quiet spread and deepen. Listen to Logi's happy crunching, the insects, an owl somewhere close. Listen to the night breeze off the river, sifting through the trees.

And hear a svartjagr's wingbeats, the peculiar hiss of air across bone and membrane. Briel dropped out of the sky, wings churning. Bounced to an ungraceful landing beside Logi, who snorted and shied sideways without letting go of his rabbit.

And there, clear evidence of Briel's distress: she did not even look at Logi's prize. Scrabbled on wing-knuckles and clawed back feet around the fire, damn near dragging her tail through the embers, and put herself between Veiko and Snow. Looked at one, then the other, and hissed.

"Oh, shut up," Snow said. But she put out her hand, and Briel snaked underneath it and put her head on Snow's thigh.

The spear behind Veiko's eyes dissolved into tingles and twinges. He closed his eyes and breathed until the knot in his throat loosened. There. He rocked onto his toes. Stood up slowly. Tossed the remaining rabbit bones to Logi. He peered into the pot. Added a little water, a double pinch of salt from his pouch. A fistful of the things that smelled like onions. Ancestors only knew what the Illhari called them. He considered asking Snow. Reconsidered. The quiet between them was not comfortable, but it was safe. Only a fool would stir it up.

"Veiko."

And of the pair of them, he had never thought her the fool. His chest tightened, as if heart and lungs had curled together into a fist. He glanced at her. Tipped his head, silent *what?*

The sun had sunk into twilight. Long, feathered shadows came off the trees, met the limits of firelight and turned solid. They crept up over Snow, covering her haunch and hip and boot. Her moon-colored hair had gone pinkish in the firelight. The tip of her jenja glowed like Briel's eyes. Her own were opaque, reflecting fire and nothing else. "You're Jaihnu, yeah?"

"Yes. But my ancestor, Taru, is Pohja."

She blew a cloud of smoke. Flicked ashes into the fire. "What's the difference?"

"The Pohja follow the takin herds. They are hunters. Wanderers. Jaihnu also herd takin, but our herds are smaller, and we keep them close, instead of following them. We have settlements. Fields, sometimes. Forges."

"Permanence."

Your people have grown rooted, Veiko. You look to the earth instead of the sky.

"The Pohja find it unnatural."

"And the Jaihnu probably find the Pohja barbaric." Odd little smile on her lips, bitter and amused at once.

"Yes."

"So which of your parents comes from barbarian stock?"

"My father's mother. Taru is *her* grandmother."

"But *you're* Jaihnu, yeah? Because the line runs through your father and *his* father."

"Because I was born in a Jaihnu village." He saw the trap too late. Wished the words unsaid.

She pretended great interest in the tip of her jenja. "We've got that in common, yeah? My father's mother comes from outlander stock, too. But I'm Illhari."

"And what does that mean?" He meant the question sincerely. Jaihnu meant one set of customs, Pohja another, but the language was the same. But Illhari meant nothing he could see in common, no, not with Dekklis and Istel and Snow all claiming it, and Aneki and Kaj. "What is Illhari? Tell me."

She hooked her shirt and tugged sideways. Bared her neck just past the too-prominent bones, where the Illhari sigil coiled crimson against the black skin.

"That is a tattoo," he said. "Not an answer."

"My mother had one. My sisters do. Even my fucking *father* has one. Listen. You want to know what being Illhari means? I'll tell you. You know about the wars, yeah? Between Illharek and the tribes?"

"Yes." Everyone did. The grandfathers told tales from *their* childhood, of fires that burned like sunset across the horizon, and ash that fell like snow from the skies. Great shuddering quakes of backlash that made canyons where there had been meadows and twisted rivers into new patterns.

"You know why it happened? The Alviri tribes thought the Dvergiri were demons. That's what their gods told them. Or their chieftains. Fact is, we scared them. We conjure, and they can't. We live underground, where they bury their dead. They say we're the same black as a rotting Alvir corpse, that we were the walking dead. Toadshit superstition, yeah? We built Illharek and called ourselves a republic while they were still chasing goats on the hillsides. We set up trade routes. We built things. We forged metal, good metal, and they needed it, and they bought it and used it to kill us."

She paused. Stared at him, as though waiting for something. Veiko shrugged. "The Illhari won those wars long before your birth. You cannot still want revenge."

"Me? No. But there are grudges. The Alviri tribes did things to us that make Taliri raids look like children kicking anthills. You know that one of their tribes executed every Dvergir in its borders? You know how many that was? *Thousands*, Veiko. They had a lot of territory. And it was the summer caravan season, so the Dvergiri were Above and traveling."

Veiko understood blood feud. Whole families could die, farmsteads burned to the last stalk of wheat. But the chieftains usually intervened before that. Forced peace, reparations, and reconciliation. Marriages sometimes. But he could not wrap his mind around thousands. That would be all the population of Cardik. That would be a whole valley of Jaihnu villages, gone.

But the Illhari had ended the wars. And they had used Tal'Shik to do it. And then they had cast her out, too. So perhaps that first blood feud hadn't ended at all. Perhaps the battlefield had changed.

Carefully, feeling his way over the words: "Your people had reason to seek Tal'Shik's help, then."

"Sure. But she cost us. Bad fucking bargain, yeah? Two hundred years ago, Istel wouldn't be in the legion. He'd've been sold, gelded, or exposed at birth. Maybe gone to feed Tal'Shik on some pole somewhere. And Kaj would've spent his whole life in a collar. Now he's as much Illhari as any highborn Dvergir, according to the law."

"The law. Yes. Your law has two faces. You say it was worse under Tal'Shik, and perhaps that is true. But regardless, the highborn will still call Kaj toadbelly and skraeling, no? Whether or not he can hear them. And they will still call you a half-blood. So I do not understand why you care if Tal'Shik returns or not, when they will deny you honor in either case."

"Honor?" She laughed. "You been talking to Dek?"

"No. Aneki. Back in Cardik."

"Didn't know Aneki knew the word." Snow's jaw squared stubborn. "Dek throws it around enough. You do, too. So explain to me, Veiko Nyrikki. Should I just walk away? Let Tal'Shik win? Is that what you mean by honor?"

"This is not your fight. It never was. It was the God's and Tsabrak's. Maybe the legion's. Not yours."

"That sounds like Aneki, too."

"I do not need Aneki to tell me what I see with my own eyes."

"And I can say for myself which fights are mine, yeah?"

As soon argue the sun out of the sky as persuade Snow to anything like reason. "You fear the black river so much, but this path you are on will put you back in it."

"And what, you won't be able to get me out this time?"

"Even noidghe can die."

"I'm *not* a fucking noidghe."

"No. Of course you are not. You are Illhari, and the Illhari do not have noidghe, although the Illhari can count Dvergir and Alvir and Talir and Jaihnu among their ranks, and some of *them* have noidghe. But there can be no Illhari noidghe, ever. Fire is hot, water is wet, ice is cold."

"Let me tell you what Illhari have. A Senate playing politics. Missing highborn men used as hostages, who're probably spiked somewhere and dead. And there hasn't been a single toadfucked caravan out of the north yet this season, yeah? That never happens. We've sent ours out. Bet me what happens to them?"

"I do not need to bet. But I still do not understand what you hope to gain from this pursuit except your own ruin."

So rare to see her at a loss for words. Eyes closed, quiet for so long that he wondered if she would answer. Then, "Why did you kill the chieftain's son?"

"We have talked about this."

"Tell me again."

"Because he was a thief. But because of his father, I could not be sure of justice, so—" He stopped. Frowned. "It is not the same thing."

"Finish what you meant to say, yeah?"

"If I had not killed him, he would have continued his harm unchecked."

"And who would he have harmed?"

"My people. It is *not* the same."

"Toadshit. If I leave this now, Tal'Shik harms *my* people. It's *exactly* the same."

A man could argue until his tongue rotted out that a village full of people he'd known all his life did not compare at all to Illharek's whole Republic. He had known the people he had saved. Had known the ones he damned, too. His family had undoubtedly paid for his crime, in wealth or blood or flesh. He had sisters, and the Illhari were not the only ones who kept thralls.

Briel *chrripped*. Scrabbled partway across the distance between them, wings half-spread and awkward. The svartjagr's distress rippled through him, mixed with his own grief, and sent it washing back.

"I would not make the same choice again. I would be wiser."

"Too late for wisdom. For either of us. I need the God. *Need* him, Veiko."

They had no habit of modesty between them. Had seen each other in every stage between naked and clothed, in situations better left to privacy. But the surge coming back through Briel made Veiko feel like he was inside

me

Snow's skin with her. A fear so deep that

I

he wanted to retch. An anger that ran even deeper, colder, like a river under ice. A need that burned in

my

his throat, in

my

his chest, in

my

his belly.

And then gone, blank, with a force that made him blink. Briel squawked and flared her wings. Made an awkward run and leap at the nearest tree and scrabbled up while Snow slowly pushed her knife back into its sheath and stood up. He expected her to arch her back, stretch, maybe go after Briel. So he was unprepared when she scooped up her pack and angled behind him. That was a woman going someplace, and the only thing in that direction was Illharek.

"Snow." He made a grab for her. Missed and rolled up onto his feet, hunter-quick, and stepped in front of her. He had his hand out, still. She stared at it. At him. Peeled him an odd little smile.

Heat prickled under his skin. Veiko let his arm fall, but he did not step aside. "Where are you going?"

Her brows rose. "I wanted to make sure you were all right. You are. Now I've got business, yeah? I found Ari. He's waiting for me, back Below."

"What, now?"

"Tal'Shik's not waiting, is she? Listen. Maybe you're right. If you can't find the God, then maybe I try and summon him. Ari and me and what's left of the godsworn."

"I will come with you." He did not like the way his voice clung to the inside of his throat.

"No." She shook her head. Hitched the pack's strap higher on her shoulder. "That lot's dangerous. They don't know you. And besides, Veiko, it isn't your fight. You just said so. Fuck and damn. You don't even think it's mine."

"We are partners."

She gave him a long look, steady and blank. Briel was no help. The svartjagr was a silent knot in the branches, two glowing eyes, that was all. Only his own thoughts for company, his own fear, black and deep as the shadows in Illharek. She could end their partnership here with a simple *not anymore*. He had no defense against that.

And then what would he do? The land between Illharek and the northern border crawled with Taliri: all the places he knew, that he had traded, turned hostile. He might head farther south, where the forest spilled into naked plains. Might head west, into the jagged mountains that were more rock than trees. Wurms

dragons, *Veiko, that's the Dvergir word*

lived in those peaks. A

fool

hunter might kill one and make a fortune on its parts.

Suicide's faster, yeah?

Or he might follow those mountains north again and find a settlement that needed a noidghe, where no one knew or cared who Veiko Nyrikki was or what he had done. Make a life, after everything.

No. He would argue with her if she cast him off. He would not slink away like a feral dog. He would stay *here*, because that was where she was.

She stretched her arm out. Laid her right hand on his chest, fingers splayed over the drum-thump heartbeat, the fluttering panic.

"I know," Snow said. "Partners. That doesn't change, yeah?"

She took her hand away and then herself. Walked past him, around him, going back toward Illharek, to Ari, to the Laughing God.

He made no move to stop her this time. Left his hands at his side, stiff as his spine. Listened to the whisper of boots, felt the air move as she passed. Imagined her dissolving into shadow, pulling the dark around her like a cloak.

It was not until he smelled the stew beginning to scorch, and turned around to tend to it, that he saw she'd left Briel with him after all.

CHAPTER THIRTEEN

Dekklis rested in a wrinkle of rock, her feet braced against one side of the stone crease, her back against the other. She flexed the fingers of each hand in turn. Breathed around the ache in her ribs. Ignored the burn and throb in her shoulders. She could march for days and leagues on Illhari roads, run the forests like a twice-cursed deer—hell and damn, she'd gone overland from Cardik to Illharek, dodging Taliri the whole way, in just over a week.

This climb—which had taken maybe two candlemarks, up a much shorter distance—might just kill her.

Snowdenaelikk would've been better suited to it. Snow would've laughed herself inside out if she could see Szanys Dekklis, highborn First Scout of the Sixth, clinging like a spider to the fluted stone columns between the First and Second Tiers.

Spider, hell. Spiders didn't need handholds.

The top Tiers had been shaped pre-Purge, when blood feud and assassination had been both legal and common methods to bettering a House's political standing. You wanted to stop traffic between them, you cut the bridges or barricaded them. But a blood feud didn't end on account of lost bridges. An enterprising assassin—or a House trooper, because there hadn't been a standing legion until after the Purge, when the Senate decided it wanted soldiers loyal to Illharek first, House second—who wanted to get from one Tier to the other cut holds into the stone. Spikes in some places, age-smooth depressions in others.

She supposed she shouldn't be surprised that some of the spikes were unrusted steel. Highborn still died

of bad fish

out of time and turn, whatever the laws said. Snowdenaelikk had told her as much. But it was Sindri's endless stories of forbidden lovers climbing across the Tiers that detailed where those handholds actually were.

In Sindri's stories, the lovers died by violence. They never died falling down half a league of jagged black stone. Never spread themselves over ten paces of Suburban streets when they hit. And if soft highborn lovers didn't fall, hell if she would.

Although it might be kinder. She still had to get down again. Maybe she'd just walk down to the garrison, bold as a rat in a midden. Let the praefecta wonder about it. Dare Dani to confront her as she came through the front gate. At least the cargo she meant to

kidnap

liberate wouldn't take that trip with her. She intended to deliver him to a First Tier destination. She only had to get herself down.

Shee-oop ricocheted off the stone. A svartjagr's hunting cry, which sank into bones and nerves.

Not Briel, hell and damn. Svartjagr, wild ones, whole toadshit pack. They'd spotted her. Sliced past the crease where Dekklis was wedged, keening. She heard the rattle of claws on the stone. The leathery whisper of wings.

A pair of hot orange eyes peered at her from the edge of the crack. Bigger than Briel, oh sweet foremothers. A second pair of eyes joined the first. She heard the third one scrabbling on the stone, hissing.

Her palms began to sweat inside her leather gloves.

Snowdenaelikk said svartjagr didn't like risk to themselves. Dekklis hoped that she managed to look dangerous, jammed in between rocks like a blister-toad, with her blade pinned uselessly between hip and stone.

The first svartjagr poked its nose into the crevice. There was a length of neck beyond, Dekklis knew, that could bring that head, and all its teeth, much closer.

"Sssss!" She did her best Briel imitation. Imagined herself much larger, drawing on memories of that violet outline she'd seen in Cardik, when Tal'Shik tried to take make an avatar out of one of her godsworn.

The svartjagr squawked, very much like a chicken, and withdrew so fast its claws scored the rock. Shards clicked and tumbled. And then came a great snapping of wings, and another chorus of *shee-oops*. They were retreating.

She listened to the inner thump and twist of her heartbeat. Breathed herself calm. The svartjagr didn't come back. Probably waiting for her up above, right where she was going to come out.

Which would be a nice trick, since she wasn't entirely sure where that would be. She had Sindri's stories for guidance, and her own sense of Illhari geography. She knew she'd come out on the First Tier. But the Tiers weren't like midtown or the Suburba. The Tiers were a webwork of bridges and catwalks, staircases conjured out of the stone. Houses might jut up three levels, and out another three, like enterprising fungi growing out of the walls. They had grown organically, randomly, sections conjured when a family could afford the additions. And most of the current structures had taken their shapes pre-Purge, when a House needed to worry about its defensibility. First Tier was a small collection of armed, oddly shaped fortresses.

This high, Dek could even feel air moving through one of the vent passages. Some of those were natural. More still had been conjured, as Illharek grew, so that the city didn't choke on its own exhalations. Dekklis wondered where that extra stone had gone. Imagined asking Snow, imagined the half-blood's lazy smile. Probably something stupid-obvious to anyone who could conjure. Motherless mystery to everyone else, something awesome and inexplicable. That was how the Academy held its power. Mystery and theatre.

That was likely how the godsworn had risen to power, too. Dek wondered, not for the first time, why the Academy had ever allowed it. Why they hadn't sent assassins and Adepts the same way she'd come up the spikes to take care of the problem. Because godsworn *could* die. Ehkla had. Tsabrak, too. Godmagic was a little like armor, yes, but its real power was fear.

That wisdom, and a half piece of copper, would get her a mug in the tavern. A soldier didn't need to play philosopher, hell, leave that to the Belaerys and the Majas and everyone else with the leisure for thinking. A soldier needed to kill the enemy. That was all.

So what are you doing, Dek?

Climbing. Ignoring the burn in every muscle she had. Hoping that Sindri's stories were right, and this path *went* somewhere.

It did. The crevice didn't end so much as it passed through a fold between two houses. It was at that point a simple matter for Dek to haul herself clear of it and to stand in what might generously be called an alley. Scarcely a body's width, wall to wall. But there was evidence here of traffic: a rotten potato, a half-eaten, far-too-green fruit. Smooth patches in the rough stone where hands and shoulders might bump the walls. She guessed that bondies used the alley to pass between houses, to deliver messages, bring food up from the markets, passing unseen in their business of managing highborn lives.

Dekklis leaned against the wall. Peeled off her climbing gloves while she breathed the ache and exhaustion out of legs and chest. Checked, for the fifteenth time, that she had all her tools, knife and blade and the little ring of metal slivers that she'd hung under her shirt on a leather thong. Lockpicks that no highborn daughter had any business carrying, that no highborn daughter would know the first thing about using.

But highborn daughters didn't keep the company she did. Snow hadn't asked why Dek was suddenly so interested in learning to open locks. She'd only narrowed her eyes and nodded. They'd had three marks of lessons before Snow pronounced her tolerable; and then Snow had given her a set of picks and a knowing, crooked smirk.

In case you need to practice on your own, yeah?

Dekklis eased out of the little wedged alley. The passages—you couldn't say streets, not here—were empty. Too quiet after the garrison's constant clatter. A House had dozens of servants, and a harem of consorts, and children who wouldn't get out during the day; and everyone who wasn't on the Senate plaza was inside, working. Doing whatever it was bondies and servants did. But you'd never know it, from the quiet. Thick walls smeared any interior house sounds to vague thumps and whispers.

Dek trailed her fingers along the stone. Looked around for some identifying feature in the rock. Yes, there: a glyph that looked burned into the rock, a dark gouge in the slash and double twist of House Qvist'a. Dek let a small breath out. Sindri's information was good. One of Stratka's two servant doors was a sharp left past the next junction, at the top of the alley. From there, it was a short walk across the bridge connecting Stratka, Qvist'a, and Tjol to House K'Hess.

Dekklis took her time. Eased from shadow to shadow. Checked windows and balconies, imagining where an arrow might land, or a spilled pot of oil. She saw places where guards could have been. No one standing there now. Dust and cobwebs. A republic at peace with itself.

There was no one at Stratka's back door, either. It was an old thing, massive and wooden, braced and reinforced with black steel. There were black streaks on the wood, as if the door had caught fire and reconsidered. Conjuror's work, bet on that, to prevent the burning. A chill crawled up her neck. Spread over her scalp and tingled. There might still be wards. Her mind spun out images: a fireball bursting out of the lock, spiders flooding out of the shadows, the dark itself eating her whole. Blink, and it was just a door again. Old as Illharek, slumped weary on its hinges.

If there's conjuring on the lock, if you even think it, then use this wire, yeah? It's not a pick, exactly.

Dek flexed her fingers and reached for the pouch at her belt. Pulled out a pair of gloves, fine and tight, and worked her hands into them. Too fine for climbing, almost like skin, and still she felt clumsy in them. She selected the smallest metal sliver on the ring of picks, the one that looked like plain wire. Uncoiled and slid it into the lock.

And then what?

Cold, burning through the gloves. The smell that came just before lightning. The lock shuddered like a dying thing. Something dark leaked out the keyhole. Ran down like oil, pooled on the stone.

You'll know if the ward's gone, yeah? One way or the other.

What if they're better than you, Snow?

That half-cocked grin. *You won't have time to notice.*

Her heart hurt, it was beating so hard. But the picks were steady in her hand. She checked the lock the way Snow had taught her. Selected one finger of metal and guided it toward the hole. Recalled her lessons and moved the metal, feeling her way around the lock's guts. There, just so, and the lock clicked open.

She let her breath out. Took a new lungful. Eased her weight down on the door's latch.

What if it's barred on the back side? What then?

Then you find another way in, Szanys. There'll be windows.

The door swung inward. Swish, whisper, the liquid slide of oil and good care. Good balance, too; it hung where she stopped it, unmoving, while she eeled through the gap. She closed it again just as quietly.

There *was* a bar on the inside, raised and hooked on the wall. So that meant either someone was out and expected back, or the bondies in Stratka were careless. Or maybe one of Sindri's love affairs was going on right now, right here, and the bar had been left up to let someone in.

Dekklis was most of the way down the hallway, just coming to the stairs Sindri'd said were there, when she remembered the rest of Snow's advice.

One question to ask about wards, Szanys, is who put them there. The second one to ask is why.

***

There was someone waiting in the shadows by the tunnel gate.

Snow knew it, *felt* it. You didn't run with Tsabrak for as long as she had without getting a sense for when shadows were occupied. She stopped on the dark fringes of the trail. Pulled the shadows more tightly around her and cursed the moon. Fuck and damn, it must be Ari, some of the baby godsworn. They might've followed her this far. She could have led them to Veiko.

She put her hand on the seax hilt, intending to leave a body in the dark after all.

The shadows moved. Took on familiar dimensions as they drifted closer. That was Tsabrak's face, Tsabrak's silhouette—Tsabrak as she'd last seen him, holding her own seax in his fist. Her heart twisted.

Not me, Snow. You have a visitor.

Then the ghost shattered, like a mirror struck from behind. Another familiar outline appeared, dusted in moonlight, coming out of the dark of his own accord.

Fuck and *damn.*

"Istel," she hissed. "Did Dek send you?"

"Yeah." He sounded faintly embarrassed. "I think she wants me out of the way."

"Why? Where is she?"

"She's got her own problems. Says they're watching her. Says *she* can't get out unwatched, but I can." Istel laughed, a near-soundless clicking in his throat. "Says to tell you, fuck you for being right."

That he could come and go, and Dek couldn't. That no one would bother with a common man. Snow bared her teeth in the dark. "Write it down, Istel."

"Can't write," he said cheerfully. "Can read a little, though."

Her laugh died. Anger filled in behind it, old and comfortable. Tsabrak would've recognized this smile.

Veiko couldn't read, either, but Veiko wasn't Illhari. Veiko thought a stylus was for spearing meat from a pot. Istel knew better, but Istel had had no opportunity to learn what it *was* for. And Dek hadn't bothered to teach him in all their years in the Sixth.

Pity Istel and Tsabrak hadn't met under better circumstances. Istel might've joined the God's side, or at least fallen in with Tsabrak. But instead it was Istel who'd put a legion blade through Tsabrak's back.

The darkness convulsed, in the corner of her vision. Tsabrak whispered, *The word you want is* killed. *He* killed *me, Snow. Say that.*

Trying to save me, yeah? Say that.

A sudden burst of mirth from the nearest barge on the Tano made her look. Men's voices, raised in drunken Alviri. The last time she'd heard so much volume in that language, there'd been riot.

Istel's flinch said he shared the same memory. For a moment she saw Cardik dying in his eyes, pinprick dots of reflected lantern light. Saw the God in the next breath, those dots turned to licking flames.

And then it was just Istel again. "Noisy," he muttered. "The hell they so happy about?"

"They're out here. They're not us. They've got beer and we don't. Take your pick." Snow watched the barge glide on the Tano's current. Shook herself into motion. One foot in front of the other, stay in the shadows. Istel fell into step beside her, faint whisper of leather and cloth. No armor, of course there wouldn't be. Istel was playing civilian. Istel had done a damn good job of it, too.

Snow uncurled her fingers and wished up a witchfire. Tiny blue glow in her palm, no tingle of backlash, even though the cave was still a few paces away. She raised her hand. And yes, there, closer than she'd thought, the open gate, propped and rusting on its hinges. That was proof enough of Illhari arrogance. No need to guard this entrance, no need to lock it. Taliri wouldn't take this route into the caves. Taliri wouldn't invade Below at all, never had, because they hated the dark and the stone overhead. Even the Alviri, at the height of the war, had never come farther into Illharek than the Riverwalk.

Small wonder the Senate wasn't catching Dek's urgency.

Snow stepped through the gate. "So who's watching Dekklis?"

Istel came through behind her. "Legion. Probably on Senate orders. She doesn't think it's her praefecta friend. She caught someone following her, up in the Tiers."

A chirurgeon knew very well that a heart didn't turn into stone and ice. She put one hand on her chest anyway, to check that it still beat. "When?"

"Couple days ago. She was coming back from her mother's house."

"What about before that?"

"All her meetings with you? She says she doesn't think so. Says you're not in chains yet, that's a good sign they don't know about you. Or Veiko."

That sounded like Dek. And she was probably right, too, damn her anyway.

Snow willed the witchfire larger, held it high. The blue light chased

Tsabrak

the shadows into the crevices between rocks. Spider lines of darkness, too small for a ghost, too small for anyone to weave into cover.

Bare stone gleamed back at her. Snow let her breath out. "But she's worried enough to send you."

"That's her story. Mostly true, yeah? But really, she wants me out of the garrison. Wants me somewhere else. She thinks I don't know she's up to something." Istel shrugged. "She's toadshit for lying."

"She is." Snow waited the requisite few beats, then asked, pretend afterthought, "Do you know what she's doing?"

"No." Bland-faced neutrality, which Istel only used when he was unhappy.

"I don't know, either," she told him. "She asked me to teach her to pick locks, last time we met."

Istel grunted. "Same day she asked me to fight with Nezari."

"Wait, what? Dek wanted you to fight who?"

Feel his glance splash off the side of her face. "Toadfucking optio."

"House?"

"Minor. S'Haati, I think."

"You win?"

"I think so."

"Then you're lucky they didn't stripe your back and throw you in a cell."

He made a spitting sound, dry air for effect. "Rurik would've. Me *and* Nezari. That lot up there—rabbits, Snow. Fucking soft, all of them. The praefecta just let it go."

Maybe it was just as well Tsabrak had never met Istel. Tsabrak had rejoiced in Illharek's soft troops. Made business that much simpler. But Cardik's troops weren't rabbits. And Rurik's Sixth didn't break discipline, no matter how provoked.

"And *Dek* told you to do it."

Istel grunted. "Not like I minded. Nezari needed a beating."

"And then she sent you to find me."

"I've *been* following you. This is just the first time you caught me doing it. I wouldn't be coming after you now, except it looked like you were going out to Veiko and I wanted to see where that was. You haven't gone out in a long time." He pointed his chin at her pack. "Didn't reckon I'd meet you on the way back in."

"Huh. Two of us."

Istel's eyes caught the light like a cat's. "Trouble?" And then, before she could answer, "Sorry. Shouldn't've asked."

Snow grimaced. "My partner's fucking stubborn. Nothing new."

"Ah," and wisely, nothing else.

The ambient air was growing cooler. Heavier. They were getting close to the main cavern. The Tano babbled to itself, water and stone. From where Snow walked, it looked black, like the river on the other side of the ghost roads. She'd walked beside that one, too, with a different Dvergir man. Difference was, she and K'Hess Kenjak had both been dead at the time.

And Veiko wanted her to go *back* to that. Fuck and damn. Better to take her chances with the God, yeah. With Ari. With the ghost she could just see, there, in the shadows. But not with Istel.

"Istel," she murmured. "Do me a favor. I know Dek said watch me, but I'm asking: you turn around, go find Veiko. Watch *him*. He'll be glad of the company."

Istel's eyes rolled toward her, gleam and flash in the dim. "You're not going back to your flat." Not asking.

"No."

He hesitated. Then, in a rush, "Where, then?" And unspoken *can I go with you?*

"Got to see some godsworn. *My* people," she said, which tasted like dust. "You're in trouble if they see you."

"And you? Are *you* in trouble?"

She put her hand on Istel's arm. Flex and twitch of muscle that said he wasn't expecting touch. Pressure as he leaned into her that said he didn't mind it. No more or less than she'd suspected. Ask this man to throw himself into the Tano for her, he just might.

Instead: "Favor, Istel. For me. Please. Go to Veiko. Keep him safe."

Istel frowned. Then he turned and went back the way they'd come, toward the open night sky. She tucked shadows in around him like blankets. He faded invisible like one of Veiko's fucking ghosts.

And left one ghost behind, all hers, all unwelcome. Ghost-Tsabrak had his arms crossed, shoulders back: waiting beside her as the members of what had been his Illharek cartel picked their way up the Tano path. Their shadows sliced through him.

Snow folded her own arms and waited with him.

CHAPTER FOURTEEN

Highborn houses followed a general pattern, however they'd been conjured or built. There was a bondie wing, separate from the main house, with its own entrance. A kitchen, close to that wing. There would be stairs nearby, or a hallway, that led into a formal area that might be for dining or entertaining. Off *that* there would be another, separate entrance, for people who didn't wear collars, so that guests and owners need not see the comings and goings of servants. Offices, a library, and a larger room that had been a house-shrine to Tal'Shik before the Purge, which most families had turned into a room for entertaining guests. Sometimes it held a fountain that had been conjured into the walls, sometimes couches. Szanys Elia had turned hers into a garden, moss-covered walls and a mosaic-lined pond studded with darklilies.

Beyond those public rooms were the family quarters, which no one outside the House ever saw, divided male and female. In Stratka's house, those quarters sat at the top of twisting stairs, a labyrinth of hallways that would have been easy to defend against invaders. The stair got brighter at the top, if not wider, the walls studded with candles that choked the place with a sweet waxy smell. Not cheap tallow, not oil, not for Stratka. That was wealth burning in the sconces, for the highborn.

House Szanys had invaded Stratka once, pre-Purge, and been stopped here, on the last landing.

Dek had gone through every Szanys account of the battle fought here, had sketched out a rough interior map from the descriptions. She'd had Sindri, too, for help—all too happy to describe this place, time and again. He had visited often as a child, being of an age with one of Stratka's sons. That was fortunate, because the battle accounts hadn't included any mention of the servants' tunnels, or the clever panels in the walls, the latches concealed among carvings. Here: a man's open mouth. There: a dragon's third claw. And *here*, just where Sindri had promised: a Stratka matron's ruby eye, winking out of a scene of battle and conquest. Twisted bodies around her, dark granite women in chips of colored glass. House uniforms, not legion. That was K'Hess blue, and Szanys orange. The Stratka matron, polished out of obsidian, stood above all of them, bare armed and bareheaded, with her palms spread. Amethyst streaked up and out of her fingers, to be lost in an onyx sky.

It was an old piece. Beautiful. And it should have been pried out of the wall, chip by chip, its glass melted, its stones cast into the lake. That had been the Senate edict after the Purge: that all Houses must destroy any reminders of godsworn. Maybe Stratka had argued that Stratka Gael had been a conjuror, that the amethyst was meant to be witchfire, that the artist had had a shortage of appropriate lapis to make the right color. But no one who'd seen godsworn fire could mistake it. The flames in that Cardik alley, where Ehkla had died, had been just that shade of violet.

It gave Dek small satisfaction to jab her fingertip into that godsworn's eye. The door's mechanism clicked deep in the wall. The panel slid back on silent hinges, shattering the image along well-concealed lines. Dek put her face close to the mosaic. Scrubbed a nail along the grout, looking for the seam. Couldn't feel it. You could admire that kind of craftwork. And you could still wonder how Stratka had got away with this thing in plain view for two hundred odd years. Grant that it ran up the staircase that led to the family wing, that no stranger would see it—but the Purge hadn't got rid of politics, had it, and rival sons might spy for their mothers.

Confining those sons to the men's harem might solve that, but according to all Dek's sources, the confinement was a recent development, since the disappearances. So either Stratka truly didn't care what anyone said, or Stratka was stupider than anyone reckoned, or everyone really thought that figure was a conjuror.

Or—hell and damn. Dekklis peered at her fingertips, at the color she'd gathered under her nails. Someone might've painted over the whole thing, for all those years, to hide it. And then someone—probably many, collared and fair-skinned someones—had scraped all that paint away again, chip by chip, stone by stone, very recently, and left only enough that a nosy interloper scratching at the grout might've noticed.

Stratka had reclaimed its heritage. Godsworn heritage.

Dekklis slipped behind the panel. Felt the tile shift under her foot, faintest sag, and the wall sighed back into place. It was solid black back here. A bondie would've come armed with a candle. Snow would've had her witchfire. Dek had her hands, spread flat on the wall. Had Sindri's—

Count seventeen steps, then left.

—directions to guide her. They were shallow steps, worn and old. It would be easy to trip, fall and break a bone back here, or her neck. Let her mother explain *that* to Stratka. So she took small steps, precise, and ignored the pressing dark. It was her imagination that the walls were a stone throat swallowing her whole.

Seven, eight.

She wondered if her own house was so full of passages. Wondered how many of Szanys's bondies came and went like this, and how many Sindris might be out there who knew the ways in and out. Something to investigate later. She supposed Sindri wouldn't be so forthcoming then.

Eleven, twelve.

If she got out of this—no, *when*—she'd ask Snow to teach her to call witchfire. Or that thing she did with the shadows. Some way to drive back the darkness.

Breathe, Dek.

At least she met no one coming or going. That, too, had been part of her planning. The consul would be in the Senate. Her daughters, too. Which meant a good chunk of the household staff would be there, in attendance, and the ones left behind would have no reason to go running up and down a dark passage in the family wing.

She had just congratulated herself on her foresight when she felt a puff of cool air on her face. Then she heard a rasp, like leather on stone. She stopped. Flattened against the wall. Saw the soft yellow glow ahead that meant candle, growing larger as the carrier came down the steps. Dekklis crouched and worked her knife out of its sheath. She laid the blade back against her arm, edge curving out.

A foot on the stairs. A leg. Dekklis moved. Took an eyeblink to mark the face: Alvir, female. A gilded collar below the face, which meant she had value to the House.

The bondie was unarmed, unprepared, utterly surprised. And dead, very suddenly.

Her corpse would be impossible to miss in this narrow passage. Better hope no one used this stair, then, in the next few candlemarks.

Dek scooped up the naked candle, which had rolled on the step and was somehow still burning. Wouldn't be if it got to the blood. She steadied the flame. Wiped her knife on the bondie's robe and sheathed it again, one-handed. Looked at the woman. She was on the young side of middle age. Pretty enough. Probably taking the back passages because she was visiting places she shouldn't.

It happened. A dozen songs Dek could name about one tryst or another. Most of the songs ended badly—the bondie whipped and sold, the Dvergir man dying of heartbreak. The reality was always less romantic. Before the Purge, the bondies died, but the men did, too, depending on their House connections. But in this enlightened age

that what we call it, now, Dek?

a man found bedding women below his station would be sent back to his mother and sisters. And what *they* might do, well. There were brothels in the Suburba who would buy a highborn contract, but more likely that man would end up in the legion, indentured first, and then as a free soldier. There were—had been—more than a few of those in the Sixth. The northern borders were more forgiving than Illharek.

Fact was, Stratka would've killed this bondie for being where she shouldn't. Fact was, they'd've done it slower than Dekklis had, and more publicly.

That make you feel better?

It didn't. But Dek wasn't a squeamish woman. Wasn't sentimental. She didn't like killing unarmed civilians, but that hadn't stopped her in Cardik, or here, or ever. She banished the knot in her gut. Stepped over the body and kept climbing.

Fifteen, sixteen.

Much easier with a candle.

She came to a small landing, where the passage branched right and left. Dekklis took Sindri's directions. The left branch ended in another panel, where stone gave way conspicuously to plaster and wood. Dek set the candle into a niche on the wall. Blocked the flame with her hand and tried the latch.

The door rolled out and sideways. Oiled hinges, hardly a whisper. A well-used door, this. Well maintained. Well hidden, too, if Sindri's stories were right, which they had been so far. Dekklis stepped into the back of a very large wardrobe. The air was dusty and thick with wool, linen, the lingering stale waft of bodies clinging to fabric. The floor felt like wood, too, not stone. She rubbed her toe across it. Not quite smooth, not quite even. Parquet tiles. Not cheap. Not too slick, either, if she had to move fast.

She paused to let her eyes adjust. There was light bleeding in, yellow and warm, that told her the wardrobe doors were already open, that said Stratka didn't mind spending money here, either, for perfume and wax candles. She wormed between the clothing. Pulled a pair of city trousers off a rack, and a plain shirt, and hoped they would fit K'Hess Soren. Got to the door and cocked her head. This room was empty. But she could hear not-too-distant voices, low enough to be male. Heard a higher one, too, fluting over the others. Please, that it was a boy or another bondie, and not one of Stratka's daughters.

She moved into the room. There were carpets on the parquet floor, and couches meant for sitting, not sleeping. A mirror stood in the corner nearest the door. Dek eyed her own reflection, growing larger the nearer she came to it. She was a small woman, for a Dvergir, almost man-sized. Endless source of harassment, in her pre-legion youth. Endless mockery in the Sixth, too, when people thought she wouldn't hear it. Calling her Istel sometimes, pretending they looked alike.

Today there was some truth to that. The bulky northern clothing blurred her near shapeless. She reached up under the sweater. Took out the scarf she'd stashed there and wound it around her head. Told herself that was a man's face staring back and not Szanys's youngest daughter.

Except men didn't stare, did they? Not in Illharek. Men kept their heads down and their eyes on the floor.

Laughter stabbed down the corridor. Several voices, all male, rose out of it, battling for volume. One shouted the others down finally.

"—hear the rest or not?"

Another swell of sound. Dek tucked the ends of the scarf into its own folds and settled it around jaw and cheek. Be lucky if she didn't suffocate in the wool, too *hot* in these motherless chambers—

A flicker of light in the corner of the mirror warned her. There was someone in the hallway. Dekklis flattened against the wall. Dropped her hand to her knife. Waited as the shape grew in the glass until the man stepped into the room. Household and highborn, from the open-necked shirt, the loose breeches, the unbound hair. He stopped in front of the mirror. Leaned forward, examining something up near one eye. His shoulders blocked most of his face. She got a smeared glimpse of his House sigil, distorted by glass and angle. It wasn't K'Hess. Wasn't Stratka, either. One of the rounder sigils, maybe Dasskli or K'Haar.

She unfolded. Two steps to cross the distance, to get one arm across his shoulders and rest the dagger's tip near his throat. It was a stupid hold against anyone with training, or anyone larger than she was. This poor toadshit was neither.

His eyes met hers in the mirror. Wide, terrified—foremothers spare her, had he just pissed himself? He had. Rot him. Well. Boots would dry. If she stepped back now, she'd risk her balance and he might discover courage. She eyed his sigil. Dasskli. She dredged memory, couldn't summon up the House politics or whether one dead son might matter to that woman's vote.

"Please," he whispered.

"K'Hess Soren," she murmured, rough and low as she could manage. "Where is he?"

He shivered against her. "Down there. Down the hall. With the others."

"Call him."

"What?"

"*Call him.* Get him down here, yeah?" She poked red out of his neck, just a drop. The knife was sharp, the flesh was soft. She watched him watching the blood run down his reflection's neck, too shocked to even squeak.

"Call K'Hess," she repeated. "Not for help. Don't you raise the alarm. You savvy me?"

Another shiver, like a dog shaking water. He nodded. And yes, that *was* piss, another round, but not only. Dekklis was glad of the scarf for a layer between her and the stink.

The man—boy, really, he might be all of Sindri's age—turned his head. Opened his mouth. His ribs stretched against her. Then an indrawn breath and a wobbly "Soren!" dragged out singsong and treble.

Dekklis winced. Only her eyes narrowed, over the scarf. There was sweat on the man's face. Bright beads against skin gone waxy and damn near grey. She'd seen happier corpses.

The voice down the hall stopped in its storytelling. Lifted and flung back, "What do you want, Birkir? We're busy."

"I need Soren." Birkir's voice cracked. Quick swallow, eyes wide in the glass. "I need an opinion."

"What, *now?*" The storyteller's voice moved. Getting louder, *hell,* probably standing up and coming into the hallway. Dekklis jabbed Birkir under the chin. Drew him backward, away from the door, out of the mirror's angle.

"What is so important, Birkir?" Definitely closer.

"Let it go," came another voice. This one was softer. Lower. Eerily familiar. An echo of Rurik's bellow in the resonance and chiseled consonants. "I'm coming, Birkir. Keep your pants up."

Dekklis rolled her forearm against Birkir's throat. Bent her elbow and applied pressure. Didn't take long, no, Birkir's eyes bugging and mouth flapping before he went limp. She swung him sideways. Dropped him onto carpets and pillows. Turned back as K'Hess Soren stepped into the doorway.

"Birkir, where—"

He stopped, openmouthed, as Dekklis stepped over Birkir's unconscious body.

There was no question of identity, not at all. Soren was taller than Rurik, and slimmer, more like Kenjak had been. But all three had the same blade of a nose, the same too-large eyes that Rurik was forever narrowing into slits. Soren's were round and wide, like Kenjak's had been when she'd last seen him.

With a pole shoved through him crotch to gullet.

She blinked the memory aside. Soren was alive, and she meant him to stay that way. She tugged the scarf aside. Bared her face and held up her hand.

Sharply, softly: "Quiet. Birkir's not dead. Won't be unless you shout. You savvy?"

Be thankful for trained passivity. Be thankful K'Hess Soren had at least a glimmer of his other brother's wits. He did not, she noted, piss himself, or shit, or begin shaking. He only nodded. She thrust the trousers at him. "Put these on, yeah? Can't have you in silks in the street. Then you come with me. Quickly. For your life and safety, K'Hess Soren."

He stared down at the trousers. "I—"

"Soren! Birkir!" Oh foremothers, coming closer. Footsteps now to go with the voice. "What—"

"Toad's *tits*," Soren snapped, and now he sounded exactly like Rurik. "Birkir needs my opinion, not yours. Wait, can't you? Entertain everyone else."

A moment's quiet. Then a subdued and sullen "Fine" and a retreat of footfalls.

Dek let the air out of her lungs. Met Soren's eyes. He licked his lips. Shaped *who* at her as he unlaced the house silks and stepped out of them.

Headshake. "Quick." And as he pulled the other breeches over his hips: "Through the door in the back of the wardrobe. *Move*, K'Hess."

"What do you want?" Still quiet, this one, not prone to hysterics. His hands were open. Spread. Dekklis reckoned he might have reach on her. Reckoned he wouldn't know that. This wasn't a fighting man. But he had a light in his eyes she didn't like, which looked a little like panic and desperation.

The hell you expect, Szanys?

"You're not safe here," she told him. "I came to get you. Now turn around—"

He pushed a hand at her, more warding than attack, and took a step backward. "Who are you?"

She resigned herself to delay and damnation. "First Scout Szanys Dekklis. Second Legion, Sixth Cohort. I serve under Rurik."

"Szanys?" Soren blinked. Questions piled up behind his eyes, so many she'd need a whole candle of marks to answer them. *Snow would approve of this one,* she thought, and, *I don't have time for this toadshit.*

If he was a bit like Rurik, he wouldn't respond well to force. Reason, then. "Listen to me. Taliri have Cardik surrounded right now. I came to get help, but the consul won't listen to my mother. *Your* mother could help, and she won't say anything. You savvy why not?"

A second blink. Comprehension pushed the questions aside. Drew his face into new planes and angles. Not a stupid man, no. But he was civilian enough to flinch when she poked the knife at him.

"We have to go." Another poke. "Turn around. Out the passage."

This time he did what she told him. Turned his back and ducked into the forest of cloaks and tunics. She followed him, closer than she liked. The man had elbows. It wouldn't take much to bring one around. Her knife could get tangled in cloaks and tunics and turn useless. It could turn weapon in Soren's hands if he got it.

He isn't Istel. He isn't Veiko. He won't do that.

But she didn't let her breath out until the latch clicked and they were back in the servants' passage. She pulled the secret door shut behind her. Candle glow spilled across the shadows on the floor. She heard Soren breathing, shallow bites of near panic that turned loud in the stone passage.

She talked to him like a green recruit, simple and steady. "Down. Take the candle. Stairs are dark."

He went, the candle clenched in both fists. He didn't seem to notice the wax collecting on his skin.

"You can put the knife away, Domina."

Foremothers, you could hear the titled inflection. Dekklis tried to imagine Rurik sounding this frightened, or this polite, and couldn't manage it. Then she wondered at the ache in her chest when she tried.

"First Scout," she said. "No titles. I've got a mother and three sisters before me."

"Accidents happen." Now he did look at her. "Like my brother. Ivar."

The missing one. "I heard about that."

"Not just Ivar." His mouth creased. "My senior-sister died last winter."

That left one K'Hess daughter, barely past her majority, badly inexperienced. No wonder K'Hess wouldn't take a step out her doors. She was afraid *she'd* die.

"How'd it happen?" Regret the moment she asked it. This man wouldn't know. He'd've been living here when it happened. He'd've got whatever truth Stratka shared with him. But there must've been gossip, and no one had bothered to tell her. Not her mother. Not her sister.

Soren's face said no one had told him, either. "It was sudden. No illness."

Never know when you need someone's death to look like bad fish, yeah? Assassination, hell and damn. Had to be.

"Sorry. I didn't know." It sounded stupid. Small.

Soren nodded, a curiously gracious gesture. "How are my other brothers?" he said calmly as he navigated the shallow steps.

"Kenjak's dead. I don't know about Rurik." And more gently: "Keep moving. Your impatient friend up there comes looking, he'll find Birkir. And he'll reckon where we've gone. —And be careful, yeah? There's a body."

"Ah." Soren stepped over the corpse. Minced past the blood on the steps. "How?"

"Bondie surprised me. I had to—"

"I mean Kenjak. How did he die?"

She weighed the answer, brutal truth against the civilian version. "Taliri," she said finally. "Godsworn Taliri. They put him on a pole."

Soren said nothing for long enough Dekklis wondered if he'd even heard her. And then: "Tal'Shik," so quietly she wasn't sure she'd heard him.

"What?"

He turned to face her and did what Illhari men simply didn't: made unblinking eyelock. "Tal'Shik. The poles. Sacrifice. That's what her god-sworn did before the Purge, to us," with the certainty of a man who remembers his histories. "What they're doing to us now."

Soren was still staring at her. Dangerous light in his eyes that made her remember Rurik again, that made her wish Kenjak had managed to get older. That made her wonder what kind of soldier Soren might make, and wish she could see that, too.

"You said," said Soren, "my mother wasn't speaking out in the Senate. You think you know why. But there's more to that story, Szanys Dekklis, and I can tell you."

* * *

Veiko was not happy when Istel came out of the trees, in almost the same place Snow had disappeared not so long before. He had some warning: Logi's head came up, and he sniffed. Then *oofed* softly and went back to his rabbit bones. So Veiko thought it was Snow coming back, until Istel walked out of the woods.

From Briel, nothing at all. Some guardian.

"Chrrip," Briel scolded, which was Briel's way of saying Istel didn't warrant a warning. He was no stranger. She sent a cascade of images, Istel at their fireside, Istel in the forest, Istel in conversation with Snow and Dek and Veiko. Unusually vivid for Briel, and very deliberate: a svartjagr's version of slow speech and clear enunciation.

See here, Veiko. This is our friend.

As if he could not see that with both of the eyes in his head.

But what he could not see was, "Why are you here?" He flushed in the next heartbeat: there were rules about hospitality, and he had just broken several.

Istel's mouth twitched. "And Snow said you'd be glad of the company." But he did not break stride. Came and squatted beside the fire and let Logi come and greet him.

"*Snow* sent you," Veiko said dubiously, because Istel had no pack with him. No preparations. Poor planning for a man like Istel.

"*Sent* might be too strong a word. I met her just outside the gate. Reckoned she was coming out to you, thought I'd make sure. Didn't reckon to meet her coming back so soon."

A not-quite-question. Veiko folded his arms. "That was her choice."

"She says you're a stubborn toadshit."

"Did she say that I learned it from her?"

Istel chuckled. "You should know better than to argue with a Dvergir woman by now, Veiko. Whatever the topic."

"You do not follow that advice with Dekklis."

"You're smarter than I am." Istel straightened. Came around the fire and made a mirror of Veiko: folded arms, chin up. "And because you're so smart, I reckon you might know what to do about this. There were people in the tunnel, coming from Illharek. Snow said it was godsworn. Seemed to recognize them. That's when she told me to go."

"The God's people," softly, because his lungs felt too small. "She thought they were dead."

"Well, they weren't that."

"Why did you leave her there?" He knew how foolish that sounded as soon as he'd said it. Saw confirmation in Istel's crooked grin.

"Because she told me to go. She isn't *my* partner. You think she'd've let me keep my hands if I'd grabbed her arm and insisted I go with her?"

Veiko recalled the look she'd given him when he'd tried that. "You could have followed her."

"Sure. Or I could do what she asked, which was come out here and find you."

"I am in no danger."

"Don't know that she is, either. She said they were her people." Istel's smile faded. "Of course, it was her people in Cardik who tried to kill her."

"It was the God, wearing Tsabrak's skin, back in Cardik. And he succeeded."

Dekklis would've flinched hearing that. Istel only gazed thoughtfully back toward the tunnel. "Way I reckon, Veiko, she told me to come find you. I have. Nothing says we can't *both* go looking for her right now."

And oh, it was tempting, to snatch up axe and pack and abandon fire and campsite and go after her. But:

"She is a conjuror, and this is Illharek. She can." He strained the words through his teeth. "She can care for herself."

Istel looked at him as if he'd grown another head. "Not what I thought you'd say."

"Briel is calm. She would not be were Snow in danger."

"So what, we stay here and . . . wait? Watch Briel?"

"Waiting and watching is what scouts do," Veiko said. "I, however, am noidghe. I will help her another way."

CHAPTER FIFTEEN

Tsabrak had set himself up in the Suburba the moment he'd cleared territory: a couple alleys and streets by the docks, that was all, but they were his. He'd been young then, not much older than Veiko was now. But he'd never abandoned the Tomb and the God's sanctuary, scraped out of living rock, stuffed so far off the road that no one could find it by chance. There was no sneaking and following in passages this narrow. Two abreast, and that was tight. Shoulder to shoulder, she and Ari. She was acutely aware of Hraf behind her, and the rest of them. Soft footsteps, softer muttering. Cheap oil lamps burned at long intervals, smearing smoke on the walls, guttering and flickering and casting long shadows.

Ari took a final turn into a cave that was at least partly natural. Smooth on one side, egg shaped, with long drips of upthrust stone, and the whisper-trickle of unseen water. The air was fresher here, fingers of cool on her cheek. A domed main room with half rooms spoking off it, two layers stacked. It might've been barracks once. The architecture had that utilitarian look about it. There was a battered table in the center, lined with benches that looked as if they'd been dragged all the way from the Suburba. Probably had.

When Tsabrak had gone north ten years ago, he had left almost thirty godsworn and allies in the Suburba. Left Stig in charge, but Stig had still answered to Tsabrak. Took his orders, clear from Cardik. They'd been running rasi mostly, with the odd crate of spice or bolt of silk or some Illhari luxury hard to find on the frontier.

There was maybe a third of that cartel left now, by Snow's count, and most of them were new faces. Young, male, scared mixed with angry. Sullen and suspicious when they saw who Ari had brought back with him.

She heard "half-blood" and "woman" and less flattering terms whispered among them. Either they didn't know who she was or they were angry enough not to care.

Ari pretended not to hear the muttering. "Need to talk to Snowdenaelikk," he said to the men at the table. They got up, wordless. Skulked to the margins of the room, where the rest of their brethren collected.

Ari jerked his chin at the table. "Sit, yeah?"

Yeah, sit, in the middle of the fucking room, angry godsworn on all sides. Fuck and damn. Reminded her of that meeting with Rata, ten days and forever ago. She missed Veiko suddenly, sharply, like a knife shoved up under her ribs. Which was all too likely in here. She should walk the fuck out, yeah, drag up some shadows and just *leave*.

And she wouldn't, because Veiko couldn't get her the God. Ari, now. Maybe he could.

There was a firedog in one corner, leaking a greasy smoke that clung to hair and skin and burned the inside of her throat. Mad patterns danced on the walls. Tsabrak lurked in those shapes, forming and reforming: his face, his profile, his hipshot silhouette.

You are my right hand, Snow. Remember that.

You're dead, yeah? But she drew herself straight, every fingerlength of her half-blood, unnatural height. Swept a slow glance around the room, stopping on every face, on every pair of eyes. Measuring attitudes, marking features. Letting everyone see the rings and the topknot.

Then she sat slowly and splayed both hands on the table. "Is this everyone?"

Ari dropped hard onto the bench across from her. "Yeah."

"This a good idea? Everyone in one place?"

"We tried scattering. They picked us off. This was the only place we reckoned they wouldn't come."

"They. *Who*, they? Not highborn. They wouldn't get through the toadfucking Suburba."

"No. Not highborn. Rata's people. All of a sudden, she wants more territory. All of a sudden, we start dying. Godsworn first, and then the regulars."

"That's good strategy."

"Feh. Rata had help. Shouldn't have been that easy. She took Stig first, and he was the best."

"Hate to tell you this, Ari, but godsworn die like everyone else. Plain steel through the gut will do it."

Ari grunted. "That how Tsabrak died?"

Through my back, not my guts. Tell him that.

"Yeah. Took a trooper's blade in the riots."

"Huh. Then he went better than Stig. We found him in the Tano. Fish had been at him, but we could see what they'd done." Ari made a noise in his throat. "They cut him open, nape to hips, from the back. Cracked his ribs. Took his fucking guts out, yeah? Both lungs. His heart. They must've peeled him open like a fucking snail."

Snow trusted that the murky firelight would hide her flinch. Fuck and damn: remember a windowless room in Cardik's Warren. Remember sigils cut into the plaster, blood running up the walls. Remember the whole room turning a throbbing violet, and the god-magic pushing against her skin. Ehkla between her knees, and Ehkla's breathless *Let me tell you how it's done, half-blood. First you must cut me along the spine. Then crack the ribs and spread them . . .*

"It's one of Tal'Shik's ritual killings," Snow said. Coolly, yeah, ice wouldn't melt on her tongue. "Spread the ribs out, put the lungs on them. It's supposed to be wings. Like a dragon."

"The fuck you know that?"

She tapped the rings in the curve of her ear. "Learn a lot more in the Academy than conjuring, yeah?"

"Fuck." Ari sat back. His hands flexed and stretched. The God's sigil gleamed like ink on the black of his palm. And then, almost soundless, "What kind of ritual?"

"Archives say it's the way to sacrifice godsworn. Usually, it's them sacrificing their own to make an avatar. I don't know why they'd bother with rival godsworn. Maybe to make a statement. Maybe they don't know what they're doing." *Maybe Ehkla didn't.* "Everyone else who's died, they go like that?"

"No," Ari said bleakly. "They died on poles. We found a whole *garden* of them in the tunnels up past the Abattoir."

"That happened up north, too."

"But not the dragon-wing shit."

She shrugged. "Don't see any avatars around, do you?"

"Not yet." The bare gleam of teeth, snarl more than smile. "This makes more sense if Rata's got Tal'Shik's godsworn working with her. *Taliri*, you think?"

"You see her keeping company with any toadbellies? I didn't. I think she's got highborn help." Snow paused, let that soak into the room. Utter silence for a handful of heartbeats.

"Godsworn *highborn*?" Ari's composure cracked like cheap pottery. "That's pre-Purge toadshit."

"Yes, it is."

"The *fuck* do we fight that?"

Snow opened her palm. Let the witchfire coil and drip through her fingers. "You've got me. Let's start with that."

"I'm glad to see you, Snow. No lie. But." Ari hunched forward. He twined his scarred fingers together, twisting and pulling until Snow winced for his joints. "We can't reach the God. None of us. We've tried every fucking thing we know. He's just not answering. And I don't know why." He blew air through his teeth. "Fuck and damn. I don't know."

Snow pressed her lips against her teeth. Veiko's axe through the God's shoulder, yeah, that might be the problem. "The God's lost a lot of people, yeah? That hurts him. Especially the strong ones, like Stig and Tsabrak. He's weak, and Tal'Shik's strong."

Ari stared at her, stone-faced. "You're saying he's *hiding*?"

Oh fuck and damn. Hiding implied that the God was afraid of Tal'Shik, which he *was*, damn sure. But Ari couldn't know that. Ari had *faith*, without sufficient wit to balance it. He should never have been a leader in the cartel. Would not have been in Stig's era. Or Tsabrak's. And he was all she had.

Use his faith, Snow. It's a tool.

Tsabrak's dead man's advice whispering in her skull. His silhouette across the table, where Ari's own shadow should be. She wanted to blink him away. Didn't dare, with Ari staring at her. With all the *rest* of them listening to her near blasphemy.

"Tal'Shik's hunting the God, yeah? You know that. And he's no fool. He's hiding from her like you're hiding from Rata. It's what you do when you don't have numbers to fight."

"So we're fucked."

"No." She took a breath. "Listen. I learned things up north. That skraeling I brought with me—he *knows things*, Ari, about talking to the gods, things that Tsabrak didn't know. Things that Tsabrak asked me to learn, so I did. And Tsabrak told me, if anything went wrong, if something happened up north, I should come back, use it, make sure Tal'Shik doesn't win. Point is, I can *make* the God answer." Cold, clear syllables, ringing off the stone like metal. "I promise you this, Ari. Get me into that shrine, I'll get the God back."

"Fuck that." Hraf's voice knifed through the quiet. Murmuring welled up in its wake like blood. "You don't belong in the shrine. You're not even godsworn. You're just Tsabrak's half-blood *bitch*, yeah?" He used the Alviri word, the one that had no match in Dvergiri.

Ari's gaze cut sideways. "Hraf. Shut it."

"Fuck that, Ari. I want to know—"

"I said *shut it*." Ari slammed his fist down on the table. Came halfway around on the bench, halfway uncoiled. "Snow wears the God's mark, yeah? That means she's been to the shrine once, and the God accepted her. And she's Academy. You know what that fucking means?"

Hraf had his back to the wall, his own hand halfway to a knife hilt. A little space had opened around him, Ari's men bleeding aside as if Hraf might infect them. "Don't fucking *care*, Ari. The God's not answering *us*! The fuck would he answer *her*?"

Ari shrank a little. Doubt shivered across his features. Snow strangled a sigh. Tsabrak would've gutted Hraf in front of everyone. *Dared* them to come at him.

You are my right hand.

There'd been a reason for that.

It was so easy, conjuring in Illharek. She'd gotten used to the tingling threat of backlash, even in Cardik, and the Wild's pressing menace. But here, Below, it was a matter of will, drawing power from air and stone. There were patterns a conjuror could see. Patterns she could feel, twist, change into new patterns.

Air to fire, stone to water.

Snow stretched her left hand out and pointed at the firedog. Hooked the essence of fire in the banked coals and ripped it out in a burst of light and heat and sparks that hissed where they struck stone floors and damp walls. Those too near the firedog jumped back and swore, slapping at their clothes.

The sparks were an accident. Blame the broken finger. But Hraf didn't know that. None of them did.

She came off the bench, witchfire coiled through the fingers of her right hand. Her left drew the seax out of its sheath. The black steel gleamed blue on the cutting edge.

"You want the God back, Hraf, you do what Ari says. Shut it."

"Or what?"

Snow smiled.

Hraf was watching her weapon. He'd drawn by now, too. He'd been a good fighter, Snow recalled. Quick on his feet, quick with his hands.

But it was wits that won fights.

She flung her witchfire at him, a glowing whip that snapped out of her right hand, stretching wire-slim before it let go. Hraf yelped and recoiled as the witchfire wrapped around his seax, slithered like a snake down around his wrist and arm. It didn't burn. Didn't do anything except glow. Hraf's eyes widened, then narrowed as he realized he wasn't hurt. And widened again when he realized he wasn't looking at *her* anymore.

Snow flicked her seax past his guard, a glittering tongue of metal. He tried to parry, tried to move himself out of the way, to retreat. But it was too late. She grabbed him, right-handed, and *pulled*, same time she pushed the point of her blade into his gut and shoved up. She let momentum push the metal deep, up under his ribs. Hraf gasped and sagged, drove the metal even deeper. His own weapon clattered to the stone floor while he clawed at her left wrist with frail fingers. Stared up into her face, all his toadshit bravado smeared to pain and terror. Tiny noises leaked out of his mouth along with a gush of blood and foam.

She ripped her blade loose and stepped clear before he soaked her with his dying.

Snow stretched her right hand down. The witchfire jumped back into it and settled in her palm like a kitten. She held it up and spun a slow circle. Blue light licked across the other godsworn. She marked the hands hovering over weapons, the shifting, sliding looks between her and Hraf, gurgling at her feet. They were godsworn, but they were young, and scared, and Hraf had been the bravest of them.

She turned to Ari last.

"I was Tsabrak's right hand," she said. "The God *will* answer me."

Ari opened his mouth. Shut it and shook his head. "Right. Then let's go."

* * *

Dekklis had intended to leave Soren at his mother's house. K'Hess was Stratka's neighbor, an easy walk across the bridge. It should have been easy to deliver Soren to safety.

But K'Hess house wasn't safe, not now. None of the houses were, after what he'd told her.

Snowdenaelikk would laugh herself sick at the irony, that the Suburba was safer than the Tiers for anyone, much less a highborn male. Then Snow would call her an idiot and tell her what Dekklis already guessed: that she and Soren were obvious, conspicuous, and that reports of their presence had run already from the Abattoir to the docks and into dangerous ears.

Rata's the rule in the Suburba now, yeah? She's got from the Abattoir to the docks. You don't cross her.

Whoever Rata was. Dekklis pictured a very tall rodent, Dvergiri black, with a tail trailing out of her pants. Long snout, chisel teeth, yellow eyes. Dangerous, sure, but something Dek could handle with metal.

That was the reason she hadn't taken Soren to the third member of their alliance. Bel might've given Soren asylum in the Academy. Damn good bet she *would* after hearing what he had to say. But what happened in there, Dek couldn't guess. Couldn't do a thing about it if Belaery flipped sides or couldn't protect him. No, it was better to dodge Rata and the cartel than trust what went on in Academy walls.

Damn good bet Snow would agree with her reasoning, at least on that front. But equally damn sure Snow would be pissed that Dek was taking Soren to *her* place.

The Street of Apothecaries, seventeenth shop from the Tano docks.

Assuming she could find it. Assuming she survived the Abattoir. It really wasn't so different than the Warren in Cardik. You dodged livestock and shitpiles. Same volume. Same stench. Same sort of people.

You mean lowborn, yeah?

She could imagine Snow at her shoulder, crooked grin and acid whispers.

Slouch, can't you?

Not really, no. Too many years of trying to seem taller, too many years of armored inspections. But she kept her shoulders hunched, as much to keep hands close to beltpouch and dagger as anything else.

You look like a mark, they'll take you.

And yes, there were eyes on her. Women slouched against the walls, arms crossed. Men crouching in shadows. Paranoia, surely, to think they were all watching her and Soren.

Who was doing better than she was, playing lowborn. Scuffing along beside and behind her, like Istel might've. She'd given him her sweater, to hide both the fine weave of his shirt and the ink on his chest. Let someone see K'Hess, consort to Stratka, and it wouldn't matter how either of them slouched. That news would get wings and fly.

Her own sigil was safe under the shirt she'd borrowed from Istel's kit. It was a northern cut, high-necked to keep away cold, coarse weave. They'd pass in Cardik's streets easy.

Not Cardik, is it, Dek?

No. Hell and damn, no. She was half-convinced Soren would cough himself blind on the blood reek and death in the air. Half-convinced she'd take metal between her ribs any moment.

"Just like a battlefield," she'd told Soren. "Watch where you're going, breathe through your mouth."

That advice held the deeper they went, through the Abattoir and into the Suburba proper, where bloodstink turned into fish and dirty water. The noise hadn't changed. Conversations shouted across the narrow streets, drifting out of open shutters, bouncing off stone and brick. Only the accents shifted, slurred Suburban native mixed with outlander. She heard two Alviri dialects. Heard what she thought was Taliri, too, across the street. She had stopped then, tipped onto her toes and looked and offended the woman behind her, who swore at her in fluent Suburban—

"Toadfucking motherless maggot."

—and damn near ran her down with a fishcart.

Once she thought she saw Snowdenaelikk, too: flash of fair hair over a dark face, which made her grab Soren and dive through the crowd. But of course it wasn't Snow. Some other half-blood, shorter and thicker, with dull yellow hair and eyes more green than blue.

No, finding Snow would be too much good fortune. Then Dek could hand K'Hess Soren off and take herself back up to the garrison before someone noticed her absence.

She tried to follow the water smell first, reckoning the docks must be close to that. Ended up on the docks, sure, but on the Jaarvi's shore, which had led to another plunge through Suburban streets, and an eventual *please, Domina* to a barkeep who was happy to sell Dekklis both watery beer and directions.

If that barkeep had lied, Dekklis promised herself, she'd go back and gut the woman and feed her eyes to Briel. Not for the first time, she cut a look up, at the hanging black overhead. No svartjagr. No sun, either, and no moon. But it must be close to the sixteenth mark now. The Senate must be out. Stratka would discover she was missing a consort, and then—

Hell. Worry about *then* when it became *now*.

"Dekklis." Soren touched her elbow as if she were hot iron and might burn him. Did not quite flinch when she turned and looked at him. He managed an uneasy eyelock, one whole breath. Then his gaze skipped past her. His chin tipped toward a cross street. "That way, I think."

That way, yes, and damn him anyway. Dek grunted not-quite-thanks at him. Shouldered past him and up that street. And then it was a slow progress, with Soren almost beside her, checking the signs. Tarnished copper, Snow had said, shaped like—

"Soren. You know what sweetleaf looks like?" Expecting a *no*, some point of commonality between them.

"Yes." And when she snapped round and stared at him. "Dried, anyway."

Foremothers defend. "The sign we want looks like a bundle. Don't know if it's dry or not."

"That shouldn't matter. The leaves have a distinctive shape. Kind of jagged on the edges, pronged." He sketched a shape with his fingers. "It gets its name from the smell when you burn it."

Rurik's eyes lit like that when he talked about battle tactics. "You're an apothecary?"

"Not exactly." His chin ducked. He developed a sudden fascination with the paving stones. "My mother indulged my interests."

Damn idiot, Dek.

Of course he wasn't an apothecary. But he might've been had he been born low and female. Might've been able to practice that trade as a bondie, even, if he'd shown aptitude. But he'd never gotten his hands into dirt or gotten anywhere near a real teacher. All his knowledge, his maternal indulgence, would've come from K'Hess's library.

That's a crime, Szanys. Or it should be.

"You'll like Snowdenaelikk," Dekklis said. "Ask her about plants, she'll talk you earless."

A sidelong glance. Soren knew about Snow what she'd told him: half-blood conjuror, no friend of Tal'Shik's, who'd once tried to save his baby brother, who had a skraeling partner. Dekklis had left off *heretic* and *criminal*. Soren was smart. He'd figure that out. And if he were anything like Istel, he'd probably stitch himself to Snow's shadow a candlemark after he met her.

Dekklis turned away before he saw her expression. Spent the scowl on signs and buildings. And there, yes and finally: a copper sign gone green, shaped like a bundle of jagged leaves.

She lingered a moment. The shop had both doors rolled back. Witchfire glowed in bowls, crowding out the firedog's more honest, sullen orange. The blue seeped onto the street, spots of cool to draw eyes and customers. Witchfire was neither cheap nor common in the Suburba. That the shop kept bowls of it like candles spoke well for its prosperity.

Unless you knew that the shop's owner's sister was a conjuror, and in residence, and the shop's clientele included at least one Adept. In which case you smiled to yourself and ducked inside and waited, at the back, for your turn at the counter. Dekklis tried to imagine Snow in this place, caught up in legal domesticity, and choked on a laugh.

And then it was her turn.

"Help you?"

Dekklis knew Snow's sisters weren't half-blood. But still, it startled her, seeing a pure-blood Dvergir behind the counter. She'd've passed this woman on the streets and never looked twice. Medium tall, unremarkable eyes.

"You're Sinnike?"

For a moment Dekklis thought she'd misremembered the name. Then the woman's eyes narrowed. "I am. Who sent you?"

"Your eldest sister."

Sinnike's brows shot up. Then her eyes flickered past Dekklis. Settled on the door. She said, more loudly, "A moment, Domina, what you want is more complicated. Let me help this other person first."

Dekklis nodded. Folded aside as another woman came up to the counter.

"Toadskin," the woman said to Sinnike. "Do you have some?" But she was looking at Dek when she said it. And kept looking, even after

Sinnike turned and pulled down a jar of suspicious grey powder and began tapping its contents onto the scale.

Dekklis pretended to study the jars and powders. Dizzying rows of them, stretched up the walls. She wondered if Sinnike could read. Guessed she could, hell, Snow would've taught her, which left Dekklis wondering why none of the jars had labels. Dek drifted toward Soren to ask if he knew what they were. Her eyes caught movement at the room's edge, a fluttering of the curtains that must lead back into the family's quarters. A man came out who looked like Veiko at first glance and clearly wasn't when he stepped into the light. Same coloring, but older, his hair silvered and bound in an Illhari queue, the citizen's mark inked black on his neck.

The skraeling caught her staring. Bowed. That was a shadow of Snow's crooked smile on his lips.

Dekklis turned and pretended great interest in a bundle of something drying over the firedog. Some kind of fungus, lacy-edged and impossibly purple, and better than staring like a child. It hadn't been obvious which of Elia's three consorts had fathered Dekklis. But everyone with working eyes who saw Snowdenaelikk and this man together would know something that only a mother should properly know.

You could condemn the mother for that indiscretion. You could even pity the daughter. But you couldn't be at all surprised if that daughter turned heretic and criminal.

The tall man drifted into her periphery. Waited, proper and diffident, until Dekklis turned to face him. And oh, you'd never see that kind of deference on Snow's face. Probably not sincere, not if Snow got anything but looks from him; but sincerity didn't matter. No highborn would care as long as he seemed polite. No highborn would come farther down than the Abattoir unless she was—what, an idiot? Desperate?

Word you want is traitor, *Dek.*

"Domina." He peeled a smile. "Perhaps I can help you."

Dekklis glanced at Sinnike. She'd finished with the powder. Was scraping it off the scale's tray and into a scrap of cloth. The cant of her neck said she knew what was happening in her shop. Her shoulders said she didn't like it. She wouldn't reprimand her own household in front of strangers, and this man clearly *was* household. Damn sure he knew that he'd just crossed a line. Bet that he made a habit of it.

Easy to see where Snow learned that, too. Well. It wasn't like Dekklis held too closely to protocol anymore these days.

Dek turned her back on Sinnike and the other customer. Dropped her voice. "You know what I'm looking for?"

"Yes." He bowed. "Though I regret to say that we don't have that which you seek on hand."

"Where might I find it?"

"I am unsure."

"And your mistress? Is she unsure?"

A second bow, a hair too shallow for manners. "I regret—"

Dekklis took his elbow. Spun and steered him away from the counter, into the corner, and *hell* with the stares she'd just got. "Where'd she go?"

"I cannot say."

"Cannot. Not will not. All right. When will she be back?"

She heard the edges of accent on that so-proper Dvergiri. "Again, Domina, I am unsure."

"You don't know much, do you?"

His eyes were darker than Veiko's, a murkier blue that collected the shadows. "I do not know *you*. Domina."

Dekklis tied down her temper. At least Snow hadn't been waving her name around. "What about Veiko? I can talk to him."

Blink. "He was here briefly. Where he stays now, we do not know. Regrets, Domina."

Hell of a time Snow picked to go visiting. She jerked her chin sideways, at Soren. "Fine. Then you take delivery. You need to keep this man. Can you do that? He knows things she needs to hear."

"He is highborn," the skraeling said flatly.

"So am I."

"That is obvious. But—" The skraeling clipped his teeth together on what he meant to say next. Watched instead as Sinnike walked her customer to the door.

"—mix that with water, yeah? Or tea. Only a pinch."

The woman was nodding, agreeing, looking, too, between Soren and Dekklis. "I will, Sinnike, thank you."

"My pleasure." Sinnike did not quite push her through the doorway. Waited an indecent heartbeat, then drew the shutters and turned to look at Dekklis.

"Who are you?"

"First Scout Szanys Dekklis, Second Legion, Sixth Cohort. And this is K'Hess Soren. Yes. *That* K'Hess. As I've been telling your man here, you need to keep him. For Snow."

Sinnike shook her head. "Fuck if I do. This is highborn toadshit. Doesn't belong in my shop, yeah?"

"As may be. But it's legally your sister's shop, not yours, and this is her business."

Dekklis was glad this sister wasn't a conjuror. Sinnike's look would've turned her to ashes right now, a smoldering pile of former trouble there on the tiles. "Get out."

"No. This man dies if I do. Maybe Illharek goes down, too. You savvy that?"

The skraeling made a small, pained noise in his throat. "Sinnike—"

She held up a single finger, *shut up*, and never broke eyelock with Dek. "Take him to her yourself."

"I would if I knew where she was. But I don't. And if I don't get back up to the Tiers, people might come looking for me."

"People. Huh." Sinnike looked sideways through the slatted shutters as if there were already troops on the street. "So who comes looking for *him*?"

Godsworn. Stratka House agents. Mostly honest to say, "I don't know."

"But someone will." Sinnike peeled an echo of Snow's crooked smile. "Will they want him alive or dead?"

Soren flinched. The skraeling winced. Dekklis shrugged. "Depends who it is. But I'll tell you: he needs to stay alive."

"I reckoned. Tell me. He have something to do with the Taliri in Cardik?" A cut-glass smile. "I see he does. —*Easy*, woman. No need for metal."

Dekklis looked down at the knife on her hip. Uncurled her fingers, one by conscious one, from the hilt. Said, through her teeth, "Snow told you, then."

"Not much. Not everything, damn sure. My sister keeps her own counsel." Sinnike blew a breath. "All right. Fine. Leave him. Not the first time I've handled Snow's toadshit."

"Thank you."

Flat stare. Flat lips. Sinnike turned a shoulder and pushed the door open. The Suburba spilled back in, light and noise and stench.

That was a clear *get out*, and Dek was out of reasons to argue. Snow's sister had vouched for Soren's safety. Best she could do was hope that Sinnike had her sister's strange honor.

Her stomach clenched. What Soren knew could ruin whole Houses. Could lead to another Purge. Or it could die with him if the wrong godsworn got him.

There are right godsworn?

Better the heretics than the highborn right now.

That's the way, Szanys. You're getting it.

"You can trust Snow. And I'll be back for you," she told Soren. "Savvy that?"

"Yes," he said faintly.

K'Hess Soren was too well bred, too well trained, to call after her. But his stare followed Dekklis out the door, pulling at her like a drowning man's fingers.

CHAPTER SIXTEEN

The path to the Laughing God's shrine was unlit, unmarked. His god-sworn carried a mental map. A visitor, even an ally, had to keep one hand on the wall, and one hand on Ari, and follow blind. Ari led her down a twisted path, turn and redouble and come back again. This darkness had no beginning to it, and no end. No moon to rise and set. No sun bleeding up the horizon. A woman got used to knowing *when* it was, just by looking up.

No witchfire down here. No candles. It might be tenth mark, or fifteenth, or a thousand years from now. All the Above, all the fields and the forests, might be blasted to stone and sand. Snow could imagine that place, clear on the back of her eyelids, as if someone had painted it. Familiar, as if she'd lived it. The Jokki burned off to a trickle, winding out of Illharek's mouth and away through rocks and bleak dust—

And then she realized that she *had* seen it before, and where, and scared herself wide-eyed.

That trickle wasn't the Jokki. It was the black river that didn't have a name. Sometimes she still felt it sloshing around inside her, until she had to cough it out.

Be careful. Tsabrak's whisper. Tsabrak's crooked, bitter smile. Tsabrak pressed up against her. His familiar heartbeat against her ribs, as if there were only skin between them. *The God's treacherous, Snow, you know that.*

And what are you?

Expecting him to vanish. To run, like Tsabrak always did, always had. But this time, the ghost stayed.

You could run, too, yeah?

Sure. She could run away, leave all this toadshit. Abandon Dekklis, Istel, Belaery. She could get Veiko and go—somewhere. Let Tal'Shik have Illharek. And then spend the rest of her life, and Veiko's, waiting for that *bitch* to come at their backs.

Fuck and damn.

Without the God's help, they'd fail. That was the truth of it. They'd lose Illharek.

The fuck do you care about Illharek?

The fuck do you care what I do?

Snow. He sounded so gentle, so sad, she could almost believe him, as if she didn't know the Tsabrak he'd *been*, with all the *sad* and *gentle* burned away. His fingers gripped her arm, pressing against the wound and the stitches, damp and cold through her sleeve.

"Step and turn a sharp left," said Ari, and she remembered where she was, what she was doing. What she was about to do, fuck and damn.

The first time, the only other time, she'd come to the shrine, she had walked out with a fresh godmark on her palm, the God's sigil, inked blacker even than her skin. Not godsworn, because the God

has no use for women

did not take women into his service that way. Veiko would've shaken his head and told her *foolish bargain, the God's battles are not yours.*

She'd thought it was. Her younger self, half-blood and angry, had imagined more kinship with Illharek's lowborn and men, with its heretics and outcasts, than she had with its privileged classes. There was money and accent and address; there was fair hair and blue eyes. One of those things, *either* one, the Academy might've forgiven. But half-blood *and* lowborn, well, that was too much.

So her younger self had been a fool, but she hadn't been *wrong*, and that was what Veiko wouldn't understand. Veiko saw things in clear lines, hard edges, sunlight and shadow. But it was all shadow down here. Murk and gloom and soft edges. You learned to see grey.

"Here," said Ari. "Mind the footing."

She smelled the water. Heard it bubbling out of the rocks, giggling past her boots. She remembered this place. It had been lit last time, sullen oil lamps smearing the dark into twilight, showing her slime-slick pillars connecting floor and ceiling. She slowed down. Told herself it was for footing's sake on the waterslick. But she strained for any light-leak on the stones. Please, that there was no one waiting ahead.

The laughter that kissed the back of her neck was not Tsabrak's. Older, smokier, terrifying and familiar.

The shrine had a solid door, metal and wood, dragged from the God knew where, bolted into the surrounding stone. There had been locks once. Tsabrak had let her in with the key he'd worn on a chain. As part of her bargain, proof that she brought useful skills to the God's service, she'd warded the door. The sigils eliminated any need for keys or locks. She could see them, faint lines sketched into the iron. Ari couldn't. He knew the prayers to pass them.

Laughing God, Smiling One, Svartjagr's Brother. By these names I know you.

She didn't need any prayer. Snow moved her hand across them, smelled dry lightning and smoke. Audible click and the door swung open, sent air like a body's last breath rolling over her.

She stepped inside. Let Ari close the door and whisper the wards back to life while she called up a witchfire. She set the blue fire gently into the brazier nearest the door. It licked among the coals and oil. Cast lazy blue across the room, smeared the carpet's geometry into blurs of red and gold. Then it hopped from brazier to brazier, spreading itself until the shrine throbbed and flickered blue. Dust puffed, settled silver on the toes of her boots. There was a trail worn across the carpet from the door to the tiny firedog in the corner. It was cast in a svartjagr's shape, coiled on its tail, wings flared for balance. Smoke had greased the ceiling over it. Lingered in the stale air. Its eyes burned with real flame, tiny wicks in tiny lamps.

"Snow." Ari licked his lips. "You sure this will work? Because after what you did back there, if it doesn't—"

"If it doesn't, they'll gut me. And you. I know. It will work, Ari."

Snow wore the God's marks, more than the godmark on her palm. She had silver-shine scars winding from shoulder to hip, a lover's trail made with Tsabrak's god-ridden mouth and the God's malice. The God had been trying to break her. She wasn't sure that he hadn't. She still twisted up out of sleep some nights. Scared Briel and woke Veiko, who never said anything. Who looked at her with those witchfire eyes, and held her if she could bear it, and watched over her until she went back to sleep.

This is not your fight.

Oh, but it was. Burned into her flesh, it was her fight. Assuming that soul-stealing toadfucker was still able, the God would answer her. They had a bargain, never mind he'd dropped most of his end. He'd promised, so he owed her, and she'd hold him to it. Veiko had taught her that much about being noidghe.

Snow peeled the firedog's chest open. There were cold coals inside, and the remnants of some small dead offering. She squatted back on her heels. Rummaged through the pouch on her belt for some jenja. She laid the sticks across the coals. Conjured fire out of air and stone and sent it twisting among the coals. The jenja caught. Smoked. Flared and burned and helixed out of the firedog's open jaws.

Then she reached a little deeper and pulled out a tiny sack of dried bluestar. It was a restricted substance, reserved for Academy chirurgeons. The stem and roots were good against fever, but the leaves and flower itself were toxic. Hallucinogenic in small doses. Deadly in larger ones. A challenge for students to get the dose right. A test. Fuck it up, and you died or spent the rest of your short life drooling. Do enough of it, and often enough, and you built up a tolerance for it.

She pinched off a couple of flowers and crumbled them into the flames. Held her breath as the smoke rolled off the coals, closed her eyes. The first puff was the strongest. You learned that. Take little bites of air until the smoke cleared a little.

Ari got between her and a witchfire brazier, threw a blue-tinged shadow across her. "What is that?"

"Incense," Snow said. "Special stuff. Bluestar. Or witchtit if you're an Alvir."

"Damn, that's . . ." Ari trailed off. Coughed, weakly. "Strong."

"You should sit, yeah?"

"Yeah." He did, gracelessly. Just folded his knees and thumped. Shook his head. Took a deep swallow of air, which he probably thought would help. "I'm fine."

Snow latched the firedog's belly again. Bluestar and jenja swirled out of its mouth. She was feeling the effects now, too. Light-headed, her bones buzzing like wasps. It wouldn't get much stronger, not for her. She'd done too much across the years. But that first time, hell, she'd damn near come out of her skin.

Ari looked like a man afraid he'd fall off the floor. He groped at the carpet with both hands. Shook his head and damn near tipped over. "The fuck," he tried to say. It came out *da fug*.

"Listen," she said. "I should've told you about this. Asked your permission. But if you'd said yes, you'd know what was coming. Better if you're surprised, yeah?"

Eyes pooling wide and black, sweat beading on his skin. "Don unnerstan."

"I know." Snow took his hand. Flipped it over and spread the limp fingers. No resistance as she pulled his knife out of his boot.

You *asked* for the God's favor. You *offered* and hoped that he came. She reckoned that Ari had done that. She bet that Ari had got on his knees and begged.

Veiko had taught her better. Spirits liked blood.

She traced the godmark on Ari's palm. Once. Then again, a little harder. Pushed the tip of the blade into his skin. Drew the sigil a third time and left blood in the wake of the blade.

Snowdenaelikk looked at Ari's face. "I want to talk to you. Hear me, Laughing God? We had a bargain, and you broke it. Now I want an accounting. I brought you a skin, yeah? So come put it on and talk to me."

Ari shuddered. Tilted sideways, as if he'd turned to liquid inside his skin, until her grip on his wrist was the only thing holding him upright.

"A bargain," she repeated, and tugged sharply on Ari's wrist. The blood welled up and dripped. "Oathbreaker, I'm calling you. *Answer me.*"

Ari's head rolled on his neck. Then his head snapped upright, and he looked at her. Flames burned where his eyes had been.

Rattle-skip heartbeat, cold sweat on her skin. Blame the witchtit, yeah, and ignore the

panic

fluttering in her chest. That smile didn't change, no matter whose face the God wore. Last time it'd been Tsabrak's face grinning while she smelled her own skin burning, the blisters rising and bursting, as if her flesh itself wept.

The God's voice rumbled through Ari's lips, a little rougher, a little lower. "Snowdenaelikk. What do you want?"

"You owe me a debt."

"Toadshit."

"Then why are you here? Ari said you wouldn't answer him. But you answered *me*."

The God bared his teeth. "Curiosity."

"Compulsion. Toadfucker. I kept my side of our bargain, yeah? And you fucking killed me."

The God hissed like a hundred Briels. "You were making deals with Ehkla."

"Which didn't cross what I'd promised *you*, yeah? Ehkla died under my knife. Coming back was her arrangement with Tal'Shik. Not my problem. So you do as I say now, and you settle your debt."

"Or *what*, Snowdenaelikk?"

She pulled Ari's hand to the carpet. Flipped the hand, palm down. The words were old, Purged and forbidden, but Bel had helped her find them. The reading, she'd managed on her own.

"Laughing God, Smiling One, Svartjagr's Brother. By these names I know you. By these names I *bind* you."

She jammed the tip of the blade between the ridges of tendon and bones, through the sigil, the carpet, until the metal stopped hard on the stone.

A man would've recoiled, screamed, wrenched himself into real damage. The God merely looked down at the wound. Frowned when the hand would not move, or the elbow, or anything from fingertips to shoulder.

"Snowdenaelikk, I don't know what you think you've learned, but." The God reached for the knife with Ari's other hand. "This won't wo— *fuck and damn.*"

There was a popping sensation in Snow's ears, the spreading smell of lightning. The shrine faded until it seemed as if Snow could see through the firedog and the walls and the floor. Until it seemed as if she knelt on the banks of a black lake under a stone sky.

Then the shrine came back, with its witchfires loyal to her. The God shivered like a wet dog. The fires in his eyes had gone pallid and yellow, like a lamp on the last of its oil.

"I am the Laughing God." He sounded aggrieved.

"A god's just a spirit with ambition, yeah? And spirits follow rules."

"Is that skraeling wisdom?"

"No. It's in the Illhari Archives. So is the binding I just used. The woman who wrote it died. You want to guess who killed her?"

"Other women, no doubt, seeking favor from another ambitious spirit. Very well. You're clever. I'm just a spirit. Now take this fucking knife out of my hand, yeah? It keeps me in one place, here and in the ghost roads. Makes it easier to find me."

Snow took the knife's hilt and twisted the blade. The God screamed with Ari's voice. She waited until he ran out of air, plus a handful of heartbeats. Then she sat back on her heels.

"You don't dictate terms to me. You listen, yeah? And you settle your fucking debt to me, with that steel in your hand, or you can fucking *rot* until Tal'Shik finds you."

"You motherless half-blood." The hatred came off him in waves, prickled hot and dry across her skin. "What do you want?"

Oh, the temptation to say *nothing except you leave me and Veiko alone.* But that would be like throwing a sharp sword down a well because you were afraid it'd cut you. There was a trick to handling any weapon. Just had to learn it. Had to practice. Had to know what it wanted, yeah, and use it accordingly.

"Tal'Shik's got people in Illharek. It's not just the Taliri."

"Of course she does."

"Then you know what they did to Stig."

"Of course I do." Smoke curled out of his nostrils, through his teeth. "I couldn't help him."

"Couldn't, or wouldn't?"

"Ask your skraeling."

"I know he cut you. I know you're hurt, and weak." She paused while the God glared at her, and peeled her own lips back. "But I think you'd let every last one of your godsworn die before you'd face her yourself. You're Tal'Shik's toadfucking ally. You betrayed all of us."

The God's eyes flared white. She smelled Ari's singed eyebrows. She squinted through that brightness, at the God's face where it pushed against Ari's bones.

"Fuck you, half-blood. I would bind Tal'Shik to her own altars with strips of her godsworn's skin."

"Then why haven't you?"

The fires damped back to orange. "Because she's too strong for me. She's always been too strong."

"That's too bad, yeah? Because I want you to find her and pick a fight. Keep her too busy to answer her godsworn so we can deal with them. That's how you pay your debt."

The God leaned toward her. Yellow light mixed with the witchfire's blue, bleached Ari's face grey. For the space between blinks, Snow saw a dead man looking out at her.

"Are you sure? Because if I throw myself at Tal'Shik for you, if I *slow her down*, she will kill me. Then she will steal *my* power, and you will have no help at all."

"So don't die."

"It isn't that fucking simple. You're not stupid."

"That's why I don't believe you."

"Tsabrak's right hand. Clever woman. I always liked you." The God stared hard at the firedog. Ran a finger along the edge of its belly, raising blisters on Ari's skin. "You're right. I owe you. And I will do what you . . . demand." His lip curled. "But if you want anything except simple revenge on me—if you want Tal'Shik *dead*—then I need something from you. Another bargain, yeah?"

Sweat ran down her ribs. "Meaning what?"

His eyes smoldered now, coals nearly gone out. "Repair the damage your partner did to me. Make me strong again. Become *my* right hand, Snowdenaelikk, and I will *kill* Tal'Shik for both of us."

Feel the trap, smell it, hear it. And step into it anyway, eyes open. "I'm listening."

* * *

Veiko did not need the drum to walk the ghost roads. Did not need the poisons, either, anymore. Needed only to close his eyes, and breathe, and loose his spirit from his flesh. It was, Taru had told him, a rare talent.

Very few noidghe can do this. You are fortunate, Nyrikki's son. The look on her face said she wasn't sure how much he deserved that good luck, or how long he might live to enjoy it.

It was a reasonable concern. Luck had its limits. It was skill that saved a man. But he had little of that, playing noidghe. Had only talent to guide him, and Helgi, who was waiting when Veiko stepped onto the glacier. Who put his ears back, teeth bared in a happy dog's grin.

Then his ears flicked a warning, forward and sideways, and he fixed a stare past Veiko's left shoulder.

Veiko sighed. Someone else must be here to greet him, and she would not be so pleased to see him.

"We agreed," said Taru, "that you would return in three days. It has been only one. You must take more time between visits. Remind your spirit that it is bound to your flesh."

"My spirit knows that." His leg throbbed where Ehkla had cut him. It had not done that in a long time. He rubbed the muscle. Rubbed Helgi's ribs, too, where the wurm's tooth had gone in. Wondered if Helgi's wound ached, too.

"The dog died," Taru said. "You did not."

"I wish you would not answer questions I did not ask."

"Then do not think them so loudly." She pointed at his leg. "It hurts because you are tired. Go back. Rest."

"It aches because I am thinking of the one who gave it to me."

"Then think of something else. Show your wits for once."

He squinted across the ice. The sun was a plain silver disk, only a little brighter than the rest of the sky. No shadow. No glare. The green-brown tundra to one side, the herd of takin spread out across it. He wondered why there was no village, why there were only animals here. Thought *that* at Taru.

She snorted. "Now you are asking worthwhile questions. The village is not your spirit's home. This place is."

"How do I destroy a spirit?"

"And you disappoint me again. A noidghe bargains with spirits. He does not destroy them."

"Does not, or cannot?"

Taru folded her arms.

"That is what I thought." Veiko gave Helgi a last pat. The dog set off across the ice, tail high, nose lifted. Hunting.

Taru appeared in the corner of his right eye. Veiko turned his head slightly. Met the icy wall of her anger.

"I have other things to teach you. Far more useful things."

"I will learn them. Later. After I have hunted down a certain spirit and killed her."

"This wastes your time. And mine."

He stretched his stride. "Then do not come with me."

For a moment he thought she wouldn't. Then she drew even with him again, jogging loosely, easily. A ghost needed no breath. And so her voice was steady when she said, "You are a child of my lineage. You have asked a foolish question, but nevertheless, here is your answer: a noidghe can destroy a spirit if that noidghe is powerful and skilled enough. It is difficult, and it is dangerous, and it comes with a price. —Do not look at me that way, Nyrikki's son. I know you are no coward, and your luck is better than it should be. But it is not something a noidghe *should* do, even if he can."

The wind sighed and sifted through his braids and hers. Veiko let out a breath. "Thank you for the answer."

"Fool," she said, but more gently. The silence settled around them. Helgi drew a few paces ahead. The wind grew stronger, gusting first from one direction, then another. In the flesh-world, it would have been storm weather. Veiko cocked a glance at the slate-colored sky.

And so he did not see Helgi's sudden wheeling stop. But he heard the dog's warning growl, and the sudden scrabble of claws. And he heard, very clearly and from far too close:

"Veiko Nyrikki."

Veiko turned around fast, with his hand on his axe. There was no shadow on the tundra: dull silver sky, no sun, no trees. And still this man cast one, which spilled around him like liquid dark. Veiko had never met him in life, no, but he knew the face from Briel's sendings.

He forced the name. "Tsabrak."

And looked closer, to be certain. The God had worn other faces before. But this man's eyes were garnet dark, common Dvergir. No fires burned in the sockets.

"A ghost," confirmed Taru, grim-voiced. Then she frowned. "No. Not entirely."

"No." Tsabrak said amiably. He did not look at her. "Not quite, any more than you are, skraeling foremother. —I've been looking for you, Veiko."

"I cannot say the same."

Tsabrak stretched his lips. "No. You're looking for *him*, yeah? You've *been* looking. And you can't find him."

Veiko shrugged. "Perhaps."

"Toadshit, *perhaps*. I know where he is. I can take you."

Oh ancestors, let his face show nothing. "And why would you do that?"

"Because I want you to help me kill him."

Veiko felt the surprise escape onto his face. "What?"

"I kill him, I take his power."

Taru made a rude noise. Spat, audibly, onto the ghost tundra. "That rule is for spirits. You are only a ghost. A little thief. You would do better to say, 'Help me kill this God before he comes looking for me to reclaim what is his.'"

Fuck you on Tsabrak's face, plain as fire. But he only shrugged. Cool-voiced, with only a little shake, "Tell me, skraeling. Do you let a woman speak for you now?"

"I have learned Illhari ways."

Tsabrak took a step back. It was not a retreat so much as a settling. The garnet eyes gleamed. "Your foremother's wrong. I didn't *steal* anything from the God. I was his godsworn, yeah? I have some of his power. Some of *him*. That's what godsworn means."

"And you gave part of yourself to him. Yes. I can see that." Taru shook her head. "A bad bargain, little dead man, to yield up part of your soul."

"You're not a Dvergir man, yeah? I got what I wanted. So did the God. It worked well for a long time. Then he did what he did to Snow." Tsabrak closed his eyes. Grimaced. "He betrayed us both with that toadshit. And then he let me die. So yeah, I kept a piece of him."

"So the God has broken the rules, and now you have. So much for Illhari bargains. But that does not say why I would help you."

"Because Snow's with him now. The God. She called him, and he came, and now they're making deals." Tsabrak folded his arms, as if the ice-flavored wind could chill him, and squinted at some distant nothing. His shadow spread a little bit, investigating the cracks in the glacier, pooling black in the ice. "And because Tal'Shik knows where you are. Her godsworn *know*. They're coming for you."

"Perhaps I will find her first."

Sudden comprehension bloomed on Tsabrak's face like a bruise. "You're *hunting* her. You think you'll get her first. Is that it?"

Taru snorted. Veiko said nothing. Stood and stared while the cold seeped up through his boot soles.

Tsabrak began to laugh. "Least I learn from my mistakes, yeah? You can't beat her. You tried once, and you failed."

Taru folded her arms and grunted. It was not quite *I told you as much*.

"I tried twice," Veiko said mildly. "Both times, she retreated before the fight was finished."

"You got lucky, yeah? Listen. I can help you find Tal'Shik. I can help you kill her. But first, you help me kill the God. When I've taken his power, I'll be strong enough to help you."

Veiko tried the Dvergiri words, first time off his lips. "Fuck you."

Tsabrak blinked. Grinned. "Listen to me, toadbelly. The God's crippled. Broken. You fucked him good, yeah?"

In this place, language was no barrier to understanding. But his difficulty with Dvergiri had never been the vocabulary. Ancestors, that image.

Tsabrak grinned wider. "You know how a god gets unfucked?"

The Illhari prayed to their spirits. Sacrificed. Poured power into them without bargains to govern the exchange. It was not a healthy relationship. Snow had said as much herself, yes, but if she wanted the God to help her, she would offer him what he wanted. Because, oh ancestors, *he* had refused to help her.

Veiko closed his eyes. Opened them again. "Yes."

"Then you know the God won't tell Snow how bad he's hurt. He'll *say* whatever he has to, to get what he wants. And you know she'll agree to it. And he'll use that to destroy her."

"She is not a fool."

"Of course she's not. She's desperate. She's pissed at the God, yeah? I know that. But he's a better choice than Tal'Shik, and she's winning.

You think Snow's going to let that happen? You think she won't do *anything* to make sure that doesn't happen?"

When he had killed the chieftain's son, he had done so for justice, and he had not balked at the price. Snow would be no different. This was a matter of blood feud for her, just as it had been for him.

Veiko looked at Taru. Met that pale, grim stare. Weighed the wisdom of asking advice, here, in front of Tsabrak. The other man might read it as weakness. And while he did not care what a ghost thought, a soon-to-be-god was another matter. A noidghe should grant no advantage to spirits.

And a noidghe should know the difference between wisdom and pride. A man should.

Veiko set his teeth. Drew cold air between them. Said, hardly louder than Helgi's constant growl, "Wise ancestor, I have need of counsel."

Taru gazed up at the sky. "If a noidghe is intent on destroying a spirit," she told the clouds, "then he should find allies to help him. He does not need to like those allies. However." She looked at him. "I must also tell you that what you intend is foolish."

"Snow is my—"

"I know what she is to you." A tiny smile, grim and wise and knowing. "So I will tell you this, too: she has neither your talent nor your luck with spirits. If you choose this alliance, you must move quickly."

CHAPTER SEVENTEEN

"I seen the troops on the 'Walk," said a voice like tarnished brass, "setting up lines. No one's getting out that way."

The voice's owner had gathered a crowd around her: two fishcarts and a wool merchant with her bondies, a scattered handful of citizens with bundles, a pair of well-dressed bondies. Every one of them, Dekklis thought sourly, was taller. She stretched onto her toes. Surely a voice that big would belong to an equally large body.

Nothing. Shoulders. The backs of people's heads.

It might just be toadshit. Rumors in crowds were as reliable as a northern spring. But the Abattoir streets were crowded, citizens clotted like the blood in the gutters, little chunks and knots on the pavement, buzzing like a cloud of flies. Bondies in Tier-quality clothing. People with midtowner accents. Farmers with empty handcarts, too, who should have been gone by sunset, out Illharek's gates. It *had* to be well after the Senate's recess.

But if it were true, hell and damn, that was bad. Barricades were worse than just troopers. And they were probably *her* fault, if a certain highborn consort's absence had been noticed. Stratka would want him back.

"And." Tarnished Brass paused for dramatic effect. "*And* I saw troopers coming up the road just after noon. Ragged lot."

"From where?" someone asked, and another voice added, "Were they ours?"

"No one else's they could be," said another bystander, with the sneering confidence of a woman who has never been out of Illharek. "You think the toadbellies got armies now?"

"You shut up, Risstael, you motherless—"

"I hear," said another woman, loudly, "that the raiders are bad this year."

"Taliri don't *march* on the roads, idiot."

"That's not what I said—"

"What colors? Which road?" Dek tried to call, and found herself drowned by more speculation. What she wouldn't give now for Barkett and Teslin to bull a path for her. What she wouldn't give for Rurik's tile-cracking shout, which would cut across a barracks full of drunk troopers at midwinter.

She had her elbows. She used them, on the rearmost. By the time she'd gotten close enough to put a face to Tarnished Brass, she'd gotten new bruises on her ribs, and muttering malice behind her, and a new admiration for the quality of her boots.

She threw her voice over the last heads in front of her. "Which road?" and shoved her way through.

A scrawny woman stood there, wearing a drover's coat and shit-crusted boots. Five slat-ribbed goats milled around her. A spotted dog circled the goats, nipping at them. It turned its teeth at Dekklis. Lunged and snapped.

And yelped when she put one of her hard-soled northern boots into its ribs. Veiko would've put an axe through her for kicking his dog. But Tarnished Brass only looked at her, head-cocked curious.

"North road."

"What colors?"

"Couldn't see colors. Ragged-assed lot. Looked like—"

"No flag?" The shape of the walls funneled Dekklis's voice back, made it bigger. Hell and damn, she did sound like Rurik. *Polished* brass, not tarnished.

The drover frowned. "No flag. They looked like they'd been running hard, yeah? Like something was after them."

Dekklis closed her eyes. Opened them again. "They the ones on the Riverwalk?"

"No. Riverwalk's all Illhari troopers. *Those* colors I can see fine." Narrow-eyed squint. A rake from crown to boots. "You from Cardik?"

"No. Davni. Taliri burned it flat last winter."

The drover woman was watching her. All of them were. Hell and damn. Snow had warned her. Snow had said, *Don't come down here, highborn.* Square shoulders, snapping out questions, bet her accent had slipped, too.

The drover smiled at her with the intimacy of a total stranger. "Davni's a toadbelly village, and you're no toadbelly. I reckon, with that accent—"

Dekklis wheeled on the crowd. "The legion did this in Cardik, right before the Taliri attacked. They tried to pen people up in the city. Blocked the bridges. They *shot* people, yeah? We can't stay down here!"

There was a new swell of muttering now, a new pitch and timbre. The crowd had grown, too. The bondies, the merchants, the farmers. Butchers with their bloody aprons, who had to be local. Who were, she noted, carrying hooks and long knives.

Incitement to riot. That's a new one for you, Szanys.

Add it to the list of her treasons.

"Not staying down here," a woman was saying. She carried a seax on her hip, and a duffel slung over her shoulder. "They can't keep us."

And another said, "Not a bunch of sheep for the slaughter."

Voices rose in agreement. Dekklis smothered a smile. Here the greatest difference between the Republic's heart and its border cities.

A native Illhari had a sense of entitlement, be she Dvergir, Alvir, half-blood, or bondie.

It was easy to fall into the crowd as it surged up the Abattoir's main thoroughfare. Easy, with those bodies already moving, to snake and slip between them. A little frightening, too, how fast their numbers grew. From crowd to mob, in a half-dozen streets.

Which made it a little more difficult, once Dekklis reached the Riverwalk, to approach the legion line standing there. About a third of them were facing into the Abattoir, more turning as the crowd's noise reached them. The rest were looking up at the bridges and ramps leading into the Tiers. A handful were stationed up near the mouth of the cave, looking up the road.

So the trouble wasn't outside, then, Taliri burning their way up the river. The trouble was up in the Tiers. The absence of K'Hess Soren seemed less and less likely the cause. This was a lot of upset for one man, whatever his birth. This action had a different root. *Someone* had ordered the legion out. The praefecta wouldn't do it without authorization. As to who had that kind of power, well. Consul. Senate. Maybe both. So the Senate was still in session, even this late. Maybe her mother had gotten them to listen. Or maybe a certain half-blood heretic had gone off and killed someone important.

Dekklis had been on the leading edge of the crowd when they'd come up onto the 'Walk. She dropped back now, stepped to the side. Let the first wave of anger sweep past her.

"Stop where you are!" slammed into "You got no right!"

"—can't keep us out—"

"—disperse, by order of the consul—"

Briel, Dekklis thought, looking up. *Briel, if you're up there.*

A finger of pain poked her left eye socket. She had a dizzy flash of the open night sky. Veiko, lying beside a fire. Logi, sitting watch. Istel, of all people, poking sticks into the flames. And then firelight on cave walls, and the smell of smoke and blood. A stranger's face, with fire where his eyes should be, and a smile peeled off his teeth.

Fear and anger, two flavors, hot and cold and so tangled together that Dekklis gagged. No help from Briel, then. And no time to sift through what she had seen. Svartjagr sendings depended too much on a svartjagr brain. Dek had her own trouble. Snow and Veiko and Istel would have to handle theirs.

And then she was back looking out her own eyes, with the headache prickling white behind them, at two lines of Illhari, legion and citizen. Somehow the conflict hadn't yet spilled into blows. Shouts only, and threats, traded across a gap just wider than an outthrust arm with a sword in it.

Her first task would be to get across that legion line. Dekklis angled through the crowd toward the edge of the 'Walk, where the cave walls sloped down and met with the floor. It wasn't a neat joining, an uneven hip-high convergence that said water had made it, and not conjuring. But that sloped ceiling meant that most of the not-yet-riot's weight was concentrated toward the middle of the lines, where everyone's head would fit.

Most of the troopers' attention was pointed that way, too. Dekklis got within an armspan of the wall before she was noticed. Then it was only the last soldier in line who saw her. Young woman, tall and spare. Dek didn't recognize her, but look at those bones. Highborn, yeah, she could bet on that. The trooper had no insignia on her, and that vibrating energy of mixed fear and excitement that said *green*. K'Hess Kenjak had had that look, Dek remembered. Kenjak would've laid hands on his sword just like that, with no thought how he'd clear it from the sheath with the stone walls so close. Kenjak would've snapped *stop there, citizen!* in that same unconvincing treble.

Dekklis stopped. Showed empty hands. "First Scout Szanys Dekklis. Second Legion, Sixth Cohort." She pulled the collar of her shirt aside. Bared the House sigil on her shoulder. "Let me pass, Mila."

"My orders are no one gets through the line."

"I'm not no one," Dekklis said patiently. "I outrank you. And I'm on Senate business."

She'd got the soldier's partners' attention, too, by now. Three young faces staring back at her. Hell and damn. There should've been a senior trooper among them at least. It might be that Istel was right about Illhari troops.

"First Scout Szanys Dekklis," she repeated. "With the Sixth. I have a report for the Senate."

That got a flicker of recognition, and a look traded among them. "About Taliri," Dekklis said, with the exaggerated patience of a woman about to lose hers. "You understand this is urgent, Milae. And above your rank."

"First Scout," the tall woman repeated. It sounded partway between an address and a question. "How did you end up in the Suburba?"

As if that were the important question. Not *what about the Taliri?*, not *let me get my commander.* Either this soldier was criminally green, or whoever'd given her orders was more formidable than a highborn scout out of uniform.

Dekklis thought about the knife at her belt, and the pair in her boots, and began to plan how she could get past this woman and her partners. Blood would start the riot in earnest.

But the Sixth also had a reputation for take-no-toadshit. A man's command. Northern. Border. Dekklis put on her best cold-eyed stare. Tried to look like someone who'd walked with ghosts and seen a dead woman sit up and talk. "Trooper. Move aside. Do it *now*."

The three shared another look. The tall one swallowed. "Yes, First Scout."

They made room for her to squirt between them and the stone wall. Dekklis nodded a terse thanks and stalked through the gap they left her. Now all she had to do was get through the rest of the lines. Well, she could do that. Here highborn and straight-backed was the camouflage.

Only a few heads turned as she passed, and one of them was Optio Nezari—the left side of whose face was still lumpy, whose nose would never recover from Istel's fists. Nezari left off whatever conversation she was having with the centurion. Dekklis pretended not to see her. Kept on marching

please, foremothers

and hoped she'd get to the Tiers before Nezari caught her.

"First Scout!" flung at her back like a javelin. "First Scout!" And then, even louder, too close to pretend to ignore: "Szanys Dekklis!"

Hell and damn. Dekklis spun on her heel. Nezari came panting up to her. Someone

a rabbit, Dek

was not used to running in armor. Sweat rivered down Nezari's temples.

Dekklis saluted. "Optio."

"First Scout." Nezari returned the salute. "I have a message for you."

Dekklis raised eyebrows. Her heart battered the inside of her chest. "For me."

"Yes, First Scout. From Senator Szanys. She wants you in the Senate immediately."

* * *

Tsabrak led them into the badlands, backtrailing the thread of the black river until it disappeared into the ghost-roads version of Illharek. The cave looked exactly as it had all the other times. Just an empty opening, a pattern of jagged stone and shadow.

Tsabrak stopped at the threshold.

"In there," he said.

Veiko stopped beside the smaller man. Ghost. Whatever. The Dvergir's head stopped at Veiko's shoulder. It would be easy, he thought, to underestimate such a small people. The Alviri tribes had once. And this man, in particular—dead or not, ghost or not—made Veiko's skin itch.

"I will follow you," he told Tsabrak. "I will help you. But the fight is yours to begin."

Tsabrak turned to look at him then. Bared his teeth. "No, skraeling. *He* started it. I'll finish it."

Then he stalked into the cave, dragging the shadows behind him like a cloak. Light followed him, a shaft of cold grey the same color as the sky. But it was bright enough that a man might see where he stepped. Enough that a man might see the black river, gleaming in its banks, winding deeper in the cave.

Taru cocked her head like a raven listening for the screams of the dying. "There is a large spirit down there," she said. "And there is blood already drawn and exchanged. If you mean to do this, go now."

Veiko loosened the axe. Loosened his shoulders, too. He rubbed the heel of his left hand across his chest. Felt the thump come up through bone. The last time he'd felt this pounding, he'd been fevered and dying. Having visions. Caught on the border of living and dead. But he had his dog with him this time, one step ahead. Had Taru beside him.

The black river ended in a lake, or began there, at the bottom of the cave. That was the same as true-Illharek. But where that cave was lit by witchfire and torch, all sharp shadows and contrast, and massive, this one was small enough a man might see across it. Tsabrak had drawn the darkness aside. Left the stone banks smooth and empty, the whole cavern rendered twilight. Of Tsabrak himself, there was no sign.

The God, however, was easy to see. He crouched beside the lake like a firedog, one hand down for balance, the other curled against his chest. Veiko saw blood on the stone. Dark smears, still gleaming slick.

The God looked up, his eyes glowing like Briel's from this distance. Then he rose, a slow unfolding of shadow. His grin split his face like an axe blade, wide and sharp.

"Veiko Nyrikki," he said. His voice rolled across the cave like a fog, filling the cracks and the whole space before rising up, swelling. "I wondered when you'd come."

Taru grunted. "Does *every* spirit know your name?"

Veiko matched her murmur. "Only the Illhari gods." Then he raised his voice, and both hands. "It seemed I must. You would not come to me."

The God's attention seized on the upraised axe. "Are you here to kill me, skraeling? In *my* home?"

Veiko shrugged. He spotted Tsabrak creeping around the lake's perimeter. The light avoided him. Found rock and water to settle on, patches of pallid illumination.

The God did not appear to notice. He stood straight now, hands outstretched in an insincere welcome. The right one still wept, dripping at intervals. Steam curled where the blood struck the rock.

Veiko took another step. Behind him, Taru muttered something that sounded like *fool.*

"I did not come to kill you," said Veiko. "*I* do not want your power."

The Laughing God's head cocked. His eyes flared and flickered. "*You* do not. Then who does?"

"I do." Tsabrak rose from the shadows, casting them off like a cloak. A heartbeat's pause as he faced his God for the first time and saw himself recognized in the God's faint recoil.

Then that heartbeat ended. Tsabrak lunged forward. Swiped at the God, and missed, and swung again, bare-handed. The God spilled out of the way. Like a thick liquid, Veiko thought, ink or blood. He jabbed his hand at Tsabrak, hooked his fingers and pulled. Blood sprayed onto the stone.

It was as if his fingers had become knives. Or claws. A sobering thought. Veiko had not known the God could do that. But he did know that blood here wasn't truly blood. He had the scars on his
soul

leg to prove it. And Tsabrak had much less soul to lose than the God.

Tsabrak tried to retreat, but the God was much quicker. He caught Tsabrak midstep. Struck him in the shoulder and threw him sideways. Tsabrak staggered for balance, and before he got it back, the God was on him. He plunged one fist into Tsabrak's belly, as if the ghost were no more solid than water.

Tsabrak screamed. The God laughed, and the whole world shivered. His hands moved in Tsabrak's gut. A second scream.

Veiko started forward. Small steps to test his footing on the stone, to test his leg. He shifted into a run.

Taru's voice followed him. "Do not let him touch you. *Hurry.*"

Tsabrak saw him. His hands reached, like a drowning man's.

The God's head snapped around. His laughter shivered and died.

"Veiko Nyrikki!" he roared, and pulled his hand clear. Tsabrak dropped like a wet sack.

Veiko did not think about mortal wounds or what those clawed hands could do to him, or how fast the God came at him. Bears were that quick. Rock leopards. Svartjagr, too, when they wanted a flatcake.

He folded sideways as the God struck. Felt the fist whip past him, the heat of it. Saw the jagged fingertips, dark with Tsabrak's blood. Then, as the God realized he'd missed, as he began to recoil, Veiko brought his axe down.

It was exactly like cutting a man. The same hitch as the metal met bone, the same spray of

not

blood. Same hot, wet, and salty where it touched his lips.

"Skraeling."

The God sounded surprised. He raised his stump between them. The blood had already thickened. Only a trickle now, running down the God's arm. Impossible to tell exactly where those bonfire eyes were looking, yes, but a man could not mistake the sudden flare in their sockets.

Helgi barked. Taru shouted. Veiko threw himself sideways and back. The blast of heat and flame missed him, only just, singeing hair and beard.

He had not known that the God could do *that*, either.

Veiko landed hard on hip and thigh and skidded. Put an arm out for balance and left some skin behind. But he did not drop the axe. Got himself stopped, got his knees back under him. Veiko had a single heartbeat to consider how much this would hurt. To wonder what Snow would do when she found out what happened. What would happen to Logi, to Briel. And then he pushed all that aside and stood up.

Then Helgi was there, his grey bulk between Veiko and the God. Veiko hefted the axe, still dripping with the God's blood.

"You took my axe again, Laughing God. What will you give in return?"

"I will eat your heart." The God's eyes flared, bright enough Veiko had to squint. "I will *unmake* you, skraeling."

Veiko chopped, sudden and savage. Helgi lunged, snapping, from the other side. The God swiped at the dog, swinging the stump of his arm like a club. Veiko heard the hollow thump, the startled yip, as the blow brushed Helgi aside like a puppy, sent him rolling toward the lake. The God spun back, impossibly fast, his hand jabbing low beneath Veiko's swing, intending to open his guts.

Faster than a bear. Faster than Briel's greed. Veiko threw himself backward, sideways. Landed badly this time, in a sprawl on the edge of the lake. He felt the first bite of black water tug at his sleeve.

The God laughed. White fire raged in his sockets. The shadows fled, scattering in his wake, washing over the place where Tsabrak had fallen. A place that was suddenly empty.

Veiko grinned.

Tsabrak lunged at the God, sudden and graceless. He looked horrible—skin gone grey, all the color washed out of eyes and hair. A man made of fog, wisping away on the edges. But that was hate in his eyes, and rage, and a fire that was no less hot than the God's. He stagger-lunged at the God's back and thrust his arm elbow-deep.

The God threw his head back. Shrieked. Flailed and twisted trying to reach Tsabrak with his remaining hand. He overbalanced, staggered left and right and twisted, falling onto his knees. Fire ran down his face like tears. Tsabrak stood behind him, with both hands buried in his back. Veiko heard a crack that sounded like ice breaking. A wet, tearing noise. Black seeped on the sand, which might have been shadows and was not, no, not here. The God sprawled flat on his belly now, his ribs cracked and spread away from his spine like wings. Tsabrak knelt on either side of his hips, rummaging through the God like a man looking for a small item in the bottom of a pack.

The God was looking at Veiko. Eyes down to coals now. Cracked smile, crumbling at the edges. "Snowdenaelikk," leaked through his lips, spilled like glass on the stone. "Breaker of bargains. There will be payment for this, skraeling. Tell her that."

"Shut it," Tsabrak said. Then he pulled the God's lungs out and laid them on his shoulders. Plunged his hands back into the God. Held up a thick reddish-black thing. It twitched and pumped.

Incredibly, impossibly, the God began to laugh. The lungs quivered on his shoulder blades.

And he kept laughing, even when Tsabrak tore off a chunk of the heart and put it in his mouth. Madness in that laughter. Malice.

The ground shivered and bucked. Veiko had felt that before, when Snow had tried conjuring too deep in the Wild and backlash had rear-ranged the terrain. He joined Helgi back on the ground, as he had then. Rode out the tremors on hands and knees.

The storm-feeling was back, crawling across his skin until every hair stood up. That was witchery. Godmagic. Spirit magic, yes, which was the same thing—but more magic than any spirit should have. The accumulation of hundreds of souls, offered up, taken, devoured by the God, and eaten by Tsabrak in turn.

There was very little left of the old Laughing God now. A little ash, a wet smear on the rock. Tsabrak seemed larger. The shadows flickered and pooled around him, moving like fine silk in an absent breeze. He was more beautiful now than he had been. Beautiful like winter or wildfire.

A sudden pain in Veiko's arm made him catch his breath. Felt like sharp things driven deep into flesh. Like a bite, or claws. He thought, for a heartbeat, that the God's hand had leapt off the stone and attacked him. Foolish. The hand was still lying where it had fallen, and the God was far past attacking anyone. But the discomfort was not his imagining. Veiko shifted the axe to his left hand. Folded his arm against his chest. He threw a quick glance down at it, found his sleeve unmarked and untouched. But there was blood soaking through the weave, spreading spots that looked exactly like the pattern a dog's jaws might make. But not Helgi, who was sitting beside him, whose jaws were much wider.

His *living* dog.

That realization brought another jagged pain, in his skull this time. And this one came with a wash of sensation: a svartjagr's dizzy vantage, smudged red impressions of darkness and terror and temper.

He shoved Briel out.

Not now.

Taru touched his arm. Tasted the wetness that came away on her fingers and frowned.

"I smell blood." And oh, that was the old God's tone, sheathed in Tsabrak's voice. At least it was Tsabrak's red-dark eyes staring back at him, and not the God's flames. "We remember how you smell, Veiko Nyrikki."

Godmagic and soul-theft hummed under Veiko's skin, crackled in his braids. His flesh pulled at him, pinpricks along his right arm. "It is no matter."

"No. No, I think it matters very much." Tsabrak flowed upright, liquid shadow growing solid. "Your body is in danger. *Her* godsworn have found you. I warned you, yeah? You have to go back."

That was sense. But that might also, by a powerful, proud spirit, be taken as acquiescence. A noidghe did not do a spirit's bidding. Veiko *would not* obey Tsabrak, in this or anything. Istel was back there, with Logi and Briel. His body was not undefended. He opened his mouth to refuse, even as Briel battered against him, even as his

soul

blood dripped down his arm.

Taru squeezed his wrist hard enough to make his fingers tingle. *Go away* in that grip.

"I will deal with this," she said, and set herself between him and the new Laughing God. She seemed very small suddenly. Very grey and dim, against Tsabrak's vivid dark. She was an old spirit, an older noidghe. She could handle Tsabrak.

Or he could eat her.

"I won't eat anyone. I'm your ally, Veiko Nyrikki." That was entirely Tsabrak's grin, razor-thin. "And you're going to need me."

CHAPTER EIGHTEEN

Nezari sent Dekklis into the Tiers with an escort of three more young and green troopers. They were very serious. Very much like stones, they talked so much. It had to be orders. Had to be Nezari's edict that they answer no questions, even those perfectly reasonable ones like *why are there troops on the 'Walk?* or *was it the Sixth who came back?* or *what are your damn names, you three?*

There was black irony. With a partner like Istel, she'd gotten used to quiet. But these three made Istel—hell, made *Veiko*—seem like chattering children. Made her feel the idiot, too, getting flat silence for answers. At least the anger burned a hole in the worry coiled all through her gut.

Until they got to the Senate plaza. Then her anger froze solid. The whole place was empty. Blood reek, blood smears. And bodies, oh foremothers. Three. And she knew them, a trio from the Sixth's First Squad, the ones who stayed closest to Rurik. Veterans, all of them. Rurik's personal guard, *dead* on the plaza. The big doors to the curia sat open a handsbreadth, spilling a narrow band of light across the pavement. Dekklis guessed that there were still senators inside if Nezari's three had brought her here on Senator Szanys's orders. *Her mother* in there, and Rurik's troops dead out here. So where was Rurik?

Pointless to ask her escort anything, like *the hell happened here?*
Battle, clearly. Legion troops cut down in front of the Senate. And from
the stiff unconcern of her escorts, they'd known about it.

"You can go," she told them. "I can find the senator from here."

The trio exchanged glances. The oldest, perhaps twenty, cleared her
throat. "Our orders—"

Dekklis didn't raise her voice. Didn't turn her head. Didn't look at
them, foremothers, she dared not, or she'd gut all three.

"*Fuck* your orders," she said. "Tell Nezari I'm delivered."

Dekklis walked away from them at a brisk legion march. The plaza
seemed larger when it was empty. Svartjagr perched on the buildings
like snake-necked, silent crows. She felt those eyes on her as she crossed
the stones. Felt the brush and kiss of strange svartjagr minds, like a
cutpurse testing purse strings. Curious. Hungry. Patient.

She cocked a glance at them. Pretended the row of ember-hot eyes
didn't bother her, staring back. One of them flared its wings and hissed.
It was bigger than Briel.

Svartjagr don't attack people, Szanys.

No. People attacked people. Svartjagr cleaned up the mess.

Dekklis took the curia steps two at a time. She got to the top without losing her breath. Marched to the doors. Laid her hand against the
wood, and pushed, and slipped inside.

Chaos. Hell and damn. Somebody, maybe several bodies, had bled
in here, too. The scented oil in the lamps couldn't mask the smell. The
flames in those lamps showed the source of it clearly, streaked red on
the floor.

People had died in the Senate before. But there'd been an actual
fight in here. Long strips of cloth on the floor that had once belonged
to someone's robes. Smaller patches from the bench cushions, and tufts
of stuffing. Score marks and scrapes on the polished floor. The consul's
chair—alone of all the seats in here, made of wood—had been split
like kindling.

There were no corpses in here at all. Only a clump of living bodies in the corner farthest from the door, near the top of the rows of stone seats. Maybe twenty women in here, of the eligible hundred. And not, she noted, a soldier among them. Which didn't make sense, given the blood, unless a bunch of unarmed senators weren't afraid of another attack. Unless the attackers were dead. Unless.

She remembered what Soren had told her, and thought grimly that she might know why these women weren't worried.

"Dekklis!" One of the senators detached herself from the group. She came down in a flutter of robes, like the wings of some strange insect. The robes were, Dek noted, too small for her, baring wrists and ankles. Her hair was improperly loose.

And she should not have been here at all.

Dekklis waited on the curia floor, with a soldier's stoicism, for her second oldest sister to cross that bloodstained floor.

And then she said, in her best soldier voice, "Maja," before that same sister had come to a stop. "The hell happened out there? Where's our mother?"

"Dekklis." Maja reached for her. Put her hands on Dek's arms and squeezed. "I'm so glad you're here. I thought, when they couldn't find you—"

Dekklis stared down at the hands on her arm. Slender fingers, delicate, that had never slung metal or dressed wounds. Smooth little hands, highborn fragile. They would break very easily. Dekklis resisted the urge to take them in her own hands and squeeze.

"Slowly, Maja. Tell me what happened."

"The K'Hess third son, what was his name?"

"First Spear Rurik."

"Yes, Rurik. He arrived just after sixteenth mark, came straight to the Senate. He barged through the doors. This is what the Reforms get us! You should have heard him, Dekklis. He spoke to Consul Stratka as if she were his equal!"

Dekklis had years of exposure to K'Hess Rurik. They had come up together in the Illhari garrison. He'd gone north a half year before she did, marching to join the Sixth, made First Spear in five short years. An Illhari, even a soft-bodied senator, would have to be deaf and blind not to know *who* he was—third son of K'Hess, brilliant fighter. As good as a woman. Cool under pressure. Logical. Not prone to those rages for which men were famous. If Rurik had indulged some of those masculine passions as he climbed the ranks—if his temper among his troops became legendary—then it was for its volume, and little else. Rurik didn't lose control. He might get angry, but he wouldn't just snap. And he'd never forgotten protocol in all the years Dek had known him, on either side of command.

"Why?" she asked before Maja could say anything else.

"What?"

"He had to have a reason if he came up here. He asked for entrance, and someone said no? One of those polished toadshits outside, maybe?"

"Dekklis!"

"Hell and damn, Maja." She wanted to sit down. Her knees hurt. Her shoulders did. Every bit of her. "The man's fought his way down from Cardik, his people are wrecked, and some overfed gate-guard pulled attitude with him."

"You weren't here," Maja said mildly. "I can't see how you'd know *what* happened."

"And you were?"

"Of course." Maja folded her arms across her robes. "We all were."

"All."

"Jikka. Disar. Me. Only you were missing, little sister. We sent for you, but the garrison didn't know where you were." Maja raised an eyebrow.

Dek had never been good at politics, never good at reading people, and her skills hadn't improved in Cardik. She was missing clues as obvious as the blood on the floor, wasn't she, clues stamped in Maja's crooked smile, in her too-bright eyes.

What Dekklis could tell, clear enough, was that Maja wanted an answer to the question she hadn't quite asked—

Where were you?

—and Dek wasn't about to tell her. She folded her arms across her chest. Wished, for the hundredth time, for armor and sword. For Istel at her back. For Snowdenaelikk, hell and damn, and tall, grim Veiko. For *Briel*, if it came to that.

She swept her eyes around the chamber again. Only a handful of senators up there, most of them looking down now. Damned if she recognized any of them. That wouldn't be surprising, given the length of her absence, given her political disinterest. But they were all young faces, somewhere in their third or fourth decades. Faces her age. Or Maja's.

"Mother," she said sharply. "Mother wanted to see me."

"*Senator Szanys* wanted to see you," Maja said. Her crooked smile straightened out. "Yes, she does."

"Then where is she?" Growing coldness in her belly, creeping up through chest and throat. "She's not dead. Maja. Tell me she isn't."

"Dekklis." Maja moved her hands on Dek's shoulders. "Listen to me. When K'Hess Rurik arrived, he demanded to address the Senate and the consul. Of course, he was told he could not. He insisted. There was a fight between the Sixth and our loyal guards here."

"No. Not Rurik. He would not attack his own—"

"But he did," Maja said gently. Her eyes did not match her tone. Glittering now, like chips of glass. "Our mother tried to intervene. She was unarmed. I'd like to think it was an accident, what he did to her."

She might not be good at politics, but Dekklis knew toadshit when she heard it. She recognized a feint, too, when she saw one. Maja meant to draw her into grief, or rage, or some off-balance place.

Like a man.

She settled. Steadied. "You're saying Rurik killed her."

"I'm saying she died in the fighting. Dek." Maja's hand rubbed her arm. "I know this is shocking."

Shocking had been finding K'Hess Kenjak dead on a pole. Shocking had been walking the ghost roads with Teslin and Barkett. *Shocking* had been what Soren had told her.

And all of those things had been true.

Dekklis closed her eyes. Let her breath hitch around the cold stab of grief. Felt the anger fill in behind it.

"She wasn't the only casualty," Maja was saying. "Rurik went quite mad. It took several of us to subdue him."

Us. As if Maja had been anywhere near the fighting.

"And you're all that's left?" Dekklis waved a blind hand. "What about Disar and Jikka?"

"They're fine. They went home. Most everyone else has, too. The rest of the Sixth fled."

More toadshit. There were only three corpses on the plaza. Rurik's closest associates, his guards, the ones he'd take as his escort to the Senate. He wouldn't've dragged what was left of the Sixth up here. Not after what was likely a running skirmish all the way from Cardik. Rurik wasn't an idiot. Wouldn't bring bloodied troops into Illharek unannounced. Wouldn't leave the roads undefended, either, from Taliri. He'd have left the Sixth in the forests, outside the gates. Which explained the legion on the Riverwalk. They were there to keep the Sixth *out*.

And Maja expected her to believe the toadshit. That, clear as glass on her face. Eyebrows arched, level lips, the perfect image of a concerned daughter. A solicitous sister.

No. Not daughter. A daughter might weep. A sister might. But a senator maintained decorum.

Dekklis swallowed and hoped Maja heard grief, and not rage, coming out of her throat. "Those are our mother's robes."

"Yes. Clean ones, obviously. They're the only Senate robes I have—"

"Jikka's the eldest."

"Jikka declined the appointment."

That wasn't impossible. Jikka had no particular love for politics. The eldest daughter of Szanys Elia preferred her books. Would have, Dek thought bleakly, gone to the Academy, except that Elia had not allowed it.

Maja might permit it now. And Jikka might not even be sorry their mother was dead, if it got her a wedge of freedom. Or she might be very sorry and soon to meet with an accident. And so might Dekklis herself if she stepped wrong. Maja didn't know her well, not anymore. Maja remembered the woman she had been—reckless, defiant, willful. Hell. Maja might even expect her to be pleased about Elia's death.

Maja expected *something*, damn sure. Her strange half smile growing stiff on her lips, eyes turning arrow sharp.

Dekklis remembered the Archives: dust and mildew, cave-cool and filled with witchfire shadows. Remembered Snow pushing a scroll in front of her.

Read it.

Remembered the archaic, elaborate script that said how the Purge had happened. Mother against daughter, sister against sister, to root out Tal'Shik's godsworn. This—what Soren had told her, what she saw now in Maja's cold eyes—was the Purge all over again. Except it was Tal'Shik and her godsworn behind this—don't call it a Purge, no, call it retreat. Regression.

The opposite of purge is swallow, Dek.

That's what Istel would say, with a flicker-fast quirk of his lips.

"Dekklis?"

Pay attention.

She drew a breath. Let it out slowly. Said, somehow steady, "Senator Szanys," and managed a perfectly adequate, perfectly polite legion bow.

"No need for that." Maja's smile said otherwise. She liked the deference. "I am still your sister."

"Where's K'Hess?" she asked, and braced herself for *dead* and *floating in the Jokki*.

But Maja said, "K'Hess? I imagine she's in her house, where she's been all winter. Why?" And then, a little more softly, "Are you looking for allies, little sister, or enemies?"

Dekklis shrugged. "I meant K'Hess Rurik."

Maja relaxed. "The traitor awaits execution."

"And the rest of the Sixth, once you catch them?"

Maja's lips clamped together. "They will be handled."

It was the way she said it, *handled*, as if the Sixth was so much debris. Dek's temper snapped before she realized it. Suddenly hot, where she'd been cold, all the fatigue washed away.

"They're still Above. That's why our troops are all over the Riverwalk. To keep them out."

"There are Taliri on the roads if the traitor spoke true." Maja shrugged. "Let them find the Sixth first. It may take time to mobilize the Illharek garrison to go to their aid. It may even be that the Sixth will break before we arrive. But the Taliri will be much weaker when we meet them."

"You're saying the Senate will let the Sixth die out there."

"They serve Illharek."

"And who do you serve?"

Maja arched her eyebrows. "Illharek, of course."

"I don't see *of course* here. Elder sister. Senator. You're Tal'Shik's, not Illharek's."

She was expecting denial, maybe. Protest. At least some pretense at shame or shock. But Maja only smiled. "I'm Illhari. And Illharek is Tal'Shik's. The Taliri are a test of our loyalty, that's all. *We* are her daughters, but we must prove our worth first. We must take the Republic back from the godless and the men."

Snowdenaelikk had warned her. "How many women died here today?"

"They were no good for Illharek. Dekklis. The consul wasn't going to act in time to stop the Taliri."

"And our mother?"

Maja's face might've been a summer sky, serene and cloudless. "Our mother would have divided the Senate even further."

"You mean, she wouldn't've sold us to heresy and superstition."

"We haven't sold anything. Dekklis. We've *returned* where we belong. The Republic was greatest when we served—"

"That's the right word," Dek snapped. "We were servants. Toadfucking bondies. That's *all* we were to Tal'Shik."

Maja's face shifted through a dozen expressions. Settled on something that reminded Dek of their mother. "Is that treason I hear, First Scout?"

Dekklis gazed steadily into her sister's face until Maja had to blink. Then, very softly, "I know my oaths."

Her biggest regret was that her knife was not a legion sword. But its metal was true Illhari steel, and it had a soldier's muscle and skill to drive it. Through stolen robes, through flesh and fat and bone.

Maja stared down at the hilt in her chest. Folded her fingers around Dekklis's. And then she crumpled. Dekklis let her keep the knife. Turned on her heel and walked back out onto the plaza. There were troopers already gathered. She walked through them, steady march. Did not look back when the shrieks echoed off the stones. When the shouts came to stop her, arrest her, *get that woman.*

A trooper knew how to march. Left. Right. Never vary, never flinch, never flag. Distractions did not matter. Distractions: the faces around her, soldiers she'd known now for weeks, who called her name and asked what'd happened. Who were not Rurik, or Istel, or anyone for whom she *would* stop.

She made it to the bridge before they caught her.

* * *

A noidghe learns early that the spirit easily forgets its flesh. That he needs time to remember how skin feels, how muscles work, once he returns to his body. A noidghe does *not* plan to return to a camp with the fire gone out and smoke heavy in the air. The inconveniently full moon bleached part of the campsite white and turned the rest into blackest shadow. Veiko's eyes could not seize on any solid shape for several precious blinks.

His kit was where he'd left it, hanging off a branch. But his bow was gone, and the arrows. The axe, too, which brought a moment's panic before he saw it on the ground between his blanket and the dead fire. Where he had *not* left it, no, but where a man might roll and grab it easily on the way from supine to standing.

If that man were not still wobbly as newborn takin, perhaps. If that man's spirit was not half on the ghost roads, worrying about Taru and the new Laughing God. Worrying about things that would not help him now, that might get him killed.

Veiko rolled onto his knees. His feet. Logi was with him, loyal and worried. He gripped the dog's scruff. Istel must be nearby. Briel must. And the attackers, unless Briel and Istel had killed them all already. He listened past the blood-thump in his own ears.

And heard the unmistakable twang of a bowstring, followed by a howl of pain, a stream of Dvergiri invective. Chaos erupted. Bodies crashing in the brush, Briel's hunting keen, a brace of wordless shouts. The bow sang again and again, moving away now, up the ridge, as Istel retreated.

Veiko eased a step deeper into the shadows. He might, if he were fortunate, creep undetected away from the campsite. Away from the smoke that any fool with a nose could follow. There was no knowing how many were here. But surely not all of them would follow the arrows. Surely some would come here to investigate the smoke. With luck, he might avoid them, climb the ridge and rejoin Istel. A hunter and a legion scout together might make short work of Illhari who were not used to forests. Unless these were Taliri godsworn. Then the fight would be much more difficult.

Logi's growl shivered against his leg. And then the dog was gone, a scuff and whisper in the brush. And then, louder: raised voices, drifting downslope.

"—up here—"

"—that's not—"

Istel had drawn them away, but Istel would not be able to take them all. Istel was one man.

Veiko set his teeth together. Abandoned silence and moved upslope, fast as he could manage. Startled a Dvergir woman in the trees, no one he recognized. She had a seax in one hand, held down and sideways—not ready for a battle, no, she was more worried about low-hanging limbs. She stopped when she saw him. Hesitated for one startled moment.

Veiko did not. Cut crossways and up, one motion, with the axe. He spat her blood out of his mouth and kept moving as she dissolved into shrieks and dying. Bad luck, oh ancestors, that she had not died at once. He might as well set the trees on fire and announce his position.

But he might draw them off Istel, anyway. Divide them.

And then what?

Hope that he and Istel were the better fighters. Hope that Logi and Briel tipped the balance. Hope, and cleave through enemy flesh until they were dead, or he was.

He met one more in the trees. This woman had two arrows in her already, bubbling blood out of her nose and mouth. She drew metal anyway, swiped at him with a seax just like Snow's. Gurgled "Here! Here!" before he chopped her quiet. He heard Logi's sharp yelp, and a louder snarl, and then Veiko broke out of the trees.

The ridgeline was all rocks and short grass, bleached white in the moonlight. Istel knelt at the apex, down on one knee, arrows thrust into the dirt beside his foot for quick draw and fire. One woman, already fallen, writhed and clawed at the shaft through her thigh. A second crossed the remaining open space as Istel nocked another arrow. The woman ducked and rolled as he let fly, and the shaft clattered into the trees. Then the woman came up cutting and launched at Istel.

There was a blur and flash where steel caught the moonlight. Then Istel was clear again. But that was blood bubbling between his fingers where they pressed against his belly. He dropped the bow. Dragged his trooper's knife out, left-handed.

Shee-oop ricocheted off trees and stars. The woman hesitated—looked up, which was instinct and fatal and foolish. Briel's tail licked across her face, and she toppled backward, shrieking.

Istel finished her. Wiped the blade on his thigh and bared teeth at Veiko, *glad you're alive* and *good fight* and *this hurts*, all together. And said, Istel-quiet, "Think that's all of them? —Oh. Fuck and damn."

Veiko took that for question and answer, for a warning. Turned fast and saw the woman standing at the edge of the tree line. Violet fire shimmered in her hands. Godsworn. Oh ancestors.

Veiko knew what she was, what that meant, what power she could use against him. Knew, and grabbed for the bow anyway, to put a shaft in her eye. He had stopped Tal'Shik that way once. He would stop her godsworn just as well.

Except the shadows seemed to have grown solid around him. Seemed to have grown weapons and armor. Seemed to be women, yes, too many for the bow. Veiko dropped it. Stepped in front of Istel and swung the axe and felt it bite flesh. Heard Briel's keening. Heard Istel curse. Heard a woman scream. Saw the flash of moonlight on metal and the godsworn's violet fire.

But he did not see the blow that felled him.

CHAPTER NINETEEN

Briel wanted Snow's attention. Pressure on the inside of her skull, bordering on pain. Little fingers of lightning that came at odd moments, blasting her concentration to cinders. Briel liked to share: a stray cat, a good breeze, a dozen different experiences of being Briel. Briel's insistence, though, her persistence—that was the worry. Snow could imagine a dozen horrors, most of them ending with Veiko dead or bleeding.

Snow stuffed that thought back into a corner. Covered it up. And worried that Briel had leaked through her blocks at all. A year ago, Snow would not have been able to stop her. Now she could shut Briel out, thanks to Veiko. She and Veiko and Briel, that was three, and anyone's guess where Logi and Dek and Istel ranked in that pack. A sending spread out among several minds wasn't as strong, as blinding, as impossible to ignore. Or maybe it was because Veiko was noidghe. Maybe it was because *she* was.

That Briel had forced her way through suggested that Veiko had got himself into trouble, yeah, but he had Istel and Logi and Briel for help. She had no one at the moment. Solitude should have made a *look-away* conjuring simple to cast and maintain, except she had a godsrotted svartjagr hammering at her concentration. She'd had to stop and reconjure twice already, fuck and damn.

Belaery could've turned the whole Suburba blind, walked from Tano gate to the Tebir to the Street of Apothecaries without anyone seeing her, or stepping on her, or ramming their godsrotted handcart into her heels. *Belaery* wouldn't be sweat soaked and flirting with a backlash-sized headache from a half-dozen failed conjurings. *Belaery* wouldn't be wishing Briel would shut up, or worrying about a partner who was perfectly capable of taking care of himself. Belaery would be worrying about herself, ever and always.

So try that, yeah?

Snow reached into Illharek's stone guts, into the moist and stinking air. Drew from the Jaarvi's deep dark, from the Tano and the Jokki. Pulled from the real fire in the corner barrels: this street was two blocks too poor for witchfire street lamps. Its residents had to make do with whatever would burn. Drop it into the barrels, keep the street lit, never mind the oily smoke.

Conjuring didn't care what the fire burned or that the air stank. Conjuring pulled and shaped that fire. Borrowed it. Changed it and bent it so that eyes followed its light, and not her. *Look away.* Then she stepped back into the street, wrapped tight in a *look away* that she needed all the more because of the volume of traffic in the Suburban streets.

There were just too many people, and the wrong kinds. Farmers should've gone home candlemarks ago. Fuck and damn, there were *midtowners* still here, when they should've gone up to their dinners a candlemark ago, with their robes hiked to just above ankles so the silk didn't drag Suburban muck. Pretty little city boots, soft soled and embroidered and meant to show disposable income. A shopkeep saw clothes like that, she reckoned a customer. A cutpurse saw them, she reckoned a target. The Laughing God's right hand, well, she just saw people talking. Information.

Snow drifted toward the midtowners, close enough to smell stale perfume over sour, to mark thin-lipped fear on midtown faces, to hear hushed and half-panicked:

"—we don't have enough coin for an inn—"

and

"—can't stay here, are you mad?"

and

"—the legion can't stay on the 'Walk for*ever*—"

Oh fuck and damn. There were soldiers on the Riverwalk, cutting one half of the city off from the other. The legion had done that in Cardik. It must be the Taliri, then, finally arrived.

Snow reckoned *that* was the reason for Briel's distress. Raiders in the forests. Veiko might have had to move. He'd go north if he had any wits. Or west. Go *away*, out of Illhari territory.

Pain rippled through her skull, jaw to crown. Settled in solid behind her eyes. That was an unholy trio of conjuring, svartjagr, her own roiling worry. She could let Briel in, find out what had happened—and lose the toadfucking conjuring *again*. Everyone on the motherless street would see her. And that was exactly what she did not want. Rata had eyes down here, which meant Tal'Shik did. And right now, they didn't need to see her. She'd spent too much of the last two weeks parading one end of the streets to the other, drawing eyes and attention. Now she needed to pass unseen.

Veiko was too smart to get caught, but sometimes smart didn't matter. She needed someplace safe so she could let Briel in. So she could reckon what to do next.

Go home.

Snowdenaelikk scuttled and dodged the crowds, messy-fast now. The conjuring snagged and tore like an old cloak. Left bits of itself on whatever it touched, so that by the time she got to the Street of Apothecaries, she was visible. She was grateful, yeah, that this street was less packed than the others. Fewer people to notice a woman-shaped shadow flitting along the wall.

She shed the conjuring altogether at the shopfront. The shutters were down. But she could hear voices inside, and shouting. Sinnike. Daagné. Kaj, oh yes, in rare volume. And light, leaking through the third-floor shutters. *Her* apartment, and someone up there in it. Not Kaj, if she heard his voice downstairs. Not Veiko, unless he'd come back, and—she stomped back the little lurch in her chest—if he had, then Briel would have found her already. So there was someone else up there.

Fuck and damn.

Snow went round the side of the building. Climbed the spikes and carved handholds, the slim iron ladder that Veiko had called *treacherous* and *foolish* and she'd called *almost impossible* with fresh stitches in her arm. The arm only tweaked a little now as she hauled and stretched and spidered up two stories. Then it was quickfoot across the roof, mind the beams and loose tiles, and down the ladder on the other side. She dropped to the balcony and heard the iron groan. Crouched and listened at the door.

No *oof*. No *chrrip*. Shuffle-steps on the other side, stranger-steps, a gait she did not know. Faint click and creak as someone who was not Veiko crept up to the shuttered door.

She put one hand on the hilt of her seax. Laid the other on the latch. Waited until it turned under her palm. Then she grabbed it and pushed hard, all her weight. Thump as the door hit someone solid, and a squawk as that someone fell back. Snow waited a breath, drew the seax, and followed her blade through the doorway.

The body between her and the firedog cast long shadows. It was man shaped but not quite, something odd about the chest and forearms—fuck and damn, *swinging* at her, that was her toadfucking *stool*.

Snow jagged sideways, blocked with the blade, felt metal bite into wood. The man swinging the stool was Dvergir, a stranger. Amateur, too: he would not let go of the stool when she wrenched her blade sideways. Let himself be dragged off his balance. And he wasn't prepared when she reached over the stool and put the first two knuckles of her right fist into his nose.

That was the thing about noses. Didn't take much of an impact to get watering eyes, an instinctive flinch. An experienced brawler might keep coming despite all that, but this man let go of the stool. Staggered back with both hands clapped to his face. Tripped on his own heels and sat down hard.

Snow jerked her seax loose. Stepped over the fallen stool and pushed the shadows aside without thinking. She wanted to see this toadfucker who'd come at her in her own motherless *house*. Then she'd take his head back to Rata and *beat* her to death with it.

The stranger looked up at her, all eyes and hands. There was blood all over the front of his tunic, seeping between his fingers, mixing with snot and tears. The neck of his tunic fallen aside, so that she could see very clearly his House sigil.

Fuck and damn. Snow lowered the seax. Caught her breath and damn near laughed out loud.

"What *is* it with you K'Hess men?"

"Snowdenaelikk?" It came out *Thowdengeyelikk*.

And he knew her name, too. Perfect. She stole a fast look around the room. Nothing touched, nothing out of place—except there, yeah, that was Dek's sweater crumpled on the table, the too-big grey and brown thing that had made her look like a walking collection of twigs.

So. Szanys Dekklis had left her a gift. Well. Snow shoved the seax back in its sheath. "You have a name?"

"K'Hess Soren." He blinked. Took his hands off his face. "Szanys Dekklis brought me."

"I reckoned that. Where is she now?"

"I don't know."

"Of course you don't." Snow thrust her hand down at him. "All right. Get up."

He looked down at his hands. At the ruin of his shirt.

Laughing God defend her from highborn manners. "Foremothers' own sake, you want help up or not? I don't care about blood, yeah, long as it's not *mine*."

He blinked again. Then he put a hand in hers, let her draw him up. He wasn't a small man, as highborn went. A little taller than Kenjak had been, a little broader, more like his First Spear brother. But he had Kenjak's same highborn modesty, which made him look at the floor instead of her face. Blood dripped, and he tried to catch it.

"Leave it." The battle-rush abandoned her. Shaking hands, shaking knees, a distinct wish to sit down and drink. She righted the stool instead. Pointed at it. "Sit, yeah? Use your shirt to stop the bleeding. And then tell me why Dek thought I needed another injured K'Hess in my life."

"I was fine until you hit me."

"You're lucky that's all I did. Could've gutted you. Could've conjured you inside out, yeah?"

His gaze flickered to her ears, her hair, and dropped like a stone to the table. "I didn't think you'd come through the balcony door. I thought Domina Sinnike would've told you I was here."

"I didn't check with her. Didn't want to interrupt the domestic dispute I heard. Bet you're the reason for it."

Soren had rucked his shirt up, had the excess pressed against his face. Flat-bellied, ribs and muscle sliding under his skin. He was older than Kenjak by at least a handful of years. Still trim, despite what must be soft living. Maybe Dek'd meant him for a gift. Something pretty to distract her. A hostage.

Right. This time Snow did laugh out loud. She tried to imagine Dek staging a pre-Purge raiding, stealing men from her rivals' Houses. Then imagined her giving that prize to a half-blood, oh, what had Dek called her? Assassin, heretic, general blight on all that was proper and Illhari.

Soren rolled eyes at her. Wriggled out of the shirt altogether and rearranged it on his face, so that eyes and mouth were clear. "What's funny?"

"You, sitting there bleeding all over my floor. Why did Dek bring you to me?"

"She said I'd be safe." Faintly accusatory, quick stabbing stare.

"Safe from who? Who'd you think was going to come through that window?"

Soren got very still. Twisted his shirt between his fingers. Seemed oblivious to the trickle of blood running over lip and chin. "House Stratka's gone back to Tal'Shik. All the daughters. The consul knows, but she's scared. They were plotting against her. She knew it. Was trying to settle things. And it's not *just* Stratka. I think—*we* think—it's all through the Houses. Second and third daughters, mostly, a system of godsworn."

"We, who?"

"The men. The consorts. Szanys Dekklis, too." Defiantly now, for all that he would not meet her eyes: "They think we don't have brains enough to wear boots, but we can see what's happening around us."

"But you haven't done anything."

He slashed the bloody shirt left and right like a whip. "I told Szanys Dekklis what I knew. I came *here* with her."

"And you're attacking people with stools." Snow caught the shirt and twisted it into stillness. "There a shortage of loose furniture in the First Tier? The rest of the consorts have no hands? What's *wrong* with you men?"

His turn to laugh, sharp and startled. Snow seized the opportunity. Leaned over and pinched his proud highborn nose and tweaked it straight again. Guided the shirt back over his face, caught blood and yelp together. She squeezed his fingers.

"Hold that," she told him. "Gently. Don't press too hard. I'm trying to save your looks."

He blinked wetly at her. "You don't understand. We can't just . . . start fights. Up there. With them."

"No? You tried before? What's the worst they'll do, hit back?"

"She said you'd say that. Szanys Dekklis."

"Yeah? What else did she say?"

"You're a conjuror. A chirurgeon."

"That's obvious."

"And a heretic."

"Reckoned she'd slip that in, too." Snow pinched the bridge of her own nose. Squinted past her fingers. "How long ago did she leave you here?"

"A candlemark? I'm not sure. Not that long."

"Was she going back to the garrison? No, wait. You don't know. She didn't tell you, you didn't ask. Fuck and *damn* you highborn. Listen. The Riverwalk's got troops on it. No traffic's getting into the Tiers. I *thought* it was because the Taliri finally got here. But from what you say, it might well be a new Purge starting. And it doesn't matter. Dek might talk her way through the lines. Or they might arrest her."

Fuck and damn. Dek could say a lot if they asked hard enough. If they knew what questions to ask. Which, oh hell, with Tal'Shik's god-sworn in the Houses—they would.

K'Hess Soren's eyes were very wide, very dark. "What happens if they *have* arrested her?"

"Then this place won't be safe. Don't worry, yeah? I know people who'll hide you."

"The Laughing God's people." Faint smile that looked more like reflex. Something you did with your mouth when you talked to people. "I'll go with you. Assuming I have any choice."

Snow wished for Aneki and Still Waters, yeah, wished for a safe place to put this man. But failing that, well, "You don't."

Ari wouldn't kill him. Ari would do whatever she asked, he was so stupid-happy the God had returned. He'd protect Soren, best he could, at the bidding of the God's right hand.

Snowdenaelikk pinched the bridge of her own nose harder. Eyes closed, deep breaths. Motherless headache. Motherless svartjagr. Motherless panic clawing its way up her throat. Hers, Briel's, maybe both, didn't matter.

Bang! on the balcony.

Soren startled almost off his stool. Snow came around the table, ripping the blade out of its sheath. A second bang, fainter. Bigger than a rock, whatever it was. Not enough force to be an arm or a fist. Something thrown. Two somethings.

And then a hiss like cold water on coals. Snow's headache spiked from bad to blinding as Briel forced the sending through all her blocks.

See the shutters from the balcony railing. See a

self

Briel-sized dent in the wood. See Logi down in the alley, blood all over his fur. And no Veiko. Of course, no Veiko.

Snow lost her seax along the way to the door, heard the clatter. Tore the shutters open to Briel, hissing and hopping on the railing.

And drops of blood, one and two and twenty, plinking onto the iron balcony. Raining blood, hell. Raining idiots, more likely. Snow poked her head out and looked up. Found Istel coming down the ladder, one-armed, too late for *wait* and *the hell are you doing?*

She put hands on his legs. Worked them up hips and waist and steadied him. Remembered, afterthought, to drag the shadows around them. Too late, yeah, half the street must've noticed by now.

"You should've stayed in the alley," she told him. "I'd've let you in."

"Don't need the whole house knowing I'm here."

"Whole street's better?"

He grinned at her. He was grey around the eyes and mouth. "Grant me some skill, yeah? You didn't hear me coming. And no one ever looks up."

"They will if it's dripping blood." She let him in. Dragged shadows and shutters after them. And turned to find Istel and Soren eyeing each other. Istel, at least, had not reached for a weapon. She wondered if he could, with his arm wrapped across his guts. Holding them closed, if Briel's sending was accurate.

"K'Hess Soren," she said. "Second Scout Istel, Second Legion, Sixth Cohort. —Istel. *He's* what Dek was up to."

"Huh." Istel's lips stretched tight. "Never thought she much liked men. 'Specially not highborn."

"Never thought she much liked anyone. Can you get to the couch?"

"This is fine." Istel sat, hard, on the hearthstones. Leaned against the wall beside the firedog. "Couch is a long way."

This, from the man she'd left Above. He'd walked all that way. Fuck and damn. She knelt beside him. Plucked at the sopping wool shirt. "Who did this?"

The hole in Istel went past skin and muscle. That was bone winking out at her, a rib where it shouldn't be. And that wasn't the worst she could see. "Rags!" she snapped at Soren. "And fill that basin."

"Leave it." Istel closed his eyes. Tipped his head back. His breath leaked through his teeth. "I'm already dead."

"I'm the chirurgeon."

"Then you know there's no point, yeah?" Istel looked at her, eyes steady and his mouth hitched up tight in the corner. He'd seen battle before. He took the bloody shirt back from her and repacked it into the wound. "Veiko needs you. Tal'Shik's godsworn have him."

Her gut dropped. She traded a hot-coal stare with Briel. "Show me."

And Briel did, with the detail that Snow had trained her to notice, and a force Snow hadn't felt since Veiko's arrival. It went on a long time.

And when it was over, the headache drove Snow to her knees. She gritted her teeth against a backsurge of nausea.

Godsworn had him. Oh fuck and damn.

"Snowdenaelikk?" in the near distance, a not-quite-stranger's voice. A not-quite-stranger's touch on her arm. Gentle man, K'Hess Soren, she could tell that from the way he touched her, from the way he asked, "Are you all right?"

"Fine," she croaked out. Bitter and bile scalded her throat. She blinked through vision hazed grey as river fog. But she hadn't gone blind with the sending. And she would have if Veiko were dead.

Believe that.

She straightened. Wiped her mouth. Color came leaking back. The firedog's yellow glow. The grey and brown of Dek's sweater on the table. Briel's hot orange stare. And a dying Istel, nodding *I told you so* at her.

She stood up too fast. Damn near collided with Soren and the basin of water. Dodged around him. Left him to set it beside Istel and rummaged through her gear. Needle, thread, powders, and tinctures wouldn't help Istel. But this. She turned, tossed a pouch at him. "That's mossflower. Chew the leaves if it hurts." And to Soren, standing wide-eyed: "Wait here. I'll be back."

He was too well bred to grab at her. Made a knot of his hands instead. "Let me come with you."

"You don't know where I'm going." She added a knife to her left boot, match to the one already living in her right. Thought about hiding more sharp metal in her sleeves and rejected the idea. Long time since she'd done that, and now, right arm stitched and aching, a half-healed broken finger on the left, she'd only just drop the fucking things. She'd never been good at throwing blades. "Stay here. Help Istel."

"I'm past that, Snow." Istel, dry as dust. "You know it."

"Shut up." She wanted to say *no one's dying*, but that was toad-shit. Istel already knew it. Dead-man smile, dead-man calm. Dead man reaching for the mossflower. He popped a leaf in his mouth. Raised a brow at her. "Take the highborn with you if he wants to help."

Fuck and damn. She couldn't look at him anymore. Drilled Soren instead. "Listen. There will be godsworn where I'm going. Way more dangerous than staying here."

"Doesn't matter."

"They've got my partner. Not your fight, highborn."

"If it's her godsworn, then it is my fight. Snowdenaelikk." He reached for her. Got halfway to her wrist and stopped. "Please."

Oh yeah, the God would love this one. "You know anything about how to fight?"

"I have some skill with stools."

"Knives are better." Snow offered him one of her spares. "Hold the dull end and poke with the sharp one, yeah? And stay behind me."

* * *

A man did not panic when he woke in the dark, alone and blind and bound and nearly deaf. A man thanked his ancestors he was still breathing, that he had woken at all, that no injury screamed out for his immediate attention. A man took account of the senses he did have and stayed calm.

Cold metal on his wrists, a collar on his neck, the clink and weight of what must be a shackle between them. Musty smell, like mildew and dust. Coarse weave against his cheek and nose. It had pushed his lips apart, rubbed his teeth and gums dry. A sack. A cloth. Something over his head. His toes and the tops of his feet hurt. His ankles felt stretched and bruised. His arms were sore, and his shoulders. The left side of his face ached. His head thumped like the morning after Winterfest.

They must have dragged him back, then. He hoped the Dvergiri who'd done it had been small and weak and found him an unpleasant burden. He hoped he'd have a chance later to thank them personally, with something heavy and sharp.

Veiko flexed his fingers. Dragged his knees under him and knelt and pawed at the sack over his head—which must have held onions once, or fish, or a hundred dead bodies, given the smell of it. Got it off finally and took a breath that was cooler and just as foul.

Fish. Stagnant water. Rotten things. The floor under his knees was dirt over stone. The wall behind him—he ran his hands across it, because even with the sack off, it was too dark in here for seeing—was a rude brick and mortar. There was a ring bolted into it, and a chain running through that to the crude metal bracelets on his wrists. The collar around his neck was a little better crafted, and looser. He curled his fingers under it until the rough edges threatened to cut him.

Then he sat, and took deep breaths, and considered.

Rata could sell him. He might spend his whole life in a collar, for however long that life lasted. Which would not be long, because he would not live as a bondie, *would not*—

No. He was more likely to die as a sacrifice to Tal'Shik. Or starve to death down here. Or flop at the end of his chain like a fish while Rata's people beat him to death.

As if you'll just sit there, yeah? Fuck and damn, Veiko.

He slid the chain between his fingers. Not much length, no, but enough. When they came, they would not find it easy to take him.

And in the meantime—it was dark in here, yes, and airless, *yes*, but any room would have a door. A way out. An opportunity. He looked for it. Crawled and crouched, then stood and felt his way across the walls until the chain tightened. Then he went the other way and, using the anchor as a pivot, scraped out the limit of his leash. He could not reach the opposite wall, or a door; but he could, at the farthest point, see a dim grey line in the black. Could imagine he felt a draft on his cheek.

And except for him and the sack, the room was empty. No bucket. No water. No straw. They didn't mean to keep him long, or they meant him to die here, forgotten.

He wondered what had happened to Logi and Istel and Briel. Wondered what they'd done with his gear, and then thought how foolish that was: no point in worrying what he would do without his axe and his kit if he died here. And then he wondered, if he did manage to escape the room, how far he would get before someone cut him down.

Patience, yeah?

Tsabrak's whisper, Tsabrak's voice, a hand on his shoulder. But it was Snowdenaelikk he smelled, the spice and stale jenja of her, real as a kick in the belly.

He thought first that it was Briel's doing, a svartjagr sending to tell him that Snow was on her way. Except it didn't feel like Briel at all. *Briel* didn't feel like anything when he focused on her. Ordinarily she was like breathing, constant but unnoticed until something went wrong. Now she was only a flicker, like a single star on a clear winter night, which meant all her attention was elsewhere.

She's coming for you.

The pair of them together could make short work of whoever waited outside. Snow would pick the locks, drive back the shadows, and together—

Together they would probably die, however many they took with them.

Children imagined that things would turn out well simply because of the people involved. Virtue and honor would triumph. Cowards would fail. A man knew better. A man knew that death was inevitable, and the best he could do was meet it without flinching. Veiko expected that if he did *not* attempt an escape, he would die like Kenjak. And if he *did* make an attempt, that he would end up dead anyway.

But he hoped, with one corner of his heart, that his partner would come, and that she'd get there in time.

CHAPTER TWENTY

Dekklis expected to die on the plaza. Expected a sword in her back and her corpse piled with the others. It had been a surprise when they arrested her. She hadn't recognized the woman in senator's robes who'd given the order:

"Put her with the K'Hess whelp."

Oh foremothers, she'd damn near stopped breathing. They couldn't have Soren yet, *couldn't* have got to him. But if they had, it didn't matter what they did to her. If they had Soren, then Illharek was dead, whether or not the Taliri came.

She realized, after they'd hauled her up and bound her wrists and started marching, that the senator had meant K'Hess *Rurik*, not Soren. That they meant to take her to where they were holding him.

Illharek had a shortage of prisons. There was a set of cells in the garrison, for troopers who broke regulations. There had been another set of cells under the old temple, under what was now the Senate chambers, for enemies of Illharek; but that system of tunnels and oubliettes had been destroyed along with the temple. Conjured, filled, bricked over. There was a stone tablet now, over the entrance, with an inscription commemorating the dead.

Dekklis supposed the new Senate would excavate that prison and fill it with dissenters by summer's end. But in the meantime, the Senate needed its legion loyal. She could grant them that much wit. And if they had some handpicked officers—young highborn women, like the motherless toadlickers holding her arms—well, that wasn't everyone in the uniform. The men would rise if they knew about Tal'Shik's return. So would a good number of the women. So it made sense they wouldn't take her back to the garrison. Which left, as possible prisons, this place.

She blinked, staring up at the gates, and refused to believe it. The Academy had profited from the Purge. They wouldn't want Tal'Shik back. Would not ally with the Senate in *this*.

Believe that.

She'd been a decade away, and so much of Illharek had rotted away at its core. Maybe the Academy was full of godsworn sympathizers. Sisters, brothers, friends to the new crop of women who called themselves senators.

No. Damn. *Think.* If that were true, Belaery would've said. There would have been *some* indication. This must be a convenient allegiance. The Adepts might not mind if a few highborn died, but they would care very much if Illharek fell to Taliri. The Taliri had no word for conjuror, preferring the word *witch* instead, and they had learned how to handle witches from their former allies, the Alviri.

But Dvergiri godsworn, now—they had a history of working with the Adepts, because war with them was too expensive. Until the Purge, anyway, when the Academy had sided with popular opinion and the rebel highborn. Tal'Shik would not have forgotten that. And this new breed of Illhari godsworn, already traitors once, wouldn't twitch at betraying an ally. They'd killed their mothers and elder sisters. Had spilled blood all over the Senate floor. They'd try it here, too, and the Academy would burn. The Adepts had to know that.

A woman met them just inside the gates. She might be a generation from half-blood, grey-eyed and a little tall for a Dvergir. This conjuror—little more than an apprentice, from her single gold ear-ring—looked them over. Raised both brows.

"Who is this?" calmly, as if there weren't two armed guards at Dek's elbows.

"Traitor," said one of them. She sounded terribly young, and a little nervous. "Goes with the other one."

The robed woman raked Dekklis with a second, longer look. Eyed the cords on her wrists. Her northerner's garb. Then she stepped aside and gestured. "All right. Bring her."

"I." Young Voice hesitated. "We were supposed to deliver her this far. That's all."

The robed woman's lip curled. "If she is so dangerous that you must disarm and bind her—and that you must bring her *here*—I would think you would not want to leave her with a single, unarmed apprentice." Her smile fell away. "Now, either escort her yourself, or leave and take her away with you."

Oh, Young Voice didn't like that. Dek watched her hands clench. Felt the anger shiver off her. But she steered Dekklis through the gate without arguing.

The robed woman left them standing in the corridor and went into a small room beside the gate. Conferred with the other woman in there. And then she came out again and beckoned as if to a bondie. "This way."

Which meant inside the second set of doors, across the little cross corridor that led around and down to the Archives. Now they were entering new territory, nowhere Dek had ever intended to go.

Not her guards, either. Clearly uneasy, the pair of them. They drew so close Dekklis thought she could wear them like a cloak.

The image amused her. She allowed the smirk onto her face. Allowed the chuckle through her teeth, which got a puzzled look from the apprentice. Which got her a shove from her guards, one and then the other. A muttered "Shut up" from the second.

Dekklis dubbed that one Raspy and held back long enough to meet her eyes. Yes, another young one. Afraid, and furious because of that, and prone to violence.

"Save your breath," the robed woman advised. She let them into a large roundish room with a fountain in the center. Water giggled down off a sculpture of—something. Smooth stone in a shape that made Dek feel nauseous, staring at it. Doorless openings studded the walls at uneven intervals, showing corridors or staircases. The apprentice selected one of them, steps going up. They climbed a coil of stairs for what seemed like forever. The guards thought so. Puffing and wheezing. You could feel sorry for them, wearing all that armor, so unaccustomed to exertion.

Or laugh at them. "Bet you're sorry you wore the full kit."

"Shut up." Young Voice sounded more like Raspy now. Maybe Dek would rename her Breathless. Maybe she'd tell Istel he'd been right about Illhari soldiers.

Oh foremothers, don't think about Istel. Too much like a knife in her breastbone, a worry so sharp she forgot how to breathe. He could care for himself. He'd found Snowdenaelikk. He wasn't going to walk into the garrison now. Wouldn't get himself arrested. He was smarter than she was. He wouldn't've killed

my sister

a senator on the floor of the curia in a fit of honor and anger. He'd scout out the situation, keep his head down, stay safe with Snow.

Which meant, inevitably, he'd come here. Because Snow would. Damn sure, when she found out they had Dekklis in the Academy, she'd come.

The apprentice stopped finally. They'd passed half a dozen doors already. This one looked like the others. Plain wood, old iron fittings. The stairs continued upward, presumably to other doors. All had big, visible locks. Dek would wager her life and Istel's that there were— what did Snow call them?—not sigils, no, but wards, that was right, on that door. That this woman, with her single gold apprentice ring, had enough skill to get through those wards, and the lock was performance.

But it clicked like a real lock when the woman put a key into it. And the door groaned, swinging open a crack.

"Step back, First Spear," the robed woman called. "Please. And put your weapon down."

There was shuffling from inside. A violent clang that sounded like metal hitting rock and losing the battle.

"You're safe," said K'Hess Rurik in a tone that suggested otherwise. "*Do* come in."

The apprentice looked very much like Snowdenaelikk in that moment. Same crooked smirk that meant another offense added to a long tally of grudges. She turned that smirk toward Dekklis.

"After *you*." Added, suddenly serious, "He has a temper. Be careful."

"I can handle him," Dekklis said loudly. Shrugged her escorts off, one and the other. Turned and offered her wrists. "Cut me loose."

They had no orders to that effect. That was obvious. Sheep-stupid stares, the pair of them. They were tired. A little scared. Not at all sure what to do.

These, *these*, were Illharek's defense. Maybe the Taliri deserved to win.

Dekklis blew air through her teeth. "You think I'll break out of *here*?"

Raspy sighed. Started to draw her blade.

"Wait." The robed woman shouldered between them. Touched Dek's cords with a fingertip and muttered under her breath. There was a moment's sharp pain, and the cords burst into flame. Burned to ash and sprinkled to the floor.

"Don't let this one near metal, Mila. She could kill you." The apprentice smiled at Dekklis. "Isn't that right, Domina?"

"My title is First Scout, not domina," Dekklis said, "And yes."

She turned her back on both guards. Walked into the room and hardly noticed the door locking shut behind her.

This place was huge. Spacious. Far more than a room, a cell, some-place to keep a dead man. This was a whole apartment, furnished with couches, a low table, a firedog set in a hearth. There was even a win-dow on one wall, a long slash that ran a tall woman's height. Illharek's witchfire ambient glowed through it, blue twilight to compete with the honest yellow coming out of the firedog.

There had been a metal pitcher and basin on the table. The pitcher was still there. It lay on its side, rolled nearly off the table. Water puddled around it. Gleamed off the floor like a mirror. The basin had been relocated to the floor. It was, Dekklis thought, a little bit out of round.

But the basin looked better than the candlestick, and *it* looked better than K'Hess Rurik. He sprawled across one of the couches, arms outspread like a man waiting for his dinner. One eye swollen shut, split lip, blood dried brown on his uniform tunic. They'd taken his armor, his weapons, the laces out of his boots. She guessed at the bruises his clothes were hiding. His hair tufted and curled where it'd escaped from its queue.

Dekklis drew up to attention. Saluted. "First Spear."

His mouth creased. He stood up, none too easily, and returned her salute. "First Scout."

Dekklis picked up the candlestick with both hands. It was sturdy iron, stuck all over with old wax.

"You could kill someone with that, sir." She looked for a candle. Didn't see one. Set the stick upright.

"That was the plan." His face writhed between a man's relief and a commander's severity. "Szanys. The hell are you doing here?"

"Here, this apartment? Or here, Illharek?"

"Both."

"All right. Start with *this* place. I stabbed my sister on the Senate floor. She killed my mother, also on the Senate floor. Or had her killed. I didn't ask which." The words tasted strange. Foreign.

Rurik blinked. "Oh."

She looked at him. "Reckoned something rotten when I saw your guard dead."

"You reckoned right." He shook his head. "I thought you'd died in the riots in Cardik."

What happened? in his eyes. *Did you run?* in the line of his tight-pressed lips.

"I got caught in the Warren when the riot started. Couldn't get back to the Sixth. I got out of the city"—

by the ghost road, in the company of dead soldiers

—"another way, came south to warn the Senate. Get help, bring it back. They wouldn't send it, sir. And." It felt like knives in her chest, like she'd never breathe again. "I'm sorry. I shouldn't've left without orders. But Illharek needed the warning. And I thought Cardik was finished."

"It is." Rurik sat down suddenly, as if someone had cut out his knees. "Taliri. Godmagic. Toadfucking *dragon*. Did you know stone will shatter when it's hot enough? Just bursts, like a blister. The shards are deadly. You were smart to run, Szanys." He held up a hand. "I didn't mean it like that. I would've sent you myself if I thought you had a chance of getting through. How did you? They were thick as ants around Cardik. We barely got out, and we paid blood for it. Surprised 'em. The main force of Taliri is maybe a day behind us if they tried to match our pace. But I reckon they stayed in Cardik, to . . . occupy. Motherless raiders dogged us most of the way here, though. They're all through the forests." Rurik's jaw worked. "We abandoned the city. All those people."

She couldn't say *you had no choice* to this man. He'd had one, and he'd chosen his troops over his charges. Chosen Illharek over Cardik. "How many dragons?"

He frowned. "I don't know. One that I saw. Why does that matter?"

She had no idea how many avatars a goddess could have at one time. Snow had always acted like one was the limit. But Snow might not know everything. Maybe the God was limited to one avatar but Tal'Shik could manage a dozen. If Snow'd killed Ehkla and *she* hadn't come back as the avatar, then that dragon must be one of the other Taliri.

"First Scout?"

"Curious, sir, that's—" *all*, she started to say, and changed her mind. "No. That's not true. I was asking because I think the dragon's an avatar, not godmagic."

Anger flickered like distant lightning. Rurik's response to confusion, predictable as sunrise. She hadn't expected to be glad to see it.

"What are you talking about?"

"If it's godmagic, that's like conjuring. Bad, but nothing Illharek can't handle. We've got Adepts. We've got godsworn, too. Most of the new senators. They might not be as good as the Taliri are yet, but I don't know how much it'll matter. Tal'Shik doesn't seem to reward skill as much as fanaticism. But if it's an avatar out there, a dragon, that might mean Tal'Shik's taken sides with the Taliri and Illharek's in real trouble."

"As opposed to the false trouble we're in now?"

She ignored his sarcasm. "The city's rotten with Tal'Shik's people. In the Suburba, in the Tiers—they're everywhere. We suspected the ones in the Suburba. But we—I—had no idea how far it'd spread until—" She stopped. Shook her head hard enough that her ears rang. "Your brother told me. Soren. He knows who the godsworn are in the Houses. They've taken the Senate, or at least a good part of it. They hear there's a dragon coming, they might think we need one. Or that we need to make more sacrifices to prove how loyal we are."

"You've seen Soren?" Rurik's face locked down. "I thought he'd be dead by now."

"No, sir. He was hostage for your mother's silence in the Senate, but he's safe now. I got him out of Stratka and into the Suburba."

"That's *safe?*"

"Got friends down there. *A* friend. She can hide him. She will."

"You have strange friends, Szanys."

"Not so many, sir. I brought this one with me."

His eyes widened. "The one from the Warren."

"She's from the Suburba originally. A half-blood. And." Dek hesitated. Closed her eyes and sifted through Snow's secrets. "She's got ties to the Laughing God."

"That doesn't really surprise me. So why go after my brother, Szanys?"

"My mother needed K'Hess's support to vote to send a cohort north. Your mother wouldn't leave her own walls after your eldest brother went missing."

"Ivar," Rurik said stiffly. "So he's dead?"

"Likely. I'm sorry, Rurik."

He shook his head. "Go on."

"Your mother thought you were dead, too. Soren was all she had left, and Stratka held him as hostage. All the highborn men are hostages now. It's like it was before the Purge."

"I've noticed. And somehow you still got Soren out." That might be a sullen respect in Rurik's eyes, underneath the more honest surprise.

"I reckoned if I did, and she knew he was safe, your mother would help, throw her vote behind sending aid to Cardik. Except I never got the chance to tell her. I don't know if she even attended the last session. If she did, she could've died in the curia with my mother."

"I didn't see her there. I came to the Senate, straight off, to report. Toadlicking senator told me I was speaking out of turn. I told her piss off and listen, and next thing." Rurik launched to his feet. Stalked to the window slit. He bunched both hands into fists. Dekklis watched the play of muscles across his shoulders. Wasn't entirely surprised when he uncoiled and punched the stone.

"Breaking bones won't help."

"I know that." He curled his fist against his chest. "They brought me here after that. I thought they'd kill me right there. So I'm guessing I'm leverage." He curled his lip. "They'll be sorry for that if they think my mother will shift policy for *me*. Unless they think they'll spike me, like they did Kenjak. In which case they will be *very* sorry." He turned, stared out the window. "Look out there. It's already started."

Dekklis went and stood beside him. The window looked out over the Arch, past it, toward the Jokki and the Riverwalk. Fire danced along the water's edge. No—danced *on* the water. That was a barge burning down to the waterline.

Rurik heaved the words out as if they were stones. "They were trying to leave Illharek. I watched it from here. The people on the boat, they were just scared. Bunch of Alviri. I watched from this fucking window while Illhari troopers shot arrows onto the deck." Anguish washed through his voice. "*Our* troopers, Dekklis. Firing on *our* people."

She'd fought with Rurik a hundred times, never seen him give in or slow down. This hollow-faced man, hell, she didn't know him.

Just *like* a man to crack when there wasn't time for it.

Istel wouldn't. Neither would Veiko.

Istel and Veiko weren't here, either. Just Rurik, whom she'd once called *First Spear*, and hell if rank mattered now.

She took a fistful of sleeve. Jerked and made him look at her. "The Senate's giving the orders. *Her* orders. Savvy that? The legion's not rotten, and we haven't lost Illharek yet. Hear me, Rurik?"

That got his attention. Just like Veiko's dog, wasn't he, to respond to his name. Or, more likely: he didn't like hearing *Rurik* where he should hear *First Spear*. Fine. Let him act like a First Spear, maybe she'd grant him the title again.

Until then, she seized on his irritation. Seized *him*. Took his hand, spread the fingers wide: split skin, knuckles already swelling. She wiped the blood aside with her sleeve. "You break your hand, you're no good in a fight."

"What fight? We're up here. Any fight happens, it'll be down there, without us. And when it's over, either the Taliri will kill us, or the traitors will."

"No. Told you, I've got a friend here. She'll get us out."

"Your heretic. In the Suburba."

"My heretic, who's also a conjuror. She *will* come."

"She'd better hurry. Can you tell her that, Dekklis?"

"She knows."

Please, foremothers, that was true.

* * *

No one came for him.

Muffled voices leaked in through the seams between wall and door. Thumps and vibrations. The occasional bleed of light under the doorway as a lantern or candle accompanied someone up the corridor.

Veiko wondered if they'd forgotten him. He spent his time testing the chain, link by link. Testing the locks and the stretch of his limbs. He knew he could stand up and take exactly four short strides and still lift his arms over his head. He knew that at five strides, his arms would not swing past his hips.

He knew that no matter how he twisted and pulled on the shackles, no matter how much bloodslick wrist and metal, he would not get them over his hands without breaking bone.

It was not worth the damage. Not if the first person he met in the corridor could best him with two working hands. Not if the door was locked, which it surely was.

He wondered if he dared cross back to the ghost roads and leave his body unattended. Wondered if he dared ask Taru for assistance. Wondered if she was all right, having been left alone with Tsabrak. Which led to wondering about Logi's welfare, then Istel's and Briel's, and then, finally, Snowdenaelikk's. Which in turn prompted him to test chains and limits again and pace like a tethered takin.

At least Tsabrak had not come to him again. He did not know whether to be pleased or annoyed. The godling owed him favors. Now would be the time to repay them. But perhaps he should be relieved that he would not be faced with a costly bargain that he would almost certainly take, since a debt to Tsabrak would be better than dying here.

He sat down finally, his back to the wall, and waited. A hunter was good at waiting. A hunter did not think of himself as prey.

A key rattled in the lock. He sat, staring and startled, and weighed the wisdom of meeting his captors awake and upright, defiant, as a warrior might.

You're a hunter, yeah?

Veiko curled up against the wall. Tugged the sack back over his head, with the edge peeled up so that he could just see the door as it squeaked open and dirty light spilled across the floor. Rotten as that intruder light was, it blinded eyes used to darkness. He squinted through his lashes and counted feet. Two remained at the door. Four more crossed the room toward him. One in boots that had seen recent mud, one pair city-clean. Muddy Boots stopped just past the range of his chain. Shifted one foot to the other, nervous. Clean Boots strode over to him and stopped. Squatted so that he saw knees and thighs doubled over.

Woman's curves, woman's sweat, woman's skin. A woman's voice breaking over his head.

"He's awake. —Aren't you, skraeling?" Clean Boots's hands dangled between her knees. Veiko noted, without surprise, Tal'Shik's mark inked onto her palm.

She continued after a breath's beat, as if he'd answered her. "You took a good hit back there. But." She tilted onto her toes. Time enough to close his eyes and smooth his mouth to level before she plucked the sack from his head. "Enough pretending, yeah?"

This was the godsworn from the woods, the one he'd meant to shoot in the eye. She was less menacing now, in the plain honest light. Bones too small for her features, Dvergiri dark hair and eyes and skin. She was even missing a tooth, there—a gap in a smile meant to intimidate.

Veiko hitched up the corner of his own mouth. He could reach her neck from here if he tried. Get both hands around it, yes, and wring it like a chicken's. The woman behind her—Muddy Boots, a woman he'd seen with Rata—would probably kill him for it. She carried one of the Illhari seaxes, like Snow's. A little smaller than a legion sword, lighter, slimmer. Fast, Veiko knew, and sharp.

The godsworn wore no knives at all. Nothing edged.

She saw him looking. Laughed out loud. "Not stupid, yeah? I won't get close to you with metal. You're a wild one. *She* says."

"What does *she* say about my aim with a bow?"

The smile hardened. Must be imagination, or poor light, that made her teeth look sharp. "That you got lucky."

"It was not luck."

Veiko sat up. It wasn't easy, with his hands bound in front of him. He'd practiced in the dark, had had nothing better to do. Smooth fold and roll from hip to knees to feet pressed flat. He squatted there, ignoring the ache in his thigh, with his hands thrown casually across his knees. He turned his wrists in the shackles. Watched with detached interest as the metal scraped across raw meat. Twist and flex, knot the fingers into a fist. Squeeze. Fresh blood dripped onto the stones.

There were dead whose names he knew. He breathed those syllables now, as he had a dozen times already.

K'Hess Kenjak. Teslin. Barkett.

No chill drafts, no creeping fog, no skin-scraping whispers. No answer. Of course there was not. He was tired. Hurt. Had sent his own spirit walking too many times recently. There were a hundred reasons the dead did not answer.

K'Hess Kenjak. Teslin. Barkett.

The godsworn's shadow bled across him. "I know about you. Some kind of skraeling bloodmagic you do, yeah? It won't work here."

Veiko raised both brows and said nothing. It was, Snow had assured him, one of his most maddening habits.

The godsworn peeled her lips off her teeth. "Or maybe you think the half-blood's coming for you. Maybe you're waiting for her, yeah? Well, we're waiting, too."

He cocked his head. "If she comes for me, you will not survive it."

"Such faith. She is *one woman*, Veiko Nyrikki. A conjuror of unremarkable talent who serves a broken god. We're ready for her."

A man could laugh at that. No one was *ready* for Snowdenaelikk.

But then, she might not come. Or she might be late. Or it was possible they really were prepared. Veiko might've wished Briel *no* and *stay away* then if Briel was listening. But she wasn't. Cool little spot of awareness, her focus somewhere else.

On Snowdenaelikk, and bringing her here, into what was surely a trap. But Snow would know that. Expect it. Nor was she a martyr or a fool. She would come for him, yes, but she would not die with him out of solidarity. That was what the godsworn did not understand. Snow would not let him die like K'Hess Kenjak had, no.

She would kill him first, and everyone with him, and apologize on the ghost roads.

CHAPTER TWENTY-ONE

Lightning flash behind her eyes, bad as it had ever been before Veiko, blinding and painful and *fuck*. Snow paused and leaned against the wall. Ducked her chin and cursed Briel—

Stop that, rot you.

—and squinted through the sparks.

It was like seeing double. The alley in front of her, narrow and familiar, and Soren's face peering into hers. His "Snowdenaelikk?" came from a very long way and snagged on the wool in her ears.

That was one layer.

And over it, under it—like the smeared features on the far side of a dark window that you realize after a moment isn't your reflection at all, but someone else outside, looking in—was plain flames against real darkness, and a sense of

panic

close-pressed stone. A collection of aches, of which

my

the right thigh was a throbbing jewel. An unmistakable steel weight on both wrists, hard pulling that meant someone on the far end of a chain who didn't care toadshit about raw flesh and bruises. And so

my
the jaw ached, too, locked against words
I
learned from her
me
and gone.

The sending ended. And now she knew they were moving Veiko someplace. Fuck and damn.

Logi whined. Pushed his nose against her chest, which made her wonder when exactly she'd slid down the wall. Explained the look Soren was giving her, anyway, snagged between fear and worry.

"Are you—?"

"No," she snapped. "Shut up and let me think."

Soren was a good highborn, obedient and patient as a cow. He waited while Logi—who was not patient, who was hurting and worried and determined not to get more than a fingerwidth away from her—licked her chin and pressed all his not inconsiderable weight against her. She smoothed her hand over his spine. Skirted the edges of the long, raw furrow on his ribs. That had been a damn lucky miss, no real damage, a little blood. It didn't even need stitches.

Logi had fared better than Istel. And Istel was better off than Veiko would be. Godsworn would drive a sharpened pole through him and carve runes into him and feed him to Tal'Shik. Or maybe they'd carve him open, like they had with Stig. Either way, they would finish what Ehkla had started. They hadn't started anything yet, of that Briel was certain. But once they'd put a stake through him, or slit him open, it wouldn't matter whether Snow got there or not. She might save his spirit, but she'd lose his body, and she wasn't noidghe enough to count that any kind of victory.

She patted Logi a final time. Dragged herself up the wall with a forearm. Rested there and looked down at her right palm. The God's mark was damn near invisible in this light, a line darker than black on her skin. She braced both feet. Traced the sigil with her left hand.

Her skin tingled when she finished. That was godmagic. That was something she could not have done two candlemarks ago, before her bargain. "You hear me?"

Soren glanced at her. Did not ask *who are you talking to?*, no; rolled his eyes at a madwoman instead and kept his well-mannered mouth shut.

Wise man.

A smudge of fog and smoke drifted across the alley, an apparition that resolved into Dvergiri beauty. Small wonder Tsabrak's mother had sold his youth up into the Tiers. Highborn looks without a House's protection, yeah, he'd've brought in a good price.

He could still twist her heart, even now, even dead.

Soren yelped. He fumbled the knife out of its sheath. Wrapped both hands round the hilt and pointed it at Tsabrak.

Snow started to reach for him, to push the knife down. Reconsidered the wisdom of it. Man saw a ghost the first time, he might get slashy. She didn't need a new cut, and it wasn't as if he could *hurt* Tsabrak.

Who laughed, very softly. *Brave man. Maybe I'll keep you when this is all over.*

"Leave him alone. And why are you here? I called the God, not you."

I am the Laughing God.

"I look like I'm interested in your delusions?"

Oh, it's true. Ask your partner how that happened.

"My partner." Veiko had said *she* should talk to Tsabrak, that *he* couldn't find the God, and now here was Tsabrak, claiming power he couldn't have. Unless Veiko had made his own bargains. Unless he'd talked to Tsabrak after all.

"My *partner*," and this time it was almost a curse. Her heart twisted into new shapes. "Did he send you?"

No. Tsabrak cocked his head. *I don't think it occurred to him. He's busy calling on ghosts. Someone named Teslin? Barkett? They're trying to answer him. They just can't. I can't, either. I need my own people to walk through the wards on that place. I need my right hand.*

"I didn't bargain with you. I bargained with *him.*"

The old God's bargains are mine now. And his debts. That means I owe you, Snowdenaelikk. Veiko, too.

"Snow." Soren edged into her periphery. He held the knife out-thrust, an amateur's grip, like he meant to skewer something. Fuck and damn, she had to keep him out of a real fight. He'd end up joining his youngest brother in the black river. "Who is this?"

Snowdenaelikk skinned a smile. "This is the Laughing God, yeah? And he's here to help."

***

It took four of them to drag Veiko out of the little stone room, the godsworn and Muddy Boots on the wrong end of his chain and two strangers for escort, who pointed crossbows at him and smiled like they wished he would try something.

He didn't. He'd seen what bolts could do to meat and muscle. Reckoned that even if they weren't professionals, well, even a child might hit him in here, a big pale shape who took up most of the corridor's narrowness.

Tal'Shik wouldn't want him dead too soon, but crippled wouldn't bother her.

And so he gave them no excuses for violence. He went along with Muddy Boots and the godsworn, chin tucked, as much to spare the top of his head a scraping as any attempt to play docile Dvergir man. He counted his strides. Five to the end of the corridor, then left. Another seven and a half until the stairs, which were wooden and creaked and moaned under his weight. Four of those to a narrow doorway, through which more than one body was not meant to pass at a time. Through which the godsworn and Muddy Boots squeezed together, so that neither would be alone with her back to him.

Gratifying, that they counted him so formidable.

And then they climbed into a much larger space, with a ceiling half again his height overhead, lost in the shadow and dust. Plain oil lamps hung from the walls, above and among columns of crates and mounds of greasy nets. A warehouse, which was a word Snow had taught him: a place for storing goods that came off the barges. From the smell in here, much of that cargo was fish. There was another narrow doorway on the left adjoining wall, open, and on the right: a big pair of double-wide doors, swung half-open. He could hear the Tano on the other side, slap-slosh against the wooden docks.

There was a pole standing tall in the room's center, metal shafted, with a jagged head that did not gleam like steel. It looked like Briel's tail-spike. Like his recollection of Tal'Shik's own tail in the otherworld, when she'd taken her wurm-shape. And it looked exactly like the tip of Kari's spear, which he had said was the tail-spike from the wurm he had killed. Everyone in the village knew that story, because Kari told it a hundred times a winter. Everyone in the village had reckoned that spear-tip for fancy forging, something Kari had got from the Dvergir trader that came up the mountain twice a year.

Veiko promised himself that, should he ever go home again, he would find Kari and apologize for doubting him.

A man should not show fear, especially not in front of his enemies. But when he considered what that barbed head would do going into a body, oh ancestors, all he could do not to balk and thrash on the end of his chain like a yearling takin. All he could do not to stumble as his knees melted and refroze and tried to buckle. Ehkla had cut him with a wurm's tooth, and he had cried out. That pain would be nothing at all against what this thing would do to him.

A man should not show fear, a man should not show pain, a man should not die like a rabbit on a spit, and he would do all of those things. Bitter surged and burned in his throat. He gulped it back. Filled his mouth with words to keep the fear in his belly.

Too loudly, too obviously a sneer: "It must be difficult to clean the pole between uses."

The godsworn looked back at him. Knew his fear for what it was and smiled. "We dip it in the Tano. The fish clean it for us. But don't worry, yeah? The pole's for highborn Dvergiri men."

He would not ask her *what will you do to me, then?* Pressed lips and teeth together and stared down at her.

She laughed and pointed, past the pole and across the room, where the shadows gathered like ghosts. There were rings bolted into the floor, sunk into the cracks between tiles. Four of them, in a rough square. The lanterns did not reach very well this far from the walls, but Veiko did not need to see to know that was blood staining the tiles. He could smell it. Blood, and death, and fear.

"We'll chain you down," the godsworn said softly. "Wrists and ankles. Then we'll crack your ribs and cut them away from your spine and pull them open. Lay your lungs on your shoulders. We do it right, you'll take a long time to die. You know what sacrifice means? The longer it takes, the more it pleases her."

Sweat prickled cold on his skin. The old scar on his thigh throbbed. He looked down at her, thankful that the Dvergiri were a small people. Thankful that his voice did not shake. Thankful that Snowdenaelikk had described that particular ritual to him with a chirurgeon's cool detail, telling him how Ehkla had died.

He made fists of both hands. They would have to unchain his hands and rebind him. The shackles he had now joined the wrists together. Both feet were still free. They would have to bind those, too, and stretch him out on the stones.

He thought about the crossbows pointed at him. Licked his lips. "You will try. That does not mean you will succeed."

The godsworn raised her eyebrows. "Listen. You fight, you won't gain anything. She'll still take you. But if you yield—ask her for mercy, yeah? She might take you quickly. Or." The godsworn leaned closer. She smelled sour, a woman who spent her days in slaughter. Old blood, old death. A joy in both. "She might let you live. Let you serve her. She's taken men as godsworn before."

Veiko let his silence answer, and his scowl. And stopped, so that the two behind him almost ran up his heels. Very close range now. The bolts would go through him completely. A faster death than sacrifice.

"Move," said the godsworn. "You want to get shot?"

He shrugged. Listened for the bootscrape and the mutter of cloth while his skin pebbled and twitched and waited for violence.

"Not stupid, are you?" Her mouth pulled sideways. Her gaze did, just past his left shoulder.

So he knew where the strike was coming from, had time to twist so that fist took him in the ribs, not the kidneys. He let the impact push him forward, mock stagger that turned real when the godsworn stabbed a savage kick at him. She'd meant to hit his knee. Drove her heel into his thigh instead, the one Ehkla had cut, the one that already hurt like fire. This time his fall was real, uncontrolled, graceless.

He landed hard on his hip. Bounced and got his knees under him. The landing had carried him closer to Muddy Boots, so that there was a little slack in the chain. He wrapped a fistful of it, pulled her savagely off balance. And then, as the other three came at him, he lunged to his feet. Oh ancestors, let him stay upright just long enough.

He got both shackled hands up, swung them like a club. Locked stares with Muddy Boots, saw her eyes round as eggs. Then his fists came between them. Something crunched against his knuckles. Sudden wet.

Momentum carried them both over. Another soggy crunch as she landed under him. A crossbow bolt clattered off the tiles. The second burned across his ribs and buried itself in the woman beneath him.

And then they were on him.

* * *

Keeping Veiko down here—in this warehouse, conspicuous only because of its empty pier among neighbors whose docks bristled with barges and skiffs—was purest proof Snow could ask that Rata was an idiot. This had been *Stig's* warehouse, and Tsabrak's before that. *Their* headquarters, when they'd brought the rasi in from Siljaan, hidden among crates of salted silverlight. It had been an open secret that everyone on the dock pretended not to know about. Tsabrak hadn't been kind to people who got in his business.

But he hadn't gone round vivisecting people, either. Quick knife in the ribs, yeah, that was Tsabrak's style. Direct, simple. He'd left the fancier killing to Snow—death that looked like bad fish or a weak heart. Death that didn't come back looking for vengeance.

Tsabrak would not, in any imagining, have taken his dead enemy's headquarters as his own. He'd have razed the building if he'd been in the mood to send a message; but he would've traded it away, more likely, for less than it was worth to someone who needed it, who'd later owe him a favor. He'd acquired most of the dock district's loyalty that way. Then when it had come time to move against rivals, well, Tsabrak had his allies bought and paid for.

Tsabrak had loved his intrigues. His elaborate plots and plans. Strategy, he'd called it, thinking long. And he'd thought himself too long, hadn't he, thought himself into a fatal knot. And still he'd come out all right; that was Tsabrak's other gift. He was lucky. From indentured to godsworn, from ghost to Laughing God, yeah, not bad.

There was another thing about Tsabrak, a quality she understood, a quality he and she shared. Never forget an insult or an offense, never miss a chance to pay it back.

Rata had offended him mightily. But then, so had she.

"Sst." Snow thrust a hand across Soren's path and stopped him. "Wait."

"Snowdenaelikk?" Soren whispered.

Logi whined.

She ignored both of them. Said to empty air, "I have a question."

What, now? Felt like a man's lips, warm and soft, against her ear. *Your partner doesn't have that much time, yeah? I told you, Snow. They'll kill him whether or not you're there. She wants him that badly.*

"Briel says he's got time." Briel had indicated no such thing, but Briel wasn't panicking, either. Snow wiped her hands on her thighs. Couldn't hold a blade, with them sweating like that. And it would come to bladework in there. If her conjuring held—*if* Tsabrak could handle the godsworn, *if* Tal'Shik didn't take a personal interest and eat the new Laughing God whole and entire—she might get all the way to Veiko before she had to use it. Then she could fight her way out with what promised to be a wounded partner. Fuck and *damn.*

"Can you stop Tal'Shik? Really?"

I don't know. Best we get there before they draw blood, yeah? Before they have her full attention.

"But if we're not. What then? You stay and fight with us? Or do you run? Because you *say* you don't want her to have Veiko, but way I reckon it, he dies before she kills him, you get your way."

Ah. The air trembled, as if there were an invisible fire burning behind it. She saw Tsabrak's face in that shimmer. Saw his knowing smile. *You think I want him dead, then? And you, too? Even though I've said otherwise?*

"I do. Question is, when's best for you? Now or later?"

Once upon a time, Tsabrak would've protested. Would've said *no, not me*, and *how dare you even think it?* Maybe godhood had made him more honest, then, because he said nothing at all for long enough Snow thought her ears might burst with the silence. Then, breath of deep winter on her skin: *I could ask you the same thing, yeah? How long before you turn on me, the way you turned on the old God?*

"You know why I did that."

I do. She felt that stare, invisible and heavy as chains. *Say I owe Veiko Nyrikki a favor, just now. I mean to pay it back while he's still living. Believe that, or don't. As for you. You are my right hand, Snow. I won't betray you.*

She squatted in the shadows and listened to the water slap against the pier. To the voices bouncing off water and walls and stone—conversations, arguments, echoes from up and down the wharf. But not from the warehouse. Nothing at all from in there.

Briel.

Whisper in the dark, wings scything through air. A tip-tilted pass over streets and alleys. The dock was empty, unguarded. There were sentries on the main street, leaning against the walls. Watching for her, yeah. Waiting. Trusting their godmagic, when Tal'Shik had never been anything but treacherous.

And what was the God, then? What was Tsabrak? She had scars from that betrayal.

Oh yeah, Dekklis would laugh at her. Dekklis would dip her chin and draw her sword and get in there—because in Dek's world, there was honor and then there was everything else. You died for honor's sake.

Damn stupid. You didn't plan to die, not ever. You didn't go into a place where dying was likely, not on purpose, not with uncertain allies and bad odds. Revenge was a better idea. Smarter. She'd done it often enough, yeah? Damn skilled at it. She had a small stack of highborn bodies to her count, and she was still breathing. She didn't want fucking *Rata* to be the one who got her because she'd turned stupid.

Snow closed her eyes. She could burn the place from here. Lots of torches around. Real fire. She could conjure a firestorm and send it roaring through the warehouse. That would spare Veiko the worst of the dying.

As if burning was better.

Dekklis could lecture about honor, but Dekklis hadn't choked on the black river. Dekklis hadn't felt the weight of that silence, or a cold so deep it went past pain. Dekklis didn't understand what a gift it was to wear a sleeve of skin and muscle. To be warm. To *breathe*.

But Veiko did. And Veiko—knowing all of that—would come after her whatever the odds, having his own attitudes about what and who mattered more than his own life.

"You," she said to Soren. "Stay here. I mean it this time. Watch my back."

She walked away before Soren could argue—assuming he knew how, being highborn and new to defiance. Fuck and damn. If she died in here, she bet Tsabrak would teach him all about it.

She drew the shadows around her, spilled them ahead of her like ink. Watched them fill in the cracks between walls and pavement. She was a competent conjuror, never gifted. Not like Belaery, who could've conjured a hole in the wall and walked through. But she had some things Belaery didn't.

She had Briel. She had Logi. She had the contents of her pouches, and her wits.

And the Laughing God's successor at her back. Fuck and damn.

* * *

The fight did not last as long as Veiko intended. Part of the reason was that four became five became too many to count, all hard feet and hard fists and an uncanny knack for finding a man's softest parts. The crunch and battery against ribs and back, yes, that was unpleasant, but he could ignore it. He could *not* ignore a toe driving up under his ribs, pushing the air aside, flipping him over like a flatcake. Could not ignore a second foot, stomping down on his exposed belly. But he could catch that second foot. Grip and twist until a woman howled and the foot flopped limp.

And then he rolled away, writhing, trying to suck air back into his lungs and avoid a new assault. Caught the next wave of violence on his shoulders, forearms, the backs of his thighs. He lurched onto his elbows, on his knees after that. If he moved fast, he might make it upright—

He didn't see who kicked him. Whose boot it was, suddenly large and coming at his face. He shied sideways, caught the kick just above his left eye. His vision spangled, then turned to red twilight as blood rivered into his eyes. A second splash of stars as his elbows wilted and his face slammed into the ground.

And then they were on him. Hands biting his arms, his ankles, fingers curved under ribs and hips. He bent his body like a bow, flexed and twisted—instinct now, pure desperation—because he did not need to see to know what came next. If they chained him to that place on the floor, he would not get up again. Let them kill him. Whatever they did to him now, any beating, was better than *that*.

A fist slammed into the side of his face, in the place the boot had landed. Veiko forgot about fighting and tried instead to stay conscious. Could not argue as they dragged him, not at all gently, and cast him down on the floor.

He had a dim awareness of the shackles coming off. A faint awareness of legs and arms stretched, of his body arranged on the stone. He blinked his eyes clear of blood and stars. There was etching on the tile, gouged glyphs whose purpose he knew, even if he could not read them. He couldn't see anyone, no, but he could feel their weight grinding down on him. Heard murmuring, swearing, the words smeared and indistinct. He blamed the bloodrush in his own ears for his deafness. Please, ancestors, his heart burst itself in his chest.

The torches flickered. Cool air kissed his cheek, stung where it touched the wound on his head.

And then the shadows spilled off the walls. A winter wind tore the flames from their torches and crushed them. And then stillness, silence, thick and rough and wet.

Conjuring, he had time to think, and *Snowdenaelikk,* and then the screaming began.

CHAPTER TWENTY-TWO

Sending the darkness ahead, that was easy. Snow gathered the shadows, wove them solid. Close your eyes, yeah, reach into stone and air and *push*. The shadows were cold, thick, and slow, but they moved. Slipped between the cracks, under the door, poured over the torches and the candles.

The guards on the door had no defense against shadows that coiled around legs and arms, against shadows that forced themselves into open eyes and mouths. Against the woman who sent those shadows against them, wrapped in the same. They never even saw her.

But they died quietly, which was all Snow had wanted. She stepped over their leaking corpses. The door was locked, but that was no obstacle. A moment's delay, that was all. The wards took a moment's further effort. There were two sets, on the frame. Snow's were the older ones, traced and cut when Tsabrak had been a man, not a god. The newer ones were godmagic, hazy purple when she looked with conjuror's eyes. They tingled when she passed her hand across them. So did her own godmark, and when she glanced at it, surprised, she saw a faint orange glow on her skin.

My right hand.

The doors opened without argument.

Snow reckoned a corridor of potential death when she stepped inside. Reckoned steel and crossbows, maybe godmagic. Found chaos instead, with women who must be Rata's cartel jogging down the corridor—*away* from the front door, and toward a bundle of shouts and yelling in the main body of the warehouse.

That sounded like a fight. Snow guessed Veiko was the cause of it. So he wasn't past fighting yet. That was good. She sent the darkness rolling ahead, running like water along the cracks in the floor and the walls.

Briel swam in that darkness like a fish. The svartjagr's sendings came in raw and violent bursts, like they hadn't since her adolescence, when she and Snow were new to each other.

This, Snow thought, was how wild svartjagr hunted together. And that Briel had forgotten the minds touching hers were not svartjagr, well, take that as its own warning. Briel was not a brave creature. But she was angry now, and she knew Veiko was up there. That was a good portion of Briel's frenzy. Not an inconsiderable part of Snow's own, well, not frenzy, exactly. Call it focus. Call it *bloody* focus, with an unhealthy joy attached.

But she didn't rush ahead. Wasn't an idiot, to march down a corridor without checking all the doors. There weren't many. This was a warehouse, with most of its space open and near the back, by the river. The rooms budding off this hall were offices, mostly, populated by desks and crates.

And a guardroom, whose dregs had not yet managed to join whatever trouble Veiko had started. There were three of them coming round the doorway, etched into flat silhouette by the firedog's backlighting. They damn near ran into her, dodged and broke like water when they got close enough even the shadows couldn't conceal her.

One behind, two in front. Had they been older, smarter, anything like Dekklis, they'd've triangulated and struck as a unit. But Snow had surprised them. And while they gaped—not long, but she did not need much time—she drew the seax and sliced one deep across the belly. Spun partway toward the second, too aware of the one still behind her.

Better she offer a shoulder than an unguarded back, fuck and damn, she could *hear* that woman coming at her.

Logi snarled, quick and savage, and charged.

Then the first one found her breath, screamed as her guts spilled out. The second one struck—quick cut, with a blade just like Snow's, with a skill that said she knew how to use it. Came in fast, feinted right, sliced her seax across Snow's forearm. Crippling if it had landed square, yeah, but it didn't. Scored across healing stitches, fresh cut and fresh blood and *fuck*. Snow slapped the other's blade aside and closed the distance. The woman was fast, but she was young: gave ground, trying to bring her seax around for another strike. Unprepared when Snow used her elbow as a weapon, stabbing first to the chest, then the jaw, before she slammed her forearm against the second guard's throat, all her weight behind it.

She felt that crunch rather than heard it. Stepped clear as the woman buckled and choked. She never even screamed as Snow hacked down with black steel, once and twice.

Nice contrast to the third guard, who was dying badly, loudly, competing with Logi's snarls for volume. No need to worry about her. Worry about a maybe-fourth lurking in the guardroom, warned by all the noise.

Snow peered inside. Lucky. No guard. There was only a table, and what was clearly Veiko's gear spread out on it. The axe, the bow, the noidghe drum, his pack untied and half-emptied. She could come back for that, yeah, once she had Veiko. Assuming reinforcements didn't come up the door at her back and trap them in the warehouse, and then it wouldn't matter anyway.

Snow coaxed a witchfire out of the black. Twined it among her fingers. Briel and the darkness had gone on ahead. She heard that chaos, shouts and screaming and Briel's keening. The svartjagr sent only red-tinged darkness. No sign of Veiko.

He was there. Wounded, probably, maybe unconscious—but not dead yet. Not ruined. Not dying.

Tell yourself that.

Snow stepped back into the corridor. The two she'd cut were burbling to a slow death. Logi had been more thorough with his kill. He grinned redly at her. Ears back, tail waving, as if he'd just brought down a rabbit for the stewpot. Snow scraped her hand over his head. Took a handful of scruff. Couldn't have Logi dashing ahead. Veiko wouldn't forgive her, she got his second dog killed.

There was one door left, at the end of the corridor, hanging open on its hinges. The screams came from that direction, echoing out of what Snow's memory told her was the main warehouse. The river smell was stronger now. Old fish. Mildew.

And godmagic, yeah. She smelled that, felt it crawling over her skin like a hundred spiders. Saw the violet flicker swelling against the conjured black.

There was someone on the other side of that doorway. Someone waiting for her.

Lightning flashed across the back of Snow's eyes. Flash and bang. Then came an un-Briel silence.

Fuck and *damn*. Snow wiped the seax on her sleeve. Slid it back into its sheath. Let Logi go, too. She needed both hands for conjuring. Might need Tsabrak.

"You hear?" she whispered. "Come in, Laughing God. Your right hand needs you."

Then she flung the witchfire through the empty doorway ahead of her. It might draw the godsworn's attention. Might offer a target. *Please*, let that work.

It did. Violet godmagic sizzled, slicing where she would have been had she been an idiot and followed too close. She dove through the doorway, rolled and came up. She called up another witchfire, filled her palm with it. Cool blue for half a heartbeat. Then she conjured it to real fire, hot and bright, drawing from air and stone. A moment's heat on her palm, and then she threw it. The ball unraveled as it flew, spread and swelled like a sunrise, so that the godsworn—snaggle-faced, toadfucking Dvergir woman—had to twist and dodge. The godsworn threw her hands up as if she meant to catch it. Snow had a moment's hope that it would be that easy, that the fire would fold around the godsworn and burn her whole.

Instead the godsworn caught the fire in both palms, as if it were a child's toy. The flames shivered, turned traitor and violet.

Laughing God, that woman had an ugly smile.

Snow murdered her witchfire. Used the sudden dark and her memory of the room to cross fast toward the far wall. She slipped on

blood

wet tiles. Had time to realize she was going to fall when the godmagic flared again.

The godsworn had made her own fire. Not witchfire, no, more like a glowing sphere of violet flames trapped behind glass. She lobbed it like a ball, two-handed.

It shattered when it struck the floor. Broke into a dozen burning strands that roped and writhed toward Snow, fast as snakes. She lurched onto her knees, swept her own hands in a *push away* that sent a fresh witchfire sheeting across the floor. Witchfire wouldn't stop the godmagic, no, but it might slow it down, tangle it, give her a moment to

what, find a new place to die?

recover.

The godmagic passed through the witchfire and left it curdled, smoking, in bruise-colored puddles. Snow had enough time to be astonished, to think *Bel should know about this,* and then the godmagic was on her. Coiling around her boots, climbing her like a trellis. Sinking through leather, through her trousers' rough weave, through her skin. Felt like snakes coiling around her, like worms eating into her. Like threads of fire, a tingling that turned to acid-intolerable so fast it stole her breath. She tasted smoke on the back of her throat, realized she would burn from the inside, that she would be grease and ash before it was over. Her vision tunneled inward, showed her a landscape of violet fire, a whole world of pain and terror. There was a darker-than-black shape amid all the violet that might've been a woman, or a dragon, or both.

Tal'Shik. Fuck and damn, *waiting* for her on the other side. That was enough to make Snow pray for a forever-burning, long death, let it never end—

You don't mean that, said the darkness, where the godmagic's glow could not reach. A shadow passed between her and Tal'Shik, there in the ghost roads. The Laughing God raised his hands, and the violet flames flattened and guttered. The dragon-woman rose up and spread wings and made a sound that Snow felt rather than heard. Like the stones themselves were melting from the inside.

And then, that fast, the pain was gone. Cold wet wash that made Snow think that she was back in the black river. She gasped out of reflex, expecting a flood in mouth and lungs. Except she was not wet and was not dead—unless *dead* meant a bruising fall to hands and knees, which jarred every joint in her body.

That was fast and *too close* and *what the fuck happened?* Tsabrak and Tal'Shik going at it, that was obvious. But that was the ghost roads' battle. On this side, blood and stone, she had a godsworn out there, with godmagic, and she wasn't sure she could conjure a clever retort right now. Wouldn't *that* be her luck, yeah, saved from Tal'Shik and still dead with a knife in her back. The godsworn had been—where? To the left—get her feet under her and stand *up*—

She could hear a woman screaming, and rattling steel over stone, and a series of meat-solid thuds, like a blacksmith at an anvil.

Snow swept the darkness aside in one violent gesture. The torches flattened and flared. She swept a blurred glance across everything. Marked the pole, tall and naked. Marked the scattered bodies, no time to count them. Marked a huddled heap of cloth and hair and spreading blood where the snaggle-faced godsworn had been, with a tall shape hunched over her, arm rising and falling. Not a hammer in his hand, no—chains, hanging from the manacles on his wrist.

Veiko, she almost said, but the name shriveled on her tongue.

Bloodmask and witchfire eyes, red-soaked rags of a shirt stuck to pale chest and shoulders. Torn trousers, smeared with blood and Laughing God knew what else. That face turned toward her. Then he was staggering like a three-legged goat, one hand stretched out for balance, the other knotted around a chain too clotted to clank as it slithered across the floor.

There was one way to stop the angry dead, Veiko had told her, but fuck and damn if she wanted to cut off his *head*.

Then Logi barreled past her, whining in his throat, and Veiko—not a ghost, not dead—folded onto his knees and dropped the chain and wrapped both arms around the dog's neck.

Relief hurt worse than any stabbing. And behind it, a deeper ache. Briel was somewhere in here, probably crisped and dead, *fuck* if Snow wanted to look for her. Not yet. Not now. Focus on the ones she could help. It looked like someone had hit Veiko with his own axe; he had a long split across his forehead that stretched into his braids and bled like a heartwound.

Stop the bleeding, that came first, and then—and then what? She looked around, took the time to actually count the bodies. Snow recognized some of them as Rata's people. But it wasn't everyone. Wasn't even Rata herself. And that meant there might be reinforcements coming, at the worst; and at the best, another round of this toadshit in the near future, with her and Veiko

together this time, yeah

in less than perfect shape to deal with it. Without Briel's eyes and help, too—and she had helped here, that was obvious. There were gashes and cuts on the bodies made by svartjagr tail and claws. Contortions to some of the corpses that meant svartjagr venom.

Snow herself bore no visible marks from the godmagic, no burns. But the echo of pain throbbed in her bones, pressed behind her eyes, flopped in her gut. She was going to have the foremother of all headaches. She bet part of that hurt was Briel's death, too.

"She is not dead." On a good day he sounded like gravel and thunder. Now he sounded like sand in a pot.

Snow looked at him. Frowned. *She.* He must mean the godsworn. They were damned hard to kill. Except what was left of this woman's face and head suggested Veiko had managed quite nicely.

"Veiko, there's brains on the tile—"

His eyes were startlingly blue against the red. "Briel," he said. And repeated, laboriously, "She is not dead. She is hurt."

How do you know? crowded against her teeth. She kept it there. Veiko had a sense for Briel, a sensitivity that she didn't. Trust the man. She left him to his dog and his headwound and walked around the room, really looked.

And there: a scrap of black against the wall, which fluttered and hopped toward her.

"Chrrip!"

There might be broken bones in those fragile wings. Snow offered a forearm. Watched with a chirurgeon's eye as Briel wrapped talons and tail around her.

"Can you fly?"

"Chrrip." Weak, emphatic, unhappy and happy at once. Briel thought she could. Briel did not want to try. Snow couldn't blame her. She reckoned Briel had earned a rest and a carry, at least back to Veiko. And after that, well, she might have to fly, because he'd have enough trouble staying upright without a double-arm's-length of svartjagr draped on his shoulders, and Snow couldn't balance them both across hers. No doubt Veiko would protest, *oh it is nothing*—but he'd need help to walk out of here. She *might* manage a simple conjuring, make sure no one saw them.

And it wouldn't matter if she didn't work on him first. He would leave a bloody trail that a child could follow. Logi was trying to help, licking and licking, but Logi would choke before he'd stop the bleeding. Toadfucking headwounds.

"Move," she told the dog. Elbowed him aside when he wouldn't. Slapped Briel, too, when the svartjagr poked her nose toward Veiko. "He's fine, yeah?"

"Fine. Yes. But." Veiko touched the wound. Looked at his fingers. "It is a bad cut."

"It's a fucking river." Snow probed the edges. A wound that size needed stitches. She had the needle and thread in her pouch, yeah, but that took time, and there were faster ways. She reached up, took a fingerwrap of her topknot. One, two, three, *rip*.

Briel hissed.

"I know, yeah? It was my head." Snow rubbed the hair between her fingers. Closed eyes and gritted teeth and twisted a little power out of stone and air and her own overstretched talent.

A tiny flame bloomed between her fingers. The hair began to smoke.

Veiko squinted. His pupils didn't match. At least half this headache was his, bet on it, coming through Briel.

"What are you doing?"

"Burning hair."

"Oh. Well. That is—" He made a sound very much like Briel, cold water on hot iron, as she packed the ash and burning fragments of hair into the wound.

"Can't have you dripping all over the Suburba. This'll hold until we have time for stitches."

"Huh." He let her help him up. Held on to her with both hands as he looked for his balance.

She'd forgotten how tall he was. Forgotten the weight of him, leaning on her, and the texture of his ribs under her hand. Remembered now, in a rush and shiver. He'd come *that* close to dead, fuck and damn, and all she'd've had would be memories.

His eyes were older than his twenty-odd years. So was the grim little smile he gave her. "I am alive."

"Wasn't sure when I first saw you. Thought you were angry dead."

"I nearly was." He tilted his head. Looked at her out of both eyes. "So were you. We are both lucky." He stared down at his wrists. "You can get these off, I hope."

"Sky's blue, water's wet. Veiko. Tsabrak's become the Laughing God. Said you knew about that."

"I know. I helped him."

"Right. Istel found me. Told me what happened." She left off Istel's condition at arrival. Veiko didn't need to carry that, too, right now.

"So he is not with you."

"No."

"Then." Veiko started to wind the chain around wrist and forearm. "We have a guest."

Snow found her seax drawn and raised before she'd managed to turn. And then she realized why Logi hadn't bothered to look at all, why Briel hadn't hissed.

"It's okay," she said, for Veiko's sake. "He's ours."

Soren stood in the doorway. He had Veiko's axe cradled in his arms like a child. A pack hung off his shoulder, its guts trailing. A sleeve. A pot handle. The bow, unstrung, poking out like a dead tree. "Passed a room on the way in. This looked important, like maybe it might belong to your partner. I think I got everything."

"I thought I told you stay back. Wait outside."

"You did." Soren shook his head, thin-lipped. He shifted the axe to one arm. Showed her his knife. It was wet. "You also told me poke with the sharp end."

"Who'd you get?"

"Don't know. Some woman running away from here. She looked." He cast around for the words. "Roughspun and leather. Cartel, I think."

Veiko cleared his throat. "Who is this?"

Snow looked sideways at Veiko. Tightened her arm around his ribs. "Veiko. This is K'Hess Soren. Kenjak's brother. Dek stole him from the Tiers. He knows who all the godsworn are up there. —Soren. This is my partner, Veiko Nyrikki."

Veiko's eyebrows pushed their way up his forehead. Ghastly effect, with the blood and ash and dogspit. "K'Hess. Your brother was a brave man."

Snow let them study each other. It kept them occupied while she reckoned what to do next. It would be safest, in the sense of furthest from trouble, to go back to the shrine, to Ari. But getting there would be the trick, yeah, there was a lot of city between here and there. A lot of people to avoid. A lot of conjuring and a lot of concussed, bloody-faced Veiko, who might collapse on her.

She weighed that against taking refuge at her sister's house, and the danger she could bring down on the household. If—big gamble—Soren had got the only runner, then Rata might not know what'd happened here until midmorning, maybe later, whenever the godsworn failed to arrive and report Veiko's death.

And mine.

Dekklis called her assassin, but Dek didn't know half of it. The God—the old God, anyway—had encouraged permanent solutions. Fires happened sometimes, on the docks. The trick was to keep them burning. Damp was bad enough, yeah, but half the district would turn out to help if there was fire. No one wanted to lose a barge or a warehouse. But let this place go up, let Rata find cooked bodies inside, and Rata might reckon Snow had, yes, come for her partner, and that a conjuror and a godsworn had killed each other and taken the warehouse with them.

Or Rata might think Snow survived. Rata might worry, and wait, and give Snow time to organize Ari and the rest of the God's people. Then they could start hunting Tal'Shik's godsworn until the Suburba was clean again. And then they could start on the Tiers.

"Soren." She shifted Veiko's arm across her shoulder. "Take him. And careful. He's heavy. You," she told Briel, "need to fly. Find Dekklis. Let her know we're alive, yeah?"

Briel hissed. But she spread her wings when Snow raised her arm, flapped and managed, somehow, to keep from crashing into the floor. One rough circuit, and she was out: through the double doors and over the water.

And to Veiko and Soren, staring at her, Snow said: "Go ahead. I'll catch up with you."

CHAPTER TWENTY-THREE

There was a svartjagr circling outside the window. Alone, which was unusual among the feral ones, and if one svartjagr looked like another, well, *this* one seemed somehow familiar. The cant of its wings, maybe. The breadth of them.

Dekklis went to the window and opened it. Called Briel's name, quiet as she dared.

Rurik started. "The *hell*."

She ignored him. The svartjagr heard her. Turned its arrow-slim head and looked. It passed the window and canted its wings and doubled back, its head pointed at her the whole time. And yes, there: spider-tracery of old scar on its wings, *her* wings.

Dekklis braced her hands on the sill. Not entirely safe, leaning out, because the sending always came with a headache, but sometimes it came with vertigo, too.

"All right," she whispered. "Give it to me."

The sending hit like a hammer, an axe, cleaving bone and brain. Worse than usual, harder: she saw herself, a distant smudge on the Academy's wall, a mote in one of a hundred separate eyes. A second shift, this time into svartjagr memory, this time still more alien: the buildings were hard edged, vivid details down to the cracks in the shutters, but the air was solid, too, etched in patterns of color and texture. There was the lake, rippling and flickering, reflecting fire. One of the warehouses was burning. Heat that painted the air red and blue and yellow.

Flash again, to a smear of darkness that was also somehow Snowdenaelikk, with Veiko, and Logi; another person, too, maybe a man—but no one Briel cared about. No one who rated detail beyond *man* and *dark*.

Dekklis shaped Istel and sent *where?* at Briel. Got back red-washed darkness and vertigo. And then Dek was leaning over the sill, gagging, and Rurik's hand was warm on her back.

"Szanys? The hell was that?"

"Briel," she said, and realized he wouldn't know who that was. "The svartjagr. She's Snowdenaelikk's. That was a sending."

Rurik took her elbow. Guided her back to the bench beside the table. "Is your friend . . . ?"

"Alive, yes, and her partner." *Istel.* Dek's guts folded and fell. She put the worry aside, focused, made herself look at Rurik and deliver a report. "It's a message. Something happened down there—a fight, I think, maybe a—"

There was a knock at the door.

Dek grabbed for the weapons that weren't there. Naked hips, naked boots. Saw Rurik do the same and grimace. And then they both, together, spread their hands flat on the table and waited.

A second knock. "Szanys Dekklis? May I come in?"

Courtesy and a familiar voice. Oh foremothers.

"Of course, Adept," she called back while Rurik looked at her with such a deliberate lack of expression she thought his face might crack.

The door opened, and Belaery came in. Alone, in Adept's robes, her topknot in a midnight coil so dark and perfectly black that her whole head looked slick and oiled. The rings scalloped silver along the rims of both ears, five on one side, one on the other. That was a message, to anyone with wits to see it. Two highborn prisoners would understand it just fine.

Do not try me. Here I have the rank.

Belaery bowed first to Dekklis, then, only a little more shallowly, to Rurik. "First Scout Szanys Dekklis. First Spear K'Hess Rurik." Polite and fleeting smile. "I hope the accommodations are acceptable."

"They would be lovelier if we could leave them. Adept." Rurik's accent was flawlessly highborn round, where Belaery's was midtowner flat. Another message. Ink and family against Academy rank and sex.

This, Dekklis thought, is how the Purge had happened. Oh foremothers, defend them all.

"We appreciate the Academy's hospitality," she said sharply. "I imagine we have you to thank for it."

"Whoever you are."

Belaery's eyes flickered toward Rurik. Lingered a moment on his face, his furious eyes. "Adept Uosuk Belaery," she said. "I am an associate of the First Scout." Her gaze came back to Dekklis. The smile hardened into a tight line. "And yes. I'm the reason you're not rotting in a proper cell somewhere. Or dead," she added, and glanced at Rurik again. "That wasn't easy with *you.*"

"I'd love to know how you managed that."

Belaery inclined her head, gracious as any domina. "I have a friend on the Adept Council. And she has a sister in the Senate with some very quick-footed messengers." Belaery shrugged. "Listen, Dekklis. We've had some of the same problems the Houses have, with god-rot in high places. A particularly highly placed piece of that rot arranged to have all highborn dissidents—that's what they're calling you—brought here for safekeeping."

"You mean, to be hostages," Rurik said. He'd folded his arms across his chest. Was staring directly at Belaery, as if she were an errant mila who'd failed at latrine duty.

Belaery sighed through her nose. Dek watched all that Illhari custom working its way across her face: exasperation, offense, impatience, with male intrusion, male insolence, just plain poor manners.

"I *mean*," she said, deliberately not looking at him, "for safekeeping, because that is what I *said*, K'Hess Rurik, until a purpose could be found for you. There was concern that hasty decisions would result in regrets later on. I didn't give the order to bring you here, but I made certain you were housed in this apartment rather than in the vaults."

"Oh, well, that's kind—"

Dekklis thrust out her arm, made a bar between Belaery and Rurik. Raised her own voice over his.

"You said that you *had* the same problems with god-rot. You don't anymore?"

"We do not." Belaery raised her chin. "The problem suffered an unfortunate and sudden illness. He did not recover, and my *friend* assumed his position on the Council."

Dekklis caught the smile crawling onto her face. "Bad fish?"

Belaery nodded, wide-eyed and grave. "Perhaps."

"Doesn't your rot have friends of his own?"

"There *have* been a couple of accidents. Some of the staircases can be quite treacherous in the dark."

Dekklis laughed outright, sharp and loud. "And no one's suspicious."

"No one's interested in having Council control fall into Senate hands, and certainly not *godsworn* hands. We also swear oaths, First Scout. The Academy will not be a political tool for any House's advancement." Belaery's eyes glittered. "We have no interest in bringing the godsworn back to power. But we also do not wish to see the Taliri take Illharek."

"So why are you here?"

Belaery nodded, a teacher pleased that her pupil had finally asked the right question.

"Three reasons. First: there's a fire in the Suburba. One single warehouse, down on the Tano dockside. That wouldn't be so remarkable, except that the fire's been very polite. It hasn't even tried to jump onto its neighbors. Which, of course, means it's conjured."

"Snowdenaelikk's doing."

"Presumably." Belaery's smile smoked away. "The Academy has rules, of which Snow has just broken a handful. Not that she ever much cared for rules."

"Who'd she kill?"

"Most people would ask *is she all right?* first. So you must know that she is."

Dekklis blinked. Rearranged her face into what she hoped looked like shock. "Is she all right?"

"Oh, don't try. I saw Briel outside. Her scars are distinctive. And her presence here suggests to me that Snow's alive, and what's more, she wants *you* to know that." Belaery went to the window. Gazed out, as if she even noticed the view. "Let's dispense with the toadshit. I know the Suburba relatively well, and I've done some scrying, and I can't find her. Snow's very good at some of the more, ah, rudimentary conjuring. Better than most of the Adepts, actually, though I doubt she knows it. We won't find her if she doesn't want to be found." Belaery leaned against the window frame. Folded her arms. "To answer your initial question, I don't know who she killed. That's actually the second thing I came to ask you."

"I certainly don't know. She doesn't check plans with me. But I can guess it's got something to do with her partner, or Tal'Shik's godsworn. Probably both."

"Godsworn in the Suburba, too. So that's confirmed." Belaery's mouth tightened. "I was afraid of that."

"Afraid." Rurik made it a challenge.

Belaery curled her lip. "Godsworn are formidable, First Spear. I thought you already knew that."

"I'm not an Adept. You people do magic."

"*We people* conjure. We do *not* wield godmagic."

"About that," Dek started. Stopped when Belaery looked and smiled razors.

"Yet. That takes time. Which we might not have if Snow's toadshit starts a war with the godsworn."

"Work faster, then," said Rurik.

Hell and damn. "So what's the third thing, Adept? That you wanted to ask me."

"What? Oh, yes." Tap tap, slim fingers on the stone, a nervous gesture at odds with Belaery's deliberate nonchalance. "There's an empty place on the Senate bench for House Szanys. I thought you might be interested."

"You know why that seat's empty? I killed my sister, in front of witnesses. Half the motherless Senate."

"Oh, I know."

"You think the other senators will just forget it? Let me sit on the bench with them?"

Belaery shrugged. "All that time in our archives, Szanys Dekklis, and you still don't understand? Sororicide, matricide—all traditional, honorable ways to rise in power. Szanys Maja took that very path with your mother, in front of those same women."

"I didn't kill Maja to take her place."

"Who else knows that?"

"Anyone who knows me."

"Which is . . . wait. Let me count. You've been absent ten long years. So those who actually know you *now* are: Snowdenaelikk. A skraeling man. This son of K'Hess here, your First Spear. Your own partner, Istel—who has not, as I understand, returned to the garrison. None of these people will contest your claim on the Senate floor. Perhaps K'Hess Rurik will even endorse it. His mother certainly will."

Maja had counted on Dekklis's ignorance. Had believed, being Maja and arrogant, that she could control her naive little sister. But Belaery knew better than that. Belaery looked at her and saw Snowdenaelikk's friend, and everything that meant. So Dekklis would be a lever against

Snow, maybe, a weapon to turn on the Laughing God. A weapon turned to many Academy purposes.

"No."

Belaery's look could curdle milk. "Snow said you were an intelligent woman, if unsubtle. So consider, Dekklis. You're legion. You could be First Legate *and* senator. You could command our troops. Defend Illharek from the Taliri. You could be the Republic's hero of the siege. The people would love you."

"The Senate would hate me."

"Some might. Some will cling to you like a svartjagr on stone. And you will have *other* friends."

Oh yes, wouldn't she. A whole conjured tower full of those friends, no doubt, robed and ringed and reliable as cats.

"No. And don't say you need me, Belaery. You don't. You'll make this deal with someone else if I don't go along with it."

"Maybe." Belaery looked grim as any trooper. "If there's another senator left untainted. The godsworn have no love for us Adepts. Surely Snow told you that."

"Snow told me that the Academy allied with the rebels during the Purge. I imagine the godsworn are holding a grudge."

"We have always served Illharek's best interests."

"You serve your own."

"We will have to teach you politics, Senator."

"Don't call me that. I haven't agreed."

"You will, because you know I'm right. Because there's no one else who can do this. Because if you don't, Illharek will dissolve into civil war and godsworn infighting while you sit in here and watch the svartjagr pick at the corpses." Hard glare. Long silence, which grew thin and then snapped. "Snow thought you had more than cobwebs and toadshit for brains. Was she wrong? Can you be so obtuse?"

There wasn't a good way to answer that. Dekklis shrugged and didn't. Held her own silence until the room ached with it.

Then Rurik cleared his throat. "If I may speak, Adept," all highborn formality, a man asking permission to address his betters.

Bel inclined her head, a study in magnanimity. Rurik didn't notice. He was looking at Dekklis. Eyes on her, hot as fever.

"Go ahead," Dekklis said, and barely bit back the *sir*.

"Thank you." For a heartbeat she thought he would bow to her, too. But then he squared both shoulders. Snapped a salute and held it. "I only wish to say that it would be an honor to serve you, and through you, Illharek, as both senator and First Legate. It is rare to meet a woman of such honor and dedication to duty."

Foremothers, what a speech. Pure highborn flattery, pure politics, pure *toadshit*. Belaery was nodding, smirking—believing it, because that is what highborn men *said*, and she didn't know Rurik.

And from Rurik, here and now, that was an order.

Give us a way out of this room, First Scout.

Because if they got out, they could do something. Bring the Sixth inside. Start *acting* instead of reacting. She'd never wanted any motherless Senate seat. Certainly not to be First Legate. But *want* wasn't the important consideration now. Duty was.

"If I agree." Her voice cracked and splintered. She swallowed. "If I agree to this, you let us both out of here."

"Of course." Sly almost-smile draping Belaery's lips, which made Dekklis want to hit her. Except *senators* didn't hit people, did they. Senators got other people to do their hitting for them.

"Because I will need commanders in the field, and I will need K'Hess Rurik most."

"Naturally."

"And."

Belaery raised both brows. "And?"

"I take your *advice*. I don't take your orders. I serve Illharek, not you, and not this Academy."

Belaery bowed, palms together. "As you say, Senator Szanys. Just as the Academy exists to serve Illharek."

Snowdenaelikk, Dekklis thought, was going to laugh herself sick.

* * *

"I can't save him."

The words drifted up with the jenja smoke, uncurled and unraveled and disappeared, so soft Veiko might think he'd imagined them. Their speaker did not turn her head when he came and stood beside her at the railing. Only pulled another lungful of jenja, and held it, and then asked him, "What are you doing out here?"

"Waiting with you." It was as honest an answer as *standing* and *escaping*. Veiko had seen death, dealt it, survived it. But he was finding it difficult to watch a friend dying slowly, beyond anyone's help.

Because of you. Think of that.

Istel hadn't made any accusations to that effect. Istel probably didn't even blame him; he had fought with Veiko and lost a fight, that was all. He might not even notice the moment of dying, being as full of mossflower as Snow could make him.

That false peace was more unnerving to Veiko than Istel's gritted silence had been while the blood leaked through bandage after bandage and K'Hess Soren had traded basins of clean water for polluted red. Patient Soren, who had not argued when Snow told him how much mossflower to put in the tea, although his eyes had rolled wide.

Much of that tea had leaked out later on the bandages. More had probably leaked into Istel's guts along with the contents of his stomach. *That* was the damage Snow could not repair, not with needle or thread or poultice or conjuring. Godmagic might, but no one had called on the Laughing God yet. Veiko wondered if Snow had thought of it, and realized that he was reluctant to ask. He might give her ideas. He might save a man's life. He might do far more harm than good.

Tell yourself that.

And so he did nothing except stand beside his partner, and watch the street below, and feel his heartbeat throb in every bruise and cut and the row of stitches above his eye.

Snow flicked the butt of her jenja into the street. Missed, by some miracle, hitting anyone. No one looked up. Veiko suspected a conjuring on the balcony, so that anyone looking would see empty iron and shuttered windows instead of a tall half-blood and a taller skraeling and a big red-furred northern dog.

"Didn't expect him to be alive when we got back, yeah? Thought for sure we'd come home to a corpse. Now I got three freeborn men living in my flat with me." Soundless laughter, lips peeled back from her teeth. "Let that get to the street, Sinnike will close up shop from the shame."

"You do not care what she thinks." Sky is blue. Water is wet. Idle conversation, which he'd never been good at, which was Snow's best defense and distraction.

"No." She found another stick of jenja. Lit it and sucked hard on the end. "I don't. And it'll be down to two men soon enough. Fuck and *damn*. I keep thinking—if I'd stayed here, yeah? Just a candlemark longer. If I'd treated him when he arrived, he might not be dying right now. And I know better. He was dead when he got here. Wound like that, there's no fixing. He knew it, too."

She would have tried anyway, except for him. Veiko knew it. She had chosen his life over any tiny chance Istel had. A man should not feel guilt for another's choices, but he did.

Veiko did not need to inquire about Snow's own guilt. Her eyes were red rimmed, red mapped. She had not, he guessed, slept more than a candlemark since their return here, and had snatched that huddled against the hearthstones, beside Istel. He wanted to tell her: *Rest, because Istel will not notice. Rest, because we will need your wits soon enough.*

And then he considered what her dreams might look like, with Tsabrak newly come to his power, and thought she might have another reason to avoid sleep.

Snow tapped the jenja against the railing. Bright cinders at first, and then drifting ash. "The Laughing God made me an offer, and I took it."

"The Laughing God, not Tsabrak?"

"The Laughing God before Tsabrak. Though it still holds, yeah?"

Veiko's ribs felt too tight. His throat did. "What did he offer?"

"Alliance. Loyalty. Power." She flipped her hand, sent the jenja smoke into mad curls. "I am the God's right hand, Veiko. That means I lead the cartels. Ari answers to *me*."

Not a surprise. And still: a man should not be able to breathe with his whole chest solid and frozen. A man should not be able to say, so calmly, "And are you godsworn now?"

"No. One step from it. I wouldn't give him that. The old God, I mean. He didn't ask. There's an intimacy in that I don't think he wanted."

The relief was short-lived. One breath, and the pain came back, knives all through his chest. "But *Tsabrak* has asked."

"He says he can stop Istel from dying. Mend the flesh. Is that even possible?"

"I do not know. Illhari gods are not like other spirits." And reluctantly, "It is the Illhari way, to become godsworn."

"And I'm Illhari now, is that it? Not noidghe?"

"That is what you have told me."

Her gaze flinched away. She folded the burning jenja into her fist, the one with the godmark. Smoked leaked out between her fingers. "If it was just me, and Istel's life in the balance, I'd do it. We need the Laughing God to stop Tal'Shik. Godsworn brings a new level of power, yeah? For both of us. And Tsabrak knows I want Istel alive. But I need you, Veiko, more than I need either of *them*. So I'm asking. What should I do?"

The Laughing God had been an enemy, he and Snow had agreed on that. But this new God was also Tsabrak, and perhaps that had changed.

Veiko had never figured out where Tsabrak ranked in Snow's affections. Lover. Betrayer. Leader and ally. They had years of association, of shared history. So much more complex than *partner* and a mere few months.

And she was asking him for advice. Oh ancestors. He could advise her to deny the bargain. Istel would die, but all men did that. At least she would be free of the God, of Tsabrak, as much as she could be free of someone with whom she had shared the balance of her life. But that freedom would not last. Tal'Shik would not simply leave them alone.

A *man* could say, from his heart, *tell him no*. But a partner owed honesty.

It felt like an axe in his chest, and it was nothing so simple, or harmless, as metal against bone. "If he can truly save Istel, then you should take the bargain. We need all our friends now. And we need the Laughing God, with as much power as you can wring from him. You were right. We need what he is, against what *she* is, if we are to have any hope of winning."

Sharp look, oh ancestors, a man could bleed to death from it. "*We* now, is it? This is your fight?"

He met that midnight stare. Held it. "If it is yours, it is mine."

Snowdenaelikk stretched her hand over the railing. Opened the godmarked palm. Ashes where the jenja had been, and blisters raised on her skin. The ashes drifted off her palm in little swirls and gusts, a response to a breeze Veiko could not feel.

"Thank you."

There was nothing a man could say to that that would not shame them both. So he touched her instead: his hand around hers, carefully, in case she objected. She did not. Laced her fingers through his and squeezed, hard. And then she let him go, which was relief and distress both. But she did not turn round and go back inside at once. Stayed beside him, her shoulder just touching his, so that her warmth seeped through sleeve and skin.

Such moments would be rare in the coming chaos. A wise man would treasure them.

ACKNOWLEDGMENTS

I thought—foolishly—that writing the second book in a series would be easier than the first one. Ha. For hashing out plot possibilities and reading many drafts, thanks to Tan and Colleen. For sharp eyes and smart critiques (and for selling the story!), thanks to Lisa. For top-notch editing, thanks to Caitlin (sorry for all the *S* names). For escorting this book into the world, thanks to Adrienne and the rest of the excellent folks at 47North.

And thanks to Loren for all the rest.

ABOUT THE AUTHOR

Photo © 2015 Tan Grimes-Sackett

K. Eason started telling tales in her early childhood. After earning two degrees in English literature, she decided to stop writing about everyone else's stories and get back to writing her own. Now she teaches first-year college students about the zombie apocalypse, Aristotelian ethics, and *Beowulf* (not all at once). She lives in Southern California with her husband and two black cats, and she powers everything with coffee.